A MACHINE DIVINE

DEREK PAUL

Follow the Author
Instagram: TheBreakingPattern
Twitter: TheBreakPattern

ISBN: 979-8-9873135-0-3

Edited by Mairead Beeson
Map by Alessia Sagnotti
Cover Art and Formatting by Miblart

For my mother,
*who read to me nightly and
encouraged me to be my best in all endeavors.*

For my father,
*who provided me a blessed life and
nurtured my passion for the sciences.*

And for my sister,
*my greatest inspiration
and influence, both in my creativity and in my being.*

And to you, dear reader,
thank you for sharing in this journey!

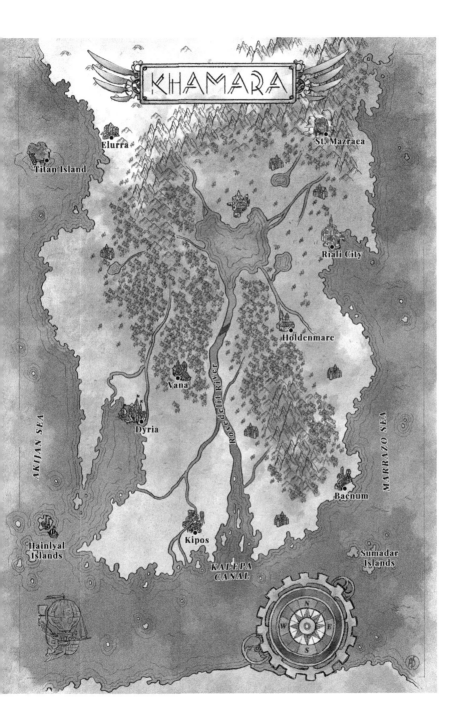

CHAPTER 1

A brief swish of light, a fluttering of emerald, her prize had revealed itself, and now the hunt was on. Callie watched as it swan-dived into a pile of cut daisy petals and fallen leaves. She crawled through the brush, counting her heartbeats. *One.* Her hands clasped tight around a makeshift trigger of rope and birch. *Two.* Her breath held the sharp air of dawn. *Three.* Trigger pulled, and the trap sprang upward. She jumped through a mist of dew and dust and let out a high-pitched whistle and then a call. "Cloud!" A stunning white fox came barreling through the thickets toward her knees. "I got one."

They made their way toward the trap that was now swinging in midair from an oak tree. Sunbeams leaked through the forest canopy, spotlighting the leather cloth, which began to shriek and rustle violently. "Seems to be a lot more than a sprite in there. What else have we caught…" Callie lowered the bag and peered inside. A burst of green illuminated her face. *Definitely a garden sprite, but something else too.* She reached in and grabbed a small furry creature by the scruff. A squirrel nipped and clawed at her hands.

"Hey! Hey now, come on." She placed the squirrel carefully into her hunting bag. "There you go, a little bit more room for ya." The fox sniffed at the bag in curiosity as Callie knelt to tie up her other traps. Five in total, a good day. The sprites buzzed and whistled as she roped them together. She stared intently at the bags as the noise continued to rise with excitement.

"Do you hear that?" Callie asked, looking at Cloud. He pointed his nose over at the sprite traps. "No," she said, "in the distance." The ground began to shake, forest trees swayed with the rumbling earth beneath them. "Stay here," she warned, dropping her gear at the base of a nearby oak. Looking up, she plotted her path skyward before jumping for the nearest branch. Her hands grasped the first one, then another higher up, her limbs acting in one fluid motion as she climbed the large oak. She perched on top and peered in the direction of the thudding noise. Forest trees bent and swayed; something massive was coming down the mountain.

Above the canopy emerged the head of a rock golem. Callie could make out the vines and foliage that wrapped around its body as it continued to bob in and out of the dense woods. "It's Drvo," She whispered to herself with a smile. She watched as the gentle giant pushed its way through the green. A sea of sloping canopy moved in rippled waves at the golem's touch. As it grew closer, she waved her arms. "Hey, Drvo! DRVOOO!" Her attempts went unnoticed as the golem slumped down the hill, focusing intently on every step so as not to disturb the forest vegetation. Its bulky body was made entirely of rock; it was a creature born and carved from the hillsides. Callie knew today was a special day for the friendly golem.

Callie took one last look around to absorb the forest she'd grown up in. Behind her was the small and humble town of Vana, which she would soon leave for a bigger and more bustling city. She'd be exchanging oaks for towers and fields of daisies for a maze of steel and travertine. Perhaps she too, a creature with a spirit shy and crafted from hillside, would come out of hiding. Perhaps she too, would know what it was to be welcomed. She let out a deep breath and shimmied down the oak to where Cloud was waiting faithfully below. The quaking thuds of Drvo's steps grew distant. She picked up her satchel and rifle, gave Cloud a scratch behind his ear, and made her way back toward town as the five sprite traps swinging from her back sang in a high screeching chorus of captured light.

Callie plopped the bags on an old wooden counter. A bullish man with copper-rimmed glasses glared down at the sacks before meeting her gaze. "And how many do we have today?"

"Four garden sprites and two moon sprites." She pointed to one of the bags. "This one contains the two moon sprites."

The bullish man shifted his glasses and peered into the bag. A soft purple light reflected off his lenses. "Nicely done, Callie! Very good. Twelve for the lot!"

She cocked her head. "Aren't moons worth three?"

"Ah, right. Ok, fifteen for the lot then."

Callie nodded in agreement. The shopkeeper smiled and took the sprites to the back room. She turned toward Cloud, who had left her side to investigate a wall of brass trinkets in the corner of the store. The shopkeeper came back out, handing her coins and the now-empty traps. "Callie, you have a real talent. Vana is going to have a hard time surviving without you."

"I appreciate the dramatics, but I think things will be just fine."

The man cracked a smile as Callie and Cloud turned to walk back into the streets.

The sidewalks were filled with a joyful chaos. The annual Midbloom Festival was Vana's greatest holiday. Strands of valencia flowers arched over cobblestone streets. Extravagant vendors, in an effort to outshine one another, placed their ripest crops on dancing mechanical platters. Brass gears flipped plates of slow-cooked meats. Outward, to catch your nose. Inward, to draw you close. Robotic arms shot out toward Callie's face, offering her bouquets of valencias and lilies as she and Cloud weaved between strangers.

She passed under a series of large floral arches, each one containing the colors of a different city. Vana, green and yellow for its lush forests. Elurra, blue and white for its arctic tundra. Dyria, with violet and black to represent the seas they tamed. The last and most excessive arch contained the image of a lion, the symbol of Riali, with red and gold in honor of the capital and its abundant harvests. Nearly every flower was a valencia. A native bloom renowned for its adaptability in appearance and grown skillfully by Vana botanists.

The deep thumping of drums beats alongside the fluttering of flutes and brass. Callie continued to lace through the crowd, spinning out of the way of oncoming traffic, her dirty white tunic swishing with the sudden movements as she made her way to her uncle's pet shop—a small brick add-on at the end of the city square.

She arrived to find her uncle gesticulating wildly in an attempt to sell an indri lemur to an elderly customer. The festival must have drawn some extra foot traffic as the feed and hunting shelves were in disarray. Callie walked over to one of the displays, the shop smelling of pine and damp animal fur. She took a second to watch a young shrew attempt to burrow its way through the glass containment before she grabbed a nearby cage and headed outside.

The squirrel nipped at her fingers as she plunged her hand into her satchel and placed him into the cage. "I know you're not happy here, little fella. You want to be back in the trees. But you got a cozy new home and a few acorns to munch on." It glared at Callie from its cage. "I know, I know. But you fell into the trap, and that's how it works. Out there, I'm your enemy, just the same as all the others. I can't make you like me, but I hope you can at least understand."

Cloud sniffed the squirrel one last time before heading over to his favorite patch of sun that peeked onto the corner of the porch. Callie set the cage beside the door and took a seat on the front step. On the other side of her was a caged land squid, its tentacles poking through the wood bars and reaching down the front patio steps. Tethered to the cage were a group of wild ahriman—batlike creatures with one large eye at the center of their foreheads—each fluttering about, curiously watching the bustling street. A miniature hippogriff nuzzled at Callie's ankles, tangling its leash against a brass buckle on one of her boots.

Callie lifted her arms back into her hair and pulled out two wooden sticks. A flood of dark auburn tumbled down her neck and shoulders, punctuated by blueish-gray feathers swooping outward like the spikes of an aerodynamic porcupine. She positioned the sticks into her leather boots, untangled the hippogriff leash, and let out a sigh as she placed her chin into an open palm. Her fingers tapped against her lips, expressionless, as she and the beasts watched from their perch. The crowded streets continued to swarm. *Vana's wildest day of the year*, thought Callie, *and the real animals have yet to arrive.*

Asher Auden had half a trunk of biology supplies to acquire before dusk settled and the festivities began. His parents were not helping speed up the process. His dad, Murphy, stopped to haggle with every store owner in Vana, and his mom, Cara, was gushing to every remote acquaintance about her son's acceptance into Langford. Asher just wanted to get it over with. He had evening plans to attend to.

"Asher! Asher!" his dad snapped for his attention. "Don't you need a seeding kit for botany class? We're right by Saint's Animals."

Asher groaned. "Yeah, Dad. But can we make it quick?"

They pushed through the crowded street and headed toward the corner store.

Asher could see Callie staring off into the crowd. A leather armband around her bicep contained small, hanging feathers that matched the ones in her disheveled hair. Her plain white tunic was stained with grass and dirt; she must have just come back from hunting. Asher's mom went barreling toward her at first sight. "Callendra! Sweetie!"

Callie's head turned briefly in shock, her eyes like a frightened rabbit's. Cara Auden knelt down and bear-hugged Callie, pinning her arms against her body and trapping her in a cage of visible discomfort. She kept up the relentless affection. "How are you, dear? Are you all ready for school?"

"Hi, Mrs. Auden." Callie attempted a half smile. "Yeah, I'm ready."

"Ooh, you and Asher, I'm so proud of you two!" Cara cooed.

Murphy added, "The only two in all of Vana to get into Langford this year! It's quite the accomplishment."

Callie shrugged and gave Asher a nod in acknowledgment.

Asher chimed in, "Not that big of a deal, Dad. Professor Fenske is the one who got us in."

His dad was taken aback. "Not a big deal? Of course it's a big deal! You're headed to Riali; you're going to be a famous scientist when you get out. And Callie. Well...actually, I'm not sure what you're studying."

Callie let out a muffled laugh. "Animal behavior. It's a dumb degree."

Cara shook her head. "You two are so negative. You both have a once-in-a-lifetime opportunity. People from all over the world would give anything to be in your position."

A booming voice emerged from the doorway. "Well, who do we have here?" Callie's uncle came walking out of the shop. "If it isn't the Auden gang. How are you doing, Murphy?"

Asher's dad gave a big smile. "Hey, how are ya, Augustus?"

"I'm good, I'm good. Happy Midbloom! Do you have a float this year?"

Asher's dad blushed. "No, not one of our own. But I did a little bit of woodwork and design on the Baenum float this year. They're quite the engineers."

"Oh, I'm sure we're in for a treat. Come in, come in!" Gus waved them into the store. "What can I do for you all today?"

The adults walked inside, Callie's uncle looking to make a sale and Asher's dad a deal. Asher lowered his hand to let Cloud take a sniff before rubbing his cheek. Awkward silence blossomed.

"So, I saw you have some shrews in. They're pretty great for gardens." Asher ruffled his hair nervously.

"I know. Don't you think about doing one of your experiments on one of them." Callie shot a glance toward Asher, who was unsure if she was joking.

"No. I. Uh. I wouldn't." Asher looked around, already looking for an escape route; a group of loud, well-dressed Riali boys provided a brief distraction from the conversation.

Callie got up from the stoop. "I bet they'll have pretty nice labs for you in Langford. Should really help you out a lot with the science stuff."

Asher sighed. "Yeah, it'll be great to have more resources. Fenske's lab is wonderful and all, but Vana just really isn't the place for a geneticist."

Callie raised her eyebrows. "Why is that?"

"Well, to be honest, it's mainly the people. They don't seem to care much about biology or education or whatnot. They're just different from me. I'm really hoping to make some new friends while I'm out there."

Callie nodded. "Makes sense, I guess."

The Riali boys in the street began to holler at a group of Vanatian girls. *The Midbloom crowd is starting to pick up*, thought Asher. He looked back down to find the mini hippogriff sniffing at his neatly buckled shoes. "Is Cloud coming with you?"

Cloud's ears perked at the sound of his name.

"Of course. Why wouldn't he?"

"Oh, I don't know. Just curious what the animal policy was like, ya know?" Asher shook his foot as the mini-griff bit into his sock.

"He'll be staying in the sanctuary during class hours, but I'm allowed to let him out under guidance. I think he'll enjoy it there. Plenty of other animals and a good amount of land at the sanctuary."

"Right," said Asher. "Well, uh, I think we both have metaphysics class together. Professor Fenske mentioned it to me."

"It's a core class."

"Yeah, I think it is..." Asher bit his bottom lip and lowered his head so that just enough of his messy black hair could cover his eyes. He stepped aside as a burly customer walked up the steps between them. Callie nodded to the customer as he walked past before turning her attention back to the bustling streets. A group of scruffy-looking Vanatian boys that Callie recognized from school had started yelling at the Rialians. "It's getting rowdy out there. Do you have plans for the festival tonight?" she asked.

"Liam and I were going to watch the ceremony and walk around a bit. Nothing too crazy. You?"

"Not really. I saw Drvo walking into town earlier, might try and catch him if he's around."

A loud crack came from the doorway as Mr. Saint swung the screen door open for Asher's parents. "Pleasure doing business with you, Audens."

"Likewise, Gus."

Callie's uncle turned toward Asher. "Asher, good luck in school this year. I'd ask you to watch out for Callie, but I don't think she'll have much of a problem."

Callie shook her head in embarrassment.

"Callendra, there's been a man standing by the door looking at that squirrel for the last five minutes. Go help him out—and try to *actually* sell the squirrel this time."

Callie rolled her eyes and half-heartedly waved goodbye to Asher before making her way to the customer and her newly caged friend.

Asher raised his arm to wave goodbye. "Thank you, Mr. Saint. Bye, Callie."

He turned toward the street but was pulled back by his mother just in time. A Vana boy had sucker-punched a Rialian, knocking him straight back onto the front steps of the porch. A full skirmish ensued. The Auden family skirted to the edges of the sidewalk, just outside the storm of dirt and dust. The well-dressed Riali boys had no hesitation when starting their brawl with the Vana locals.

Perhaps they're drunk, thought Asher. *These outsiders always seemed to treat Vana as their stomping ground during Midbloom, acting as if their money means more than Vana's dignity.*

He tried his best to discern meaning behind every fist. But a dirty farmer's tunic or iron-pressed vest aside, who would want to walk around caked with blood on such a bright and joyful day? Groups of adults flocked to pull the fight apart, each boy with blackened eyes and fat lips. The Vana boys were being scolded by their elders as the Riali boys sneered, both groups continuing to shout and curse.

"Come on, time to get home," said Asher's father. They had begun to head back when Asher noticed a sudden cessation of the yelling. He turned around one last time. The fighting boys and the bustling Midbloom crowd all around them stood frozen, eyes glued to the sky, as a dark shadow crept across the dense streets. From the clouds emerged a massive airship, making its descent into the center of Vana's town square.

CHAPTER 2

A crowd gathered beneath Arthur's light blue airship, its elaborate gold stitching catching the sun and shimmering over them. Its giant basket held a tiny propeller engine that hummed as he hovered above the town square. He shouted over it, warning children to jump out of the way while he descended. The burner flickered on and off until the balloon rested gently in a small, grassy park, where the Vana townsfolk greeted the spectacle with applause. Arthur opened his basket's side gate and walked out to meet them.

His outfit was as flashy and ornate as his entrance. A dark-red vest with gold buttons under a tan tweed overcoat fitted his tall, slim build perfectly. A modest, black top hat covered his medium-length, wavy brown hair, and—though he was only in his mid-thirties—he held an engraved, gold walking cane topped with a bright emerald in his right hand. In his left, he dragged an upright antique chest wrapped excessively in chains and locks.

The children, who had run away to avoid being squished, began to circle him again as he pushed over the chest, allowing it to come crashing down in a dramatic dusty thud. Arthur waved his staff, motioning for them to retreat.

"Hello, everyone! Men. Women. Children…" He flashed a smile and waved his cane playfully. "What I have here in this chest comes from the deepest corners of Khamara: evasive flying lockets forged from the caves south of Baenum. I have spent months capturing these lockets but have had no luck breaking them open. I have come to the beautiful city of Vana to ask for your assistance. Please, would you please, open these lockets!" Arthur waved his cane over the chest. The chains unraveled and the box shook to life, exploding open in a dazzling display of fireworks. A fountain of streaming blues and greens laid a foundation for larger rockets that burst into brilliant flowers in the sky. The crowd cheered and gasped. The fireworks continued as dozens of winged brass cubes came hurtling from the fiery spray. They buzzed rapidly above the heads of the children, who all jumped and grabbed for them.

Arthur snatched one from midair and gave it a shake. The gears of the brass box slowly came to a halt, and the wings went still. He handed it to a young girl, her palms outstretched. "Hold this still for me, will you?" he asked the beaming girl. He tapped the emerald end of his staff against the box, unlatching a series of mechanical gears. The box sprang open. Inside was a bright ruby pendant in the shape of a rose. The girl hugged Arthur's leg, and he gave her a pat on the back before she ran off, pocketing the flying locket and ruby for safekeeping.

Arthur scanned the bustling town square for familiar faces. He left his airship behind, knowing it to be safe with the kind, albeit curious, Vana townsfolk inspecting the craft. He loved Vana's Midbloom Festival, but he was not here for pleasantries. He was in search of a bar.

His top hat poked out from the crowd like a sore thumb in a sea of Vanatians dressed in various degrees of tans and beige. Luckily for him, his destination resided in the city square, only a brief walk through the chaotic streets.

The bar was quaint, furnished all in timber harvested from the Vanatian forests. Each chair, each table, each everything, was elegantly handcrafted from fine Vana lumber by fine Vana carpenters. The patrons appeared to be an even mix of residents from several cities. The Vanatians wore simpler clothing, loose-fitting, with generally bland colors. Much more pragmatic for the woodworking and harvesting industry. The Dyrians, the wealthy tamers of the sea, were in their dark, tight leathers, their vests strapped with knives and other trinkets. And, of course, the always fashionable Rialians who, like Arthur, wore more extravagant and formal attire—women in lacey dresses, men with black hats and dress coats.

A beautiful Dyrian woman standing by the bar pounded back her drink as an elderly Vanatian man rambled on beside her. Her jet-black hair was tied into two braids on either side of her face. She wore a fitted red leather outfit with intricate gold and silver guards around her shins, forearms, and shoulders. The outfit was covered with black holsters—daggers around her left thigh, a pouch on her right, a black studded belt with a silver buckle that secured her rapier and pistol, and two black leather straps across her upper stomach. Beside her, the gregarious Vanatian man grew more animated in his storytelling. His gray beard was comically long for his short stature. He wore round spectacles like a badge of academia, which accented his freckled face and beaming smile. His outfit was indistinct, consisting of brown robes with long drooping sleeves, beige tights, and pointed leather shoes. The woman gazed idly over his head, making little attempt to hide her disinterest in the conversation.

Arthur walked up to the odd couple with his arms outstretched. "Samira! Professor!"

Professor Fenske's mouth dropped. "Mr. Winston, so good to see you." The professor stuck out his hand to quickly shake Arthur's.

"Good to see you, too. Samira, lovely as always."

Samira flashed an annoyed smile and cocked her head to the side. "Hi, Arthur. Nice of you to join us. Did the children enjoy their Riali trinkets?"

He laughed and pulled up a stool. "Ah well, I cannot come to the Midbloom empty-handed. Have to keep those spirits up somehow!"

"I'm sure it was a long flight. Do you need a drink? My tab is open."

Arthur thanked her for the generosity and flagged down a bartender. "So, Samira, how have you been?"

"Busy. There's a lot to be done, but I couldn't miss Midbloom."

"Of course, neither could I. How is your father holding up these days?"

"Nothing you need to worry about. Princess Nora has done an excellent job keeping the world safe by adding extra security."

Arthur raised his glass. "For the best, I am sure."

"Arthur, about Riali," Professor Fenske said, stroking his long, gray beard. "I've been waiting to hear back from

Dr. Redding regarding his cellular reprogramming trials and—"

Arthur shook his head. "No, my apologies, Rupert; I have not been in touch with Redding or the happenings at Langford. However, I did hear from my friends at the university that you selected Asher Auden to attend, yes?"

"Correct!"

"It was an obvious choice, I suppose," said Arthur.

"Of course! I have never come across a student as brilliant as Asher. Truly remarkable."

"And he made you rich," Samira cut in.

The professor scoffed, "Well, not me personally. But certainly, the city is grateful for his contributions."

"Right," said Arthur. "His work on altering genetic crop growth. I heard he played a large part in that project."

"A part? Gods no," said the professor, setting down his drink. "Asher Auden did it all himself. He singlehandedly created new strains of lily fruit and honey pears that can grow in Vana's soil. And the Valencia flowers this year? Those are courtesy of him as well. It's all led to quite the boom for Vana."

"And Dyria as well, from what I hear," said Arthur, nodding at Samira.

"It certainly hasn't hurt the export industry," Samira grinned, taking a sip of whiskey.

Arthur prodded them again. "And Callendra Saint? I was informed she was accepted as well. I am familiar with the girl, but it seems an odd choice; she does not strike me as the big city type."

The professor nodded. "You're not alone in that thought. She's a peculiar girl with a peculiar mind, but a brilliant one, nonetheless. A bit, uhh…independent.

Yes, independent, perhaps more or less for the better. But I think she will flourish once away from Vana."

"Good, Riali could use some brilliant independent thinkers," said Arthur.

"Yes, they could," said Samira dryly.

Arthur and Fenske both let out a nervous laugh before Arthur continued. "So. On to business. How has the princess felt about the new tariffs? She has not said much publicly."

Samira shook her head. "Yeah, we're not too thrilled on that one. Nora has been weak in her response in order to appease the capital. It is an insult for the capital to be blaming Dyria for the recent piracy attacks along their coast. Dyria did not invent piracy, you know."

"No," answered Arthur. "But they did perfect it. These attacks, they are not Dyrian?"

"I've seen these so-called pirates firsthand. They are not Dyrian, nor any band of former Hainlyal Islanders. They are coming from the Marrazo Sea, probably Sumadar."

"But the ships they use," Fenske butted in. "They are made of Vana lumber, which is the ideal material for Dyrian ships. How would any pirate out east get a hold of Vanatian wood without going through Dyria?"

Samira grew visibly frustrated. "If you're insinuating the Raol family has anything to do with this, rest assured my father's company has been disbanded and is upholding its end of the treaty. It is not us!"

Arthur pushed on. "The craftsmanship also appears to be advanced."

"Not Dyrian advanced," Samira muttered. "And now only Dyria has to pay these ridiculous sanctions until the attacks stop? Bullshit. Clearly, this is the capital's way of stepping on our throats. They're worried they won't be able to compete economically. They want to monopolize shipping in Khamara. They've even been locking in exclusive trade rights with other cities!" Samira fumed.

"I understand your frustration, and it gets worse." Arthur stared down at his glass. "After the tariff announcement, a string of attacks has been made on land against Riali's more prominent members."

"And they suspect Dyria?"

"No. The attacks were made using biochemical weaponry. No official word on the motive of the attackers, but—"

"But given the current climate and the nature of the attack, it seems logical to assume it would be a Dyrian extremist acting in retaliation," Fenske said, nervously fidgeting with his glasses.

Samira snapped, "There are no terrorists in Dyria! Ever since we locked my father away, our piracy has dropped to zero. All our operations are by the books, exactly how Riali wants it!"

"I know, I know." Arthur raised his hands and put them on Samira's shoulders. "We will have this resolved. Some of the most brilliant detectives in Riali are working this case. Once we have more details, we will be able to renegotiate the tariffs. In the meantime, I think Princess Nora has the right idea. Cooperation builds trust, and trust is more important than ever right now."

"Agreed," Fenske nodded.

Samira took a sip of her whiskey and stared into the glass. She had spent years transforming her father's former piracy armada into a legitimate trading company. His conditional surrender and her success as a trade merchant had led to a better life for Dyrians and citizens of the surrounding islands. For it all to be undermined by new tariffs brought about by two-bit pirates and a bioterrorist would lead to an inevitable regression. She finished off her glass and watched the streets outside. Dusk had begun to set in. The festival would be starting soon.

The crowd became denser and more constrictive as Callie pushed through to the front. Excitement soaked into the city's wood frames like whiskey aging in a barrel. The sidewalks were packed to capacity as giant elaborate floats paraded through the streets, mesmerizing the townsfolk who waved at the marvelous towering creations. A new Dyrian airship hovered inches off the ground as pirates and tradespeople swung from sail ropes, waving to the crowds below. Clunky steam robots tumbled down the street, tossing flowers and candy to the cheering onlookers. The smell of slow-cooked meat caught Cloud's nose as he turned his head and let out a low growl. Callie looked up to see the burly customer from earlier manning a vendor cart.

"Hey, watch that fox of yours, girl. Put a leash on him or something."

The man stood beside a fire pit where a squirrel was roasting over an open flame. Callie scratched the back of Cloud's head. "It's alright, buddy, let it go."

The crowd packed in even more tightly. Callie was too short to see over the onlookers, but she could tell exactly what had happened from the sound. *Brghh...brghh...brghh...brghh.* The ground shook as Drvo delicately stumbled onto Main Street. Adults and children ran up alongside the rock golem with Valencia flowers outstretched in offering. Drvo walked closer to the village's center and knelt down in a patch of grass near Arthur's ship. The children shuffled into a disorganized line beside the giant, who sat patiently on the knoll with his mossy palms opened skyward. One by one, they placed flowers into his hand, taking their time to touch the granite fingertips in awestruck wonder. Drvo carefully grabbed the flowers and planted them onto his body; each then bloomed instantaneously, twice as big, and twice as bright. A purple flower on his shoulder. A yellow one for his chest. A red for his neck. A white for his thigh.

Callie walked up to Drvo. He smiled a big stony grin. She was never sure if he recognized her, but it didn't matter; she was happy to see another creature happy. She opened up her satchel and grabbed a long-stemmed valencia to place in his palm. He let out a low grunt of approval as she brushed her fingers alongside his granite arm. Cloud sniffed at an orange flower near his waist as Drvo placed Callie's flower just over where his heart would be.

"Callie! Hey, Callie!" called a voice from off in the distance. Callie pretended not to hear the call and walked away, Cloud at her heels. "Callieeee!" The voice was closer now and had no intention of letting her escape. She forced a smile and turned to her pursuer. A big, goofy boy with short messy hair came bounding through the crowd, his beige work shirt half unbuttoned and drenched in sweat.

"Hey, Liam."

Liam stopped and leaned forward, hands on his waist to catch his breath. "Hi, Callie! So glad I caught up to you."

"Oh?" she asked, tilting her head slightly.

"Because you're leaving tomorrow! Just, you know, wanted to see how you were doing before you and Asher got up and left us all behind in Vana."

Callie watched as Asher came walking slowly behind Liam.

"I'm good, thanks." She looked over at Asher, who nodded to her. Liam continued to ramble. "You goin' to miss this place at all? It's pretty here. All kinds of cool animals and stuff. We got Drvo." Liam pointed to the golem. "What does Riali have, ya know? Just a bunch of steel and fancy factories."

Asher shook his head and grinned. "Liam, you've never *been* to Riali."

"Yeah, but I know all about it from, like, school and stuff. It's the capital, along the Marrazo Sea, it's big—"

Callie interrupted, "Vana's pretty great, Liam. But I'll be back on breaks, and I'd never miss Midbloom."

"Great! Yeah, I'll actually be up there in a few months for a koroka match! It's against Langford, so you'll have to show me around."

A pair of hands came from nowhere and slapped both Liam and Asher on the back. "Boys!" Arthur exclaimed. "And lady!" He bowed his head toward Callie.

Callie cracked a smile. "Hi, Arthur."

Asher had jumped from the slap but quickly regained his composure before turning to face Arthur. "Arthur! I saw you land earlier! What are you doing in Vana?"

"I never miss Midbloom! I will be going back to Riali shortly, but not before stopping over in Callie's old hometown for a quick trip to help out with an almiraj problem." He smiled at Callie.

She didn't really consider Elurra to be her hometown—she really didn't consider anywhere to really be home—but Arthur only meant well, so she played along.

"I've never seen an almiraj. Are they aggressive?"

Arthur laughed. "Not at all! They are known to attack the occasional livestock if it wanders too close to its den. We just need to do some basic warding and make sure the population is not getting out of hand."

She nodded as Arthur continued, "Riali might have some in the sanctuary, so you might get a chance to see one there! You and Asher are going to love the capital. Delicious food, beautiful architecture. The people are wonderful, truly. You two are both going to do so well!"

His excitement was contagious to both Asher and Callie. Liam, on the other hand, looked away awkwardly.

"Well, I hope you all enjoy Midbloom and the beautiful Vana air for one last night. I would love to chat more, but I am on my way to help the mayor with his ceremony."

The group said their goodbyes to Arthur as he made his way to the stage. Asher turned toward Callie. "We're going to head up to the stage for a closer look if you want to join us."

She shook her head. "I need to be getting back to the shop. I haven't packed for tomorrow yet."

Liam didn't take the hint. "Ah, come on, it's your last night here. Plus, Asher has worked all year on creating these berries that behave like kane shrooms and—"

"It's nothing," Asher interrupted, but Liam continued to ramble.

"They're awesome, they make you feel so connected with everything, and you have these fun little visions, nothing too—"

"Liam. She said she needs to get back to the shop and pack."

Liam looked between Asher and Callie in bewildered confusion. Callie rolled her eyes. "Uh, thanks for the offer, but really, I need to go. I'll see you guys later." She turned with Cloud to disappear into the crowd.

Asher smacked Liam on the shoulder, "What the hell was that?"

"What the hell was what?"

"No one knows about these things. We still barely know if they work, and you just want to give them away?"

"I was just being polite."

"Well, congrats on that one. I'm not sure offering hallucinogens is the best pickup line."

"I wasn't trying to pick her up with hallucinogens; I just thought it'd be fun to have someone join our party."

"So you ask Callie Saint?" Asher rolled his eyes.

"She practically lives in the woods, no way she hasn't stumbled across kane mushrooms!"

Asher laughed. "Alright, whatever. Let's move to the front. This thing is about to start."

A loud blast of trumpets pierced the air. The crowd pushed up toward the stage at the center of the town square as the music swelled in anticipation. Asher and Liam were just close enough to watch Mayor Hegelson take the stage. He was a well-dressed man with tan skin and a slicked-back mane of white hair, who looked entirely comfortable standing in front of the press of people. He had a charming smile and, while not quite as flashy as Arthur, he had a knack for being charismatic. He waved to the crowd until their cheering subsided.

"Happy Midbloom, Vana!" Mayor Hegelson placed his hands down on the podium as the last of the applause faded. "Today, we gather to celebrate the anniversary of Vana's construction. Where others saw nothing more than trees punctured by jagged mountains, our founders envisioned a protected oasis turned into a thriving city. They carved deep canals from the nearby rivers and surrounding hills. They cultivated the land, bringing with them various crops from all across Khamara. And they used the wood, the strongest wood in the world, Vana wood, to build, to trade, and to create the beautiful city we celebrate today." The audience began to cheer again, but the mayor lowered his head and raised his hand.

"But, as the elders among us still remember, this oasis was not always protected. These fields were not always tilled with love and compassion but with the sweat of enslavement. Under the regime of Cha'rik Kai, the wood palaces of our founders turned to embers, our paradise was reduced to a prison camp, our Vanatian women and children sold like livestock, and our men enslaved, selected for cruel genetic programs, or simply murdered. Entire mountains were leveled in the vain pursuit of ore, the best of our timber felled until our forests were laid bare, our rivers dammed and drained." A heavy silence fell over the crowd.

"Happier were the dead and those unborn who never endured the darkest days. But the night is never eternal. And through the suffering, we grew strength. We found that, when given the choice, a burden shared is a burden halved. Vana united alongside the seven cities of Khamara: Riali, Dyria, Saint Mazraea, Kipos, Elurra, and Baenum. An unprecedented alliance rose up and resisted the rule of Kai. Together we endured, we fought, and we won.

"Today, we celebrate the Midbloom, not just for the abundance of life this land has provided. But we celebrate for our families. For our friends. And for our allies all across Khamara who join us now. As we celebrate our unity with the forest, so we celebrate our unity with each other." The mayor outstretched his arm to the seven guests behind him, each sitting in front of a giant wooden cage.

"Behind me are representatives from the seven cities. In front of me is our great Drvo, given to us as a gift in a time of rebuilding from the monks of Saint Mazraea. May the gods allow our friendships to flourish as brilliantly as does the Midbloom." At once, the trumpeters started to back up, the crowd erupted in applause, and the seven emissaries turned to the cages behind them.

Asher and Liam looked at each other and raised the berries to their lips. Liam murmured, "You ready?"

Asher smiled a devious smile and dropped the berry into his mouth. Liam laughed and followed suit.

Instantly their faces went from smiling to puckering. "Oh my lord, these are really sour!" Liam shook his head.

Asher agreed. "I know; I had no idea. To be honest, I didn't put much thought into how they would taste."

"Yech. Well, let's see if you got the rest of the recipe right." There wasn't any immediate effect, so they turned their attention to the stage. Mayor Hegelson dropped his arms, signaling a release. In unison, the seven guests pulled on ropes, and the giant cages unhinged, the walls separating in opposite directions. The heavy wood frames exploded in a cloud of dirt as they slammed against the ground.

The tarps on top of the crates whisked away to reveal giant, green, hovering orbs, spinning, revolving, glowing bright and illuminated with the occasional streak of blue and purple. Each orb held thousands of sprites gathered into a massive cluster, which soon disintegrated as the sprites burst from their groupings and flew through the streets in every direction. They rocketed over the crowd, the occasional straggler zipping in between the festivalgoers in pursuit of nectar. They were a river flowing and glowing above the streets of Vana.

Asher and Liam reached out to touch the sprites as they slipped through their fingertips. Children attempted to catch them in mason jars. Hundreds of the sprites began swarming around Drvo as he stood up, arms outstretched; they circled his limbs, nestling into the blooming flowers. His entire body radiated greens, blues, and purples, with only his wide stony smile still visible for the crowd to see. The sprites settled into the valencia arches. They found their way into the flower crowns of young girls. Houses, shops, sidewalks, and every flower now pulsing like tiny touchable stars. The festival roared on. Drunkards lifted up their libations, lovers kissed in the ever-glow, children were lost in their games. The city was ablaze—buzzing with life.

Asher and Liam followed the glowing river as the sprites made their way through the streets and back into the deep, dense woodland. The forest was noticeably colder than the city, but Asher could feel his body begin to heat up. His limbs grew heavy and his touch more sensitive; the berries were starting to kick in. He turned to Liam. "How are you feeling?"

Liam smiled and wiped a runny nose. "I'm good, I'm good. I'm happy, and I feel, I don't know, cosmic?"

Asher let out a laugh and yawned. "Great. No stomach pains?"

"No, not really."

"Perfect, and are you feeling warm?"

"The opposite, I'm pretty cold."

"Ah, ok, that's normal, too."

"Asher, are you going to sit here and ask research questions the whole time? Or are you going to enjoy the moment? Look at all this beauty. The sun is gone, but the forest has never been brighter. The trees are moving; the flowers are dancing."

Asher was busy examining his hands, noting the sensation of a peculiar moisture around him, and losing himself to thought. He had spent all year working on this creation, splicing a psychoactive gene found in kane mushrooms into the sussberry, a common berry often used as a mild stimulant in teas. While the kane mushroom was elusive and difficult to cultivate, its psychoactive properties had been used to treat various mental and central nervous system disorders for centuries. He hoped that combining them could enhance each other's properties while also making them easier to cultivate. *But how would the two interact? And did I even manage to get the potency right?* Those were the questions. It appeared he and Liam had experienced a similar response time. Now that they had a baseline to work off, maybe it was time for him to up the dosage and take a second berry?

Liam protested the idea. "What are you doing? A second one? Really? I'm almost twice your weight and I'm feeling it just fine!"

"Don't worry, I know what I'm doing. I feel great, too. You know what, Lamb? I'm really glad you're here on my last night." Asher was quick to change the subject.

"Yeah." Liam let out a deep sigh, seeming not to mind Asher's quick subject change. "I'm gonna miss having you around. You made this place a lot more fun."

"I'm not dying, you know. Just going off for a bit. I'll be back."

"I know, I know. You're going to go off and be a big bad scientist. Change the world. Save some lives. Me? I'm stuck being a lumberjack like everyone else in this place."

"Hey now, you're studying forestry part-time at Oakard Academy. Besides, you love it here!"

"Of course I do, but I've never actually been anywhere else."

Asher and Liam stopped and sat on a large rock beside a creek. They watched as the city became a distant glow, its streets spiderwebbing with the green radiance of fluttering sprites.

Asher kept his eyes fixed on a family of sprites buzzing over the creek. "Well, why don't you come to Riali? There's plenty of factories. Someone of your size and stature, it'd be easy to get a job."

"Bah, that big city life isn't for me. I mean, yeah, I haven't traveled much, but this is what I know. You know?"

"I guess. But not knowing is what I'm most excited about. I love my family and home, but I'm bored. I want something new. I want to start over, maybe make a name for myself or something."

"See, that's what I'm saying! You've always had that mind for it. Asking questions and whatnot. You've always cared about what's next, and you've always made a plan for everything. I'm not like that. I'm just good at doing what I'm told."

"You're hardworking, and you're more intelligent than you give yourself credit for; you'd do fine!"

"It's not about that. Of course I'd do fine. But what difference does it make if I'm doing fine here or doing fine over there? At least here, I have people I know. I have this beautiful forest; I have a job that I'm good at. Riali people, they aren't like me. And they might not like me because of it. And I might hate that big city with all the smoke and machines. Nah, you know just as well as I do that Vana is my home. I'm simple. You're not. That's what it comes down to."

Brghh...brghh. Drvo's footsteps marching back into the woods grew louder. The vibrations made Asher uneasy as his kane shroom fever grew more intense. He played it off and tried to focus on the conversation. "You give me a lot more credit than I deserve."

"Oh, and why's that?"

"I'm not fearless, and I definitely don't have everything planned. I'm pretty nervous, actually. What if I'm not as smart as I think I am? What if I'm too weird and don't make any friends? I don't think I even know how to make friends. I've never had to do it before. Like, what do you say to someone? Nice shirt, want to take magical berries by a river?"

The boys laughed. The laughter felt good, but Asher's vision started to blur; the greens and blues of the sprites began to change to bright reds and oranges. He looked over at Liam, who seemed unfazed.

"Are you seeing anything different?"

Liam shook his head. "Are you tripping out?"

"I'm not sure...everything is starting to turn red."

"Oh, I'm definitely not seeing red, but it is starting to get cold, and everything I touch feels weirdly wet. Let's head back."

As they hopped off the stone, Asher slipped into the creek, soaking his ankles. The water began to boil and steam around him. He let out a gasp, but Liam didn't seem to notice. Asher pulled himself from the creek and looked up at the forest. The trees were engulfed in flame. Panic set in as an inferno raged. Loud, pulsing heat choked him. "Are, are you seeing this? The whole forest, it's on fire!"

Liam looked down at Asher, who had fallen backward into the creek. Asher couldn't make out what he was saying.

"I...I can't...I don't know what's going on." Tails of fire whipped from the tree branches, lapping Asher's face. Liam grabbed for Asher and began guiding him away from the creek. Asher cowered away from the flaming forest.

*Brghhhh...*Drvo staggered into the clearing, his entire body wrapped in flame. Asher froze in terror.

"Asher, c'mon!"

He couldn't hear Liam's words. The only sounds in his ears were those of the inferno as he watched the giant crumble into embers and the forest dissipate to smoke and cinder.

CHAPTER 3

Tan tweed vest: Check. Beige, long-sleeve shirt: Check. Wooly flat cap: Check. Pocket watch: Check. Leather shoes with matching black socks: Check and check. Asher Auden was dapper. His usually messy black hair was slicked over to the side at the behest of his mother so she could see both his green eye and his blue eye. She held back tears.

"Asher, you look so dashing! You're going to make a great first impression on all those Rialians."

"Mom, please, I don't think I can handle any more affection."

Asher stepped away from the mirror to finish closing his trunk, which was brimming with clothes and lab supplies. His father barged into the room. "Everyone ready to go?"

"Yep, all set."

"Cara, are you crying again?"

Asher's mother scowled. "Don't you make fun of me. I know you'll be bawling your eyes out soon enough. And you need to change your clothes; we are not going out in public with you looking like that!"

Mr. Auden raised his hands in defense. "Hey now, I'll get cleaned up here in just a minute."

Asher looked up from his packing. "You've been at it all morning. What are you working on? Looked like some kind of chair last time I saw."

His dad smiled. "It's a throne. A captain's throne."

"Oh, fancy! Is it for one of these Dyrian merchants or something?"

"It's for Samira's ship."

Asher's jaw dropped. "Samira Raol? Nicely done, Dad! That better be one heck of a piece."

"Yeah, we'll see. She approached me last night after seeing the work I did on the Baenum float. She's only in town for a few more days, so I gotta make it a quick order. Alright, let me go clean up real quick and we'll head out. Oh, also, Liam's in the kitchen."

Pieces of black hair poked out from under the edges of Asher's cap as he gave it a tug. He flung a satchel across his shoulders and began to drag the heavy wooden trunk out his bedroom door as his mother tidied up behind him. Sunlight spilled into the wood house, bouncing off shiny brass appliances and glass cabinets. Bittersweet nostalgia began to set in as he looked over the house for one last time. At the kitchen counter sat a bulky teen scarfing down breakfast. Liam looked over at Asher. "Well. Good morning, sunshine!"

Asher cracked a smile. "Gooood morning..."

"How ya feeling?"

"I'm alive."

"Ha! Something like that. What was that little episode about?"

"I think I might have internalized too much of Mayor Hegelson's speech; it was a bit dark, after all."

"Well, at least you can get some extra rest on the train ride. You've got a long way to go to get to Langford."

Asher stole a muffin from Liam. "You're looking alright."

Liam kept his head down as he continued to shovel food into his mouth. "Yep. Destroyed your parents' bathroom after I dropped you off but otherwise, I'm great! You did a good job on those berries. Really man, felt like a new universe opened to me. Everything was so beautiful and—"

"Oh, Liam, you're up early!" Asher's mom barged into the kitchen. "Did you enjoy the Midbloom last night?"

Liam gulped down his food. "Morning, Mrs. Auden. Yes, ma'am, Asher and I had an excellent time. Great food, the floats, the fairies—"

"They're sprites," Asher interrupted.

"Yeah, yeah, the sprites, the music. It was a great time! Asher saw some real interesting fire displays—" Asher hit him on that last remark.

"Great, I'm so happy you two were able to enjoy it. We're off to the station, did you want to join us?"

Liam shook his head. "No, ma'am, I have koroka practice later. Just thought I'd stop by and say goodbye before you all took off."

On cue, Murphy walked back into the room wearing a cleaner set of clothes. "Cranked the car, time to get out of here."

Liam jumped off the stool and gave Asher a bear hug. His barrel chest smelled of cedar as his grizzly arms pressed the air out of Asher's lungs. "Gonna miss you, Ashy."

"Gonna miss you too, Lamb. We'll keep in touch, alright?"

"Yeah, definitely. Don't get into too much trouble without me. Riali doesn't know what it's in for."

Asher laughed. "Whatever you say. I'll see you around." They gave each other a few pats on the back before breaking off the embrace. His dad grabbed the trunk as his mother gave Liam a quick kiss on the cheek.

Asher walked out the door and turned to look back at the place he'd called home for the past seventeen years. The sight caused his limbs to tingle with the prick of a thousand needles. Excitement, nervousness. Adrenaline coursed through his veins; his head was a whirl of grayish fog. Whatever anxieties had plagued his mind the night before had now been fully realized. He wanted to throw himself on the floor of the house, to plant himself into the comfort of the only home he'd ever known. At the same time, he knew what waited for him was something so much more. A city of greatness that would bring out his fullest potential. This small town, this humble carpenter's farm, was a cage—a comfortable cage—but a cage, nonetheless. It was a place that had never fit him well. Always different, always special. It was time, he thought, to see the true limits of who he was—and what he could become.

He had a train to catch.

"Are you sure Langford doesn't have any public phones?" asked Asher's mother.

"Only local, nothing that I could use that would reach Vana, Mom. But it'll be fine, I'll write to you."

"You better," Asher's mom said, teary-eyed. He gave her one last squeeze before giving his beaming father a hug goodbye as well.

"Love you, see you in the winter!" He waved goodbye and ran toward the train.

The platform was packed with Vanatian lumberjacks bustling about their business of securing timber to flatbeds. A steam whistle screeched as the passengers finished piling inside the obsidian black train. Brass handrails welcomed the travelers. The booths were a dark-red leather adorned with hand-carved rosewood. Tiny lamps and chandeliers provided a soothing ambiance while the dawning sunlight poured through large rectangular windows.

Asher made his way down the aisles. His parents took too long to say goodbye; he was never going to find a decent seat. The first several rows were wealthy Dyrian families and Riali businessmen, no doubt on their way to the capital for vacation or to conduct new business dealings. He scanned the aisles as his bulky trunk clanged against the copper edges of booths. Full. Full. Full. Thick smoke began to billow outside the window; he could no longer see his parents. They had been watching him through the windows as he awkwardly attempted to find a place. Full. Full. Full.

The train began to creep. He continued his search from one train car to the next until he spotted an open booth. Across from it sat a man in a long trench coat, black boots, and a faded black cap. Beside him, Asher could make out what appeared to be the top of a glass mason jar. The man turned to face Asher as he prepared to put down his trunk.

The man's voice was low and sounded like stale cigars. "That booth is taken, boy." Asher could not make out his eyes, just a protruding chin and thin lips. "This seat is for Shelly. And Shelly ain't too fond of sharing seats with strangers." The man pulled a double-barrel shotgun from his side and laid it on the booth across from him. The slightest of smirks appeared on his face as Asher pulled his flat cap down over his eyes, picked up his trunk, and continued on down the cars.

The train began to pick up speed alongside Asher's heart rate. Full. Full. Full. Not a good start to his first great adventure. Asher was in the last car near the last of the booths before he found refuge. Callie. Her wavy auburn hair was buried in Cloud's snow-white fur while his fluffy tail curled gently around her neck. The feathers in her hair were gone, replaced by a powder-blue headband. She wore a long, matching, powder-blue dress, a white shirt, and white gloves. Definitely the fanciest attire Asher had seen her wear. She appeared to be sleeping. No matter, she was a familiar face.

Asher knocked on the wood paneling of the booth across from her. Cloud shot up from the seat like a rocket, sending Callie's head against the brass latch of the window. "Shit!" She rubbed her head in a daze of confusion before looking up at him. "What the hell, Asher?"

Asher dropped his trunk. "I'm so sorry. I didn't mean to...I just...Can I join you?"

Callie relaxed her look. "Sure." She patted the space beside her, and Cloud jumped up, resting his head against her lap. Asher pushed his trunk under the seat and threw his satchel down before collapsing into the booth. Callie and Asher stared out the window in silence and watched the dense Vana forest slowly give way to the grassy green hills of the east.

The train came to rest at a station in a small town called Holdenmare, a midway point between Vana and Riali. Callie and Asher had passed the journey reading: Callie was deep into *Beasts of the Eastern Sea* while Asher spent the time studying *Recombinant DNA Techniques with an Emphasis on Genetic Splicing*. By now, the scenery had begun to transition from grassland to fields of flowing wheat.

The stop in Holdenmare was quick, only a few short minutes to let a handful of passengers on and off. As the train started up again, a scrawny boy sporting glasses and a cowboy hat began to bumble down the aisles of their car. Callie looked up from her book and let out the faintest of groans. Asher turned around and immediately made eye contact with the frantic boy, who smiled and walked toward them. He dropped his bags and outstretched his hand. "Hi there, I'm Felix Donegal."

Asher looked over at Callie before turning back to Felix. "Hi, Felix. I'm Asher, and this is Callie and Cloud." Callie gave the boy a nod.

"The train seems to be a little crowded. Guessing it's from all the tourists visiting Vana's Midbloom. Mind if I join y'all?"

Asher smiled kindly and scooted over. "Not at all!" Callie went back to her book.

Felix continued the idle chat. "What business y'all got goin' on in Riali?"

"Callie and I are from Vana and are heading into our first year at Langford."

"Oh, no way. Congrats! It's actually my second year at Langford. Studying law."

"Really? How do you like it so far?"

"It's fantastic. The city is beautiful, very progressive—a big change of scenery from anything you'd see in Kipos. Not sure how I feel about all the stuff that's been going on lately, though, really tragic stuff."

Asher gave Felix a confused look. "What kind of tragic stuff?"

"The attacks." He looked at the two of them. "Wait. You ain't heard about the terrorist attacks?"

Asher shook his head. "Vana media isn't always up to date with current affairs."

"Ah hell," said Felix, throwing up his hands. "Y'all Vanatians must have been too busy with your festival to have heard about it. There were two chemical terrorist attacks over the past week!"

Callie looked up from her book. "I heard about it." Asher looked at her with questioning eyes. "I overheard Arthur Winston talking to Mayor Hegelson, saying something about an accident involving toxic chemicals. Nothing serious." She returned to her book.

Felix shook his head. "Yeah, well, at the moment, my suspicion is that it's Dyrian extremists, probably the Raol Company."

Asher laughed. "No way Dyria would attack Riali. Why would two of Khamara's biggest cities go after each other?"

"Look, I'm studying law to become a detective. The evidence suggests that these attacks were intended to specifically target several prominent members of elite Riali family lines, many of whom are responsible for the financial regulations that led to the Dyrian tariffs."

"Wasn't the first victim some candy shop owner?" asked Callie.

"Well, that's not confirmed to be related, just suspected."

"And hasn't Riali had issues with Sumadar pirates? Why wouldn't you assume them first?"

"Yeah, I guess that makes sense too."

"Or, you know, an accident like the papers all report," she said, clearly annoyed.

"Ok, those are all fair points. Regardless, the sheriff is handling this case personally. We'll have an answer soon, so we'll see who's to blame."

Felix was cut off as the train began to shake violently. Callie's eyes widened, and she threw her book into her bag and pressed up against the window. Asher spoke up first. "What is it? Earthquake?"

"No, look!" Callie pointed out the window.

Asher slid over and cupped his hands around his eyes like they were binoculars. "What the...? What are those?"

A herd of giant, four-legged creatures stampeded across the expanses of the wheat field. They were over fifteen feet tall and had an armadillo-like appearance: a crown of large spikes protruded from the head, with smaller spikes extending downward to the tail. Their dark-green skin faded into white around the belly, mouth, and inner legs. Each arm ended with three sharp claws that dug deep into the dirt. Each step sounded like crashing timber. Asher couldn't make out the teeth.

"Those are feylooms," Callie said with excitement. "They're native to the Riali region. They evolved in recent years to graze on the wheat, but in extreme circumstances, have been known to be omnivores as well. There used to be more ripe, tall grass that they feasted on, along with endo leaves, but as Riali became industrialized, a lot of the vegetation around the capital vanished."

"You sure do know a lot about feylooms," Felix piped up.

Asher smirked. "Yeah, animals are her thing."

Callie kept her eyes glued to the window.

Asher spoke up again. "So, how far out do you think we are from Riali?"

Callie adjusted herself further back into the seat. "Well, judging by that giant city skyline up ahead, I'd say we're here."

CHAPTER 4

Asher slid over to take Cloud's spot, who let out a tiny, disgruntled growl before Callie calmed him down. Outside the window, Asher could make out the massive skyline of the capital, illuminated by the glow of dusk. The train exited the lush fields and entered massive farmlands which stretched deep into the southern horizon. Wide rivers intertwined from the west, pouring into the city's surrounding channels and bay. Tiny traveling boats looked like ants circling around the large merchant ships that waded slowly through the channels, their white sails furling against the boom while being towed to shore.

The city was on elevated land and surrounded by walls of pure white marble stone that rose thirty feet high. Every two hundred or so yards, the marble walls were punctured by skyward marble towers that resembled large double-edged axes. Behind the walls emerged massive stone buildings and billowing iron smokestacks, which pierced the serenity with thick, black clouds. Above them were airships, some ascending, some descending, and some hovering low with flashing lights that advertised the latest gadgetry. At the center of the city, Asher could make out two looming, mammoth structures—the Citadel and Langford University.

He noticed they had started to lose speed. They were now entering the gates of Riali, which were open in anticipation of the train's arrival. Iron gates laced with intricate designs of roaring lions welcomed it like arms greeting a dear friend into a home. Soon the freight was swallowed up by the enormity of the city.

Three to five story buildings made of handcrafted stone rose in every lot. The structures were built full of columns and arches, many with circular dome tops; it was a beautiful, infinite style of architecture that appeared to lack defined edges. Large bowing windows plastered the walls, emanating a warm glow and giving a certain luminosity to the evening fog that filled the city. The train passed under large granite bridges which interconnected the buildings at various stories.

Back on ground level, just outside the train, the sidewalks were bustling with the kind of energy only a Saturday night in a big city could bring. The women wore tight corsets and bodices of assorted cloths and leather, their necks accented by gold jewelry or the occasional leather choker. Younger women's dresses were cut short at the front, with frilly trains flowing down the back to their ankles over knee-high leather boots laced in bold shades of reds and pinks. Peeking out of the boots were stockings, which rose to mid-thigh. The women whose dresses cut off at the shoulder would wear sheer arm sleeves that began midway up the bicep and ended midway to the forearm, *a peculiar covering of the elbow*, thought Asher. Some wore white gloves. All wore rings and bracelets made of precious metals. The outfits were decorated with elaborate designs and adorned with thin gold chains. Leather belts bedecked with tiny pouches hung around their hips. Most of the women had their hair pulled up in a puffy bun style, with a few tasteful curls wisping down the side of their faces. Their hats resembled something closer to headbands than actual hats, containing little to no brim but instead an occasional thin sheer veil. Some were encrusted with ornate diamond pendants; others displayed flowers or large black feathers.

"There is no way I am dressing like that," Callie murmured, seemingly as a promise to herself more than a statement for the boys.

The men dressed in complex layers as well, but not without utility. Slacks and leather boots were universal. Their vests were less ornate than the women's dresses but still contained brass buttons and chains: chains for stopwatches, chains for glasses, chains for various tools of their trade. Underneath the waistcoats were shirts of predominantly white, beige, and black, held together by bowties. Almost all left their jackets unbuttoned. Most headwear was top hats and bowler hats, some accented by goggles and glasses, giving Asher a sense of each man's line of work. Short, clean haircuts seemed to be the prevailing style, alongside barbershop-precision beards, all of which made Asher a bit self-conscious of his more unkempt look and inability to grow facial hair.

The animals, too, were odd, at least to Asher's eyes. People in Vana rarely kept pets—Callie being an exception—and when they did, they were nothing like the Rialian pets he could see. The animals appeared to be *modified*: dogs with purple polka-dotted fur, miniature cats with kitten-big eyes.

He could make out what seemed to be a large, robotic man made entirely of brass gears wearing a trench coat. A young girl in a blue dress waved to the robot, who removed his top hat and bowed deeply. As he did, he produced a flower from his hat and handed it to her. She let out an excited squeal as she clutched the flower. The robot twirled the top hat back to his head and went on his way, blending into the bustling Riali night.

The train slowed enough for Asher to get a sense of the many shops: your standard tailors, cobblers, watchmakers, and tea shops. Caution tape wrapped around the side of a quaint store in the center of the street. The entire walkway was blocked off, guarded by armed soldiers. *A candy shop?* He questioned as he pressed closer to the glass. Inside, he could see a throng of soldiers and detectives scouring the shelves and rows of confections. A brief glance was all Asher could afford—shattered glass, tattered shelves, and what appeared to be melted lollipops. *What happened here*, thought Asher, *and how could anything at a candy shop possibly warrant the military?*

The train came to a stop at Riali's Central Station. Asher grabbed his bag and hopped off the car alongside Callie and Felix, Cloud following closely behind them. More armed guards greeted the passengers at the end of the terminal.

"What is this about?" Callie asked Felix.

"Retinal scans," said Felix. "They're IDing all newcomers to Riali. Standard precautions since the terrorist attacks."

Asher stepped forward as a guard shoved a brass scanner in their face.

"Eye, please," said the guard.

"Which one?" Asher joked, pointing at his blue eye and then his green.

The guard scratched his head. "Uhh...the green one."

Asher smiled as the guard scanned his eye, asked him a series of questions, and then ushered him along with the group through the terminal.

Steel signs rotated on oversized mechanical gears. Callie was the first to find it. "There." She pointed upward at one of the signs. "Shuttle to Langford, it's over here."

Asher and Felix followed her through the station. The all-glass dome ceiling felt as if it were a mile high; the floor was perfectly squared marble. Every table, bench, handrail—all were crafted from gold. Asher had never seen this kind of wealth before; Vana was a place made almost entirely of wood. Here, everything was metal and machinery. Machine tellers, machine vendors, the people themselves carrying briefcases that resembled machines. Asher watched as a robot with spring-loaded arms launched itself in front of Callie, attempting to sell her sweets. "Oh, excuse me!" spoke the offended robot as she swatted its metallic hand away, Callie's face flushing with embarrassment, not having realized the robot's level of sentience.

While Langford was within walking distance from the station, their heavy bags and long day made it mutually understood that the bus was their best option. The platform was packed, predominately with who Asher assumed were students—well-dressed but also looking somewhat disheveled from their travels.

Once the bus arrived, Callie headed straight for the back with Cloud. Asher and Felix followed suit and found a seat together. Felix began to chat about his hometown but was cut short as a massive building appeared in their view. The Citadel was twelve stories high and composed primarily of cement and stone. The perimeter contained seven interconnected, spiraling towers, each unique in its décor, ranging from two to four stories high and varying in distance to each other. At the heart of the Citadel was a pyramid-like structure, which started as a large, square base and narrowed with each subsequent floor. However, unlike a pyramid, at the fourth floor, the structure transitioned into three distinct pieces. The centerpiece was circular and consisted of many columns. The two outer sections retained their pyramid-esque shape, with the occasional balcony and overhang jutting from the side. They were curved on the side facing the centerpiece, and bridges at every few stories connected the three. At the top of the building, the centerpiece came to a circular peak, while the two outer structures stopped at sharp points, giving the building a look of having horns.

Felix leaned over to Asher. "That's the Citadel. It was originally constructed before the dark days as a great Hilezkorra temple."

Asher nodded. "Yeah, I've heard about it. What all goes on in there?"

Felix continued, "Well, it was reconstructed and expanded upon when Cha'rik Kai ruled. There's still the occasional service, but now it's mainly just a government building. The president lives there. It's used as an embassy and where the representatives meet. Of course, it hosts big events, and some businesses and trading groups work from the offices. There's a cafeteria and a library too, but not as big as the library at Langford."

"Right. Yeah, I guess I knew all that to some degree. It's just the enormity of it; there's nothing even close to that in Vana." A small silence took over as they admired the architecture. "But it's beautiful," Asher added.

Within a few minutes, the bus pulled up to Langford University. It was just shy of being the same height as the Citadel and acted as its counterpart: Langford, a symbol of science and progress. The Citadel, a symbol of faith and tradition. The two pillars of science and faith holding hands at the center of the nation's largest and most prosperous city.

As they piled out, it became clear who were first timers at Langford. Several students stopped in awe of its magnitude. Four equal towers on each corner, connecting to a massive structure of concrete, stone, and glass. The new arrivals exhaustedly hauled their luggage up stone steps toward large, gaudy doors of wood and iron. Asher entered the front chamber and quickly became overwhelmed by the bustling halls filled with students.

He watched as friends reunited and others searched frantically for clues about where to go. At the end of the hall was a series of tables, each with a big block sign that read: A-D, E-H, I-L, M-P, Q-T, U-Z. Each table had long lines of students extending throughout the hall of the chamber. An older-looking gentleman in a well-worn suit stood at the front of the doorway, shouting orders. "Go to the table that corresponds to the first letter of your last name. Your *last* name. The tables have your semester schedules. I repeat, go to the tables whose letter corresponds to your last name!"

Anxiety continued to spread over Asher. He had never seen this many people his own age in one place before. Callie turned to him. "Guess I'll see ya later."

He waved goodbye, seeing a hint of nervousness in her usually calm exterior. Despite Felix's odd looks and attire, Asher felt grateful to have him by his side as they walked up to their respective line. Felix continued to chat idly, droning about horse wrangling on the Kipos frontier. Asher wasn't paying much attention; he was too focused on staring at the predominantly Riali student body. Their chatter was a loud static that flooded his ears. He watched as one group of boys shouted at another across the rows of students in what was a clear fraternal bond. Packs of girls congregated, sharing schedules and dorm assignments. And their attire! Asher was wearing his best yet felt nowhere near as well-dressed as the students around him.

In a separate line, Callie attempted to bury herself in a book. She was used to being alone, but this was different. Her head felt light and dizzy, and her vision began to blur. She tried to focus on the words, to get outside her nervousness, but her eyesight had become splotchy. A whine from below took her attention from the page. She looked down to see Cloud, as anxious as she was from the surrounding crowd of unfamiliar faces. "I know, buddy," she said reassuringly. "We'll be in a room soon."

A few students carried cages of various reptiles and rodents. Another girl walked by with a gregorian hawk. A group of girls in front of her looked down at Cloud sheepishly, then back up to Callie. She forced a friendly smile, but they looked away quickly, unwilling to acknowledge her. *Right*, she thought, *don't be weird, just read your book.*

Langford had approved Cloud to be in the facilities after a series of requests from Professor Fenske at Callie's prompting. But for all of Cloud's sleek and graceful beauty, he was still a snow fox; his home was in the wild. She reached down and stroked his silky head. The touch soothed them both. "You are even more out of place in the crowds of Riali than in the forests of Vana."

Cloud licked her hand and stood closer to her side.

Asher walked up to the table and met a worn-out but friendly-looking professor. His young face was framed by round glasses and disheveled brown hair. He had a warm and inviting smile.

"Last name please?" said the professor.

"Auden."

"Auden…" said the gentleman, thumbing through his files. "Ah, you are Asher Auden!"

"That's me," said Asher.

"I'm Professor Redding, Director of Biological Research." He reached out his hand. "Professor Fenske sent you with glowing remarks."

"Oh, wow," said Asher, shaking his hand. "Yeah, he's told me all about your research in cellular reprogramming. I was looking forward to meeting you and hearing more about it."

The professor's smile grew wider. "Yes! He has helped me solve a few recombinant DNA dilemmas. But it is a conversation for another time. I am sure you are exhausted from your travels; here are your papers." Redding handed Asher a folder and room key. "You will be in the Southwest tower, room 501. In your file are a schedule, a map of the school, various brochures, and some other goodies. If you have any questions, your resident assistant will be at the end of the hall and will help get you all moved in and set up."

Asher thanked the professor and fumbled to stash the file in his overstuffed satchel.

"I look forward to seeing you in class on Monday. Nice meeting you, Asher!"

"It was nice meeting you, too, sir!"

Asher stepped out of the line and waited for Felix, who grabbed his belongings and headed over. He looked at the folder Asher had given up on cramming into his bag. "Looks like we won't be in the same dormitory; mine's over on the opposite end." Felix pointed to the northeast tower on the map.

"Dang, that's a bummer." Asher wasn't sold on Felix, but it was nice to know at least one friendly face. "I guess I'll see you around?"

"Yeah," said Felix. "It looks like we have religions class together. And you should come find me at the cafeteria tomorrow for lunch!"

"Sounds good, I'll do that."

The boys parted ways, and Asher was truly alone for the first time. It had been a long day of traveling, and the sun had finally set. He was looking forward to unpacking and going to sleep. He walked up the stony steps to the fifth floor of the southwest tower. Each floor was filled with its own moving-in day chaos. Students lugged heavy bags up steep staircases. Asher walked through dim hallways, lit only by wisps of moonlight from high windows, then finally through the giant wooden doors to his floor.

The corridor smelled faintly of mildew and body odor. Loud music was coming from the first door on the left— his room. Asher approached the door, which had been left cracked open. Inside were two skinny beds, one smashed against the window adjacent to the entrance, the other against the wall on the left side. Beside the bed on the left, a boy was putting away clothes in a closet. He was roughly Asher's height, with short blond hair. His shirt was untucked and unbuttoned, revealing his bare chest in a display of brash immodesty or perhaps just deserved confidence. The boy turned and made eye contact with Asher, who had stopped in the doorway. Asher dropped his trunk and hurriedly went to shake the boy's hand. "Hey, I'm Asher."

"Nice to meet you; my name is Nico." The boy had bright blue eyes hidden behind thin-rimmed glasses and short, trimmed facial hair. Asher picked up his trunk and walked it over to his side of the room.

"Looks like we'll be rooming together. Are you from here?"

Nico turned down the record player and went back to unpacking his belongings. "From Riali? Yeah, my parents have a place out west in the city. What about you?"

"Vana."

"Vana? Really? Not many Vanatians at Lang U. Is this your first time in the capital?"

Asher nodded yes. Nico continued, "Well, hey, I can always show you around. What are you studying?"

"Biology. Molecular genetics specifically, but biology is generally my area of expertise." Asher said, immediately becoming worried he might be coming across as boastful.

"Oh, cool, always in need of biologists in Riali. No wonder they selected you. I am studying mechanical engineering. I know it seems a little generic, but I was top of my class in mathematics, and I am pretty good at building things, so I figured it made sense."

"Definitely, always good money in engineering, too."

Nico smiled. "You sound like my dad."

Asher laughed but was unsure if that was a positive thing or not.

"Hey, what are your plans tomorrow? Last day before classes start up. I can show you around a bit if you would like? I am pretty familiar with the place."

Asher tried to play cool. "Yeah, that would be great! This place is enormous. I was going to finish picking up some books I needed and maybe try and find my classrooms so I don't get lost the first day. But otherwise, no plans."

A loud knock rang across their open door. A large, older student strolled in. "Gentlemen!" The boys turned to face the hulking figure. "Which one of you is Nico, and which of you is Asher?"

"Nico here," said Nico raising his hand.

Asher stuck out his arm for a handshake. "Asher."

The man shook their hands. "Asher, Nico. Nice to meet you. I'm your resident assistant. Do either of you need any help unpacking or anything?"

The boys shook their heads no.

"Great! Well, you are the last room on my list, so let's go over the ground rules real quick." He looked at the two of them. "No excessive noise past sundown, be respectful of all residential corridors, no more than four people allowed in one room, and shower every day. Oh, and illicit substances are strictly banned when they are in my line of sight. Got it?" He said with a wink.

"Is that it?" asked Nico.

"Yeah, just about," said the assistant. "But if there is anything you need, my room is always open. The last one down the hallway."

"Thank you," said Asher. "Nice to meet you!"

The assistant smirked and waved off the thanks. "Welcome to Langford; see you gentlemen around."

He left the room, and the boys continued to put their things away. "So, the whole drinking and drugs thing..." said Nico.

"Yeah?" Asher raised his eyebrows

"That rule is being broken," said Nico slyly.

"Fine with me," Asher laughed. "Just don't get me kicked out."

"Not going to happen," said Nico, taking a bottle of liquor out from his suitcase and waving it invitingly. "Want to join me out in the hallway? I think it is about time to meet some of the guys cohabiting with us."

"But the resident assistant just said to keep alcohol out of sight...?"

"It will be out of sight," said Nico pouring the liquor into a thermos.

"Uhh..." Asher fumbled hesitantly.

"Here," Nico offered the thermos up to Asher with a smile, "let's go make some friends."

CHAPTER 5

Asher woke up the next morning, ready to be productive. Nico was still asleep as he quietly crept out of their bedroom and down the hallway to the community bathroom. He showered quickly so as not to keep any of the other boys waiting. He made some brief and awkward introductions in passing as he combed his hair and brushed his teeth. When he got back to his room, Nico was still lying in bed but was now awake and fully clothed.

"Morning!" said Nico cheerfully.

"Good morning."

"You ready to get educated about your educational institution?" Nico cracked a smile.

Asher shook his head playfully. "Are you going to be my guide?"

"Of course!"

"Great! Where to first?"

Nico jumped from the bed, slung a pack around his shoulder, and began to walk out the door. "First thing is food. First thing is *always* food."

They walked to the cafeteria but didn't sit at any tables like the others. Instead, they grabbed muffins and scarfed them down while walking through the school's long, winding corridors and sub-buildings. Nico gave an impressive presentation of the school's history and backstory, all the while stopping every few minutes to greet a friend and introduce Asher. He began to receive the impression that—while it was also Nico's first year at college—he was quite the socialite around Riali. Or, at the very least, a fairly well-known figure.

As they were walking through the anthropology wing, Nico headed straight for a group of three girls in mid-conversation. One was a shorter brunette with a frilly red dress. The other was a taller blond girl, around Asher's height, wearing a similar gold dress with a blue ribbon tied around her neck. The third girl was easily the most attractive person Asher had ever seen in his life. Jet-black hair and clear blue eyes. A golden gloss across pouty lips. She had a lean, athletic frame, which was accentuated by a black bodice and complimented with a gold-rimmed, heart-shaped pendant. She wore a wispy, dark-purple skirt. Fragile black lace covered her wrists, and her fingers were adorned with gemstone jewelry.

Asher was stunned by her beauty, but Nico appeared unfazed. "Hey everybody, how have you been?"

"Nico!" The girls all smiled cheerfully.

"I cannot believe we are finally here, right?" said the raven-haired girl as she threw her arms around him. "We have been talking about Lang-U since we were kids."

Nico laughed and ruffled his hair. "Yeah, I know, crazy. Time flies, but I am just happy to be out of the house and on my own finally."

"Definitely, I am so ready for the Uni life. Who is your friend?" she asked, pointing over to Asher.

Asher smiled sheepishly and waved. "Hi, I'm Asher."

"He is from Vana!" Nico interjected.

"Vana? Ew. Who the heck lives out in Vana?" said the blond.

"I would have expected a little more dirt and beige. I wouldn't peg you for a Vanatian," teased the brunette.

"What brings you to Riali, Asher?" asked the dark-haired girl.

"I came here to study biology," said Asher, unsure of how else to respond. "I have to look the part, right?"

The dark-haired girl got uncomfortably close to Asher's face. "Hmm…" she said, examining him closely. "I think I prefer your green eye."

"Thanks?" Asher blushed.

"What is wrong with them anyway?" asked the blond.

"It's heterochromia," said Asher. "It's like a genetic thing, makes my eyes two different colors."

"Well, I am Autumn," she said, sticking out her hand. "This is Avee and Kiara," she continued, motioning to the blonde and brunette, respectively.

"I am studying chemistry. Maybe we can work on homework sometime when you are not too busy getting dragged to parties by Nico."

"Both sound like a good time to me!" Asher couldn't help but cringe at his own over-eagerness.

Autumn snickered. "Yeah, we enjoy our grandeur." She looked back at Nico. "We are headed over to the sanctuary. See you guys around?"

Asher and Nico said their goodbyes. Once the girls were out of earshot, Asher let out a sigh but tried his best to hold his tongue so as not to say anything inappropriate. Nico looked over at him with a big grin. "So...what you think?"

"There are no girls from Vana like that. That one girl seems really cool."

"Autumn? Yeah. We have known each other since we were kids. Our families are friends. She is practically a sister to me."

"Well, I hope you don't mind me saying this, but your sister is incredibly attractive."

The boys laughed and continued their tour through the school. Asher was becoming slightly overwhelmed by all the new faces and Nico's knowledge. *Do all the students know this much?* He had to ask. "How do you know so much about the school anyway?"

Nico was quiet for a few seconds, leaving Asher with the quick fear that his question was out of place, before finally answering, "So, my parents are alumni. They are also pretty big donors and good friends with Director Dolent."

"Really? That's awesome."

"Yeah. Actually, you know the mathematics wing we passed? The one on the west side of campus?"

"Yeah?"

"Well, that is the Catalano Corridor."

"Right," said Asher.

"That is my family. My last name is Catalano."

"Oh, that's really cool!" Asher said, pausing to think. "Is that why you're into mathematics? Your parents must be mathematicians or something as well, right?"

Nico laughed half-heartedly. "Sort of. My dad owns CAT Robotics. He does not do as much engineering anymore, but he certainly has the best engineers in the world working for him."

"I imagine so." Even Asher, with all his small-town knowledge, was aware of CAT Robotics. They made countless industrial machines and had a heavy presence in the agricultural industry. He didn't want to dwell on Nico's wealth, though. "Do you plan to go work for your family as an engineer?"

Nico shook his head. "I'm not sure, maybe. I grew up hanging out with engineers, and my dad taught me a lot about math. It certainly is my strength. But I have always considered opening or running my own company or perhaps going freelance. You know, make my own way kind of thing. But to be honest, I don't really care. I do this to make them happy. I have always looked forward to coming here, just not exactly for the learning. It feels liberating to be out from under their roof, even if it is only a few miles away."

"Oh yeah, definitely," said Asher.

"I will make the grades if that is what it takes to keep them at bay. But it is my time to do what I want."

Asher listened intently as Nico continued.

"Maids, butlers, tutors—every single day, I was constantly watched. Constantly taught. Constantly drilled into being better than everyone else. And yeah, I did better than everyone else at my school. But what does that even mean? What does it matter? So what if I can count numbers faster than you or her or him?"

"Well, it doesn't appear like you were completely locked up or anything. You seem to know a lot of people."

Nico smiled. "Damn right I know a lot of people."

The boys were now standing outside of Asher's molecular genetics classroom. Asher went to peer inside when the door suddenly flung open and revealed a disheveled Professor Redding. The professor bobbled and then caught a series of empty glass vials before gaining his composure. "Oh, hey boys, you surprised me! Asher! What brings you here today?"

"Hi, Professor. Just scoping out classes before tomorrow."

"Ah, right. And you are?" Professor Redding reached out to shake Nico's hand.

"Nicholas Catalano, sir. My friends call me Nico."

"Catalano?"

"Yes, sir."

"Tremendous! Your parents are wonderful people. And will you be attending my genetics classes as well?"

Nico laughed. "Definitely not. I am an engineering student."

"Suitable." Redding smiled. "I am sure you will make your parents proud here at Langford."

Nico shrugged. "I will certainly try."

"Well, it was nice running into you boys. I am headed out. Hope you two are as excited for the semester to start as I am. Mr. Auden, I will see you tomorrow."

They waved goodbye as Professor Redding walked down the hallway, precariously juggling his overstuffed satchel and lab wares.

The boys headed back to the cafeteria, the room was the largest in the university, and Asher finally got a proper look around. The roof was held up by stone and brass pillars, the ceiling was lined with clanking oversized fans, and one wall consisted entirely of giant stained-glass windows. The other three were lined with stalls, each station serving different types of food. One for salads and smoothies, one for heartier feyloom meat, one with soups and sandwiches, one with pasta, one with desserts, and on and on; a litany of meal options Asher had yet to explore.

They meandered to a grill serving indri burgers and selected their choices on a floating glass menu, then watched as an avalanche of whirring machinery sprung to life. Brass counters rotated to the back of the shop, where puffs of fire ignited. A small robot wheeled a sloshing cask of pink liquid to one, and Asher could make out an oversized knife slicing violently through a head of lettuce. Mere seconds later, they approached the window where their meals appeared—*impressive efficiency*, thought Asher.

Nico took a bite. "Bleh, mustard? Who puts mustard on a burger!" He slid it back through the window. "Hey! No mustard!" Robotic eyes peered through the windows angrily. A quick sound of mechanical chaos resounded before spitting out a new burger. Nico took a second bite. "I forgot to tell them no pickles…"

"For someone so familiar with the school, you're quite bad at knowing how to order food here."

They turned back to the dining hall. In the furthest corner, Asher spotted Callie sitting by herself, reading a book and eating some leafy meal. He wasn't used to seeing her without Cloud. He continued to scan the room until he saw Autumn hanging around an athletic-looking group of boys, one of whom towered above the rest. He appeared to be well over six feet and two hundred pounds, all muscle, with dirty-blonde hair and sharp blue eyes. Nico caught Asher staring. "That monster is Roman Volkov. He is a bit of a celebrity at this school."

Asher broke his gaze. "He's a big guy."

"And an insane athlete. Do you watch koroka at all?"

Asher shrugged. "Sort of. My best friend at home plays on Vana's team."

"Cool. Then you will have fun watching Roman. He is Langford's star center. We nearly went undefeated last season because of him, and it was only his first year."

Out of the usual lunchroom chaos came a loud chorus of students shouting Nico's name. He waved to the group and turned to Asher. "Found our table. Come hang out over here!"

"Great!"

Asher turned to check on Callie one more time and watched as she packed her bag to leave. He was excited to meet more people. Nico's friends stood up to greet them. Asher recognized two girls from earlier. "Kiara, right?" he said, pointing to the brunette. "And...?"

"Avee," said the blond, smiling.

Asher was relieved. "I'm Jackson," said a small boy with sharp features. "Asher is from Vana," Kiara informed Jackson.

"Vana, huh?"

"Yep,"

"What is it like there? The girls hotter than here at Riali? Or are they all rugged from the lumberjacking?"

Kiara slapped him on the shoulder. Asher laughed and scratched the back of his head. "Yeah, uh, it's a pretty place. Thick forests and a lot more nature-centric than here. Definitely not nearly as industrialized."

"Yeah, yeah, but he was asking about the girls," said Nico.

Asher laughed again. "The girls are pretty, but these Riali girls might have them beat." He accidentally made eye contact with Kiara, who proceeded to blush. He hadn't meant to; if he were being truthful, Autumn was the girl on his mind, but the damage had been done.

"Dang right," Avee said. "No one finer than us Rialian gals."

"What do you all do there for fun?" Jackson asked.

Asher shrugged. "Guess it depends on who you are. Farming, hunting, playing koroka. I kind of work a lot. I study biology and chemistry, so I spend a good amount of my free time in the lab."

"Do you guys party at all?"

"Do we *party*?" Asher asked sarcastically. "Of course. What else is there to do in a small town? Need to be a little careful since everyone knows everyone, but we go out into the forest and have small gatherings or wait until one of our parents makes the trek to Dyria. But I mean...don't you all know about the Midbloom Festival?"

"Oh yeah, guess we can't discount Midbloom. The biggest party in Khamara!"

"Exactly," said Asher. "Vana knows how to have a good time."

Avee spoke up. "You mention you're a science nerd. Have you ever tried to make your own moonshine?"

"Nah, not moonshine. It wouldn't be hard, but I've never really bothered trying to make it."

"Wait, you said *not* moonshine. What *have* you made?" Nico interjected.

Asher looked away nervously, "Uhh...umm...well...plenty of stuff for school, like mosslings and sapphire oranges. One time I made a strawberry-flavored banana."

"A kid from Vana gets into Langford for some bananas and moss? I am not buying it, there has to be more. You even just said you spend most of your free time in the lab. What else you got?"

"I uh…" Asher wasn't one to boast, but if ever there was a time, he figured now would be it. "I modified strains of various crops that grow better in Vana soil. It increased yield about six-fold in several essential fruits and vegetables. I also—"

"Whoa, wait a sec." Nico cut him off. "You were the one behind the modified crops in Vana?"

"Yeah. I helped with the project."

"You are the reason Dyria has had so much economic success recently."

"What? No, I don't know about that."

"No, yeah, you are. About a year ago, Vana not only quadrupled crop yield, it also was able to make crops that lasted several *weeks* longer before spoiling, which led to an exodus from the surrounding villages into the cities. The abundance of food led to a new influx of industrial workers in Dyria and lumber workers in Vana. To top it off, the increased accessibility of Vana wood made more ships for Dyria. At the current rate, Dyria is set to overtake Riali in overall exports within the next few years. It's a *whole* deal."

"Uhh," said Asher nervously. "I think you're giving me too much credit. I had Professor Fenske helping me."

Jackson shook his head. "In any case, something is about to go down. Dyria has been attacking Riali with chemical weapons to try and overtake business. Your work pretty much caused the recent events."

"That is not true at all," Kiara jumped in. "There is

absolutely no indication Miasma is anything but a lone wolf."

"Conveniently going after all the merchants and traders?" said Avee.

"And the owner of my favorite candy shop—" said Jackon.

"I made something else!" Asher blurted, desperate to change the topic. "Something I haven't told anyone about yet."

Nico looked at him from the corner of his eye. "Oh boy, what do you got for us?"

"Well, I recently spliced sussberries with the gene that produces hallucinogenic properties in wild kane mushrooms."

The table fell silent. The din of silverware clattered around Asher's head.

"*You* made berries that make you trip like kane mushrooms?"

"Yeah. I tried them the other day. They work." He ran his fingers nervously through his hair, "Maybe a little too well."

"Holy shit!" Jackson's jaw dropped, "How the heck do we get our hands on these magical berries?"

"Oh well, I didn't bring any with me," said Asher.

A palpable disappointment spread over the group.

Asher felt like he had let them down; he shouldn't have said anything about the berries.

"Could you make them again?" asked Kiara.

Asher thought for a moment. "Well…yeah. I mean, sure, I could make them again. They don't take long to create. I just don't know if I have the resources."

A slight glimmer of hope came over the table again as all eyes went to Nico, who gave a devilish grin. "Asher, buddy. Listen. Resources are not an issue."

Asher wasn't sure if Nico was making a joke. "That would be a lot of resources. I had an entire lab back in Vana to work with. I sort of had free rein over there for, well, for reasons you can imagine. We'd need a place safe from the eyes of teachers. One where they wouldn't know what we're working on and safe from others tampering."

"Easy," said Nico. "I can make it happen. Just get me a list of everything you need, and we can get started on those magical berries. Only if you are interested, of course?"

Asher looked around the table. All eyes had shifted back to him. His berries were simply gene-splicing practice, a fun project he'd only intended for himself and Liam. The berries were never meant to be produced to a higher degree, and he had no idea what side effects might occur in a more varied population. *What if someone had epilepsy or a heart condition? What if someone had a fragile mental disorder?* His own mind had turned against him after all.

"Or were you just making this whole thing up?" Avee scoffed.

"What? No, I can do it," said Asher defensively.

"Great!" said Nico.

Jackson nodded aggressively. "You might get bored in a small town because there is nothing to do. But we get bored in a big town because we have already done everything there is to do."

Callie had heard rumors and stories of the Langford sanctuary, of its breadth and extravagance, its many compartmentalized ecosystems. She had explored the gardens briefly on move-in day but knew there were still far more mysteries to unravel and sites to behold. For starters, it housed the largest and most diverse population of animals of any zoo in Khamara. The sanctuary was a place of complete tranquility, a paradise for the rescued and rehabilitated.

She stepped out of the school and onto a vast porch made of dark-gray stone. The walkways were shaded by large, arching oak trees. Ivy crept alongside the stone pathways, dripping over walls and trellises. The first thing to catch her eye was not the lush vegetation or exotic birds fluttering overhead but the sheer number of staircases. Small, thin steps led up to terraces only a few feet higher or lower than the previous terrace. Multi-tiered areas leveled off in every direction, crisscrossing paths in a confusing maze of stone. Fountains and streams poured from one level down to the next, filling up small ponds. Rows of bright flowers lined the paths, guiding Callie from one area to the next in bursts of color.

Callie headed to the giant fountain at the center of the sanctuary, where a robot dressed in a top hat and overcoat was feeding fish. While his body resembled the shape of a human, his limbs were made of thin metal rods and the joints of hundreds of tiny gears, with very little covering over the mechanisms. The head and chest, on the other hand, were less exposed, covered in a type of bronze plating that was rounded at the edges giving the robot a barrel chest and a bucket-shaped head. The eye sockets were perfect circles with tiny bright blue lights peering from the center, and the chest held a small circular glass covering that displayed complex inner workings.

She walked up to the robotic groundskeeper. "Hello there! Fonzworth, yes?" The robot turned to Callie with movements far more graceful and elegant than the other machines she had encountered.

"Why hello! Yes, I am Sir Fonzworth. And you must be?" he said in a remarkably human and gentle voice.

"Callendra Saint." She struck out her hand, "You can call me Callie. Professor Mara Jones told me you were the assistant groundskeeper?"

"That is correct. Are you the same Callie with the beautiful snow fox?"

"You've met Cloud?" she said excitedly.

"He has been an absolute delight! The kindest and most joyous creature I have met."

"I'm so happy to hear he's doing well. Speaking of which, have you seen Professor Jones? I was hoping we could go visit him together."

Fonzworth nodded. "I have. Mara is down in the arboreal tortoise exhibit. Would you like me to show you the way?"

Callie gave a quick nod and followed the robot. They passed iron cages holding griffins and Elurra-bred tigers. She would have preferred to see the magnificent creatures in their natural habitat, but she was grateful to observe their splendor up close. She pointed to a griffin with an injured wing. "Fonzworth, what happened to this one here?"

He stopped and took a closer look at the cage, his mechanical mind whirring. "Ah yes, Frederick here was brought to us a little over a month ago. He was found in the woods of Uppig. The theory is that he survived an attack from a titan boa. We had to amputate significant portions of his left wing. Sadly, he will not fly again, but he has a safe home here."

The two entered the tortoise exhibit, where a woman with piercing green eyes and high cheekbones was vigorously shoveling manure from a large stall into a wooden barrel. Her attire was out of place given the manual labor; she wore a beige skirt hiked up above her knees, a matching wide-brimmed hat that hid the upper half of a messy bun, and a frilly white shirt that was rolled up to her elbows.

She was lost in the rhythm of her work until Fonzworth caught her attention. "Excuse me, Professor."

"How goes it, Fonzly?" she asked, remaining focused on her task.

"Apologies for the interruption, but you have a visitor."

She shoved the pitchfork deep into the manure pile and leaned on it as she turned to her visitors. "Ah, Callie, good to see you! You're back early."

"Hi, Professor. Yeah, I finished getting all my errands done."

The professor flicked manure off her leather gloves. "Here to pick up Cloud?"

Callie initially met Professor Mara Jones while admitting Cloud to the sanctuary. It was she who had pushed the board to accept his presence at the university under the condition that he wouldn't roam the halls of Langford. Instead, he would be caged in a large, comfortable area of the sanctuary during class hours and free to move about the outside grounds under Callie's supervision.

"Yeah, I was gonna let him out to run around for a bit before I head back up."

Mara finished scraping her gloves clean before taking them off. "Great! Fonzly and I will walk over with you. I'll show you a shortcut from here." Mara wiped her brow with the back of her arm and walked swiftly past them.

Callie's attention turned every which way as they passed rows of various creatures and exotic beasts. Mara's eyes, however, stayed straight as she continued to talk. "Were you able to find all your classes?"

"Yeah, I found them all. I did a good amount of exploring, but I think I'm done for the day," Callie said with hesitance in her voice.

"How has everything been so far?" asked the professor.

"Good," she said. "A little much, I guess," she added with more honesty.

"It's a big place, but you'll get used to it," said the professor confidently. "It's an adjustment from what you're familiar with back in Vana, but you'll adapt. The people are great, the education is second to none, and our food isn't too bad, either. Although, I do prefer the food in Baenum a bit more. Have you ever visited Baenum?"

"I'd never left Vana until yesterday."

"Oh, let me tell you something. Baenum might not be the prettiest with all their mining. But it's where I met Fonzworth here."

"Yeah?"

"That's right. How do you feel about the food there, Fonzly?"

"To be frank, Professor, I don't really have much of a preference."

"Fair enough, but the Baenites are elegant creators nonetheless—and are just as inventive in their own right."

She rambled on about past adventures as the trio continued to trek along the winding, tunneling path until reaching the sanctuary's winter division. The area was underground, with crisscrossing wires strewn from brass lantern to brass lantern, illuminating large iron enclosures. Cloud's enclosure, however, had a window up top to let in the sunlight. The area was spacious, filled with various toys, and was near the snow bears and saber-tooths so he would have company. Despite the conditions, Callie couldn't help but feel guilty about putting her best friend in a cage.

As they approached, they found Cloud pacing back and forth. Callie looked at him with concern. "Something isn't right."

"It's his first day; he is still adjusting."

"Maybe. But he should be jumping to see me. This isn't like him."

Mara opened the door. Cloud ran to Callie's side and instantly took a hunting stance, his whiskery snout pointing down the hallway. *Something is definitely wrong.*

"What is it?" asked the professor.

"That's his hunting stance; he uses it to alert me of potential game." *But more often than not, it means danger is near.*

"Perhaps he caught the scent of a frost doe or snowshoe rabbit?" Mara said, sounding a little more concerned.

"Perhaps," Callie replied as the four of them cautiously headed in the direction Cloud indicated. A loud crash came from the end of the hallway. Mara turned to Fonzworth. "Have you logged the visitors today? Do you know who else might be here?"

Fonzworth spoke up. "No, I am sorry, Professor. My logs do not appear to be up to date. There has been a particularly high volume of guests due to the new arrivals."

They walked to the end of the hallway, where a large wooden door was cracked open. Cloud stopped short and began to growl. "What's in there?" asked Callie.

"Those would be the eres."

"You have an ere in the sanctuary?"

"Two, to be precise," said the professor urgently, "Fonzly, could you grab the tranquilizer? Callie, you might want to head back to the university for now."

Callie scoffed. "No way, I am absolutely seeing this!"

"Alright, but do exactly as I say." Mara cautiously cracked the door open to investigate.

Cloud slowly backed up against Callie and then began sniffing around the hallway. After a brief second, Mara swung the door open and proceeded into the room.

It contained two large cages made of heavy industrial steel, which had turned green from oxidation. A small window near the ceiling provided the faintest light. The room was cold, damp, and made of large, smooth stones. Callie walked up to an enclosure and peered inside. The beast was roughly twenty-five feet tall, pure white, muscular, and had four curved horns that lined the outside of its head like a crown. Its ears were a quarter the size of its horns, and its face was pointy, which gave it a look that reminded her of an oversized Cloud. Unlike Cloud, however, its albino fur was short to the point of near-nakedness, and the tail was long and slithered across the ground like a large flat python. She couldn't see teeth, but she knew eres were omnivores—the true danger lay in their sharp claws, which could shred predators or prey with one swipe.

"These are generally tamed by druids..." Callie said. "And there's not many of them left."

Professor Jones walked up beside her. "You are correct. We were gifted these from druids in the outskirts of Saint Mazraea. Eres tend to do better in the colder mountain climates."

Callie reached beyond the green, rusted bars to touch it, but Mara yanked her hand back. "We've had difficulties taming them."

"Well, yeah. For starters, they enjoy the sunlight."

"You're correct, but they sleep in the caves. We had to make a choice," the professor rebutted, with a tone both defensive and impressed.

"They sleep in the caves at night to avoid the snowstorms, otherwise they search for sunlight during the daytime."

"I understand that, but if we are to house untamed eres, then we need to use a cave-like environment that mimics their resting state."

Mara and Callie walked over to the second enclosure.

"It's gone," shouted Mara. Callie inspected the empty ere cage as Mara hurried toward the door. Fonzworth had returned, "I have some unfortunate news, Professor."

"What now?" asked Professor Jones, exasperated.

"The darts and gun are here, but the tranquilizer cartridges that load into the darts…they're missing."

CHAPTER 6

ara snatched the tranquilizer gun out of Fonzworth's hands and sprinted back into the sanctuary with Callie close behind. Fonzworth locked the door to the room, still holding the one ere, and ran to catch up with them as they stormed toward the center of the garden.

"Fonz, lock the entrance to the school. We can't risk having any students caught out in the open with the ere. And no heroics!" Mara ordered. "Callie, go with him and take Cloud with you." She grabbed Fonzworth by the shoulder to emphasize her final instruction: "And find Redding." She looked at Callie. "If you run into the ere, look him in the eye and do not show any fear. Do you understand?"

The professor grabbed a long metal chain before emerging from the tunnel back into the sanctuary. She could see the ere off in the distance, sunbathing in the open garden. A panicked scream pierced the air. The ere lifted his head up in the direction of the scream. A group of young female students had come out of the garden within fifty yards of the ere. The ere began walking toward them. Mara shouted to get the ere's attention. "Hey, HEY!" It didn't work. The ere began loping, picking up its pace as it drew nearer to the students. "Don't run," said Mara under her breath.

Students hanging about the various terraces turned to get a view of the commotion. Fonzworth ushered students inside. "Nothing to see, go inside. Quickly now."

As if on cue, the group of girls bolted toward the university, triggering the ere to give chase. Mara sprinted in pursuit, hooking the metal chain onto a bolted fixture on the center fountain. The ere plowed through the garden in a bright explosion of dirt and flowers. Sharp claws uprooted thick trees. A pond emptied as it leaped from one terrace to the next. The beast had the students on open ground as they sprinted for the door. A group of teachers waved madly for them to hurry into the school. The ere lowered its horns and began picking up speed, preparing to ram.

Callie watched the scene unfold and did quick calculations. The girls would not make it. She charged in a dead sprint, Cloud several steps ahead of her. She slid to a stop as they reached a point between the girls and the ere. Callie looked the ere in the eye and let out a furious and stern, "STOP!" She held out one hand, and with the other, she lifted her satchel as if threatening with some great weapon. Cloud lowered his head and growled. The ere skidded to a halt, piling up dirt and stone as his claws dug into the pathway. The ere looked at Callie and then to Cloud. It was unsure of what to make of the two. Callie continued to stare down the beast while the windows of Langford filled with curious students. The ere let out a screeching roar that reverberated against the walls of the school. Callie did not budge. The students made it back inside as Fonzworth stood guard over the door, looking as if he wanted to join Callie in her attempt to face down the beast, but respecting the orders received from Mara.

A loud popping sound came from behind the ere. The beast turned around frantically. A second loud pop sounded as Mara hit the ere between its eyes with an empty dart. Professor Redding appeared behind Callie. "Time to go inside now," he whispered as he walked past her, eyes set on the ere. Callie and Cloud slowly backed up as the ere focused its attention on Professor Jones. The ere began to growl as it stepped assertively in Mara's direction. She stepped backward in caution. *What is she doing?* thought Callie. *There's no tranquilizer, those darts will only antagonize it.* Mara took one more shot at the ere, which skimmed its shoulder, then threw the gun to the side. The ere began walking faster. Mara seemingly tripped over a stone and began to crawl backward. The ere charged at full speed. Fonzworth held onto Callie's back, "She knows what she's doing," he reassured her. The ere threw itself in full force. Its feet left the ground, its horns were lowered. Mara rolled quickly to the side and out of the way from the killing blow.

A thunderous explosion of steel and concrete erupted as the ere crashed into the center fountain, missing Mara by inches. She quickly pulled herself up, grabbed the chain, and proceeded to leap onto the back of the stunned beast. The ere began shaking himself free of the concrete, but it was too late. Mara had wrapped the metal chain around the horns and neck of the ere. It began struggling, bucking its hardest to get the professor off its back. She tried to soothe it but quickly settled for simply holding on.

A series of three loud pops occurred. The ere turned around in an increased fury. Professor Redding stood stoically by; the rifle raised to fire at the now woozy ere. The ere gained its composure and charged at Professor Redding, the chain's slack lessening with each step. Redding didn't bother to move as the chain tugged the ere back, sending Mara flying. The ere landed with a heavy thud, kicking up dust and debris. Mara groaned in pain as she pushed herself up to look at the now sleeping monster and then over at Redding, who was holding her tranquilizer gun. "Ah, there you are, Redding," said Mara as she reached out her hand.

Redding lifted her up. "Professor Jones. Apologies if I was a bit late." He handed Mara's rifle over to Fonzworth. "How the heck did this thing get out of its cage? I saw it from my window just as Fonzworth arrived."

"I'm not sure," said Mara, wiping her sweaty bangs back under her gardening hat.

Professor Redding had a concerned expression as he rubbed his chin in thought. "Hmm...well, let us get the big guy back in his cage."

"Thank you," said Mara exhaustedly as she looked over the courtyard, now covered in dirt and rubble. "The director will not be pleased with this mess."

Redding turned back to the school and watched as Fonzworth began ushering students from the windows and back to their interrupted destinations. "Why did you not tell me sooner that you needed more tranquilizer?" asked Redding.

"I didn't know I was out. I think it may have been stolen."

"By whom? That is a highly potent compound, not one meant for partying. Even a fraction of a canister could knock a grown man out for hours."

"I'm not sure," said Mara. "But I believe whoever did may also have been the person who let out the ere. It's one of the most dangerous creatures in the sanctuary—that's a little more than just casual troublemaking; it's homicidal."

"I guess we will need to double down on security and make more of the tranquilizer in case it occurs again."

"Yeah..." said Mara hesitantly, staring at the downed beast. "I guess so."

Asher fell into the school routine quickly. His first class of the day was Ancient Religions with Professor Lucas Creed, a tall man with buzzed hair and a strong jawline. Asher found him to be respectful of each major theology without giving too much weight to any one of them in particular. He was a fast speaker and a little bit of a chaotic thinker, which made following along somewhat difficult. Callie was in the class and sat on the opposite side of the room. Aside from exchanging passing pleasantries, they hadn't spoken much since the day they arrived. He had seen her become resistant to her newfound fame, watching students who approached to talk about her heroics in the sanctuary slink off at her dismissal of the deed.

Asher and Nico shared second period, a social dynamics class taught by Professor Aleksei Ederra. She was young, foreign, and very attractive. The class was intended to teach various cultures and etiquettes of other cities, as well as prepare students for the end-of-semester cotillion. Though it was a required course, Asher and Nico considered this their most useless class and paid it little attention.

Third period was Mechanical Engineering with Professor Gorton Crow. Professor Crow had a worn, unwelcoming look. His outfits, while nice, were all black. His face was in a permanent scowl, and he spoke in a low gravelly tone that suggested disinterest. Asher was unsure if the professor disliked teaching an entry-level engineering course or if he was just generally disdainful of all people, particularly students. He learned to not ask questions after the professor threw a book down on a table and told the student to look up the answer.

After third period was a small break just long enough for lunch, then botany, and then Metaphysics, two classes he always wanted to rush through so he could get to his favorite period of the day, Molecular Genetics.

The class was a doubleheader taught by Professor Redding. The first half was lecture, and the second half was lab. Professor Redding's appearance was just as disoriented as his lectures, but his passion for the subject was undeniable and, for Asher, highly contagious. His glasses refused to stay on his long pointy nose as his hands scrawled swiftly across the chalkboard. The course would be challenging but rewarding. While many of the other students stared mindlessly into space, Asher shared Professor Redding's enthusiasm. And their mutual adoration for Vana's own Professor Fenske made Redding a quick friend of Asher's.

Asher utilized the social aspects of lunch and dinner hours to their fullest. He had begun memorizing the names of Nico's friends. They seemed to be generally accepting of him, although he could sense that they still hadn't made up their minds on welcoming an outsider into their tight-knit group. He glanced around the evening cafeteria and saw Callie eating noodles alone, but then Felix came up beside her and started to chat. *Good*, thought Asher, *I'm glad she has at least someone here for her.*

He sat down at the table beside Nico and Kiara.

"Are all of you Vanatians lunatics?" asked Kiara, nodding over at Callie.

Asher smirked. "Nah, just Callie. Animals are kind of her thing."

"Still, pretty wild if you ask me," Jackson piped in. "That ere was not going to get through the doors; she should have just hidden out of the way. I'm not sure if she is dumb or just wanted the attention."

"She's not dumb, and she definitely doesn't want attention," said Asher defensively.

"Elizabeth Crann said she was weird. That she tried to talk to Callie about the ere thing and she shrugged it off, like she was full of herself or something," Avee said.

"Elizabeth Crann is just jealous she is not the only girl with pretty red hair in the school," said Kiara, rolling her eyes. "Besides, Autumn said she seemed nice. I think she talked to her in class? That is how I found out she is Vanatian."

"She is probably the one who let the ere out of the cage," said Jackson.

"Why in the world would she do that?" asked Asher.

"For attention, maybe?" Jackson shrugged.

"Did you not just hear Asher? She's not the type to want attention," said Kiara, annoyed.

"No," said Avee. "I am calling it now that Miasma was behind this."

"Miasma?" asked Asher, looking at Nico for an explanation.

"That's the name they gave the terrorist because they have been using gas to attack their victims. The attacks have not been very successful so far—the compounds used have not been strong enough. Most of the victims have been high-profile targets that ended up in critical condition with burned lungs. All we know at the moment is the killer wears a gas mask."

"It is the Dyrians, I am telling you," said Avee. "There are all these pirate attacks off the coast, and now we have assassination attempts on the wealthiest people in Riali? Definitely Dyria."

"Or maybe a Vanatian since the two cities seem to be such good pals?" Jackson said, looking at Asher slyly.

Nico threw an orange slice at Jackson. "You are an idiot."

"Hey now, just kidding. I did see Sheriff Price out in the courtyard yesterday, though. So it is certainly not nothing."

Nico looked decidedly uncomfortable with the conversation and decided to change it entirely. "Everyone going to the koroka game Sunday? We are playing against U-Kip."

"Ah, heck yeah! Roman is going to singlehandedly rip Kipos apart!" said Jackson.

"I would, too, if my parents altered me to absolute perfection," said Avee longingly.

Kiara turned to Asher. "Do you know how to genetically alter bodies? I have a few upgrades I would like to make."

Asher laughed nervously. "Uh, no, I don't think that's quite possible yet."

Kiara looked at him questioningly and then over at Nico. "You haven't told him?"

Nico shrugged and shook his head.

Kiara remained dumbfounded. "How much do you know about genetic altering?"

Asher answered hesitantly, "I mean. I don't know, I feel like a good amount. It hasn't really been done in humans, to my knowledge. What do *you* know about genetic altering?"

Avee tagged back in. "You are supposed to be the bio expert. I cannot believe no one has told you about all the altering in Riali! And we are supposed to trust this guy with magical berries?"

"Yeah, ok, I am officially confused about what we're talking about here," Asher admitted.

Nico took pity on Asher and filled him in. "It is a little bit of an open secret in the upper echelons of Riali society, but a lot of people here and at Langford had *slight* genetic altering before they were born."

"Whoa, what? Like in-vitro human genetic altering?"

"Yeah. Something like that."

"So Roman, he's genetically enhanced to be that big?"

"Mmmhmm. Yeah, basically."

"Are you altered? Wait, are you all—"

"Yes, but not like Roman," said Nico. "Most people who have alterations are just screened to eliminate any genetic diseases."

"Can people have other alterations aside from being big like Roman?"

"Were you genetically bred to be so primitive?" Jackson cut in angrily.

The air between them on the table had become tense, and there was a clear look of frustration on some of the faces, none more so than Jackson's. Asher had not considered his small stature and determined quickly that perhaps not all members of Riali were given such benefits as Roman. "Right, sorry..." Asher's brain raced to think of something to say that might lighten the mood. "So I've seen the labs here at Langford. They seem pretty perfect for making the magic berries."

Nico jumped on the change of topic. "Awesome! Have you seen Redding's personal lab yet?"

"Not yet. Why?"

"It is bigger, and he only uses it twice a week. Kiara saw the admin schedule when she was doing assistant work in the office. I think it would be perfect for you."

"Yep," confirmed Kiara. "He is there every Tuesday and Thursday and possibly on the weekends, which gives you plenty of time to sneak in and do your magic. I also managed to grab a spare key for you. You know, just in case."

Asher tried to look excited, but he couldn't help but be terrified. He really didn't plan on getting expelled for doing something this stupid this soon.

"Look. The berries are discreet, so worst case scenario, we somehow get busted breaking in, no big deal. My parents practically own those labs; the worst we will get is a slap on the wrist."

Asher looked down at his hands, which were nervously fidgeting with his fork. "Ok. Yeah, I'm in. When do we want to go?"

Nico smiled. "I was thinking of giving you one last tour tonight."

"Bah!" Nico jumped out at Asher, causing Asher to nearly drop his satchel.

"What the hell, man?"

Nico laughed and gave a playful punch, "Ah! Don't be a pansy, Auden."

Asher rolled his eyes, but he was grateful to finally have an opportunity to ask a question that had been eating away at him, "So, Nico?"

"Yeah?"

"Why was everyone at the table the other day acting weird about the genetic alteration thing? It's all still pretty new to me."

"Oh. Right." Nico sighed. "Well, it is an expensive procedure. Very few people can afford to have alterations, and the few that do, don't have anything special. Like I said, most Rialians—Jackson and Avee, for instance—only have alterations that prevent genetic diseases.

"I have an inclination for engineering because my parents paid for a mathematics-heavy predisposition. I have a slightly greater temporal gyrus than most and presumably have a greater understanding of mathematics because of it."

"So they think they're lesser than you because their alteration isn't as drastic?"

"I don't know what they think. But yeah, basically. It is kind of one of those things that everyone knows but no one talks about. It is not necessarily a good or bad thing to be born altered. But it can be used as an indication of wealth. And in Riali, wealth does matter. I am not the only one with these kinds of alterations here. Roman was going to be big no matter what, but he was also altered to have more speed, strength, and agility. His whole body was tailored while it was an embryo. Kiara was altered to be almost identical to her mother, both in looks and creativity. Autumn was predisposed to be pretty and talented. Stewart from our social dynamics class claims he was altered to have a massive—"

"Whoa, what? Really?"

"Nah, I doubt it. I think he just started that rumor to—"

"No, I meant Autumn."

"Autumn? Oh, yeah, her parents are super rich. Big entertainment moguls. She is the great-granddaughter of Bella Hawthorne, after all, one of the greatest singers to ever live. The body came with the vocal cords—that girl can sing. Smarter than you would think too."

Asher's mind was blown.

"Almost every elite at Langford has some altering done. Whether it is intelligence, looks, athleticism—all of them have been tweaked one way or the other. Our lot in life was decided for us before we were even born."

Asher wasn't sure whether to feel disgusted or jealous. "Are you glad your parents did it?"

Nico laughed. "Without question! I don't want to be normal. Who wants to be normal?"

"Well, it all makes sense now: your parents altered you to be this weird!"

The great doors of the sanctuary were propped open, and a rush of warm air came over the boys as they stepped into the dusk and headed to the garden. "So, how many berries do we need again?" Nico asked.

"About ten or so. But we'll need a few different ones so we can pick out the best seeds."

As they came around a hedge, they saw Callie up in the distance playing fetch with Cloud. "Oh shoot, there is your girl!" said Nico, just loud enough for Asher to hear.

"She's not my girl, and she also shouldn't see us grab these sussberries."

"Why is that?"

"Well, for starters, we don't have permission to take these. And secondly, she kinda knows about the magic berry thing…"

"What?" said Nico in a hushed yell. "Why would you tell her about this?"

"It wasn't me! My friend back in Vana brought it up with her."

Nico kept his eyes fixed on her and Cloud as they walked up.

"Callie!" said Asher more excitedly than he'd originally intended. "How's it going?"

She turned and saw the two boys approaching while tugging a large stick from Cloud's mouth. "Hey, Asher. Doing good."

She appeared disinterested.

"This is my friend Nico. We're roommates over in the third tower."

"Cool," said Callie.

Nico spoke up. "Pretty awesome, what you did with the ere and all."

Callie threw the stick aggressively, and Cloud ran after it. "It was Professor Jones's idea. I didn't do anything."

Nico backed up to the bush and quickly plucked a berry.

"What are you two doing out here?"

Nico shot to attention. "Uhh…just wanted to walk around and get some sunlight. You know, classes and all, makes you feel like you are in prison."

"Yeah, I get it," Callie said, turning back around to greet Cloud in his full sprint.

Asher bent down to pick a berry when Cloud crashed into his knees. He clenched his fist and shoved it into his satchel as quickly as possible before addressing Cloud. "Oh hey, buddy!" Asher scratched his head.

"It's probably nice for him to see a familiar face in this sea of new people," said Callie.

"Right." Asher tugged on the stick half-heartedly.

Nico snuck behind Callie to grab more berries while her attention was on Asher, who noticed the plan and continued to distract her. "So, how's Cloud holding up overall? Does he like the sanctuary?"

She pursed her lips in thought. "Mmm, yeah. Besides almost getting shredded by an ere, I think he's doing alright. The other animals have been accepting, his cage is pretty big, and he gets to run around out here when classes let out."

She looked back at Nico, who jolted his hand back to his side, his eyes wide as he pretended to investigate the berry bush closely. Callie raised her eyebrows and kept her eyes on him while she talked. "How's the science stuff going for you, Asher?"

Asher focused on the back of her head as he quickly snagged a sussberry for himself. Cloud began to sniff at his pockets. "Oh, the science? The science is good." He shooed Cloud away before Callie could see the results of his sleight-of-hand berry theft.

"Good." She scratched Cloud behind his ear as he dropped the stick. She picked it up and prepared the next toss. Nico walked out of the range of her throw and back toward Asher, his hands dripping with blackened juice.

He shoved his hands in his pockets. "Beautiful sunset here in Riali, huh?"

Callie looked up at the skyline. "There's a lot of smog here. The smoke is why we have all these deep purples in the sunset. It also makes the stars harder to see at night."

Nico looked at Asher, who confirmed they'd had enough.

"It was good to meet you, Callie. You Vana folk are an interesting bunch. You should come hang out sometime," Nico said hurriedly.

She turned and let out what appeared to be a smile. "Yeah, it was nice to meet you, too."

The boys walked back to the school; the sun had given way to night. "Do you think she noticed?" asked Nico.

"No clue," said Asher. "But we need to get these berries preserved as soon as possible."

The boys walked through the winding corridors, which were now mostly empty as students had cleared out for the day. They reached the eastern exit of the school and went down a covered path into a secondary building. It was all stone and was two stories tall—fairly small in comparison to the looming towers of Langford's central structure. The boys checked around to see if anyone had seen them.

"Ok, these are the private offices for a few of the professors. A couple of rooms might be occupied but just act like we belong and beeline it to Redding's personal lab."

They walked through the cramped corridors, which were trashed with scattered papers and various discarded machines. The walls were lined with large sheets of sketching paper, covered in frantic, scribbled notes. The office windows were mostly darkened. A handful of offices emanated a bright light into the dimly lit hallway. Asher caught quick glimpses into the rooms and saw professors' noses deep in their work, too busy to care about what was going on outside of their doors. Asher and Nico reached the end of the hallway and opened a door into what had to be the largest room in the building.

Nico flipped a switch, and a row of lights turned on, revealing an all-white room filled with several long steel tables. The walls were covered in large wooden cabinets and work benches. Most of the lab was kept meticulously clean, with very little clutter. The cabinets held all the supplies Asher could ever need—tubes, beakers, Petri dishes, titration distillations, the list went on. Asher was in his own heaven.

Nico saw how his face lit up. "You really are some kind of nerd."

Asher ignored him and quickly began rifling through the cabinets to locate supplies.

"Do you have everything you need?" asked Nico rather impatiently.

Asher continued to carefully examine the various cabinets and cases. "Yeah. Yeah, we have more than we could possibly need. Just need to find a clear, low-traffic area where we can hide our own equipment."

Nico wandered toward a workbench where glass jars filled with purple liquid were set on a timed burner. Criss-crossed tubes ran between a titration device and a large glass vat. Asher finished emptying his satchel's worth of supplies into the back of a nearly empty, floor-level cabinet. Nico picked up some of the chemicals by the workbench. "Hey Asher, what is Redding working on over here?"

"Not sure, and not any of my business."

"What is Azaperone?"

Asher got up from the cabinet and began walking over. "It's a type of anti-psychotic sedative. Why?"

Nico shrugged his shoulders and put the glass down to examine another.

Asher picked up a glass beaker labeled *Reserpine* and examined it closely. "What the...?"

He dropped the glass at the sound of heavy footsteps outside the door. There wasn't time to hide. The lab room door swung open.

CHAPTER 7

Professor Crow flung the door open, his tall, hunched stature silhouetted against the darkened hallway. He stepped toward them carefully in his clean black boots, hands behind his back, pocket watch and chain wrapped tightly on his black vest in a meticulous fashion. "What are you doing."

A simple question framed as a statement. His voice was low and gravelly.

Asher's eyes widened.

Nico stepped up confidently. "We were hoping to catch Professor Redding at office hours. Looks like we got the wrong day..."

Crow stalked even closer, getting in Asher's face. "And the door to his lab just happened to be open?"

Asher and Nico both nodded their heads.

"Why are you touching his things?"

Nico was calm and collected. "Asher was curious. He is a molecular genetics major and was nerding out about the lab, so we were taking a quick look around."

Nico gave Asher a look. Asher took his cue. "Yeah. Yeah, it looks like a complexometric titration with a fast sulphone black indicator. It's interesting stuff. We haven't gotten to that part of class yet, so—"

"Open your bags," Crow interrupted sharply.

Without hesitation, Nico and Asher threw their bags onto a workbench and opened them up for Crow to see. Before investigating them, he brushed the boys aside to get a better look at the titration. He studied it carefully, turned over the glassware to read the chemical names, and watched the liquid drip from its long plastic tubes into the large glass vats. The silence lingered heavily before he stepped over toward the satchels and began his careful search. "You know better than to be in here. Why are your hands black, Mr. Catalano? And you, Mr. Auden, you are touching things that do not belong to you. I will need to report this to Professor Redding and to the rest of the board."

Asher desperately looked to Nico, who walked calmly over to Crow and began speaking in a hushed voice. Asher could not make out the words, but the Professor let out a series of "hmm" and "I see" comments. He then closed the bags and threw them back at the boys. "Consider this your only warning. I catch you in this building without a pass again, I will have you sent straight to Director Dolent. And that is regardless of your intentions and affiliations, Nicholas. Do you understand?"

The boys nodded.

"Good. Get back to your dormitories."

The boys speed-walked to the main building. When they got to their room, they slammed the door behind them.

"What the hell was that?" asked Asher, throwing his arms up at Nico.

"I am sorry, I am so sorry. Honestly, I was not worried about any of the professors coming in, let alone Crow. I have no idea how that happened."

"I thought it was safe! That was your job!"

"I know! I know. Look, we will figure something out."

"Figure something out? No way, I'm not interested. I'm not getting kicked out of Langford for being stupid."

"Totally understandable."

"What did you say to him anyway?"

Nico looked down at the ground. "So, I kind of need you to come with me to something tomorrow night."

"Ok..." Asher said suspiciously. "What kind of thing?"

"Well, first to meet my parents."

"Alright. Sure, I'll meet your parents."

"And then to a meeting thing with some of their friends."

Asher's face was now a look of pure incredulity. "What is going on, Nico?"

Nico looked back up at Asher. "What have you heard about the Maurinko Society?"

Nico's home was behind a large iron gate in a neighborhood behind a larger iron gate. They had taken a fifteen-minute chauffeured taxi ride from Langford, through the back roads of Riali, down the cobblestone streets of the upper west side and away from the polluted alleyways of downtown. He had never seen a mansion this close before. As they ascended marble steps, he tried his best to hide the awestruck wonder from his face.

The house had three stories in the back and two in the front. The second story was all glass, which bulged outward and loomed over Riali. The structure was a beautiful mix of classic marble stone arches and high-level engineering; steel support beams were decorated with flowery metallic designs, while giant stone statues stood on either side of the massive entry archway.

"A little roomier than the dorm, I'd imagine," Asher said. Nico rolled his eyes. The door swung open as they approached, revealing an elderly man looming in the doorway.

"Hi, Hanley," said Nico casually. "Mom home?"

"Nicholas, what a wonderful surprise!"

Asher looked more closely at the giant, who easily stood seven feet tall. He was dressed in a traditional butler's outfit, with the wings of his suit held together by a gold chain. His chest appeared large and bulky, but his waist was thin. Something was particularly off about his proportions.

"Hanley, Asher. Asher, Hanley," said Nico quickly before peering past the butler, who stepped aside to let them through the door.

A beautiful, blond-haired, middle-aged woman wearing a blue silk dress came bounding through the large foyer. She opened her arms in an expectant hug. "My baby!"

A look of embarrassment washed over Nico's face. "Mom, this is Asher Auden, my roommate."

Mrs. Catalano stuck out her hand. "Nice to meet you, Asher. I hope Nico has not gotten you into too much trouble yet."

Asher smirked. If only she knew. "Not yet, ma'am. He's been showing me around, introducing me to his friends. We've had a great time!"

"Good," said Mrs. Catalano as she welcomed the boys inside. Her body dripped in diamonds and gold. Elegant chains and jewelry sloshed around her wrists, neck, and waist as she walked the group down the colossal corridors.

"Such interesting eyes you have, a blue one and a green one!"

"Thank you, it's called heterochromia, it's hereditary."

"Fascinating! And I presume you are from Vana, yes?"

"Yes, ma'am. How did you know?"

"Your dialect," she said, smiling. "We Rialians prefer a more, uh, *proper* pattern of speech."

"How so?"

"For instance, if you have not noticed, we use far fewer contractions. Also, you talk with a slight drawl, not as fast as we do."

Asher had grown up thinking Rialians spoke with a great deal of eloquence but had since become accustomed to the language around him without paying much mind to his own. He wondered if his informal speech patterns were noticeable to other Rialians, too.

"So," she asked, "how do you like Langford so far?"

"It's definitely a change of pace from Vana. But the classes are great, people are nice. Things have been going well."

They made small talk until they reached a heavy wooden door lined in gold leaf, with copper handles and its own knocker shaped like a wild cat. Mrs. Catalano clinked the door knocker, then proceeded to open the door without waiting for an invitation. The room was round, spacious, and littered with schematics and tinkered machines. One glass wall drenched the room in sunlight, while the others were partially blocked by bookcases, chalkboards, and scientific instruments. The bulk of the room appeared to be on a large platform. Peculiarly, it was raised a foot higher than the room's entrance and appeared to contain an intricate system of hydraulics beneath its surface. On the platform was a long red-oak desk flooded with papers and blueprints. Harold Catalano's head was down at the table, reading a schematic. Mrs. Catalano let out a gentle cough to announce her presence. Her husband lifted his eyes just above the brim of his spectacles, then flashed a small smile.

"Ah! He returns!" He carefully folded his glasses and stood up from his desk, a tall, but not imposing, figure. His frame was thin, adorned in a sophisticated brown suit, dark-green bowtie with a dark-green top hat. His matching patterned scarf was comically long, nearly wider than his suit, and drooped down to his boots. Nico had clearly inherited his charismatic disposition from his father, as well as his sharp facial features—Mr. Catalano was equally thin-faced with prominent cheeks, a sharp jaw, and a pointed nose.

He walked around the desk and took a step from the platform to give Nico a hug. Mrs. Catalano introduced Asher as Nico's roommate, and the two shook hands. Mr. Catalano did not seem to pay Asher much attention and turned his focus back on Nico. "You are back sooner than expected. How are classes? Is Gorton Crow teaching you anything new?"

Nico glossed over some of what he had been doing at school for a few minutes as his dad pried for details. Mr. Catalano eventually turned back to Asher. "And are you an engineer as well?"

Asher shook his head. "No, sir. I'm studying molecular genetics."

"Ah, a different kind of engineering."

"Yeah, you could say that..."

Mr. Catalano walked back onto the platform and peered out the glass wall behind his desk. The sun was setting. Mrs. Catalano bustled around the room, sifting through the chaos in attempt to help organize, chattering as she sorted. "Asher is from Vana."

"Vana? That's wonderful. What is a Vanatian doing studying genetics?" Mr. Catalano turned from the window and went back toward his desk. "Ignore me; that may have sounded impolite. I am just a little surprised, is all."

Nico and Asher followed him onto the hydraulic platform.

"Biology has always fascinated me. I have been able to build things since I was a child. Small things. Big things. Small things that build big things." Mr. Catalano let out a tiny laugh and pulled on a lever beside his desk. "This house, for instance, is my design."

The room began to spin. Asher looked through the glass flooring below at the hydraulics and pumps rotating the massive platform, the setting sun a fixed point of reference through the slowly revolving glass wall.

Mr. Catalano continued, "But biology has always been a mystery. Iron. Steel. Electricity through copper? Simple mathematics. Rudimentary and barbaric compared to the interlocking of adenine and thymine, guanine and cytosine." He pulled on another lever, and the ceiling slowly opened to reveal a glass dome. "It is not just this room that is moving. This whole house is a one-of-a-kind machine. Our bodies, though, our bodies are an ancient marvel." Nico appeared bored by the antics, but Asher stood in amazement at the whirring room.

Mr. Catalano watched him closely. "Sunlight bounces its way into the greenery, stripping electrons from water to produce energy and oxygen. But I am preaching to the choir, am I not? I am sure you are aware of the nature in which vegetation proceeds."

Asher snapped out of his daze. "What? Oh, yeah. Yeah, I'm pretty versed in ecosystems."

"I do not doubt it, but do you ever consider the design of these systems? After all, this universe was once a dark, vast nothingness until a sudden burst of light created a smoldering rock of fire. A burning coal, formless and devoid of life. It cooled and sculpted into pools of various chemicals. Chemicals that collated and found a way to replicate. Little specks of dust, primitive cells. Growing increasingly complex, all from the long, repetitive millennia's hammering of sunlight and rainfall."

He walked against the movement of the platform so that his body appeared to stay in place. "These cells grew to realize two options: consume each other or band together. And so intricate self-sufficient systems were built by some form of intrinsic wisdom."

"Intrinsic wisdom?"

"Yes," said Mr. Catalano, stopping his walk, allowing the room to spin him in a slow, dizzying circle. "These systems cannot exist without laws, no?"

"Scientific laws..."

"Of course," said Mr. Catalano. "But *laws*."

"These systems are not perfect. Energy is wasted. Designs are flawed."

"Perhaps the flaws only add to the majesty and perfection of it all."

"I prefer grand machinations that do not result in pain and death,"

Mr. Catalano laughed. "Of course. As do I. But here we are, wrapped in all these cells. Bound by an ancient and shared fundamental code, energized through sunlight and water. And yet, despite all these basic, elemental building blocks, consciousness exists. Is consciousness not the greatest achievement of evolution?"

"As I said before, I prefer machinations that do not lead to pain and death," Asher responded half-jokingly.

"Right! And as I said, perhaps the flaws, including pain and death, only add to the majesty. Consciousness, once it has fulfilled its primary purpose of self-preservation and a furthering of the gene pool, goes and lends itself to only one other act."

Asher now stood at the outside of the room, staring deeply at Mr. Catalano, who stood at the center, staring back. "Consciousness grapples with the purpose of creation by creating! The creation of machines. The creation of art. The creation of family. The creation of life. And, without being conscious of destruction, how can we have creation? Without knowing the pain of illness, how can we be motivated to create medicine? Without understanding the agony of loss, how can we be inspired to tell stories of our past and those who have gone before us? Pain fuels consciousness; consciousness breeds creation. And creation? Well, that is our divinity."

The room clicked to a halt. Mr. Catalano smiled, "I have a few friends in the genetics field you may be interested in meeting. I would love to introduce you sometime if you would be so inclined?"

Asher nodded, somewhat stunned. "Yes. I would love to meet some fellow geneticists!"

The sun behind them was now a sliver on the horizon, and the room was lit dimly by just a few hanging lamps.

Nico rummaged through a few of his dad's papers. "Dad, the engineering is going great and all, but our dorm is a little too small to put any of my ideas into practice. I have been working on a new minicopter design, and I really want to give it a shot in my free time."

His dad sat down at the desk across from his son. "You can always come back here. We have everything you need for your personal projects."

"I know, but I don't have time to come back here every weekend. Ideally, I would like to walk over to a lab after class and start building. I tried talking to Crow about us using a lab, but he was not too keen on the idea."

"Ah, Gorton's an old hag, no use in asking him. If you need a lab, I can get you one. Under one condition."

"Of course!"

"You need to maintain perfect grades. I know you love to tinker, but I do not want it to take away from any of your studies. Understood?"

"Not a problem," Nico assured him.

"Ok then, I will send Hanley down to Langford tomorrow to set you up with a lab and access to whatever resources you need. But I will be keeping an eye on those grades. If you start to slip, I am putting your project on pause. I also want to see how your minicopter turns out. I really do not see a practical use for a machine primarily designed for transportation having such little loadbearing potential, but I would be happy if you were to prove me wrong."

Asher hadn't realized Nico's plan up until this point. He'd just managed to get Crow off their back and obtained them an open lab space for the semester. Asher didn't even care about the berries; he was just excited to have resources at his disposal.

Mrs. Catalano called out from the stagnant entryway. "Who is hungry? We have stuffed hen downstairs. It is about time for supper."

"Sounds delicious," said Mr. Catalano, ushering the boys out of the office. "But first, Asher, there is one thing I need from you in this agreement as well."

Professor Aleksei Ederra was facing the board, deep into the details of proper ballroom dance etiquette. "Be sure to check your posture. You need to elongate your back and neck and be as straight as possible."

"That is not the only thing Aleksei is going to elongate," Nico whispered.

Asher stifled his laugh.

The professor looked over her shoulder for a brief second and went back to the board. "When holding hands with your partner, place your palms outward. Your fingers will not interlock. The man's left hand is cupped over the woman's right shoulder blade…"

Nico leaned back to Asher. "I'd be cupping a lot more than Aleksei's shoulders."

Asher snorted.

The professor spun around. "Listen up. You might not think this is important, but when you are embarrassing yourself at the end-of-semester cotillion, you will be disappointed that you did not pay attention!" She looked over at the now silent class, huffed, and went back to her presentation.

Asher tried to whisper back to Nico, "The only thing I'll be disappointing on cotillion night is Professor All-sexy—"

Nico broke into laughter. The professor spun around again and threw a piece of chalk at him. He raised both hands in the air. "I am sorry. My fault."

A few weeks had passed since Asher first met Nico's parents. Since then, the two had been riding high. They spent their evenings in a private lab off the south side of campus, Asher working on the berries and Nico on the copter designs. Asher found himself becoming accepted into Nico's friend group. Classes were engaging but not particularly challenging. With the exception of Professor Crow and his shifty eyes, Asher found himself on good terms with most of his teachers. Life in Riali was generally faster-paced than in Vana, but he had adjusted with relative ease. He was picking up on the social cues and quirks of the others. He was putting on a face and attitude that reflected and aligned with their expectations. He had even adopted the hobbies and habits of his new friends. However, despite all the effort and achievement, Asher still felt that he was an outsider, constantly needing to prove himself.

Nico had briefly explained the Maurinko Society. What Asher understood was that it was a secret group composed of the wealthy and the powerful, who wore thinly veiled masks at meetings as a formality. The masks were elaborate and adorned with various symbols and engravings signifying the status of the members while doing little to protect the identity of the wearer.

Asher was captivated by the pseudo-mystery and the exclusivity. Nico was far less impressed. He explained that it was nothing more than a social event for rich people to network with other rich people. While the society did invest heavily in the mathematics and science industries, their contributions made very little real-world impact. Conversations generally revolved around culture, commerce, and current affairs. Keeping each other in the know and ahead on trends was how they retained their wealth. Time was spent on predicting events, not creating them. But Asher saw it as a place of opportunity, perhaps potential investors for his future endeavors or maybe people to network him into a great laboratory.

Nico's father had requested Asher attend a gathering. Since it was Mr. Catalano supplying Asher with the new laboratory, it would be the least he could do to express his gratitude. Of course, he was by no means an official member, but Nico had told him that the Maurinkos were looking for more people with backgrounds in biology and, to his knowledge, that no native of Vana had ever been invited to such an affair before. Asher didn't question it.

After class, the two left Langford and headed for Nico's house. As they arrived, Nico handed Asher a simple black mask that covered the areas around his eyes and nose. They were greeted by Hanley, who ushered the boys into the dining room area. Roughly twenty to thirty men and women, dressed in their finest, were mingling in the large formal dining area. A long table stood as the room's centerpiece, beneath glass chandeliers and surrounded by various gold artifacts.

Nico leaned in so only Asher could hear. "Do not ever say your name or address anyone else by name. Right now, it does not matter. They already know your name. And I will tell you theirs when there is no one in earshot.

But as a rule, it is supposed to be a *secret* society, so, you know, be secretive."

Asher nodded. "Seems like an odd formality for a networking event."

"Right. It is only a formality, though. See those people hovering around my parents?" Nico stealthily pointed a glass of champagne in his father's direction. "They all saw you next to me and are wondering who is in the plain black mask. Your mask indicates that you are new, a guest."

"Interesting. I don't recall this lesson in Ederra's class."

Nico smirked and took a sip of champagne, "No ballroom dancing required, thank goodness." Careful to keep his voice down, he began describing the other members and identifying them by their masks. "The green mask with the red horns, that is General Volkov, Roman's father. He is the commander of Riali's forces."

Asher followed Nico over to a table of appetizers. "Do you see that light-blue mask with the black feathers? That is Dr. Mionaar Rafe. He was one of the chief pioneers behind the genetic alteration program—one of the top scientists in the world."

Asher's heart rate shot straight up at the thought of meeting Dr. Rafe—he had so many questions for him. The boys walked across the room, past a man in all black, wearing a pure white mask. He had greased black hair and stared directly at the boys for several seconds until they passed. Asher turned to Nico. "Was that Professor Crow?"

Nico shoved a crab cake into his mouth. "Yep. Old Crow used to be a top engineer in Riali, actually helped CAT Robotics for a bit. He retired and joined Langford and is on the University board now, second to Director Dolent, doing admissions. Makes him a useful guy to have around. Pretty unpleasant, though; I would hardly call him a friend of the family."

Asher stood by the appetizers, staring out across the crowd. Hanley walked up to the boys. "Be sure to grab your champagne, good sirs," he said, bowing deeply. "The toast is coming up soon." As he bowed, two robotic arms, each holding a silver plate of champagne glasses, emerged from his back. Asher grabbed a glass skeptically as the butler moved on to the next guests.

"He's...a robot?"

"Well, yeah," said Nico. "Didn't you meet him last time you were here?"

"He didn't have the arms last time!"

"Oh, right. He really only has the extra set of arms out when he needs them. Otherwise, they retract back into his body. My dad and I designed him when I was younger. His core processor is from Baenum. We wanted him to look as realistic as possible, but I don't think we quite got his proportions right. In any case, great butler. Very useful."

"Certainly...handy."

Nico groaned.

Asher turned around and stumbled, nearly dropping his glass.

"What is wrong with you?" asked Nico.

Asher nodded to the back door. "Look!"

In the doorway stood an eight-foot-tall humanoid creature, its skin devoid of any pigmentation or hair. Its exaggerated height was exceeded only by its drastic lack of muscle mass, as though it were suffering from malnutrition. Its body's disproportions were further skewed by long arms hanging just shy of knee-high iron combat boots. Its chest was bare, apart from a ceremonial-looking cloth supporting what appeared to be a selection of either short, curved swords or elongated knives. Its naked torso was incredibly thin, with a prominent ribcage poking from underneath the cloth. A single Hilezkorra pendant hung from its neck, and its head was covered in a wraparound helmet, which left a slit just wide enough for seeing.

"That is a guardian," said Nico. "All the high priests of Mazraea have one."

"It's a monster," Asher whispered back.

"Just do not get on the bad side of the priest, and you will be fine," said Nico.

Two dark figures emerged in the doorway behind the guardian. In the front was a man in a heavy cloak and cassock adorned in elaborate gold chains. An old, thick book was held in place by chains like an oversized necklace. He wore a mask made of pure gold with minimal embellishments.

"That is Father Bianok," whispered Nico.

"And who's that behind him?"

A girl dressed in purple clerical robes walked several paces behind Father Bianok. Silver hair, fair skin, high cheekbones, lips hiding a big smile. A bright flowery yellow mask did little to hide her youthful beauty.

"That? That is the love of my life. Sister Lilly. A disciple of the Father." Nico sighed.

Father Bianok waved the guardian off to stand by the door. He continued to the buffet table with Sister Lilly on his heels. "I am going in," Nico said to himself.

"Wait, don't leave me," said Asher. Too late. Nico grabbed a second glass of champagne off Hanley's plate and walked toward the clerical pair.

"Father." Nico bowed. "How are you?"

"I am well, young student. Such lovely hospitalities this evening."

"Yes. Welcome to the home. I have someone I would like for you to meet. He is a foreigner in this city, just like you." Nico pointed over to Asher.

Asher saw the high priest begin walking his way. *What in the world...?* He made his best attempt to avoid eye contact.

Nico turned to Lilly with his extra glass of champagne and a self-satisfied smirk. "Sister, I am so happy to see you back in Riali. How was your journey?" A big bright smile crept across the priestess' face.

"*Achhmm,*" came a low, lofty voice behind Asher.

"Oh, hi there. I'm—"

The priest cut him off. "No names, my son. I am simply glad to hear you are interested in the First God."

"Right," said Asher. "Yes, I've been fascinated by the Hilez gods for some time."

"You are from Vana, aren't you?"

"Yes."

"You poor soul. The acolytes in Vana have not been very successful. So much debauchery with the Midbloom. That whole city has been drunk off its own success the past year. How could a soul ever thrive in such a backward culture?"

"Well, I'm certainly glad to be here in Riali. Learning and soaking up as much as I can."

"You will make a grand student. Such a young and open mind. The celestials will certainly bless you with true knowledge and enriching experiences. Tonight, you begin a new walk, one that will illuminate the way of righteousness. Take this path and be rewarded with a life full of splendor and purpose. But stray off the upright path and find yourself emptied and in ruins."

Asher nodded. The priest grasped onto his gold chains and leaned in close enough for Asher to taste his breath. "I can see it in you now, boy; you have been given a gift from the celestials. Do not squander it. Or their fury will be swift and their vengeance just."

"Yes, Father, I will not disappoint."

A loud clink rang out beside the table. When he had everyone's attention, Hanley set the glass down and pulled out a chair at the head of the table for Nico's dad. The guests all shuffled to their spots. Asher beelined toward Nico, who had grabbed them seats near his father at the end of the table. Once everyone had reached their places, a heavy silence lay thick in the air. All eyes were on Harold Catalano at the head of the table. His mask was mostly thin metal, dripping in gears and gold. Charlotte Catalano stood on the opposite end of the table, her mask similar in extravagance but with a touch more style, as it matched her puffy white and light-pink dress. Harold stood, arms raised in a gesture of order. The room hushed, and everyone raised their placed chalices of wine.

Mr. Catalano spoke: "Welcome, brothers and sisters, to the Maurinko social."

CHAPTER 8

Mr. Catalano spoke with a low and dramatic tonality. "We are grateful to be in your presence this evening as we gather in fellowship together in honor of the First God. Thank you to both the familiar souls and the new masks. The seven cities of Khamara are strong and prosperous due to your efforts and wisdom." He took a sip of wine, and the group followed suit. "It is with a heavy heart," he continued, "that I report that a member has been murdered by the recent acts of terrorism that claimed the lives of two others in our capital. May the First God have mercy on our brother who has passed in these horrific events, and may all the gods have vengeance on the one responsible for such a tragedy."

The group took another synchronized sip of the wine as Mr. Catalano went on. "While the motive for the attacks remains unconfirmed, the high elders have chosen to divert considerable resources into pursuing the terrorist so that he may be put to swift justice. The council has also been implementing measures to ensure the capital's economic success and to deter the threats that undermine our current trade relations."

A chorus of small cheers was released from the group as they took another sip.

"In the meantime, we must take direction from the First God, and see that our pain leads to advancement and that we better ourselves in these trying times until the day of the enlightened one."

Asher gave Nico a quick side-eye. *What madness have I been dragged into now?*

"Please, let us rejoice in the sorrow of our God as he brings new order to his subjects. And we, as his subjects, bring new order to his creation. May our unity bring greatness to the cities of Khamara. May our prosperity bring blessing to the world. And may our lives echo in eternity. I hereby pass blessings onto this evening's nourishment and commence our fellowship."

"So let it be," the room proclaimed in unison as they drank from their chalices.

The table buzzed with conversation and the tinkling of silverware. At its center was a revolving conveyor belt of intricate copper plates carrying large cuts of meats, tureens of creatively prepared vegetables, and an assortment of wines and side dishes. Asher hadn't seen such extravagance even at the Midbloom festival.

Mr. Catalano made small talk with Nico, asking him about school and the minicopter project. The language between them was almost robotically formal, neither addressing the other by name or relation and speaking only of their projects and progress, maintaining the façade of anonymity for ritualistic sake. Mr. Catalano, seemingly in a positive mood, was quick to move on from his conversation with his son and direct his attention toward Asher.

"Black mask. Thank you for joining us this evening. How is everything so far?"

"Wonderful. A great group of people and even better food!"

Mr. Catalano smiled as several eavesdropping guests began to turn their attention to the conversation. He pointed with a fork to a man sitting across from Asher. "This green mask here is a doctor of sorts in Riali. He treats almost every Maurinko member personally. He is also on the cutting edge of modern genetic research. I would love for you two to chat."

The man in the green mask dropped his cutlery and lifted his chalice to Asher. "Pleasure to meet you, young Vanatian."

Asher recognized the man as Dr. Rafe. Asher lifted his glass in acknowledgment and they both took a sip.

"Doctor, I hear you have helped with the genetic modification program," Asher said hesitantly. He looked over to Nico for reassurance, who seemed unfazed by the conversation, instead occupied with stuffing his face full of turkey and mashed potatoes. Asher continued, "I hope I am not being intrusive, but are you splicing DNA for recombination or simply finding gemmules to assist in the over-expression of desired traits?"

Dr. Rafe finished chewing on a piece of juicy brisket before dabbing the corners of his lips with a napkin. He smiled and spoke into his wine. "You sure are knowledgeable for someone with your background. You must have studied under Professor Fenske, yes?"

"Yes, he and Professor Redding worked together on my admission to Langford."

From the corner of his eye, Asher saw Crow give a passing glance in their direction before taking a sip and turning away.

"Rupert is a brilliant mind. I love his work in antisense molecules and nitrogen fixation. He has done great work increasing plant life and crop yield out in Vana. But to answer your first question, the genetic alterations are primarily coming through RNA interference. You are halfway correct; we have been able to modify the expression of desired traits and limit the expression of others. But we've seen the most success in the alterations of proteins by modifying the precursor RNA. Our labs have been working feverishly to sequence the DNA of various animals and anomalies in an effort to identify desirable traits. But unfortunately, our ability to incorporate these traits has been...limited."

Asher stopped eating to think. "What kind of splicing have you been using?"

Dr. Rafe sipped from his chalice and eyed a platter of meat passing on the conveyor belt before returning his attention toward Asher. "Primarily viral proteins and enzymes. We have been modifying the building tools of a retrovirus—incorporating its reverse transcriptase, proteases, ribonuclease, and integrase."

Asher nodded. "Have you considered isolating the actual DNA-cleaving enzymes within the host cells and restructuring their target sites?"

Dr. Rafe ceased his dining and leaned into the table with curiosity. "And how do you suggest tailoring a host enzyme's splice site?"

"Well, I've done it before."

Dr. Rafe's green mask did little to hide his astonishment. "You have created spliceosomes with direct targets?"

Asher shrugged. "In fungi, yes. I haven't tried mammals yet."

"How? How did you do it?"

Asher let out a wry smile. "It's less about finding and locating the splice sites of the target gene and more about finding a unique targeting site within the junk DNA and then making sure expression is reached. Too many of the desirable genes have similar splice sites. There's too much room for error."

"Hmm," Rafe nodded, clearly impressed. "That is good in theory, but in practice, you would never be able to get an expression of junk DNA in humans—there's too much to sift through. But I do like your line of thinking." He shook his knife playfully at Asher. "There may be a future in my office for you yet."

Asher smiled and returned to eating, not wanting to press his luck with the conversation. A large, stocky man with a decorated suit and gold mask interjected, "I have no idea what you two brainiacs are babbling on about, but the good doctor here will talk your ear off. Now tell me," he said, dropping his head and making eye contact with Asher and Nico, "do you two boys plan on going to the koroka game tomorrow?"

"Of course, sir," Nico said. "I was not able to go to their practice tonight, clearly, but I caught a few glimpses earlier in the week. Our star looks even quicker and stronger than last year!" Asher recognized the man behind the gold mask: Roman's father, General Volkov.

The General smirked. "Yes, he has the physical gifts; he was certainly born with many advantages. But it is his mind that must be valued. Our loss in the playoffs last year was due to his strategic errors; truly no excuse for the abysmal performance from a center, from a leader. In any case, yes, he is talented, but if that head of his gets any bigger, it might weigh him down!"

The table around them let out a polite chuckle.

"I'm excited to finally see the Langford team in action," Asher said. "But I'll be a little conflicted about who to cheer for when Vana comes to town in a few weeks."

The General looked up at him, "Sounds like a win-win to me. You get to celebrate with the winner while reveling in the chaos."

Asher shook his head, "Or perhaps a lose-lose. I just want what is best for everyone."

Dr. Rafe chuckled, "Such youthful bliss. One day you will understand that bittersweet is always the best of outcomes."

"Oh?" asked Asher curiously.

"Sure, there is happiness in victory. But there is a lesson in defeat. And with wisdom comes enlightenment, and enlightenment provides a much greater lasting joy."

"Forgive my youthful ignorance," said Asher humbly, "but if that is the case, then I can only hope that my pursuits of chasing happiness provide enough relief for the inevitable anguish of obtaining wisdom. I believe I will follow the advice of the gold mask. I will enjoy the chaos."

Callie had no interest in sports. They were all needless brutality, an unspectacular spectacle. But Felix had dragged her out. He had made the Langford practice squad and Kipos, his hometown team, was the first up against Langford. She walked through cramped passages to the section of the koroka arena reserved for students. Chanting reverberated off the metal and concrete walls, and she could smell the crowd's lingering body odor as she made her way toward the seating area. The concrete passageway opened to reveal a glass barrier and the field. As she approached the barrier, she took a second to look behind her at a sprawling student section before trudging up the rows, searching for a place to sit.

Asher spotted Callie walking up the bleachers and waved to grab her attention. He had never seen her at a game before back in Vana, but with the amount of excitement and buzz going around, he figured she had gotten drawn into the fervor of it all. She caught his eye, but she wasn't sure if he was waving at her or not, so she gave a half-hearted wave back, just in case. Asher nodded and motioned for her to come over. She accepted the invitation.

"Hey, how's it goin'?" Callie gave Asher a light pat on the back as he attempted to give her a hug.

"Hey, Callie!" Nico shouted, pushing Asher aside. "You made it out! You ready to see Lang U kick some ass?"

Callie's eyes widened in a facial expression resembling that of a shrug. "Surrreee!" The excitement and buzz of the crowd began to reach a fevered pitch as the teams walked onto the field.

The Kipos team came out first to the loud boos of the stadium. They were a rugged bunch, large and scruffy, with the exception of two smaller women who were most likely runners. The stadium's boos quickly subsided to cheers as Langford entered the field. At the center of the pack was Roman, his figure looming over the rest of the team. He threw his arms up to accept the crowd's welcome. Five members from each team walked to the center of the field to greet each other while the remaining players made their way to the trenches on the sidelines.

Each wore a metal suit containing three rigid cylindrical tube-like cables which ran from their lower backs to their shoulders. Aside from the suit, they were each armed with one tonfa baton. The object of the game was simple— pull the cables off the backs of the other team's players.

When one cable was pulled, the remaining cable tubes would lock in place, and lights around the suit would flash and pulsate. The player must then return to their team's starting position within an allotted time, where their remaining cables would unlock, and their suit would stop flashing, allowing them to rejoin the battle. If a player lost all three connection cables, they were out for the remainder of the game. The last team standing won.

The field, however, was less straightforward. It was fifty yards of varied terrain laden with obstacles and rotating, multileveled platforms. There were plenty of hooks and jettisons capable of snagging cables, along with hiding areas for other players to make a sneak play. Each team had five players, typically including one or two smaller players capable of climbing, running, and hiding to preserve their cable count, while bigger guys took on the bulk of the hand-to-hand fighting. The audience was pressed against all sides, hovering above the fighting pit.

The Kipos and Langford players shook hands and walked to their starting points: Langford to a glowing red circle on one end and Kipos to a green circle at the other. Large rotating platforms above them began to whirl. Several menacing cactus-like pylons extended from the ground and began to spin. The countdown started.

"Five…" The crowd joined in.

"Four…" The entire stadium was on its feet.

"Three…Two…"

Asher, Nico, and even Callie were prepared for the roar.

"One!"

The noise of the crowd rocked the stadium as the teams' suits lit up and the players took off.

On the Langford side, the two smallest members darted away from the group and began scaling the pylons and platforms. Nico leaned in so Callie could hear. "Those are the runners."

Callie feigned a smile of interest. Felix was supposed to be one of the runners, but she spotted him over on the bench.

"Roman, he's the center," Nico continued. "The other two next to him are the guards."

They watched as Roman headed straight for the center of the field, flanked by the two guards. The Kipos players approached in a similar formation; from Roman's angle, their runners were nowhere to be seen. He didn't seem to care; he ran straight for the Kipos center.

Both were giants of equal proportion. All players held their tonfas except for Roman, who kept both hands free as he charged at the Kipos center. He stood his ground and spun his tonfa, preparing to strike, and just as Roman came within striking distance, he swung downward at his head.

Roman caught the player's right wrist with his left hand, stopping the blow. Roman's brute strength seemed to catch the Kipos player by surprise. With his right hand, Roman grabbed for the center's throat, picked him off the ground by the suit, and slammed him into the ground. The Langford guards defended Roman's back as he wrestled and pummeled the Kipos center.

A single Kipos runner leaned down from a spinning platform in a desperate attempt to pluck off one of Roman's tubes but was immediately met by both of Langford's runners. The Kipos runner opted to back out of the confrontation, and the two Langford runners gave chase. The Kipos runner had incredible agility, moving from platform to platform without even a pause, but her speed was no match for the Langford runners. She neared the edge of a platform and raised her baton in an effort to fight them off. But, with two Langford runners against her, she didn't stand a chance. Two brutal thwacks to the back of her knees landed her even closer to the platform's edge.

As the Langford runners muscled in, she dove between them and roared, "*NOW!*"

At her call, the second Kipos runner appeared from underneath the platform's edge and placed his tonfa between a tube of each Langford runner. He dropped off the platform, hanging on to his baton and sending both Langford runners plummeting to the ground, ripping out a cable from both of them.

A groan rang out among the crowd as the two runners crashed into the ground. Rattled, they sprinted across the field and back to their starting location. The Kipos runners headed straight to the center battle, taking advantage of their greater numbers.

Nico cheered with the crowd as Langford survived Kipos' temporary double-team advantage. Callie watched with anxious breath. Asher, though, his attention was focused on Roman—analyzing his quick movements and how he seemed unhindered by a towering build. *Far from perfection,* he thought, *but a glimpse into what is in store for human evolution.*

The match continued chaotically, with an early advantage favoring Kipos. The first player out was a Langford runner, then a Langford guard. Kipos' cable advantage began to snowball. The third player out was the Kipos center. The fourth, a Langford guard. Fifth was Kipos' female runner. And then Langford's last runner.

The fight was now three versus one. Roman still had two cables, as did each of the Kipos guards and the remaining Kipos runner. The two guards circled Roman, who stood in the middle of the field with his tonfa now out in front of him. He smiled confidently as the guards began to distract him with short stabs and feints. With his attention diverted, the Kipos runner lay at the edge of a revolving platform, holding the baton by its head to use the handle as a hook.

Roman sensed the oncoming threat and reached up, grabbing the runner by the arm and yanking her down to the ground. He bashed her faceguard, put his foot on her throat, and yanked the baton out of her now limp hand.

Seeing their opportunity, the two guards dove at Roman, who now held a baton in each of his hands. He switched his attention from one guard to the next instantaneously, blocking one with one baton while attacking with the other. He was just as agile as he was powerful. Spinning the batons by their handles, lining them alongside his arm to block and punch with the short end, then flipping them around for forceful swings and counterstrikes. He managed to catch one guard in the facemask, spinning the player backward. Roman quickly bashed at his cable with the long end of his baton, knocking out the metal tube. The crowd went wild.

The unconscious runner remained on the ground, her baton still in Roman's hand. He released her from under his foot and quickly kicked off one of her cables. The Kipos team sent out another player with one cable to carry the runner out and take her place. However, since Roman had successfully disarmed the other player, the new runner was not allowed a baton.

Roman made quick work of the existing guard's cable with a barrage of tonfa strikes, then turned his attention to the new player. The runner wisely chose to evade rather than fight and retreated up onto the platforms to wait for his teammates to rejoin the battle.

Roman did not pursue. Instead, he raised both batons in the air to hype up the crowd. The crowd responded in an uproar.

As the three Kipos players made their way back to the center, he regained his focus and began moving in on one of the guards. Roman with two cables, each Kipos player with one. The runner made a risky dive for Roman's legs. Instead of swatting the runner's tube and potentially losing his two-baton advantage, he used his baton's handle to snake around the back of an oncoming guard and plucked at his cable. At the same time, the second guard managed to swat off one of Roman's cables. A one-for-one exchange. Roman walked back to the starting point, as slow and deliberate as time would allow, trying to catch his breath before resetting the suit.

As soon as his suit reset, the crowd went ballistic. Two versus one, Roman with his two tonfas.

As Roman walked back to midfield, the runner jumped out from behind a pylon, trying to set up an ambush. Roman managed to keep his front facing toward the runner while keeping his eye on the platform above, where the guard was attempting to swat at his back. The runner held onto Roman's right arm tightly and made a play for the tonfa. Roman pulled the player toward him, kicked him in the chest, and then released the baton to send the runner flying. He then spun around and used the handle of his second baton to latch onto the guard's suit and yank him down to ground level. Roman kicked the last cable off the guard as he faceplanted into the ground below.

One versus one. Looking up at the now advancing Roman, the Kipos runner placed the baton back on his hip and took off through the maze of revolving platforms.

Roman laughed. "Aw runners, true to their name." He casually began to climb the spinning platforms, cautiously ensuring no last-second trickery or obstacles snagged his final cable. "Such a coward, you can't just hide all night!"

The Kipos player emerged on top of the highest platform, which revolved above the others at a second story, extending near the edges of the arena for the whole audience to see.

The Kipos player raised his arms as Roman made his way onto the platform. "Gotta give 'em a show," he grinned.

Roman stalked his opponent in a slow and steady advance.

"I like it," he said. "Good style. I will make it even more interesting." He threw down his baton at the feet of the Kipos player. "It is all yours."

Roman raised his palms and made a "come at me" gesture. The Kipos player was nearly a foot shorter and fifty pounds lighter. He looked at the baton hesitantly before kicking it off the platform and bringing his focus back to Roman.

The runner made fast jabs with the long arm of the baton to keep Roman at bay. He tried to catch the jabs, but the runner was too quick and kept painfully swatting at Roman's legs, hoping to trip him up or hurt him enough to slow him down. After having his hand swatted away, Roman lunged. He grabbed the runner by both arms and threw him to the edge of the spinning platform. The crowd was on their feet, cheering wildly.

From the ground, the runner turned to bat at Roman in a last-ditch effort to defend himself, but Roman knocked the baton away. The runner rolled on his back to protect his cable, lifting his feet to desperately kick at Roman. Roman pounced and began pummeling him in the face and stomach, then spun to the runner's side and grabbed him by the suit's collar.

He lifted him off the ground and dangled him over the ledge of the platform. Fear washed over the Kipos player's face. Roman let out a sly smile before letting go. As the runner fell, Roman grabbed the final cable. The cable yanked free from the player's shoulder and locked into the lumbar socket—leaving the runner suspended, twirling helplessly in air.

The stadium lights exploded in an array of red and gold for the home team's victory. The audience's cheers became deafening. Nico was hanging off both Asher and Callie's necks. "OH MY GOD! OH MY GOD! Did you see that? That was insane. He is an animal!"

Asher was in awe of Roman's athleticism. The power, the agility—it was unreal.

"He just carried the whole team," Nico screamed. "What a madman!"

Callie was considerably less impressed. "Yeah. He's a big guy and he's pretty great at pulling on things."

Roman continued to hang onto the Kipos runner until a second revolving platform spun beneath them. He safely dropped the defeated player, removed his helmet, and walked over to the center of the revolving platform to take in his moment of glory.

Nico laughed and turned back to Asher and Callie, "My Vanatian friends, we have a night in store for us now."

CHAPTER 9

The koroka afterparty took place at Roman's suite. He had his own penthouse, which spanned the top floor of a housing complex down the street from Langford. Callie arrived late, wanting to check in on Cloud before meeting back up with everyone else. She entered the condo and was greeted by an open, circular room. Staircases lined with brass handrails on either side of the entrance spiraled up to the soaring ceiling. Callie could see a few partygoers hanging over the sides, drinks in hand, rows of bookshelves behind them. Brick walls were lined with various tapestries to help dampen the room's natural reverberations, and the floors were constructed of a rich, dark wood that Callie quickly identified as Vanatian. Along the walls were curving couches and chaises, all of them bright red with brass buttons.

Unsurprisingly gaudy, thought Callie, *look at all that brass*. Brass pillars, brass piping, brass windowpanes. The edge of the ceiling was lined with brass lamps, connected by hanging brass chains, and at the center of the ceiling was a brass chandelier dripping with crystals that cast rainbow sparkles across the room. Directly below it was an oversized, hand-carved, Vanatian wood table, cleared off for a group of students to play drinking games.

It was Felix who had invited her, but he had yet to arrive with the rest of the koroka team. She could feel the stare of strangers bearing down on her as she made her way to the kitchen.

"Callie!" shouted Nico's familiar voice. She turned to find him with Asher and two other girls she recognized from class, Avee and Kiara. Nico handed her a chalice.

"A chalice? So fancy."

"Oh, you want to see fancy?" asked Asher slyly. "Check out the booze wall."

A few rows of opal buttons containing the names and logos of distilleries lined the kitchen wall. "What's this one?" asked Callie, pointing to one with a flame.

"Ooh, my favorite. Watch!" said Kiara, grabbing Callie's cup and pushing the button. A long robotic arm extended from the wall and poured out a steady stream of blue liquid.

"Hmm... ok..." said Callie.

At once, a small flame appeared from under the robotic arm, setting the drink ablaze.

"Oh, my lord!" said Asher, watching as Callie took back her cup of fiery blue and green sparks.

"That is certainly something." She looked up at Nico, who was grinning at the miniature firework display.

"I'll take one of those!" said Asher grabbing a cup and handing it to Kiara.

The flames died down, and Callie took a sip as the group around her recounted the game. She scanned the room. There had to be twenty to thirty people at the party, and most appeared to be Roman's friends. She noticed Asher's eyes lingering on a girl for a second too long, a girl she recognized as Autumn Vasiliev. Autumn waved at him, and, trying his hardest to play it cool, Asher waved back awkwardly, took a quick sip of his blazing drink, and quickly looked away.

Nico smirked. "You sly dog. Pretty sure Autumn is Roman's girl, but if you want the help…"

Asher shook his head violently. "No. No, definitely not. I'm good."

Too late. Nico and all his unabashed charisma spun around to address Autumn and her group. "Ladies! How is your evening going?" He was greeted by a series of eye rolls and hellos. "Autumn, I like the jersey. I see you took a few creative liberties," he said, striding toward them and leaving Asher unsure of what to do.

"Why thank you." Autumn did a quick curtsy, holding the sides of her outfit: a jersey that was far too large for her but was tastefully cut down the side and sewn together in the back, giving it the resemblance of a dress. "I did it myself from one of Roman's old uniforms."

"Looks great! I certainly hope you washed it. I can only imagine the smell from that man."

Autumn rolled her eyes. "Did you see him put in the work tonight? So proud of him." She beamed as the other girls swamped her with compliments and praise for Roman. Callie took advantage of the break to go explore the rows of bookshelves upstairs as Nico motioned Asher over.

Asher relented and walked over to the edge of the circle, careful to keep his presence quiet. Autumn noticed. "Hey! Asher, right? Nico introduced us during orientation. You are the kid from Vana."

"Hey! Yeah, definitely. And you're Autumn." Asher was cringing at the sound of his own voice. Autumn didn't seem to mind.

"How are you liking Riali so far?"

He had started getting used to the question. "It's good, much different. A lot more buildings..."

"And the people are treating you alright?"

"Haven't been poisoned to death yet, so I got that going for me."

Autumn stifled her laugh as the rest of the group looked over in a mix of humor and disgust. Asher realized the poor taste of his joke. "Oh, oh, I'm sorry. I didn't mean to offend anyone."

"No, you are fine," said Autumn reassuringly.

Avee stepped into the conversation. "No one here is scared of Miasma. If Sheriff Price has not caught him already, then surely Grimm has blasted that bastard's head off by now."

The group cheered at the thought of a dead terrorist and discussed the idea with colorful language and half-baked opinions.

Nico interrupted the conversation. "Asher brought a party gift for all of us."

"Oh?" Autumn raised an eyebrow. Every expression she gave made Asher melt. He composed himself.

"Uh yeah, sort of, I guess. Nico and I have been in the lab working on something."

"Ok, now I am super curious. What have you two been up to?"

"Asher made magical berries!" Nico exclaimed.

The group all laughed at the sound of it. Asher fumbled in his pocket and pulled out a baggie full of the grotesque berries.

"Not *magic* magic. Just, they're hallucinogens. I spliced the gene that makes the psychoactive component of kane mushrooms into sussberries, so now it produces the psychoactive compound on its own. Every gram of berries is about equivalent to a gram of mushrooms. If you've ever done something like this before, you should know what you're in for."

"Wow." Autumn's eyes were wide with shock. "I am not sure if I am more amazed that you and Nico would come up with such a devious plan or simply impressed that you pulled it off. Do these actually work?"

"To be honest, Asher has not tested out the new batch, but we are confident they will work." Nico, ever the salesman, immediately stuck his hand in the bag and popped one into his mouth. "You will love it!"

Asher shrugged and chewed up a berry as well. "They ought to work, and they're safe." Seeing the confidence of the two boys, the rest of the group held out their hands for a taste.

Asher plopped down on a couch beside Callie. He could feel each fiber of the couch beneath him as if they were individual cells comprising a great body. *This is a great batch*, he thought.

"Are you ok?" asked Callie.

"Yeah, I'm doing good. I'm doing really good," he smiled.

She smiled back. "Good."

"We're a long way from Vana, aren't we?"

"We are. Do you miss it?"

Asher thought about her question but could not bring himself to speak. His attention shifted to the sounds of the elegant Riali music as it reverberated against the brick and through his bones, surrounding him like a warm blanket. *Bella Hawthorne,* thought Asher, *such a lovely voice.* His eyes wandered over to Autumn again. He wondered if she, too, inherited such a perfect voice.

A large bang at the front door interrupted his reverie. The whole party turned to see what was causing the commotion.

"WHAT IS UP!" Roman stormed into the room with several of the other koroka players. Felix, the last to enter, was carrying Roman's gear and carefully hung it beside the doorway before making his way to the kitchen. Callie got up from the couch to go greet him but checked to see if Asher was alright one last time before she left. He gave her a thumbs-up before rejoining Nico.

The party had turned into a full ovation. Roman made the rounds, greeting friends, high-fiving strangers, and recapping the game with whoever brought it up. Once he finished his necessary introductions, he walked over to Autumn, Avee, Kiara, Jackson, Nico, and Asher, sneaking up behind Autumn and grabbing her by the waist. She jumped, then turned around furiously. "Don't do that!" she screamed before lighting up at Roman's face and giving him a playful slap on the shoulder. Asher felt the slightest twinge of jealousy as she leaned in for a kiss.

The group was quick to make room for Roman and gave him praise—and none more than Jackson. "Roman! My god, you were a one-man army out there tonight. They are going to be telling stories of you in Kipos like you are the god damned bogeyman. Children will have nightmares at the sound of your name!"

Roman laughed. "It was nothing. They were gassed and overconfident. I was able to flip them at the end."

The group continued to marvel at his celebrity until Autumn whispered something into his ear. "Oh? Wait. What?" Roman turned back to the group. "Ok, who has the mushrooms?" A few of the girls snickered.

Autumn spoke up so the rest of the group could hear, "My new friend Asher." Nodding toward Asher, she continued, "He invented a type of magic mushroom sussberry hybrid sort of thing."

Roman reached out to him. "Nice to meet you. I'm Roman."

Asher shook his hand, which engulfed his own and felt like calloused sandpaper. "Nice to meet you as well, Roman. Great job tonight. If you want to try them, they're berries I spliced with kane mushrooms, so they'll provide a little bit of a trip. Is everyone feeling alright?"

He looked around the group, analyzing their reactions and facial expressions. The group unanimously gave thumbs up.

"No pressure or anything," Nico chimed in, "but Asher and I have been working on these in a lab my dad provided. Almost got busted by Crow on the first go around…"

Roman laughed and picked two berries from Asher's bag, "You were creating drugs near Crow's office? That is some high-level stupidity. You might not be the dumbest person in the world, Nico, but you better hope whoever is, doesn't die."

Nico gave a wry smile and raised his glass, "Then let us toast to your health!"

Roman shook his head and then downed two berries to the sound of the group cheering. Asher figured two berries for him should be sufficient and safe, given his size. He had taken an extra one himself and began to sink into his feelings. Every person and object in the room had sharp defining lines that waved in and out. The music had transitioned into a more pulsing sensation. Laughter became contagious. Asher was in a general sense of euphoria and was particularly elated to see all the other students responding well to the berries. He felt one with the group, perhaps the first time in months that he had felt such a strong, genuine connection with those around him. He was grateful for his growing friendship with Nico, his mutual hometown connection with Callie, and excited about the potential relationships with all those around him. He could see that same love and happiness across their faces. Roman may have been the hero of the day, but Asher felt like the hero of the night.

Asher continued to retreat into himself. Nico and Kiara attempted to keep him social, but he couldn't shake his memories from his last night in Vana. He missed Liam, but the fire...why did only he see the fire? The more he thought about it, the more he could see it again tonight. Nico? Fire. Kiara? Fire. Roman? Autumn? Swirling infernos. He excused himself and went to the restroom. A large swivel vanity mirror moved automatically closer to him as he leaned in. *Not helpful.*

He turned on the water and watched as it emerged from the cracks of river stones. *Like Vana,* thought Asher. *Liam would appreciate this sink.* He turned back to the mirror, "Ok, Asher, sober up. For five seconds, come on, you can do it. Sober up for just a few seconds here. You're fine. You're going to be fine." For a few seconds, the room appeared normal. Lines, sounds, all the emotions and feelings slipped back into reality. "There you go, Asher, much better."

The fire left his vision, and the panic subsided. He opened the door and walked back into the party.

Nico approached him. "You alright, buddy?" Asher stared into his face. Nico's body was no longer on fire; it was the opposite. It was a dark, bruised purple. As if he had been suffocated.

"Yeah…" he said. "I took a little extra, wanted to push my body and the effects, but I'm good. Are you ok?"

"I am feeling great!" said Nico, his skin becoming darker shades of blue and purple.

Asher looked around the room. His friends were all laughing and smiling as their skin turned the shades of ice and suffocation. He looked back to Nico. "My skin! What does my skin look like?"

Nico laughed. "You are tripping out! You have a few zits, but otherwise, your skin is beautiful. No need to worry."

Asher continued to stare around the room as the bodies of his friends took on the appearance of asphyxiated corpses. "I think I need to lie down."

He pushed past Nico and found a seat on the couch, where he began to melt into the furniture. He closed his eyes in defiance of the image—friends around him all wearing the faces of cadavers.

It was no surprise that Roman was the talk of Langford the following week. However, what was not expected was Asher's own popularity, which began to skyrocket as word of his berries spread around school. Groups of students approached him, asking him if he had any more for sale. Nico became the intermediary, pricing out and distributing the supply. Asher could care less about the money, but the profitability of his little side experiment was certainly nothing he would have expected back in Vana.

He was in the break room of the dorm studying for an upcoming exam when Roman approached him. "Asher, how is it going?"

He looked up, half surprised. "Oh hey, doing good, just studying. What's going on?"

"Nothing much. Hey, so I kind of have a favor to ask."

Asher smirked; he knew it was about the berries. He'd had this same conversation multiple times this week. "Yeah, what's up?"

"You are some kind of bio genius, right?"

"Uh, I don't know about *genius*."

"Yeah, no. You are definitely a genius. Do you think there is any way you could possibly make an undetectable compound that might give me a little...help on the field?"

Asher was taken aback, even if he couldn't help but be intrigued by the science of it all. "Hmm. It's possible. We could make an anabolic steroid that gives you a temporary boost in strength and agility. It would exit your system in a few hours, but it would definitely give you some kind of edge."

"Yeah, yeah, exactly! That is what I am looking for, nothing too crazy. Just something to get me through a match. I will be honest with you, I barely won that last match. I know it might have looked like I was in control, but I was drained. I nearly collapsed. I could hardly make it up to the top of the platform, let alone finish off that runner." Roman looked around nervously. "Kipos is not even that tough of a team. If I am not able to go a full match, Langford is toast. We would be lucky to even have a positive win-loss ratio by the end of the year. And I am not sure my body can do what it did this past weekend for another several matches. It is too much."

"Yeah, yeah, I totally get it. I might be able to cook something up for you."

Roman looked relieved. "Oh, thank the First God. My dad would kill me if I started chickening out on games."

"Isn't your dad the General for Riali?"

"You have met him, haven't you?"

"Nico introduced me to a certain group of people."

"Ah. You don't need to be coy with me," Roman laughed. "He took you to a Maurinko social, huh?"

"He did. I met a whole bunch of interesting people."

Roman lowered his head and looked Asher in the eye. "I tell you what. You make me something for these upcoming koroka matches, and I will show you what these Maurinkos are really about."

"What do you mean?"

"Why do you think they invited you into their group, Asher?"

"Nico's dad wanted me to join. I...I needed to join in order to secure a lab for us."

"That doesn't make any sense, you aren't doing them a favor by joining. You realize people are willing to literally give up their firstborns to join the Maurinkos? The connections. The power..."

"What do they want from me?"

"Same thing as I do, I suppose. They are just not as straightforward."

"They want me to make pharmaceuticals?"

"Not quite. What do you know about the catacombs?"

"Never heard of them."

"Nico has not told you about the catacombs underneath the Citadel? Ok. It will be easier for me to show you why you are being vetted by the Maurinkos rather than telling you."

"What exactly goes down in the catacombs?"

"It is a work in progress at the moment, but ultimately the pinnacle of what the Maurinkos hope to achieve. It is a glorious monument to both man and the gods of Hilezkorra. It is a collision of biological and mechanical engineering, perhaps the greatest unknown marvel in the world."

Biological engineering? thought Asher. *What is this place?*

"Look," said Roman, leaning in. "Talk it over with Nico. He does not have catacomb access, but I will take you both there—and I will give you a glimpse of your future."

Asher gazed off into the distance, still thinking about what could be…growing?…being built?…underground. "And you just need something to get you through these games?"

"Yeah. Whip something up for me, it should be simple for someone like you, and I will show you something that Nico's money could never buy. The closest held secret of the Maurinkos."

Asher snapped out of his daze. "Alright, but just this once. I don't know how safe prolonged use of something like this might be, and I wouldn't want to get you hurt or get Nico and me in trouble at the lab." He struck out his hand. "If that's good with you, then you got yourself a deal."

Roman grinned and shook. "Great. Afterward, I will take you to a real Maurinko meeting as well, none of those boring socials. Nothing ever happens there."

"Sure."

"Oh, and one last thing," said Roman. "I am going to need a few more grams of those berries."

Asher smiled and nodded. "Of course."

The next night, Asher and Nico met up with Roman outside Langford's main entrance. Nico had been hesitant about the plan, telling Asher that the catacombs were off-limits to any non-high-ranking Maurinko members. Still, he was excited. He had heard of the catacombs, but they were merely a childhood myth in his mind; he was only half convinced such a place existed.

Asher and Nico tried their best to appear inconspicuous. Roman, on the other hand, remained his large, unabashed, hulking self. "Gentlemen," he said, greeting the boys. "Are you all ready to take a little field trip before the Maurinko meeting?"

Nico rolled his eyes and followed along.

Roman grinned. "This place could be your home someday, Nico. Maybe not your *working* home like Asher, but, you know—"

"Shut up, Roman," interrupted Nico. "I get it; your family outranks mine. I could not care less. But I do want to see what all my family's resources have been going to over these years."

"Wait," said Asher. "Did you just say this place was *my* future?"

"He meant future employment for you, Asher. For me...he means something completely different."

Asher felt uneasy at the thought as they walked off Langford's ground and approached the nearby Citadel. He saw its two oversized doors first. They were open, and the waning moon was reflecting and bouncing off the intricate workings of interwoven steel and gold. A large archway of glass windowing framed them, flanked by two towers, each with four pointing spires. A series of smaller gates and defensive towers covered the perimeter.

While the Citadel did not rise as high as Langford, it was an equally impressive structure. It consisted of three levels; the lower level opened to a grand lobby. Its magnitude gave Asher a feeling reminiscent of taking his first steps into Langford. Roman described the building as they walked through, their shoes click-clacking against the white marble floors. At the end of the lobby was the sanctum, where the masses of Riali came to watch the Hilezkorra high priests perform their weekly sermons. Various public rooms and vendors lined the lower level. The middle floor was not much more than a glorified office building for various governmental branches and employees. The top story was split between a monastery and governmental services and held a few rooms for housing preachers and servants and a couple of areas for private worship. It also contained the House of Assembly and presidential suite. The roof held an eagle's nest, an observation post that visitors could use to admire the Riali cityscape.

They were now at the center of the massive, spiraling tower of the Citadel, where the walls were lined with doors. Roman led them to a nondescript door that opened into another lobby containing a receptionist who, Asher presumed, acted more as a guard. He spoke casually to the receptionist, who eyed Asher and Nico suspiciously but eventually relented and came from around the desk to open another door. Roman lifted his hands, inviting Nico and Asher into the room.

As they walked in, Asher was immediately greeted by a strong gust of cold air. The room was dark and poorly lit. The boys stepped out onto what appeared to be a metallic, grated ledge. Asher peered over the edge and saw an enormous cavern, descending at least several stories.

"This is the great 'Maurinko marvel'?" Nico asked sarcastically.

"Just wait for it," said Roman, grinning ear to ear.

The guard shut the door behind them, and the ledge the boys were standing on began to descend, carrying them to the floors below. They watched as metal staircases wound downward into the vast cavern, snaking past walls lined with various plaques, decorations, and doors.

The moving platform came to a juddering halt several levels down. Roman swung the gate open. "First stop."

The boys walked out into a hallway that pulsated in a dark-blue light. The walls were covered with metallic cases which radiated navy, turning the level into a river of neon blue lights. Asher wanted to peer into one of the cases but instead chose to follow closely behind Roman, who seemed set on where they were going. Roman stopped outside one of the metal cases near the end of the hallway. "Gentlemen, I present to you my great-great-*great*-grandfather: Victor Volkov."

Asher walked up to the metal casing. Lengthy paragraphs were engraved into the side while a glass window took up the bulk of the machine's front. He rubbed fog off the glass to peer inside.

"Oh my god." He stepped back instinctively. "These cases. They're filled with people."

Dozens of glowing dark-blue cases were pressed against the wall. Asher ran back to the ledge and looked up and down, trying to count all the entrances emitting blue halos. Then slowly, he walked back to the case containing Victor Volkov. "All these people...these are all frozen members of the Maurinko Society?"

Roman stepped next to Asher and joined him in peering into the glass. "You are looking at immortality," answered Roman.

Asher looked over at Nico. Nico wasn't focused on the minute engineering of the cyrobaric chambers as Asher had imagined. Instead, Nico's eyes scanned over the vastness of the catacombs. "How?" Nico wandered around the ledge of the floor, staring into the glowing abyss beneath. "How does this place exist? There have to be hundreds of people spanning several centuries. All of that within these walls. I heard the rumors but this...this is incredible. There must be an entire engine room devoted to powering all these chambers. The energy to sustain this would be impossible."

Roman stepped toward the icy tomb. "When my grandfather here passed away, doctors had no idea what he died from. He was one of the very first to request to be frozen. They dipped his body into a frozen man-made lake. A few centuries passed, and they developed better and more sophisticated technology. The engravings on the side explain his name and a little of his life story. But there are also significant notes on his symptoms."

Asher leaned in and began reading the symptoms: headaches, nausea, blurred vision, loss of consciousness.

"An aneurism," he whispered. He turned to Roman. "Your grandfather died of a brain aneurism."

"We know that now," Roman said, placing his hand on the glass and looking deep into his great-great-great-grandfather's lifeless eyes and body full of tubes. "But we still don't have the technology to cure him. His passing was quick and sudden. Dr. Rafe says any kind of procedure now would be risky and could irreversibly damage his mind. He suggested that we wait a few more decades until medical technology has advanced a bit more."

Asher began walking to the next case and the next, examining their bodies and their symptoms. Long metallic hoses connected the metallic caskets, and smaller tubes went from the casing into the arms, head, and body of the Maurinko.

"This is why the Maurinkos are interested in me?" asked Asher. "You think I can help you all achieve immortality?"

Roman shrugged. "What else would we be doing with some kid from Vana?"

Asher looked over to Nico. "This…this is resurrection, not medicine. These people are *dead*."

Nico shifted from one foot to the other. "I know. I know it is crazy, but the Hilez gods are all about resurrection and—"

"What?" Asher interrupted. "I mean, I don't even know if I believe in these gods. The Maurinkos, I mean you guys, *really* believe in them. Don't you think this is a bit too literal?"

Nico shook his head. "I don't know, Asher. I really don't. The Maurinko society is about shaping the world and its events. Economic and cultural power. In a world of chaos and disorder, they want to establish the authority to which all turn for answers. The First God and the gods of Hilezkorra are established and provide a context in which their goals can operate."

"And so how does immortality play into all of this?"

"The First God promises eternal life to his believers," said Nico hesitantly.

"Nah," said Roman as he pulled away from his grandfather's tomb. "You clearly have not been paying much attention at the meetings. The Maurinkos are not concerned about belief or disbelief. The scriptures speak of men transcending into celestial beings. That is what they want. Immortality is an inevitability. What they want is to join the order of the second gods." Roman walked over to the ledge to join Nico, his voice hushed. "One day, these founders will wake up, and they will get to witness and experience the world that they helped put into motion. We are all replaceable cogs, but they see themselves as so much more. They *are* so much more. *We* are so much more. We are not the cogs. We are the cog makers. And this machine runs because of us."

Asher wandered off and walked down one of the metal staircases. He could see at least five other floors emitting the same blue lights and, at the very bottom of the cavern, one doorway giving off a dark-red glow. Asher shouted up to Roman, "Hey, what's on the bottom floor?"

CHAPTER 10

Roman walked over to the ledge and shouted down to Asher. "Those are mostly original founders. Their chambers are in locked rooms; they chose to maintain anonymity even in death."

"So no one knows who is in those VIP suites?" joked Nico.

"Someone probably knows. Just not me," answered Roman. He turned back to Asher and shouted down again, "Hey! Don't go down there!"

Asher stopped and looked up at Roman, puzzled.

"We're running behind for the meeting, we don't have time to go through each level."

"Alright," yelled Asher. "Coming!"

The three left the catacombs and entered back into the secret side lobby. The receptionist handed them long robes and masks and prompted them in a dull, dry tone, "You're late."

The boys threw on the robes and adjusted their masks before heading through one of the other doors of the lobby.

Nico and Roman led the way, with Asher trailing behind, examining the decor and ornamentation of the long, winding hallway. It seemed to be an odd cross between the catacombs and the Citadel. Stone bricks, ancient artwork, and elaborate tapestries reflected the design intentions of the Citadel. But, like the catacombs, the hallway was windowless, dimly lit, and somewhat unfinished, with exposed metal framing, air ducts, and walkways. Asher wondered if the unmarked doors that lined their route were dead ends or if multiple passageways led in and out of these secret, restricted areas.

At the end of the hallway stood the Mazraea guardian, its hand gloved with what appeared to be a weapon. Long knives extended from the gloves, curving like fingernails and elongating its already lanky appearance. Asher hadn't yet seen the guardian up close. Its helmet left only the smallest of openings for its eyes to see through, ending halfway down the creature's head. Its nose was nothing more than two large slits through the center of its face, and its lips were cracked and blackened.

Asher made no effort to hide his fear from the guardian as it leaned down to sniff the boys, only standing back up when Roman pulled out a gold pendant. Roman knocked on the guarded metal door, and a brass panel slid open.

"Glory be to the First God."

The man on the other side echoed Roman's words, and the door opened.

The room was sparsely decorated, with only a large wooden table seating twelve in the center, leaving just enough room for roughly fifty Maurinkos to line the surrounding walls. There were no windows or electric lighting, and as Asher's eyes adjusted to the dim candlelight, he began to recognize a few of the masked people: Dr. Rafe at the opposite wall behind General Volkov, Professor Crow slouching in a corner, and Sister Lilly, busy examining—or perhaps playing with—what appeared to be a belt of small skulls around her waist.

Roman walked over to a figure Asher assumed to be his father and leaned in to apologize for his tardiness. His father quickly shooed him away with a flick of his wrist. Roman obeyed and pressed his back against the wall. On the other side of the room was a second door. Nico walked over and stood beside a figure who looked like his mother; Asher stayed close to Nico's side.

The mood of the room was significantly darker and more somber than what Asher had experienced at the Maurinko social event. A heavy silence hung in the air, punctuated only by a smattering of hushed whispers.

Father Bianok stood from the table, his long robes and chains hanging heavy against his small frame. He bowed his head and lifted his arms in a sign of prayer; the room followed. "Oh, bless us, First Father, the immortal one. You are outside our time but inside our world. Bless us so that we may use our pain for advancement. Alleviate our weaknesses and eliminate our enemies. We gather today to determine the course of this world so that it may take shape in your great image and, in turn, immortalize ourselves alongside the celestials above. Let us not falter in execution or grow weary from selfish distractions. Grant us your wisdom and guidance. Glory be to the First God."

In unison, the room chanted, "Glory be to the First God."

Father Bianok took his seat, and a hooded man began to speak. "For the first order of business, I would like to propose new provisions to the Khamara financial bill being introduced in the House this week. The recent tariffs on Dyrian imports into Riali have caused considerable economic damage to Dyrian shipping industries, but Princess Nora has now shifted to strengthen trade relations with Baenum and the outlying Sumadar posts, as well as to increase their militaristic presence in the Marrazo Sea. If they succeed, they'll be able to sign exclusive seaway contracts, effectively bypassing the tariffs."

Another man jumped in, "Heavens, the last we need is Samira Raol uniting the Hains and the Sumas."

"Exactly," rejoined the first speaker. "As agreed upon in prior meetings, we have permitted Sumadar pirates to capture several of our aging shipping vessels. Crann Exports has used the insurance funds from the stolen vessels to temporarily undercut several key Dyrian agricultural trade agreements between Baenum and Sumadar. We have also been pushing a campaign to convince the public that these acts of piracy are potentially stemming from the Hainlyal Islands in hope of delegitimizing the Raol Trading Company and create political hesitancy for any other city looking to establish trade relations with Dyria. However, this campaign has primarily only bore fruit within Riali. Since the current trade agreements are temporary, we must continue to create friction between the cities and all the islands in the Marrazo Sea if we are to maintain their reliance on the capital. To do this, I am proposing—"

A hissing sound interrupted the man. The room buzzed with a low murmur before he launched back into his speech. "I propose we use our alliance with the Hilezkorra priests of Saint Mazraea to influence—"

The hissing sound intensified. Asher looked up; it was coming from the air vents.

"GAS!" shouted one of the Maurinko members, pointing to the vents.

Terror overtook the room. Sounds of shrieking reverberated inside the packed room as people rushed for the doors, soon discovering they had been locked from the outside. Purple gas poured through the exposed vent.

Asher quickly removed his robe, jumped onto the table, and attempted to shove it through the vents, blocking the airflow. He turned to Nico. "Give me your robes!"

Nico threw Asher his robe, but the gas was too much. Asher became light-headed and dizzy. He crashed down on his knees. He had a few seconds of consciousness left to analyze his symptoms: his vision was blurred, his mouth was dry. He could see some members covering their noses and mouths in a futile attempt to filter out the poison. His vision went black as he collapsed backward onto the table.

"Get up. Come on, wake up. We need to get out of here."

"We're not dead?" Asher mumbled, slowly opening his eyes to see Nico shaking him.

"No shit. Now, get up. We need to go."

Asher was still on the table. He sat up and examined the room. One of the doors looked like it was knocked clear off its hinges. The majority of the room's occupants had cleared out, although a handful were still lying on the ground, Professor Crow among them, clutching his arm in pain.

Asher and Nico walked toward the central lobby as several members snuck through the various side doors of the hallway.

"Did anyone die?" Asher asked.

"Keep your voice down! And, no. I don't know, I don't think so anyway. It doesn't appear that anyone died." The boys walked hurriedly down the corridor. Asher saw a side door partially open; he stopped and looked through the opening. He saw various members scurrying off down the hallway.

"Don't follow them," said Nico. "My dad told us to go through the front. Too many people out one door could draw attention; a lot of members are going to want to hide."

"Makes sense. Did someone wake you up?"

"My parents. They shook me awake and told me Father Bianok's Mazraea guardian broke down the back door after the gas had knocked everyone out."

The boys walked into the lobby as Asher realized what has been bugging him about the gas. "You know, we would be dead if this was a nerve agent. This had to be an incapacitating type, maybe some kind of anticholinergic compound."

The lobby was fairly crowded with a few other unmasked Maurinkos regaining their composure. A hand shot out and pressed against Asher's chest. "Boys," said a low, composed voice. "I'm Sheriff Price, this here is Vance Grimm, and this is General Volkov."

"Hi..." said Asher and Nico nervously.

The sheriff was disheveled but well-dressed, a top hat resting on messy hair and a heavy five o'clock shadow covering a strong, chiseled jaw.

"I couldn't help but catch the tail end of your conversation. It's my understanding that you two were in the room where the chemical attack occurred?"

Asher looked at Nico, who looked right back at Asher. Asher chose to speak first. "Yes, Sir. We were."

Sheriff Price asked the boys for their names, contact information, and their version of events. General Volkov looked on, nodding occasionally as the boys skirted around the details of the meeting.

"Boys," said Price, "Do you have any ideas as to why someone might have wanted you, or someone else in that room, dead?"

"No," said Nico. "We get along with everyone. Like we said before, we were just having a scripture study."

"I don't think they wanted us dead," interrupted Asher. Grimm leaned forward. Asher's eyes were still recalibrating after the dim hallways and the effects of the gas; he could not make out the face of this man who stood in the back. Still, he could sense that something was off about his demeanor. *He's hostile*, Asher thought. Violence lingered around him like cheap cologne.

"Why do you say that?" asked Grimm. His voice was the raspy sound of whiskey and cigarettes.

"Well…the gas they used. It didn't kill us."

The shadowy figure stepped closer to the boys. "That's not what you said earlier."

Sheriff Price looked at Grimm suspiciously as he continued, "I believe what you said was that the gas used was an anticholinergic compound."

Grimm's gaze was unsettling. He wore a brown trench coat and faded black cap pulled down low. His face was thin and scarred, with big ears and a prominent chin.

Asher could see what looked like a shotgun strapped around his chest. "How do you know what kind of agent was used?" he asked again.

"It's...I just..." Asher wasn't sure how to phrase what he wanted to say. "Before I fell unconscious, I analyzed my body. I felt my saliva production slow down and dizziness overtake me. It suggests there was something suppressing my central nervous system, something capable of quickly moving through the blood-brain barrier. When we woke up, there was a bit of a gap in our memory, suggesting amnesia. My guess is some sort of anticholinergic compound used as an incapacitating agent. Had it been a nerve agent, I would have had a higher saliva production. We would have noticed a constriction of our pupils upon waking up. And, given our proximity to the gas, we most likely would have at least urinated ourselves."

Grimm measured Asher up and down, his face expressionless as if Asher's words held no meaning. The silence continued to fester. "Was it Miasma?" asked Nico bluntly.

"If it were Miasma, you would be dead," Grimm grunted, then turned his back on them and walked away.

"I think that's enough questions for now," said Sheriff Price. "We'll contact you if we have any further information. I suggest you both see Nurse Kimona at the infirmary. Thank you for your time."

The boys walked past the men, Nico making eye contact with the General, who had remained silent and stone-faced during the encounter.

Asher and Nico rushed back to the university, not saying a word. A million thoughts and questions raced through Asher's mind. Nico appeared to be equally rattled but perhaps not as concerned with the hows and whys. Asher started off small. "Do you know anything about that Vance Grimm guy? Just looking at him made me feel awful…"

Nico sighed. He had zero desire to talk but simultaneously needed to process what had happened. He chose to entertain Asher. "Grimm is a bounty hunter. Possibly the most successful bounty hunter in all of Khamara. It's been rumored that the Maurinkos were planning to bring him in to stop Miasma since the Sheriff's Department has been slow in catching the terrorist. He always carries a shotgun and a glass jar."

The boys reached the infirmary, rang a bell on the desk, and took a seat outside the office.

"Why the glass jar?" asked Asher.

"Because he rips the eyes out of his bounties and stores them in the jar to collect his reward. It's easier than bringing back whole bodies. He uses small mechanical spiders specially built from Baenum that seek out his targets and rip out the ey—"

"Got it!" interrupted Asher, sparing himself from the gory details.

"Price, Grimm, and Volkov are the three most dangerous men in Riali. I would not want to be the one to catch their ire. If that attack was Miasma, then his life is fast approaching its end."

"But we were just caught in the crosshairs, right? We have no idea if it was Miasma, or who the terrorist was aiming to kill, or if they were trying to kill at all. The entire society is made up of high-profile members…"

The infirmary door swung open, and out stepped Nurse Kimona. She was young and attractive, and, were the boys visiting for reasons other than their current circumstance, they would have perhaps enjoyed her attention. She gave Nico a hug.

"Ohh, boys, I heard what happened. What a terrifying experience. Here, come into my office!" She grabbed each of their hands and led them into the infirmary.

From what Asher could tell, Nurse Kimona was good at her job. She took their vitals, looked for any abnormalities in their breathing, checked their pupil dilation, and tested sensory responses. After they reassured her that they felt fine, she requested they take a quick blood test to see if they could determine the toxin used in the attack. The boys agreed.

She set out a series of six vials and then turned to grab consent forms. As she did, Asher grabbed one of the empty vials and pocketed it. Nico eyed him suspiciously.

"Huh, that is odd; I swore there were three vials each. My mind must be flustered with everything going on. You two sign these, I'll be back in one second!"

"I need you to create a distraction when getting your blood drawn," Asher whispered to Nico as the nurse walked over to the supply closet.

Nico had no hesitation, "I got you."

"Ok, who's first?" asked the nurse sweetly.

Nico raised his hand sheepishly, "I will go first, but just to warn you, I am a bit scared of needles."

"Nothing to be embarrassed about, Mr. Catalano, happens to the best. I'll be sure to go easy."

As she neared his skin, Nico jumped out of the seat, spilling over her tray table of supplies, "AHH! Get away!!"

Asher and the nurse shot up at the unexpected outburst. "It'll be quite alright, calm down, it'll be over in a bit."

Nico wailed as the nurse attempted to wrestle down his arm. Asher took the opportunity to scour the medicine cabinet, snagging various bottles and supplies. Nico looked over while continuing his spectacular commotion. Asher lifted a finger and pointed toward the door, mouthing the words *one more time*. His eyes widened with exasperation at the request before nodding in understanding. He settled back down as Asher backed away from the medicine cabinet and walked back to his chair.

"I am feeling quite faint," said Nico as the nurse finished the blood draw. Asher slunk back into his chair, the distraction appearing to have worked. "Just sit down and relax as I grab your friend's blood here," she said in an effort to calm him.

"I think," said Nico slipping from the chair, "I think I am going to use the restroom real quick." The nurse had already plunged the needle into Asher and was filling up her first vial as Nico made his way to the door. "Please don't, just stay in here," Nurse Kimona begged.

Nico slammed his body into the door as if he were a drunkard. A series of crashing sounds came from the hallway.

"Is everything alright, dear?" yelled the nurse.

"Oh," shouted Nico, as sounds of furniture clattering and items falling reverberated down the hallway. "Oh, I think I might faint. Oh no! Oh my!"

A dramatic thud sounded from outside the door.

The nurse looked up at Asher, "I am so sorry."

"It's fine, you should go check on him."

She thanked him, put down the first vial, and ran out the door. Asher quickly grabbed the empty vial from his pocket and pressed it to the needle. *Just a few more seconds, Nico, you're doing great, ya big dummy.*

The vial finished filling. Asher yanked it out and placed it in his pocket before the nurse walked back in, dragging Nico's collapsed body. He opened an eye to check if the job had been done well. Asher reassured him with a covert thumbs up. Nurse Kimona finished and handed the boys a chalk-like nutritional drink to help with their headache. The boys thanked her for the assistance and headed back to the dorms, sipping on their drinks before quickly tossing them out.

Nico turned to Asher. "How did it go?"

"Your performance? Nailed it; you got a real bright future in theater."

"Thanks," said Nico smiling widely. "But seriously, get what you need?

"Yes, we did," said Asher twirling the vial of his blood.

"Great, great...so why exactly do we need the blood?"

"Because I doubt the police will tell us what was in the toxin. And I'm just a bit curious about what was used, that's all."

"And you are going to do what with it? Make an antidote?"

"No. I don't know. Maybe? Let's just see what it is first."

"Yeah. We can bring the information to my dad and the Maurinkos. They will know what to do."

"I'm good with that plan. Although I do hope we don't all find ourselves locked in a room being poisoned to death again."

"Hmm..." said Nico. "You just gave me an idea."

CHAPTER 11

The weather had started to cool. Callie walked through the garden, admiring all the changing colors, as Cloud strolled alongside her, sniffing at the piles of dying leaves. A group of girls chatted at a nearby picnic table. Callie continued through the hedges, paying no attention to the group until a dark-haired girl broke away and approached her.

"Hi. You are Callie, right?"

Callie eyed the girl suspiciously. "Yeah, I'm Callie. Hi."

"I'm Autumn," said the girl, sticking her hand out to introduce herself.

"I know. We're in religions together."

"Yeah, we are!" said Autumn, "I love your fox. What is his name?"

"This is Cloud."

Cloud was too distracted by a group of buzzing bees over his head to be bothered by the sound of his own name.

"He is very beautiful."

"Thank you," said Callie continuing her walk.

Autumn joined her. "Where are you from? You don't seem to be a Riali native."

She was unsure what Autumn was implying but kept her response cordial. "I'm from Vana."

"Oh, you're from Vana! I had thought perhaps you were from Dyria."

"What does that mean?"

"I just...I don't know, it's not like it would be a bad thing."

"Why would it be a bad thing?" asked Callie sharply.

"It's not a bad thing! It's not a bad thing! Well, in any case, that explains why I've seen you hang around Asher Auden. I suppose you two know each other."

Callie snorted a small laugh at the question. "Yeah, I know Asher. Why?"

"Just curious. I know he is from Vana, too. I have been seeing him around at parties, and we have a few classes together. Seems like an interesting kid. Plus, he makes these berries..."

Callie shook her head. "I know about the berries, but I can't get any for you if that's what you're asking."

"What? No. No, I was not trying to score anything from you or anything. I also see him all the time with Nico. I think he is an interesting guy. Super smart, seems to care about people, that kind of thing."

Callie looked up in disbelief but chose not to speak her mind. "Sure, he's a good guy. His head gets the better of him sometimes. Back in Vana, he would get bored easily, and he and his best friend would get into trouble. He never meant anyone any harm, though. He just...I think he has a hard time identifying with other people. It's like he needs to prove himself all the time."

Autumn nodded.

"I thought you were with Roman?" asked Callie.

Autumn got nervous and began to fidget with a leaf she had plucked from a nearby branch. "Ha, Roman? Yeah. I am. We are, or whatever. I don't know... we are a bit on and off."

"Right...But Asher?"

Autumn laughed. "No, it is not like that. I mean, maybe Asher can help me with some chemistry homework sometime or something, but yeah. Yeah, Roman is great, but I think he sees me as another one of his trophies. It feels like he doesn't care much about me, or my day, or any of my thoughts. I didn't mean to get so personal so quickly. Please, do not tell anyone I told you this... I haven't told anyone else. I...Roman reminds me of my parents. He looks down on me, like I am lesser."

"Oh," said Callie.

Autumn shifted the topic. "I know most of the people at this school already, we all grew up together. But you and Asher are a mystery. I do not know many people from Vana. The people from Riali, we are all pretty much the same."

Callie whistled to call over Cloud. "Or maybe all people are the same."

"Maybe," said Autumn. "But I have not seen many girls wear feathers in their hair like you. Your hair is super pretty, by the way."

"Thanks. I don't think the feathers are really a Vana thing, they're more a me thing."

Cloud came running toward the girls. "May I pet him?" asked Autumn.

"Sure," said Callie. "He's friendly."

Autumn knelt down and let Cloud sniff her hand; Cloud leaped backward.

"Everything alright?" asked Autumn.

"Yeah," said Callie. "He's been acting strange ever since we got to Riali. I think he's still getting used to the new environment. Adjusting and all."

"Right. I watched as you two took on the ere."

Callie shook her head. "We didn't take on anything."

"Oh, I disagree. To put yourself in harm's way for people you have just met, that is—"

"Please stop," interrupted Callie. "I've heard what the others have said about me. I'm not dumb or seeking out attention or whatever else it is they think."

"I was being sincere. I think both you and Asher are interesting people. Far more interesting than these rich hoity-toity jerks in Riali."

Callie gave Cloud an ear rub.

"In any case, you are always welcome to come hang out with my friends and me. We could use a fresh face in the group."

Callie smiled. "Thanks, I appreciate that."

"Of course! But seriously, you should try one of those magic berries sometime."

Callie laughed as Autumn walked away. She looked back at Cloud, "You don't like anyone here, do you, boy? I don't blame you. I'm fine with it being only you and I as well."

The final bell rang, and Asher marched to Professor Redding's office on a mission. He knocked and entered.

"Hi, Professor, would you mind if we talk? I just have a few questions."

"Sure thing!" said Redding enthusiastically. "Pull up a seat. Do you have questions about the new biosynthesis lectures? The isoprenoids tend to trip up a lot of the freshmen."

"No, Professor. I'm good with the new material."

"Of course you are. Then what can I do for you?"

"What do you know about aerosol anticholinergic compounds?"

"Knockout gas?" Professor Redding leaned forward in his chair. "What do *you* know about incapacitating agents?"

Asher looked down at his feet and then back up at the professor. He hadn't come this far to chicken out. "I know it's what Miasma used on his latest attack. I was there."

Redding leaned in closer and rubbed his stubbled chin, a look of concern filling his eyes. Asher continued, "I took a sample of my blood and tested it. It's full of halothane."

The professor sighed. "This is really a matter for the authorities, you know. But I'm never one to starve a hungry mind…" He leaned back and stared at his desk in contemplation before diving in. "Halothane is a chiral compound that operates as an anesthetic. It works as an NMDA receptor antagonist, activating the 5-HT3 and twin-pore potassium channels and inhibiting sodium cholate and the voltage-gated sodium channels. In ether form, it's often used as a sedative. It can be lethal in high quantities, but if I recall, no one in the last attack was killed?"

Asher nodded. "That's correct. No one, to my knowledge."

"Its effects occur very quickly on contact. Had it been mixed with a catecholamine, it could have shut down the function of organs such as the lungs. Or it can be combined with a more lethal drug, one that is less detectable whose effects take longer to process."

"So...do you think perhaps the plan was to knock people out using the halothane ether mix and then introduce a second type of gas, like a catecholamine or a carbamate, to kill the group?"

"I am only speculating. I cannot know the motives of a madman."

"But there is a possibility the plan was foiled?"

"The last attack has not been widely reported, but my understanding is yes, that is what the authorities are saying."

Asher sat in silence, processing the new information before moving to a new topic. "One other question for you, Professor."

"Please, do not let it be something illegal..."

"It's not! I don't think, anyway. I've been thinking a lot about death. I've always been fascinated by life. How it was created, why things act the way they do. But I've never put much thought into death. As biologists, we are tasked with curing diseases and bettering the human form, but should the ultimate goal be to eradicate death?"

"Hmm...this might be a question better suited for Professor Creed, but I'll give you my thoughts." Redding sat up in his chair and looked Asher in the eye. "For starters, death is nothing to fear. If many religions are right and death is just a passageway to eternal life, then great! This version of immortality lets people move from a reality whose existence they can confirm empirically to a reality whose existence they have long postulated. If they happen to be wrong about the afterlife, then what awaits them is not anything more than a cessation of sensation. A nothingness they won't have the consciousness to be bothered by. Which means no more pain, suffering, or the endless upkeep of the human condition."

Asher thought for a minute before speaking. "If death is nothing to fear, given that it's either blissful eternity or a dreamless sleep, then should the option for an unending corporeal life be provided?"

Redding shrugged his shoulders. "Perhaps. Unless it is life that should be feared."

"Why would we fear life? All life seems sacred on some level. The beauty and complexity of human life, in particular, makes existence itself something of a miracle."

Redding nodded. "Sure. There might be some value in existing simply for the sake of existing. But that does not really take into account quality of life."

"Quality is relative. Even in pain, people can find joy and happiness."

"What if death brings relief to a particularly terrible or painful existence? Or, perhaps more importantly, what if the death of one individual can stop the pain and suffering of countless others?"

"Like in war?"

"I will choose a more specific example. Cha'rik Kai brought about the pain and suffering of millions. Should he have been granted immortality alongside the civilizations he enslaved?"

"So you're saying immortality will be abused?"

"I am not saying that either. Certainly, the moral arc of history has bent toward positive progression with the advances of humanity. We are not nearly as barbaric as our ancestors."

"You think Cha'rik Kai would have changed for the better?"

"Kai was deeply religious. Granted, his beliefs were a perversion of the Hilezkorra faith. He took the concept of the First God and the idea of eternal life both a step too far, believing that as man now is, God once was. And as God now is, man must become. He was obsessed with human perfection to the point of...well, you know. His methods were nothing short of pure horror. A man like him would never stop at immortality alone, and a man like him would be the least deserving of such a gift, as I am sure most everyone would agree."

"Ok then, but his ideas died with him, which goes back to your previous point that morality continues to progress through the ages. So—in the event we achieve an immortal civilization—if human morality continues to advance at the pace of technology, would the correct moral choice be to bring the dead back to life?"

"Assuming we live in a completely equal and fair society and the deceased gave prior consent, then yes, bringing back the dead could be considered moral. But to bring them back as immortal beings would require a complete restructuring of their anatomy and consciousness in order to assimilate them into that now advanced society. In doing so, they are arguably no longer the same entity they once were prior to their consent, but by not doing so, it would no longer be a fair and equal society. So that hypothetical scenario could never actually exist."

Asher looked down at the floor. Redding sensed his feeling of defeat. "I'm sorry I cannot give you more of a direct answer. Even in a black-and-white world, truth lies somewhere in the gray. But what I can say is that a technological singularity is rapidly approaching. That science lives separately from mankind as an accumulation of knowledge. As scientists, it is our job to continue the advancement of these technologies in order to increase the quality of life for the others that come after us. Immortality seems to be just one point in our inevitable progression as a species."

Asher looked back up at Redding. "Inevitable, sure. But we have no idea the consequences of becoming gods."

Asher and Nico spent their nights in the lab. Asher's side was meticulously clean and organized as he worked on Roman's performance enhancer and the lucrative berry project. The other half of the lab was chaotic, disjointed with scraps of metal strewn across from Nico's minicopter project as well as his new creation, a prototype skeleton key capable of opening any door regardless of how intricate the lock. Asher chose not to tell Nico about his conversation with Redding. He didn't want him to know he was conflicted by the central message and ideology of the Maurinkos. Not that Nico's mind was preoccupied with religion and philosophy.

"Moment of truth!" Nico shouted across the lab.

"No way! The gyro is ready?"

"We shall see." Nico slipped on a clunky metallic gauntlet that was crisscrossed with exposed wires and small pistons, then placed the gyro at the center of the room. It was circular, somewhat flat, and about six inches in diameter. At the center was a large, rotating blade housed in a safety cage.

He began flicking switches on the gauntlet. The gyro sputtered and whirred. "Here we go!"

Nico raised his hand, and the tiny machine slowly began to hover above the table.

Asher was impressed. "This is insane. I've never seen anything like this!"

Nico began going through his gestures, and the craft hovered around the lab, moving toward Asher's bench. Puffs of black smoke billowed from tiny pores in the brass siding. Once it reached the airspace above Asher's bench, Nico opened his fist, and the square landing opened into four triangular claws. The minicopter slowly picked up an empty glass test tube from Asher's bench. Nico delicately waved it back over with the tube still in its claw. Without taking a step toward the machine, Nico grabbed the test tube from the claw and then guided the minicopter back to a safe landing on the table.

Asher's mind was blown. "How in the world?"

Nico was laughing maniacally. "I did it! It works! I am a genius; everyone will bow down to me!"

Asher gave a half-hearted bow. "Yes, yes. You are a genius. That's incredible!"

Nico continued to fly the minicopter around the room in various aerial maneuvers, opening the claw and moving around objects, testing the limits of its heights and agility. After a few minutes, the copter began to spark and smoke.

"No. No, no, no..." Nico tried to rein it back to the landing area, but it failed to respond and crashed into a stack of glass jars. The boys cringed.

"What happened?" asked Asher.

"Overheated. The energy is too much for its size. I am not sure of any workarounds at the moment. It looks like about five minutes of flight time is all we have for now."

"Still," said Asher cheerfully, "I'd consider this a success."

"Definitely," Nico nodded proudly.

The two finished cleaning up the lab before heading out. As they walked through the courtyard, they heard yelling.

"Want to check it out?" asked Nico.

Asher shrugged. "Sure."

The two snuck through a few rows of hedges and saw a couple bickering underneath a lantern-lit gazebo.

"Is that...Roman and Autumn?" Asher whispered.

"Yeah, I think so."

Autumn shook her hands in front of Roman's face as if explaining something.

Asher whispered again, "Ok, now I feel a little bad about snooping. We should get out of here."

At that moment, Roman punched one of the wooden pillars of the gazebo just behind Autumn's head. She flinched as the structure shook.

"Holy shit," said Nico. "Maybe we should wait just a second longer."

They had a hard time making out the couple's words, but Autumn seemed to begin speaking in hushed tones to calm Roman down. He kicked the wooden side railing of the gazebo, snapping it clean in half. Asher thought he might tear the whole structure apart. Autumn looked at the damage and then looked up, spotting the boys. Asher ducked down behind the hedges.

"She saw us. We really need to go."

"Agreed," said Nico.

The boys continued back to the main Langford building, walking through rows of trees, gardens, and intertwining pathways lit by the night sky. They had entered their dorm when they heard a loud, shrill scream. Nico looked at Asher. "What is with this night?"

Asher shrugged and immediately started running toward the source of the scream, Nico right behind him. They arrived at a mob of people circling around something. It appeared that the girl who had screamed was shaking and crying and being held up by another girl. Professor Creed was coming down the hallway, pushing students out of the way so that he could get closer to the scene.

Nico turned to one of the students in the crowd. "What is going on? What is it?"

"It's Professor Crow."

Puzzled, Nico and Asher pushed their way to the front of the crowd. They reached the inner circle around the same time as Professor Creed.

Creed shouted at the mob, "Go get Nurse Kimona. GO!" Several students ran off in the direction of the infirmary. Creed knelt down beside a body dressed in black. Asher looked down at Professor Crow's face, a face that had become swollen with purple veins and bulging eyes, his body rigid and void of life.

CHAPTER 12

The school's atmosphere had shifted in the week following Professor Crow's death. There were the murmurs, there were the mourners, and there were the morbidly curious. Asher hadn't particularly cared for Crow, but he also didn't feel like he had the right to judge his character. He was a strict professor who nearly got him expelled and was singlehandedly tanking Asher's grades, but none of his general creepiness seemed to warrant the permanence of death.

Regardless, mechanical engineering classes continued. Their new teacher, a stout woman with silver hair and bronze-rimmed glasses, sheepishly illustrated the finer points of reciprocating engines. Minutes felt like days until the final bell rang. The students poured into the stone hallways.

Asher was by himself, walking toward his room, when a hand touched his shoulder. Instantly, sharp blue eyes pierced his.

"Autumn, hey!" he said, caught off guard.

"Hey! Do you have a minute to talk? There is something I wanted to ask you."

"Sure. Here or…?"

"Preferably a place a little quieter now that classes are out."

"Ok, I'll follow you."

The two wound their way through the crowded hallways until they reached the sanctuary. They made idle chat until they reached the orchard, which by now was burrowing in for its cycle of winter hibernation. They wandered aimlessly through rows of apple trees, at one point stopping to watch Professor Jones toss feed into a leopard cage. They walked near the broken gazebo, and the shallow conversation quickly took a turn. Autumn stopped and turned to Asher. "I saw you and Nico the other night."

"Yeah, about that…" said Asher, scratching the back of his head and attempting to find an excuse for their snooping.

"No, don't worry about it. It's fine. We were loud, and Roman was being all sorts of crazy."

Asher began fiddling with a leaf he had plucked from a nearby tree. "Is everything alright with you two?"

"No," she said bluntly. "Not really."

"What's going on?"

"Roman and I, we have known each other since we were kids. There was always this weird inevitability that we would be dating. We have been on and off again for a while now."

Asher nodded but didn't quite understand. "Is your family friends with his family or something?"

"Yes, actually." She walked over to the gazebo to get a closer look at the broken railing. "We both had a lot of expectations placed on us. Roman meets those expectations. Me…not so much."

"I can't imagine how you aren't meeting the expectations of your family. I've seen you in chemistry class, you're brilliant!"

"Thanks," Autumn blushed. "But it is more than that. Roman was always destined to be a great athlete, a warrior, a leader. It is what his parents trained him for; it is what they had him programmed for."

"Oh? And what did they program you for?"

"It is a little embarrassing to talk about...people who are not from around these circles are not really familiar with how a lot of Riali tends to operate."

"You mean the genetic modifications?"

Autumn sighed. "Well, I am not exactly the image of what my parents had in mind. They wanted me to look and act a lot differently than who I became."

Asher walked around the railing and into the gazebo, trying his best to face Autumn.

She continued, "I am related to Bella Hawthorne."

"The famous singer? That's pretty awesome!"

"Right. But I am more than just related. My genetics are almost an identical match. My parents approached the state lab, requesting just the minimum—something that would allow their child to be free of disease and guarantee my health. At the time, my parents had already burned through most of my mother's inheritance, so they were not able to afford even that smallest level of alteration. But the lab offered them a discount if they consented to having my likeness mirror that of Bella Hawthorne."

"Like a clone?"

"Not exactly, but as close as they could get. The hair, the eyes, even the body type in hopes I would be able to mimic her voice."

Asher leaned against one of the gazebo rails and looked out over the gardens.

"In return, my parents also attempted to raise me like my great-grandmother. But I never quite got it right."

"Like you aren't able to sing well or…?"

Autumn laughed. "No, no, I can sing. It is more like I hate performing. At first, as a kid, I really enjoyed all the attention. My parents would put me in rooms with the powerful and wealthy. I would sing and dance, be the evening's entertainment. We even made pretty good money from it, and my parents were able to obtain more influential friends."

"And that is how they became friends with the Volkovs?"

"Exactly. I would often perform for Roman's family and their friends, which is how Roman and I know each other. Then, of course, we went to the same schools and whatnot. We were just always around each other."

"What happened? What made you stop singing?"

"It's not like that; I still love to sing. But when I became a teenager, I started hating the pressure. I started to despise the attention. I felt more and more like a singing monkey and less like an actual person."

"That makes sense. And your parents?"

"They obviously were not too happy with my decision to stop performing. They would still force me to do shows from time to time, but I would do what I could to mess up and put on a lackluster performance. Eventually, people began to talk, saying I was nothing like the original. Older folks even talked about how I didn't really look or act anything like Bella. My parents were embarrassed by it, and Riali labs took it as a failure as well. My parents lost a lot of money and blamed me for it. They nearly disowned me."

"Are they not proud you're here at Langford? You seem to be doing so well!"

"They don't really help pay for it. I had a connection with Director Dolent from when I was younger and still performing, so that helped. I don't really perform much anymore, and I don't plan to. Roman though, he still remembers what I can do."

"And he wants you to go back to performing?"

"He just accepts his role a little bit more than I do and wants the same from me. He might not be putting me in the same box that my parents put me in, but he is putting me in his box, conforming me to his expectations."

"Seems like a pretty restrictive way to live."

"I am just a little sensitive to it, I guess."

"For someone who doesn't like preordained destiny, it's certainly odd you're dating someone you feel you were destined to date."

Autumn laughed and gave Asher a side-eye. "Maybe you should stick with biology and not psychology, mister."

Asher looked down, blushing.

Autumn continued, "Also, I am not sure what Roman wants with you, but be careful with him. He is quick to judge and has a temper. And more so, he has a lot of connections. I do believe he is a good person at heart, certainly a better soul than myself, just…he puts the world on his shoulders. For better or worse."

Asher nodded. "I can relate."

Autumn placed her hand gently on Asher's arm. "I felt like I needed to tell you these things. Most of the people here in Riali would not understand. They would think

I am ungrateful for the life I have been given. They think I am entitled."

"I don't think that," said Asher quickly.

Autumn beamed up at him; his heart fluttered. "Thank you, I appreciate you for not judging me like the others. But about what you and Nico saw the other night. Please don't go around telling others that Roman and I are having relationship issues. I would not want any more drama in my life."

"Totally understandable," said Asher, smiling back.

A loud thud against a wood plank of the gazebo interrupted the moment. Autumn quickly withdrew her hand from Asher's arm and spun around to face Roman.

"Roman!" said Autumn, shock in her voice.

Roman appeared to have forced a smile on his face. "Hey, guys!"

"Baby, what are you doing here?" Autumn asked coolly.

"Avee told me she saw you walking out here. Just wanted to see what you were up to." He looked at Asher.

Autumn spoke up first. "We were going over some notes from class. Just wrapping up."

Asher began to leave the gazebo, but Roman walked over and blocked the entryway, leaning one arm against the post. Asher stopped, his eyes slowly scanning upward from Roman's chest to his face.

"Hey, Asher, I have been meaning to ask you," Roman shifted his weight playfully. "What is the status of that little project of ours?"

"It's done! I just need to add a stabilizer and it's good to go. I can actually get it to you later tonight if you want?"

"Absolutely, that would be perfect! We are playing your hometown this week, after all."

"Ohh, in that case, maybe I should wait one more week!" Asher joked.

"No, no, I'm good for them now. Also, do you have any more of the berries? I am going over to a friend's house later today and wanted to show them."

"Yeah, yeah, not a problem!" Asher rummaged through his satchel and pulled out a bag full of decrepit magical sussberries.

"Awesome, thank you!" said Roman as he grabbed the bag. "How much do I owe you?"

"All of them?" asked Asher. "Uh, you know what, those are on me."

Nico would be upset at Asher's lack of salesmanship.

"Right," said Roman. "See you soon then. Autumn, I'm heading over to the field, did you want to join me? Maybe study during our practice?"

"Sure!" Her voice was perky and cheerful.

Asher watched as the two walked away, his mind a whirlwind.

They met underneath the stadium. Even in Vana, Asher had never seen the underworkings of a koroka pitch. He was surrounded by a jungle of metal cogs and revolving gears. The floor was littered with various sprockets and parts strewn across dormant platforms waiting to be attached to their metal pylons. The walls were lined with large flywheels and pistons, connecting to a network of metal arms that reached up to hatches on the ceiling. A side door opened, and a flood of dusk entered the dimly lit koroka cellar.

Roman appeared, descending an iron staircase, "Asher, thank you for meeting me here, I have such a busy schedule with practice and all."

"Not a problem," said Asher, "I have everything ready for you."

"Fantastic," said Roman, hanging up his metal koroka suit against a wall hanger, "and these will give me the boost I need?"

Asher pulled out three vials as Roman approached.

"They are a cocktail of both short- and long-acting drugs that will increase your overall size, speed, and stamina."

Roman leaned in to get a better view of the concoctions. Asher continued, "The long-term effects are caused by one-part synthetic testosterone—to help muscle size and muscle recovery—and one-part synthetic growth hormone—which will cause you to grow a few more extra inches in height. For the immediate effect, I have added a stimulant. The stimulant will increase your heart rate, blood flow, and body temperature. So not only will you get a temporary athletic boost, but it will also impact the overall delivery of the hormones. Lastly, I added erythropoietin, which will increase your red blood cell count and, therefore, increase your endurance."

Roman snatched the vials from Asher's hands and stared deeply into their dark-green substance.

"And how do I take it?"

"Intravenously," said Asher. "Enough for three doses. I suggest spacing them out, so perhaps make them for game time only."

"We will see," said Roman, "I would like to test them out at a practice first."

"I'm not making you anymore after this. We agreed this would be a one-time deal."

"Yeah, sure," said Roman flippantly. "Anything else? I have a date I need to get to."

"Autumn?" asked Asher.

"What do you care? And no, she's out with friends, so I made some plans with Avee," he grimaced. "Keep that between us, though, ok?"

"A lot of secrets around here," Asher said, rolling his eyes.

Roman pocketed the vials and turned to leave the stadium's metal dungeon. "You are catching on."

It was a slow school day. Redding had just wrapped up his lecture, and the class had moved on to labs. Asher and Felix spent hours watching bands creep up the agarose gel. Redding made his rounds through the lab tables, looking over his students' shoulders and eventually making his way back to the front of the classroom.

He sat down and shuffled some papers around. A cake had appeared on his desk earlier in the day. He flipped over a note which read: "To the best professor at Langford, we're all appreciative of your hard work, thank you!"

"Class?" he asked. A few heads popped up from the workbench. "Who am I to thank for this lovely cake?" Asher watched as no one in the class answered, shrugged, and went back to work.

As the class continued with their labs, he took a slice from the cake and examined the odd blackish, blueish coloring. It smelled of sussberries, but the coloring was off.

He took a quick look around the room to make sure no student noticed him plunging into the cake. It was spongey and fresh, but the berries tasted bitter and a bit more sour than usual. Perhaps overly ripened fruit, but not bad overall. He took another bite. An odd cake but delicious nonetheless. He took a few more bites and had nearly finished the slice before he began feeling dizzy.

Heart attack? No. Stroke? Unlikely.

His fingers began to go numb, and his vision blurred. He put the cake on a table behind him. He took a sip of water from a nearby cup. The room started to spin and distort. He was certain now he'd been poisoned. He stood up to speak.

"Class?" he asked one last time, his voice no more than a whimper.

Asher looked up again. The professor was leaning heavily on the desk, his eyes in a thousand-yard stare. Asher could see dark stains dripping from the corners of Redding's lips. "Professor?" Asher said back to Redding. No response. The drool began to pool and foam. Asher stood up from his desk. "Professor!"

Redding fell to the floor, his body convulsing violently. Asher rushed to his side with the rest of the class behind him.

"Go get Nurse Kimona! Tell her to bring a poison kit. NOW, HURRY!"

Professor Redding continued to shake violently on the floor. His eyes spun back into his head, his mouth filling with foam.

CHAPTER 13

"Roll him over on his side, keep his mouth clear," Asher barked at Felix.

Felix did as he was told while Asher rummaged behind Redding's desk and picked up the half-eaten slice of cake.

"He's vomiting," said Felix, trying to push the professor onto his side.

Asher inspected the dessert. It was freckled with berries—and there was no mistaking where they came from.

He leaped back into action, rifling through Redding's drawers and cabinets.

"What are you looking for?" asked Felix. The rest of the classroom gathered around the scene, watching in shock and horror.

Asher didn't say a word. He continued to fling papers and beakers.

"C'mon, c'mon, where is it?" Asher's search grew frantic. There was a large, locked drawer at the bottom of the desk; it had to be in there. He scrambled his hands across Redding's desk to find his keys and then fumbled with the drawer's lock. It opened.

In the drawer lay several purple vials of sedative used on the ere. But no tranquilizer gun. Asher ran across the room toward his lab bench and grabbed a clean syringe, then back over to Redding's body.

"What are you doing? What's even in those vials?" asked Felix nervously.

"He's having a seizure. His heart rate and body temperature are rising. I'm going to try and counteract the effects with a sedative." Asher looked back over to the cake resting on top of the desk. "It's only going to get worse. If we don't slow his nervous system down, his whole body will go into shock and his heart will stop."

The students looked at him incredulously. Felix spoke up. "We need to wait for Nurse Kimona. You don't know what you're doing."

Asher pushed him aside. "He only has a few more minutes before full cardiac arrest sets in." He plunged the needle into Professor Redding's chest, directly into the heart. *One vial can knock out an ere,* thought Asher, *I will need to be precise with how much I dispense.*

The class watched as Asher stood over the body. He knew that neither kane mushrooms nor sussberries were fatal on their own, but the berries he had created were an unknown lab-built drug—the full effects of which could possibly lead to an overdose. Whoever thought to put them in a cake would most likely think it just a prank, but still, a terrible one to pull.

Redding slowly stopped convulsing and his mouth cleared of foam. Felix put his fingers on Redding's neck to feel his pulse. "He's not dead."

A full day passed before Asher decided to stop by the infirmary. He brought Nico along for the visit. It was a bit busier than he remembered. Still, there was a cleanliness and an orderly appearance as Nurse Kimona took charge of her assistants.

"You two again. What are you boys doing back here?" she asked. Nico flashed a smile but let Asher do the talking.

"Hi, Nurse Kimona. We're here to see Professor Redding. Is he allowed to have visitors?"

"Certainly. He woke up earlier today. Professor Jones already stopped by, so he should be good for a few more visitors. I'm sure he will be happy to see you!" She narrowed her eyes at Asher. "I was told you were the one who administered the tranquilizer?"

"Yes," Asher confirmed, trying to avoid her piercing gaze.

"I'm not sure if that was the dumbest thing I have seen or the most brilliant. Nonetheless, the professor is doing better, and that is all that matters. Right this way."

They walked through the hallways of the infirmary until they reached the professor's room. They walked in to see Redding sitting up in the bed, reading the paper, a bouquet of freshly picked flowers from the sanctuary beside his bed.

"Hi, Professor," Asher said softly.

Redding looked up. "Boys! Thank you for coming to visit! Here, come take a seat." His voice seemed cheerful, which took both Asher and Nico by surprise.

"How are you feeling?" asked Asher as he took a seat beside the bed.

"Oh, I am much better. I should be out of here by tonight. The nurse has done a good job keeping me hydrated with these IVs. Whatever got into me seems to be flushed out of my system by now."

Nico looked out the window; there was a gorgeous view of the sanctuary down below.

"That's good to hear, I'm happy you're recovering. Will you be in class on Monday?"

"I plan to be." The professor folded up his newspaper and laid it down on his chest. "Asher, you know I have to ask. How did you know to use the ere tranquilizer on me?"

Asher scratched the back of his head nervously. "It was clear you had ingested some kind of stimulant. Your eyes were dilated, your heart rate was through the roof—I thought you were going into cardiac arrest. At the rate your blood pressure was climbing, I felt it could have been fatal to wait for the nurse and her team."

The professor nodded and rubbed his chin. "And you knew I had tranquilizer locked away in my desk drawer how...?"

Nico came back from the window and sat beside the bed with Asher. "I think it was more of a lucky guess. Right, Asher?"

Asher nodded. "Right. Honestly, I was just looking for anything that could help. It was a desperate attempt."

Professor Redding paused to think about what the boys had said. "Such an odd unfolding of events. But I am incredibly lucky to have had you there, Asher. The nurse tested my blood. You were correct; I had gone into shock from a psychoactive-stimulant overdose. The cake that was found in my office, I've yet to test it, but I suspect it will be the culprit."

Nico was quick and without tact. "Do you know who made the cake?"

"No. I don't know who would try to poison me or why. Even if I had any enemies—which I don't, that I know of—I don't see why they would use such an odd form of poisoning."

A knocking interrupted the conversation. The boys turned around to see Nurse Kimona walking in with Sheriff Price. The sheriff's rugged appearance was out of place in the pristine corridors of the infirmary.

"You two again?" The boys rose from their seats and awkwardly greeted the sheriff. His eyes remained on them suspiciously. "I'll need to speak with Professor Redding privately. But you both, it would be best if I never run into you again—I'm not a believer in coincidences."

The boys nodded their heads in agreement and made their way out of the room. Nico turned and whispered to Asher, "We need to get to that cake."

"No way, absolutely not. Tamper with evidence?"

"If not, they'll find the berries, and it will get linked back to us."

"But it wasn't us! We should go back into the room right now and talk to the sheriff and the professor. They'll understand."

"Are you crazy?" Nico's voice was a hushed yell. "The skeleton key is ready to go. The nurse said Redding won't be up until tomorrow. We go into the room, flush the cake down a sink, and be on our way."

"Look, if we get caught throwing out the cake, that's imprisonment. If Redding tests the cake and finds out about the berries, half the school is a suspect. Sure, we get kicked out of school for distribution, but it beats prison."

The boys had made their way back to the lobby when Roman appeared. "Nico. Asher."

He forced his way in front of Asher, his massive body blocking Asher's path. Annoyed, he looked up at Roman.

"What's going on, Roman?"

Roman smiled. "I tried those enhancers at practice earlier this week."

"How'd it go?"

"They are fantastic, but the effects wore off quickly."

"Yeah. I told you, they're a short-term dose. You'll want to make sure you take it just before game time. You need to space it out, though. You should probably hold off on taking them for the game this week and try again next week."

"It only lasted about half an hour. I need a full hour at the very least. What if I up the dose?"

"Well…no, I don't advise that, not at all. There's a lot of nasty side-effects from messing with hormones—"

"I'm out of them." Roman interrupted. "I already tried the full vial."

"What? You're out already?"

"Yeah, I'm out, and I need more. A lot more."

Asher shook his head. "I gave you enough to last three weeks and you took it all in a few days? You did exactly what I told you *not* to do. That can't be good, Roman."

"My dad has a VIP booth at the stadium. I will let you and Nico be his guests the week Vana comes to town if you want?"

Nico's eyes raised in interest, but Asher waved it off. "What? No, I don't care, I'm not making you more, I told you it was a one-time thing."

Roman grabbed Asher by the collar and shoved him against the wall. Nico put his hand on Roman's shoulder, but Roman raised his other hand, and Nico quickly backed off. "Look, Asher. Let's just get down to it."

"No," said Asher. "This aggression is a side-effect of the enhancers. It's already taking a toll on you."

Roman shook him slightly. "You are going to make me more, and you are never going to speak to Autumn again."

"Wait...what?"

"What the hell does Autumn have to do with this?" asked Nico.

"Everything," said Roman. "Now look. You make more, and you stop talking to Autumn, or else Sheriff Price will hear all about your berry-making operation."

Nico turned his head and cursed under his breath.

Asher didn't flinch. "Sure. I barely even know Autumn, and why would you tell Price about the berries? It's not like you haven't bought a bunch yourself."

"Because if another teacher goes down in this school, they will be looking at the one making the poison, not the cake."

"You made the cake? You piece of shit!" Asher knocked Roman's arm down and proceeded to tackle him to the ground by sweeping his leg—a move he had used on Liam many times during their childhood. The other students began piling in the hallway to see the commotion. Nico went to pull Asher off Roman as Asher attempted to swing an elbow into Roman's jaw. Roman blocked the hit and threw Asher off with ease, then got up and shoved Nico out of the way.

Asher took the opportunity to jump on Roman's back and attempt a chokehold. He cranked his arm tight, pinching the carotid artery and lowering Roman to his knees. The crowd in the hallway had now grown out of control as the other students watched the fight. Roman raised his hand behind him in a desperate attempt to grab hold of Asher. His face turned purple; his arms flailed before finding a shirt and, with one hand, he flipped Asher over his back. Asher stood up to face the now furious Roman. Nico stood behind Roman, cautious and defensive.

"Roman, come on. We are all friends here." Roman spun around to swipe at Nico, who dodged the blow, wanting no part in this fight. Asher lifted his hands to defend his face, but Roman sent a punch straight into Asher's gut. The wind left Asher's lungs, leaving him doubled over and defeated. Roman bent down to Asher's ear and grabbed him by the hair.

"I knew you were going to be difficult. I had to do what I did because I need you to understand something. This is my school. And you will do as I say."

CHAPTER 14

A double-decker bus arrived from the Riali train station, with Asher eagerly awaiting at the steps of Langford. The doors swung open, and the Vanatian koroka team piled out. Asher immediately spotted Liam and blindsided him with a bear hug. "Liam!"

Liam hugged back with his one free arm. "Ash! Brother, you have no idea how long I've looked forward to this."

Liam had a few hours to spare prior to the game, so they sat with the Vanatians in the Langford cafeteria and caught up with a few more friends. Once they'd finished, Asher took Liam outside to walk around the sanctuary.

"Let me get this straight: your roommate inducted you into a secret society that's currently being hunted down by a terrorist who kills via poison gas attacks, which may somehow have ended in the death of your mechanical engineering teacher. And then you saved your genetics teacher from a magical berry overdose given by the pissed-off koroka center who I'm about to play?"

Asher nodded. "Yeah, pretty much."

"Anything else I should know?" Liam asked incredulously.

"Yeah…" Asher plucked a leaf off a nearby fig tree. "That center is on a time-delayed steroid I developed in a secret lab paid for by my roommate's ultra-wealthy parents."

"Right. Of course."

"Well…I figured you could use a challenge."

Liam laughed. "Ok, so on a scale of one to ten, how badly do you want me to bash him in the face with my tonfa?"

"Hmm…like a twenty."

"Done."

Asher's smile faded. "The longer the game goes on, the less the effects of the drug will be. But even without any chemical help, Roman is no joke. He basically beat Kipos singlehandedly. He beat the hell out of me and Nico. I've seen him rip apart a gazebo."

"Ahh, so don't be a nerd or a structure made entirely of cheap Riali wood, got it."

"No, seriously, he's violent. Be careful with him. He's a hothead, and the steroids might wear off by the end of the match, but he's more agile than he looks, and he's got about twenty pounds on you. The Langford guards will sacrifice themselves to keep him alive. He carries the team."

Liam laughed again. "I don't need your help strategizing, Asher. I got this. I'll whip his ass for you."

"Thanks."

The two continued their walk through the sanctuary. "This place must be heaven for Callie. How's she been doing?"

Asher's face turned a shade of guilty red. "Honestly, I haven't kept up with her all that much. She seems to be doing well. Cloud has a cage somewhere out here. I've seen her talking with a few people. She sat with Nico and me for the first two home games, didn't see her at the last one."

Liam gave Asher a disappointed look. "You don't talk to her? You're both Vanatians. You come from a school with only a hundred people in your class, and almost every single one of them stayed in town after graduating..."

Asher shrugged. "I don't know. We've always been different. She hangs out with other people than I do."

"She has a group of friends? That's cool. Who are they?"

"Oh. Uhh, honestly, I don't really know." Asher chewed on the thought. Why *hadn't* he kept up with her? He hadn't even checked in on her since Roman's koroka after-party. It certainly wasn't intentional; he was just so busy with his current endeavors. Remembering something, he perked back up. "She'll be at tonight's game! She has a friend on the koroka team. You can say hi to her yourself."

"That friend any good?"

"Not really, more of a bench warmer. But I'll invite her to come sit with me so we can cheer you on. You can dedicate Roman's last cable to her!"

Liam smiled at the thought. "Looks like you're living the dream here. I mean, it's a slight nightmare with all the poison and whatnot. But overall, this place is gorgeous. You're on your way to becoming a famous scientist. You're doing good, Asher. I'm proud of you."

"Thanks. We'll see. There's still plenty to go. It'll be a good start to see you beat the hell out of Roman."

The stadium was packed. The student section, the teacher section, the visitors, the team trenches—chanting reverberated off the concrete walls; the energy of the crowd had reached a fever pitch. Oakard Academy, the premier university in Vana, and Langford were the only two undefeated schools left in Khamara.

Asher made a point to find Callie prior to the match. She agreed to join him and Nico at the game, and the three found some free seats in the section reserved for university students. Large glass panels separated the various spectator sections, with private booths at the very top for the ultra-wealthy of Riali. *A booth just for Maurinkos*, thought Asher, as he spotted Nico's parents, General Volkov, and Doctor Rafe.

The teams came out to roaring applause, Oakard led by Liam, Langford by Roman, their koroka suits glowing and ready for battle. The two teams met in the middle to greet and shake hands. Various multi-level platforms and obstacles raised from the ground and began to whir.

The terrain was different for every game, randomizing the set-up so that the home team's strategic advantages were minimized. The stadium lights flashed. The starters made their way to their respective ends while the bench players cleared to each side of the field. The stadium's lights changed to a dark blue and dark red as the audience counted down.

"FIVE!" The lights pulsed. "FOUR!" The players braced for launch. "THREE...TWO...ONE!"

The air siren wailed, and the teams bolted toward each other. The two Langford runners took off through the course while the two guards remained by Roman's side at centerfield.

Oakard had a more unusual strategy: all their players, except for Liam, took to the obstacles, leaving Liam to run straight for the center alone. He was quickly confronted by Roman and his guards. Liam grabbed for his tonfa, but Roman and the guards rushed him before he could attack. He peddled backward, luring them deeper into Oakard territory.

Roman used his baton to direct his guards as they closed in, taking cautious swipes at Liam's cables. Before they could get in good reach, both Langford runners fell from one of the overhead platforms. The two runners had lost their first cables and sprinted off back to reset. The Oakard guards and runners dropped in behind Roman and the team. It was five versus three in Oakard territory, closer to the Oakard reset point. As soon as the Langford guards turned their backs to face their counterparts, Liam went in for the kill and pulled cables from both of their packs.

Five versus one.

Roman charged at Liam in desperation. Liam sidestepped and used his baton to sweep Roman's legs, then took a shot at Roman's ribs before a guard pulled Roman's first cable.

His suit flashing, Roman lifted himself off the ground and walked over to Liam, grabbing him by his suit's collar.

Liam lifted his hands and sneered. "That one was for Asher."

The referee blew her whistle; another reset foul could get them kicked out of the game. Roman quickly let go of Liam, a look of hesitation and anger in his eyes before he ran back to base with Oakard in pursuit.

"An incredible early lead for Oakard Academy, who are up fifteen cables to Langford's ten!" the announcer boomed over the speakers.

With Oakard's tight formation and cable advantage, the battle became an all-out brawl. The crowd went wild.

A Langford runner tried to sneak from a platform above and swipe a cable from Liam, but he was too quick. He grabbed the runner off the platform and slammed them hard into the ground. The Langford crowd booed at the particularly brutal hit on their player. Liam ignored them, rolled the unconscious body over, and pulled a cable before the ref whistled to pause for injury.

After a small rumbling on the Langford bench, Felix came out in a suit matching the cables of the fallen runner. Callie stood up and cheered as he took the field.

"That is the most excited I have seen you at one of these games," said Nico. Callie glared menacingly at him, shrugged, and sat back down. He laughed and turned his attention back to the game.

Oakard held on to their early lead for some time, but the close quarters and all-out war-style gameplay played to Langford's strengths. Roman proved too powerful to stop, knocking a guard out cold and forcing a substitution. The Oakard players became visibly tired and worn.

Both teams were down to their centers and one runner each. Liam and Roman met at centerfield to square off. Felix had been hustling back to the center from a reset when he saw the other Oakard runner sneak up behind Roman.

"Roman!" Felix yelled, throwing his tonfa as hard as he could at the runner's legs and tripping her a foot shy of reaching her target.

Roman turned around and quickly yanked the runner's last cable. Liam, seeing his opportunity, lunged for Roman's back. But, before he could finish the strike, Felix tackled him full force.

Callie jumped out of her seat. Nico turned to her, "Whose side are you on anyway?"

"Shush. Is anyone hurt? That didn't look good."

The altercation was brief. Liam shoved Felix's face into the ground and yanked out his last cable. Felix got up, facemask filled with dirt and grass, and limped off the field in defeat.

It was one-on-one, Liam against Roman, each with a single cable remaining. They circled each other in the center of the field, tonfas in their right hands, left hands outstretched. The cheers from the crowd grew louder.

Liam pointed upward with his baton to the highest revolving platform and yelled to Roman, "Let's give them a show, yeah?"

"Wherever you want to dig your grave is fine with me," answered Roman.

The two began climbing up opposite platforms. The crowd's roar was deafening, every spectator now on their feet.

They met atop the most elevated, revolving platform on the field for the whole audience to see. A true sudden death.

"What is with you Vanatians?" asked Roman. "You think so highly of yourselves. Go back to playing with your plants."

Liam smiled. "Funny you should say that; I just finished building your coffin. Maybe your daddy can pay for that, too."

Roman's face became an expression of rage. He advanced toward Liam, who continued his taunting, "You alright, Roman? You're not looking so great. In fact, you're looking a little tired, maybe even a little...*smaller?*"

Roman spun his baton and took a swing at Liam's head, but he dodged out of the way with a laugh, "you sure you have the stamina to keep up?"

Roman continued dueling aggressively with Liam. "You dumb lumberjack piece of shit."

Liam was on the defensive now. "Whew, boy," he said, jumping to avoid falling over the platform's edge. "I swore your hits were a lot harder earlier in the match. You must really be drained! You sure what Asher gave you wasn't poison? He must have given me the good stuff."

Both boys went in for a strike and caught it with their free hand, interlocked in their stalemate.

"You think beating me will help your friend?" Roman said, no longer yelling.

"Yes," said Liam. "Because now you know I'm always a train ride away from kicking your ass."

Liam pulled inward, surprising Roman and tripping him over his leg. Roman sprawled across the platform, nearly falling over the edge. Liam lunged for the cable, but Roman quickly turned on his back and blocked the swipe. Liam jumped onto Roman and let loose a series of tonfa strikes while using his free hand to try and lift Roman's head high enough off the ground to get behind his back and yank out the final cable.

A scream came from the crowd. Liam continued his violent barrage of punches as Roman desperately tried to knock him off without offering his back. The screaming grew louder and more intense. Roman grabbed the ledge of the platform and thrust himself over the edge, bringing Liam down with him. They crashed on another revolving platform that reached the edges of the field, closest to the crowd.

Both boys got up slowly, ready to spring back into action, before pausing in confusion. Between them, a large cylindrical canister was spewing a dark-purple gas. The platform revolved around the edges of the stadium, spraying the fumes over the players and audience.

The stadium lights went up. The gas was dense and dispensed perpendicular to the crowd, directly at the spectators.

Roman turned and jumped off the platform. Liam, however, went straight for the canister and kicked it off the platform toward centerfield—the furthest point from the onlookers. He then ran for the edge to jump off near the Oakard bench. As he prepared to jump, his knees drove into the platform, and his body collapsed.

The stadium descended into mayhem. Dark-purple vapor poured across each of the audience sections. Students rushed toward the doors, but they didn't budge.

"They're locked!" shouted Asher.

Panic washed over the crowd. Nico reached under the bleacher for his satchel and pulled out the minicopter.

"I got this," Nico said, turning to Asher and Callie. He handed Asher his skeleton key. "This will get the door open. Just press it into the lock; it will do the rest. Go! Get everyone out of here!"

Asher shook his head and handed the key to Callie. "I gotta get Liam. Can you handle this?"

Callie nodded. "Yeah, I'll get the door open." She grabbed the key and pushed her way through the crowd.

When she got to the door, she briefly examined Nico's odd-looking skeleton key, then shrugged and stuffed it into the lock as best she could. She could hear it whirring as it figured out the locking mechanism of the massive stadium door.

The doors clicked and flung open. Students began pressing against her to get out. She shook the key loose and ran to the other sections of the stadium to unlock more doors.

Meanwhile, Asher went to the edges of the bleachers and leaped onto the field below. He grabbed Liam and started dragging him off the field.

Nico maneuvered the minicopter toward a second gas canister which appeared on another koroka platform and tried to get the tiny copter's claw to grasp the canister's slippery surface.

Asher noticed that the gas was a similar color to the tranquilizer he had used on Professor Redding. "Ok," whispered Asher to the unconscious Liam, "it's a long shot, buddy. But I think you've gotta take one of my berries. It's going to speed your heart rate back up. Ok...Ok...we can do this..."

Asher grabbed a sussberry from his coat pocket. He lifted Liam's head with one hand and crushed it in the palm of the other, letting the dark liquid slide down Liam's mouth. "Good. Good, keep swallowing. Hang in there, Liam, you're gonna get through this." Asher mashed two more in his palm and let the juices drip into Liam's mouth.

By now, Callie had sprinted to the second seating section of the stadium. She used Nico's key and was thrown back against the wall as a tide of panicked spectators came pouring out of the doors, followed by a cloud of suffocating gas. Callie pulled her shirt over her mouth and moved on, pressing through the crowd to get to the next locked door.

Nico finished directing the canister-toting minicopter to the center of the field, a point where Nico hoped the gas would be too dense to disperse evenly and rise. He looked back over at Asher, who was buried in the gas, carrying Liam through the field. Asher yelled across the stadium and pointed up at the glass rooms which held the wealthy spectators. The rooms appeared to be in a panic, with people attempting to unlock the doors. A dark-yellow gas began pouring into the booths from the air vents.

Nico and Roman both had family in the booths.

His eyes widened. Nico sent the minicopter speeding at the glass, attempting to break it. The glass spiderwebbed but the copter shattered into a hundred tiny parts in the process. He looked back over at Asher with a face of terror.

Asher pulled Liam into the ground-level control room. Nico jumped the barrier and followed suit. Asher handed him the last berry. "Take this, the gas is starting to pour in, but the berry will keep you conscious."

Nico ate it and began working furiously at the control board. It was massive, full of circuits and switches that monitored every detail of the stadium, from the lights to the obstacles.

Callie had opened every section except the VIP box seats. She sprinted through the stadium's hallways but stopped short as a wall of yellow gas crept toward her. She backed up and peered into the stadium, which now in a haze of purple gas. Thinking quickly, she turned and followed the rest of the screaming spectators outside. She circled the stadium's exterior and found her spot. She began to scale the walls of the stadium using the steel beams and pipes that latticed the outside of the structure.

If she could reach the top, she might be able to find a way around the gas that had blocked her in the hallway.

Harold Catalano finished smashing the last of the broken glass out of the VIP boxes. Nico had maneuvered the koroka platform as close as he could to the shattered booth window. Mr. Catalano began helping people onto the platform, dropping several limp bodies before he grew too weak himself and collapsed on the platform beneath. Asher tugged on Nico and yelled, "We've got to get out of here!"

Nico pointed back at the booth. "My parents!"

"I know, I know, but we can't go into that smoke."

"NO! WE CAN'T LEAVE!" Nico yelled. A group of gas-masked paramedics rushed onto the field as the canisters sputtered and finished dispensing their poison.

"They're up there!" shouted Asher, pointing to the platform. A few of the paramedics began pulling the boys away while strapping masks to their faces. Asher felt the cool rush of oxygen, his brain unable to differentiate reality from fiction.

"WHAT'S HAPPENING? WHAT'S HAPPENING?" Nico lashed out against the paramedics restraining him. Asher lay back on the stretcher; he knew now there was nothing left to be done except let his system filter out the berries and other poisons. Nico, on the other hand, grew increasingly violent as the paramedics pulled them out of the stadium with other bodies. He looked up and watched the bodies convulsing on cloth stretchers as paramedics attempted to pump oxygen into their lungs. His eyes scanned the bodies for a sign of his parents.

Callie made it to a metal maintenance walkway, which wrapped around the outside of the stadium. She was roughly three stories up, the winds whipping against her violently at this height. Several hatches punctuated the stadium's exterior, designed to give repair people access to the structure's inner workings. If she could make it to the center, there might be a maintenance door she could use to open the area and reach the remaining spectators. She rounded the corner and stopped abruptly at the sight of a tall, cloaked figure.

The figure's face was covered by a complex gas mask that was connected to a series of tubes. Four leather straps held the mask tightly in place, two wrapping around the top of the head, two going down around the neck. Everything joined to a metallic vest that held rows of purple, green, and yellow canisters. Callie tried to look into his eyes but could only see a bright light emanating from tiny round goggles.

The tattered cloak flapped in the wind as Miasma stood still, his head cocked to one side as though puzzled.

Callie took a step closer. "You. Why are you doing this?"

The mask emitted a low, muffled sound that Callie took as laughter. Miasma grabbed a purple canister off the metallic vest, ripped out a pin, and casually dropped it from the palm of his studded leather glove. Callie gave a fierce look and slowly backed away as Miasma took off through the cover of smoke.

CHAPTER 15

The skies over Riali were a deep gray. A week had passed since the attack at Langford Stadium. A few dozen were injured in the ensuing chaos, with seven casualties in total. Mr. and Mrs. Catalano were among the dead.

A vigil was held in memorial for the murdered. Professor Creed was the first to address the weeping masses, followed by Father Bianok. Nico sat in front, Asher by his side. Nico stared straight ahead in silence, his eyes welling with tears that would not release. Asher had a hard time speaking with him lately since the attack. He had become closed off and reserved. The light that was once behind his eyes was gone. Asher wondered if that light would ever come back.

He looked around. Callie was in the back, a glassy-eyed stare on her face. Kiara and Avee wept loudly. Autumn's tears dripped onto the sleeve of a somber Roman. Professor Redding and Professor Jones stood stoic among the sea of other teachers. Sister Lilly was in the back, perusing gravestones like grocery aisles. Asher spotted Dr. Rafe, expressionless and observant.

There must be at least a hundred people here, thought Asher. He couldn't be the only one who felt uncomfortable in such a large group. Being out in public brought flashbacks of the stadium. The screaming, the smell of gas, the limp bodies. The heightened fear his body felt from the cocktail of chemicals that raced through him. Miasma had released a chemical attack against an entire stadium of innocents. He couldn't wrap his head around it—*any* of it. For once in his life, Asher was left with a head full of questions that he was unsure he could answer. Most of them, of course, were simply: *why?*

The heaviness of the ceremony began to weigh on Callie. She looked around before giving Cloud a gentle poke with her toe to get his attention. He perked up and followed her as she slipped out the back toward Langford, lost in thought.

When she was out of hearing range of the crowd, she began to talk out loud to her fox companion. She knew he didn't understand most of what she had to say, but he did seem to understand the emotion behind her words. She started off slowly, with sporadic curse words, choking back statements like "I tried!" and "What else could I have done?" The talking picked up into a full ramble.

Out of breath and out of words, Callie stopped near a tree and fell to her knees. The grass was cold and wet beneath her. The early winter air chilled the back of her neck. Wisps of dark-red hair brushed her cheek. Cloud turned to stare into her teary eyes. A moment passed before he pushed his head into her stomach, gently forcing her arms around him. She sunk into the ground, holding onto him, and burying her face into his fur. They lay there, still, in the silence of the Sunday, letting time wash over them.

A few hours passed; Callie looked up at the towers of Langford as the sun began to set. A shadowy bulb-like figure floated off in the distance, growing larger as it drew near. She lifted herself off the ground and began walking back toward the center of campus, her eyes locked onto the airship. As it came closer, the dark-red pattern and distinct gold stitching became clear—*Arthur.*

Callie picked up her pace as the balloon descended near the back of the courtyard, coming perilously close to Professor Jones's greenhouse and levitating just short of the second-floor balcony. Callie hid behind some nearby shrubbery so as not to be spotted.

"You could just knock, you know." Mara Jones' playful voice rang through the courtyard as she opened the balcony door.

"Of course," said Arthur opening the gate to his ship. "But I never know when I might need to make a quick getaway when I'm dealing with you!"

The airship was skillfully hovering just a foot away from the greenhouse balcony. From its basket, Arthur extended his arm and presented Mara with a bouquet of flowers. She reached out to grasp them, their hands meeting two stories above the ground. Mara examined the flowers, seemingly unimpressed.

"I have more gifts for you coming from Baenum," Arthur said quickly. "They are on a freight as we speak. Should be here in the next few days."

"Oh?" said Mara, a little more curious now. "Is it euthpars?"

"Uhh…ahhh." He glanced around sheepishly. "Not quite. Those remain a bit too elusive for me. But there will be a few more snaphopper lizards for the courtyard."

Mara smiled brightly. "Thank you, Arthur. That was very thoughtful. Really, why don't you come inside?"

"I really can't stay for long. I just wanted to drop in and say hello."

"Right. I figured you didn't cut your trip early just to see me."

"Urgent matters."

"Who are you here to see?"

"Sheriff Price, General Volkov, a few others."

"You are here about the attacks?"

"What else would bring me back to the city?"

"I feel like we have enough capable men on the job. You are not a detective."

"I am not. But these attacks could well have greater implications for the whole of Khamara. I just need to make sure *someone* is a voice of reason in these talks."

"Good luck on that one!" Mara scoffed. "I am not sure how much sway reason holds over money and politics."

"This is about the safety and unity of our nation. There will be no adventures to be had when it is all burnt to the ground!"

"I think I have had enough adventure this past semester to last me a lifetime."

"Oh, you can't possibly mean that, Mara! What about the time we trekked through Suluu? Or our dig in Mazraea? Or, you know, our getaway in the Laalyars where we ended up getting lost and finding our way to Titan Island?"

"We have had these talks before, Arthur. I am happy here. I've found where I belong. And you…"

"I do not belong anywhere, Mara."

"You belong everywhere, Arthur."

Callie shifted uncomfortably, deciding the conversation had become too personal for her to continue eavesdropping. She and Cloud headed back to the sanctuary and hung around the koi pond.

About an hour passed before Arthur strode by.

"Well, if it isn't Ms. Callendra Saint!"

Callie failed to suppress a smile. She hopped off the edge of the cement fountain and went to give him a hug.

"Arthur! How are you?"

"It is good to see you! I am good. Just got back from Saint Mazraea and now visiting Riali for the weekend. How have you been enjoying Langford?"

Her smile faded. "It's been...good."

"Hmm..." He sat down on the fountain and rested his cane on his lap. "Your tone suggests otherwise. From what Professor Jones has told me, you have been excelling in class and even stopped an ere attack in your first week! Not to mention your heroics at the stadium. It sounds like you might be ready for my job soon."

"Yeah. I mean, the learning and all of that is fine. Just not sure about the people. And these attacks. I don't know. Riali just isn't really for me."

"Understandable," Arthur nodded. He twisted his cane around and examined the bright emerald jewel on top. "This place was never my cup of tea either."

Callie watched as Cloud wandered off in the distance, smelling the begonias before being shooed away by Fonzworth. She turned back to Arthur. "Is that why you're always leaving? Traveling?"

"Partly. Also, because there is just so much more to see. Riali might be one of the most advanced cities in the world, but by no means is it the only one with culture and class. And the cities this planet has built! Your birth town, Elurra, do you remember it?"

Callie continued to stare off into the distance. "No. Not really. I was only four when I left. I remember snow, red cliffs, and clay houses. And I remember leaving, watching as the snow melted and the forest grew denser. Until I reached Vana."

"Elurra is a beautiful place. Cold, yes. But they have massive structures, a rich culture, and their wildcats grow to be the size of grizzly bears."

"Yeah...I know they've tamed them, and I've been told sometimes they even ride them."

"Yes! I have seen it! I am not sure what all Professor Creed has taught you, but it is said that some of the Ajke priestesses have connections to their big cats. A telepathy of sorts!"

Callie let out a muffled laugh. "Alright, Arthur. Take me to Elurra so I can learn to read Cloud's thoughts."

Arthur looked over at Cloud, who was biting at the bees buzzing over the orchids. "Well..." he said, "I do think it would be good for you to see it someday."

The two of them sat in silence, taking in the serenity of the garden around them. "Mara has done a fantastic job in the sanctuary. I have never seen it so lush and so vibrant."

"She has some help," said Callie, nodding over to Fonzworth.

Arthur stood up and tapped his cane against the ground. "That she does!" He beamed.

The two said their goodbyes and went their separate ways. Callie placed Cloud back into his cage and went up to the dormitories. The students had started filing back in from the funeral. She spotted Asher and Nico drinking hot drinks in the small lobby.

"I saw Arthur." Callie blurted out the news before getting into a normal conversation range. She sat down on a couch between the two.

Nico looked over at her. "Arthur Winston?"

"Yeah."

He went back to staring at the steam wisping from his cup.

"Did you get a chance to talk with him?" asked Asher.

"A little. We talked about the semester and such. He's back in town from Saint Mazraea."

Asher blew into his mug and looked up. "How do you know Arthur?"

"He is not one of *them*, if that's what you're implying," said Nico.

Callie rolled her eyes at the pseudo-secrecy.

"I wasn't," said Asher. "But I guess if he was, he'd probably be far from here."

Nico sank back into the couch. Asher didn't mean to be insensitive; the words had escaped him without thought. He tried to salvage the conversation. "I mean, Baenum just sounds like a better place to be this time of year in general and all."

"Right," said Nico sharply.

"Well, he did mention that he was going to see the sheriff," Callie interjected.

Nico's eyes lit up. "Arthur is back in Riali to meet with Sheriff Price?"

Callie regretted her words. "Uhh yeah, I think, maybe? He didn't say it exactly."

"What did he say?"

"Oh, I don't know." Her voice became noticeably nervous.

Nico backed down and spoke softly. "Please. Callie. Honestly, I just want to know what is going on with the investigation. No one has told me anything."

She shook her head. "I was interrogated, but other than that, I don't really know anything. It's not like they would tell me anything."

"What did Miasma look like? What could you see?" prodded Nico.

"It's not like that…you guys know most of the story."

"And you didn't notice anything else?" asked Asher.

She sighed. "I was on top of the stadium. The hallways had been flooded with gas, so I tried to find a back door to the box suites. When I climbed up the outside of the stadium, I saw Miasma on the walkway. But he was hooded and cloaked and wore a gas mask. And he almost immediately opened a canister of gas to hide his escape."

"I would have chased him down," said Nico.

"I'm sorry…" said Callie, looking away.

"No. No, please, don't be sorry. You did everything you could," said Nico.

Asher let out a deep breath. "Callie, you saved hundreds. Whether others recognize it or not, you stopped Miasma."

"I don't want that," she said, preparing to stand up.

Nico put his hand on her back. "Callie. Thank you. Thank you for putting yourself on the line." She turned and looked Nico in the eye. He continued, "But it is my turn now. I am going to hunt him down myself."

Asher's eyes widened. "What?"

Nico took his hand off Callie's back and turned toward him. "This has gone on long enough. I am finding out what the sheriff knows, and I am hunting Miasma down myself."

"And how do you plan on doing that?" Asher asked, stunned.

"Well, we know Arthur is going to meet with the sheriff. Might be a good starting point to insert myself into that meeting. Arthur will undoubtedly be getting caught up to speed with the recent events."

"I know how to find out where they're meeting," said Callie staring straight ahead, her eyes glossed over in thought.

Both boys turned their heads toward her.

"No," said Asher sternly. "You can't be serious. Both of you."

Callie looked up at Asher. "I want Miasma behind bars, too. I was powerless on that bridge. I won't be the victim. I won't be the prey. And if there is anything I can do to help—to redeem myself—"

"Asher's right," said Nico. "You honestly do not owe anyone anything. You saved countless lives, and this is going to be incredibly dangerous."

"This is for me," interrupted Callie defiantly. "I don't need you or anyone else telling me what I can and cannot do. If you're going after Miasma, then I will help. If I change my mind, then I'll let you know, but it won't be because I'm scared."

Asher shook his head, took a deep breath, and turned away from them both. An eternity passed as he calculated options, the risk, the reward, the logistics.

Chase down a dangerous terrorist caught between the Riali police force and the Maurinko society? I would only get in the way.

Well, perhaps not, I've gotten further in diagnostics than either group and survived two separate encounters.

And what about Nico? I couldn't let him go alone.

And now Callie is the braver of us two? What would Nico think of me? What would the Maurinkos think of me? No, I need to earn my place, both as Nico's friend and as a trusted member of the Maurinkos.

They are my future, and Nico is my closest friend here, tying my entire Riali life together. This terrorist was nothing more than some basement-dwelling, two-bit chemist—nothing I can't handle.

The whirling thoughts came to a halt as Asher let out a deep sigh. He turned back around and looked each of them in the eye. "Ok. Where is this meeting?"

The boys could hear rustling behind the large wooden doors of a sanctuary holding pen. "Are you grabbing Cloud?" asked Nico.

"You'll see!" shouted Callie from behind the door.

Nico and Asher turned toward each other and shrugged.

Asher grew anxious. "We need to be a lot more secretive than this. Fonzworth might catch us out here past curfew."

"Coming…"

Callie emerged from behind the door with her hands clasped tightly. "Nico, can you lock the door back up?"

"Sure thing." Nico locked the door with his skeleton key.

Callie whispered into her cupped hands and then opened them, revealing a small, winged creature. Its body was simply one large eyeball surrounded by dark, blueish-gray skin. It had tiny claws on the bottom and wings jutting out either side. Nico was revolted. "What the heck is that thing?"

"An ahriman," said Callie, smiling.

Asher walked up to it. "You used to sell those at your uncle's shop back in Vana."

"Yep. This is Gregory. And I've trained him to be my eyes."

Nico gave a look to Asher and back to Callie. "You mean eye?"

"Right," said Callie, shrugging off Nico's sanity check.

Asher shook his head. "Alright, so are we good to go now?"

"Yeah, over here toward the greenhouse."

"Why would they meet in Professor Jones's greenhouse?"

"They aren't. It's where Arthur's staying. He'll be leaving to go to the meeting, and we can follow him there with Gregory."

"Wow," said Nico. "Ok, that is actually really smart."

Callie shot him an offended look, and he gave her a defensive yet charming smirk back.

The three of them hid behind sanctuary hedges, waiting for Arthur to emerge. "Why is Arthur staying at Professor Jones's greenhouse?" asked Asher.

Callie gave him a look that required no verbal explanation.

"What?" asked Asher, puzzled, then "Ooohhhhh..." as the explanation dawned on him. "I did not know that was a thing."

Nico nodded in agreement. "Yeah, I honestly did not see that one coming…"

Callie rolled her eyes. A few minutes passed before Gregory came flapping back toward Callie.

"Ok, he's on the move. Let's go."

They peered around the hedges and watched as Arthur walked out of the sanctuary. Once he was out of sight, they continued onward, making sure to keep their distance by letting Gregory lead the way.

They walked to an outer tower of the Citadel. It was made of old stone with large, arching windows spiraling around the outer edges and an eagle's nest at the top for guards. The ahriman slipped through an open window, and the three waited outside until it flew down and gave an all-clear signal. Nico used the skeleton key to open the tower, and the three crept quietly through the winding hallways.

Gregory led them to a door silhouetted in light, with muffled sounds seeping out through the wood.

"This must be it," said Asher, turning to the other two. "We should try and see if the room next to this is clear."

Nico unlocked the neighboring door, and Callie pushed the ahriman through the crack. It came back a few seconds later.

"It's clear," said Callie, pushing open the door. They walked into the room and shut the door behind them. All of them saw it at the same time: a small ventilation shaft near the top of the adjoining wall was their way into the meeting.

Nico turned to Asher, "Quick, lift me up."

"What? I can't lift you up!"

"Why not? Just use your legs."

"What legs?"

"Don't tell me you skip leg day!"

"Only if anxious pacing counts as leg day."

"Well yeah, in that case, you should have calves the size of a granite god."

"That's fair..." thought Asher out loud.

Callie grabbed three stools and placed them beside the wall for them to climb and peer through the shaft. They had a decent view of the room with the two men in it, and the voices became more distinct and clearer.

"Thank you for coming so quickly, Arthur."

"Of course, Sheriff. The news of the attack at Langford Stadium rang out across Khamara."

"You were in Saint Mazraea?"

"Yes. I've been staying there for the past few months, tracking a lead on some potential new sources of diakti crystals."

"Right. Well, things have been getting out of hand. The General was a direct target of the stadium attack. He is adamant the attacks are stemming from the new sanctions against Dyria. Dyria is claiming no responsibility. And Grimm? Grimm just wants blood. He couldn't care less about the nature or motives of the attacks."

"And you?"

"Doesn't matter what I think. What matters is the evidence."

"Of course. What does the evidence say?"

"Several of the attacks have now used both non-lethal and lethal gases. While the first target was a lowly candy shop owner who survived for a few days following an unseen assault, the remaining attacks have all been high profile in nature."

Arthur rubbed his chin. "So politically motivated? Was the shop owner some kind of test run, perhaps?"

"Right," said Sheriff Price. "The attacks have increased exponentially in scale, and each sequential event has only been more successful and more efficient."

"It appears the terrorist is growing bolder as well, becoming more ambitious with each attack," said Arthur.

The meeting room door swung open. Asher could roughly make out the appearance of two men entering.

"General Volkov, Mr. Grimm. Thank you for joining us."

The General grunted at the sheriff and nodded at Arthur. "Winston. Glad you decided to join us commoners back here in Riali."

Arthur laughed. "It's a pleasure to be home, Sir—even during these troubling times. How's your health?"

The General let out another grunt as if to wave off the petty small talk. "Has the sheriff brought you up to speed?"

"Almost," said Arthur. "Does the investigation have any leads on suspects?"

The General took a seat. Asher could see the fourth man, Grimm, pacing around the room, examining the surroundings.

Sheriff Price butted back in. "We have our list. Volkov and Grimm have been keeping an eye on Dyrians and Vanatians in Riali who may be sympathetic to the political and economic causes. I have added to the list any persons who may be seeking to enrich themselves for personal gain."

"You all seem certain the motivation is for economic gain," said Arthur.

"Isn't it always?" asked the General.

"Every target but the first has been high profile. The richest of the rich," Sheriff Price continued.

"So, we are dealing with some kind of socialist or anarchist?" asked Arthur.

There was no answer except for some low-level murmuring that Asher could not decipher.

"Hmm..." Arthur tapped his fingers on the edges of his cane's emerald. "We have the police force, the military, and a world-class bounty hunter on the case."

Grimm let out a throaty laugh at the acknowledgment.

"I take it you didn't call me here for my own detective skills..."

"No," said the General. "We did not. The sheriff wanted your input on our diplomatic relations and possible fallout."

Arthur looked over at Price with curiosity.

Price leaned in. "You have spoken with Princess Nora and with Mayor Hegelson."

"Yes," said Arthur shortly. "And what else do you want me to say? That Dyria and Vana are thrilled with the sanctions?"

"Well, let's be blunt. Would the princess ever consider an attack against the capital?"

Arthur laughed at the thought. "Ha, Nora? No. Definitely not. There has been great movement to discredit her leadership, particularly her soft stance toward the sanctions."

A heavy thud sounded against the table as Grimm laid his shotgun down. He continued pacing around the room, his glass mason jar of eyeballs clinking against his belt as he walked.

Arthur looked at him with skepticism before turning his attention back to the other two. "Princess Nora is a brilliant politician and governor. If anything, the attacks would be coming from Samira. But chemical attacks…that doesn't really fit her MO."

"Samira Raol?" asked the General, now interested. "Does the princess not have control over the Raol fleet?"

"Hardly. That alliance is paper thin. While the sanctions hurt Dyria some, they hurt Samira and her fleet the most. She has spent years legitimizing her father's organization and turning it into the premier trading post it has become. The alliance between her and Nora has been built on her father's conditional surrender, as well as the exile of the King and Queen. If Nora found out Samira was behind these attacks, it would mean all-out civil war in Dyria."

"Neither Nora nor Samira would take that risk," said the sheriff, chiming in. "What good would these attacks have on the sanctions anyway? Even if they kill every last member of the Rialian elite, Riali would appear weak by removing the sanctions."

The General added, "Ever since the war between Dyria and the Hainlyal Islands ceased, Dyria has grown into an economic and militaristic powerhouse. The alliance between Samira Raol and Princess Nora has given Samira and her company access to Vanatian wood and carpentry. To top it off, Vana's recent agricultural boom has done wonders for their export industry. Dyria wants to overtake Riali as the premier trading hub of Khamara, and these recent terrorist attacks are nothing more than a cheap ploy to weaken our economic standing."

Arthur shook his head. "That is nonsense. A weakened Riali doesn't help anyone in Khamara. A terrorist's motive is almost always fear. Fear and chaos."

Grimm spoke, his voice the sound of gravel. "Miasma grows bolder with each attack. Each one has increased in size, scale, and complexity. If his goal is fear, then the damage is done."

"Which means weakened trade, market instability, and of course, demands to remove sanctions. Dyria has only profited from these attacks."

The General was sounding more and more like the Maurinko Society. Asher whispered to Nico, "Are the other three Maurinkos?"

Nico shook his head no; they continued spying through the ventilation grate.

"Yes, General. But my point is that these attacks are trending greater in scale," said Grimm.

"Are you suggesting that a larger attack than what we saw at the stadium is imminent?"

"That is precisely what I am suggesting, Sheriff."

"A single person could not carry out a city-wide attack; the coordination would be impossible," said Arthur. "This is an unfounded concern."

"Which is all the more reason to expect Hainlyal pirates. Samira and her fleet are the only non-governmental force in the world sophisticated enough to pull off attacks on this scale. Backed by the financial resources of Dyria, they could dismantle Riali from the inside without Princess Nora and her administration getting their hands dirty. Arthur, you must inform the other cities that Dyria is the aggressor here," concluded the General.

Grimm stopped his pacing and knelt beside the door. Callie carefully stepped down from her chair, took it off the tabletop, grabbed the ahriman, and placed it into her satchel.

Sheriff Price dove back into the details. "The canisters used in the attack were filled with two types of gases..."

Callie tapped on the boys' legs, but they ignored her.

"Professor Redding has confirmed that the knockout gas was an anticholinergic sedative derived from lulekuqe. However, the lethal nerve agent used in the luxury box attack was belladonna altissima, a chemical found only in nightroot, a rare plant native to Vana soil. Arthur, Riali will be proposing new national legislation requiring the sales of all biological substances across providential borders be thoroughly registered and documented. Which means full access to distribution records."

Asher shook his head. *Lulekuqe isn't right; that sedative isn't powerful enough to knock out a full-grown human. At best, it is a local anesthetic.*

"You want the entire trading ledgers of all cities?" Arthur protested. "That is a significant amount of legislative burden, especially on Dyria. They will accuse the capital's trading companies of undermining their own trade agreements. They will never accept that legislation."

Callie tapped on the boys' legs harder this time; they looked down to see what she wanted. She pointed to the door. A small, shadowy figure scurried outside. The boys' eyes went wide. Asher turned to the vent and looked back into the meeting room. Both Grimm, and his shotgun, were missing.

The boys slowly got off the stools. A slight screech from one of them caused the shadowy figure to stop outside their door. The three backed carefully toward the center of the room, behind a workbench. A whirring sound came from the door. They dropped down behind the furniture as the door swung open and the lights turned on.

The sound of Grimm's boots landed with a heavy thud. A mechanical spider scurried up his leg, around his body, and stopped in the palm of his hand. He stood still as he looked around the room, then reached into his belt for a second spider. The spiders' eyes lit up red, one in each palm. A smile crept across his face as he threw them into the room.

CHAPTER 16

Asher, Nico, and Callie all held their breath and listened as the metallic clacking grew closer. The spiders scanned the room, careful and methodical. Vance Grimm pulled his shotgun over his back and readied it. Callie took the ahriman from her satchel and tossed it gently upward. Gregory beelined for the door toward Grimm, who took careful aim with the shotgun. Before he could take the shot, a spider jumped off the ground and tackled the ahriman.

"What the…?" Grimm walked over to the frightened creature, who was locked in a losing battle with the metallic spider.

The spider stopped its wrestling and looked over at the opposite corner of the room. Nico took out a minicopter he had been working on since the attack and sent it across the room. The spiders stopped their advancement and ran to tackle the copter. A blast from Grimm's shotgun turned the tiny machine into a pile of metallic dust.

"Show yourself." Grimm's cold, taunting laugh filled the room. "Or not. You'll be hearing from Shelly either way."

Asher stood up from behind the desk with his hands in the air, shortly followed by Nico and Callie. He had begun walking toward Grimm when a spider locked onto his foot and tripped him. He fell on his backside, trying to swipe the spider off his leg, but its claws pierced into his ankle as it scrambled onto his face. Grimm whipped around and pointed his gun at the other two before they had a chance to take a step.

"Get up," he growled at Asher, keeping his shotgun focused on Nico and Callie.

Asher stood up slowly as the sound of a miniature buzzsaw began emanating from the spider's body. Grimm launched two more spiders from behind his coat. They crawled up Nico and Callie's legs and latched onto their eyes. Grimm readjusted his shotgun and poked it into Asher's belly.

"I remember you," he said quietly, drawing his face toward Asher's. His teeth were stained dark-yellow. A foul odor oozed like a cloud from his body, and his breath was a concoction of tobacco and bourbon. Asher's left eye was being scanned by the mechanical spider, while his right attempted to make out what it could of Grimm's face. Deep scars, thin lips, protruding chin, mangled nose, sparse hair held in place underneath a black cap.

Grimm read from the spider's back: "Asher Auden. Seventeen. Vana. What else…" He clicked a few tiny buttons, causing the buzzsaw to get within centimeters of Asher's eye.

"Please don't. Please don't," Asher pleaded.

"Biology expert. And you…yes, I recall you being a witness to both Miasma attacks. In the thick of it for them."

Asher stood frozen. "We helped stop him. We were there, they know this, the police know this."

"The whole city and school were at that game. Every student in Langford would be guilty by the criteria of being at the stadium!" Callie shouted. "You can't hold that against—"

Grimm shot Callie a menacing look to interrupt her outburst.

Nico stepped forward, "And he was with General Volkov during the other attack as well; just ask him. Your accusations are ridiculous. Do you even know who I am?"

Grimm turned from Asher and began walking toward Nico. "My memory is a little hazy. Perhaps my friend here will provide some insight."

Nico's eyes widened as the spider on his eye opened its chest to reveal a tiny buzzsaw.

"What the hell is going on?" asked the General in a scruffy voice from the doorway.

The others had filed into the room, the General and the sheriff with their guns drawn, Arthur clutching his staff. They observed the scene.

Grimm didn't move; his face and gun were locked on Asher. "Some eavesdroppers in need of interrogation."

"I know these students," Arthur said. "I asked Callie to meet me here with Asher. These two were present at the time of the Miasma attacks. She has a firsthand account of the terrorist."

"Yeah, I'm familiar with these students as well," said the sheriff. "Grimm, please stand down."

Grimm cut a sharp glance over at Price. "Sheriff, this one is a Vanatian and some kind of biology expert. And now you're telling me that the other one claims to have had a firsthand encounter with the terrorist and lived?" He turned toward Callie and pointed the shotgun at her face.

"Vance, they're unarmed. Stand down and let me take it from here," said the sheriff sternly.

"They attacked me. They had some little flying creature—"

"It's fine, Grimm," interrupted the General.

Grimm lowered his gun and clicked a button on his belt. The spiders stopped whirring and returned to him. He grunted and bumped his shoulder aggressively into Sheriff Price as he passed.

"Nicholas Catalano. And...who are you?" The General pointed at Callie.

"I'm Callie Saint."

Callie walked hurriedly to the injured ahriman, inspected its wings, and then cradled it close to her chest.

"Asher and Callie here are Vanatians," Arthur said. "These three helped stop the attack at the stadium."

The General nodded. "Right. And these two were also witnesses to the attack at the Citadel?"

Price nodded. "Yes, we've spoken to all three of them about their experiences. Why did you call them here, Arthur?"

"I know these two from Vana. I wanted to hear their stories. Thought it would help me get a better understanding of the situation."

Price turned toward Nico. "And why were you three in this room prior to the start of your meeting with Arthur?"

Nico spoke up in a respectful and charismatic tone. "We were getting some studying done beforehand. I'm familiar with this tower and thought this would be a good room for us to stop inside before we met with Arthur later. We had no idea there was another meeting going on, we had no intention of intruding."

The sheriff dragged a seat from across the room and toward a table at the center. "Go on, y'all take a seat." He stared over at Arthur. "What were you wanting to know, Arthur?" The air was tense. Arthur sat down at the table with Price and the three students. He pointed the emerald end of his staff at Asher first.

It was a quiet Sunday morning. Callie was hanging out around the sanctuary gardens with a book in hand. Cloud was a few feet away, watching the koi swim about the pond and doing his best to resist the urge to strike.

"Ms. Saint!"

Callie lowered her book and watched as Mara approached. "Good morning, Professor."

"All by your lonesome?"

"Yeah, just studying," she said, lifting up her book.

"Ah." The professor nodded and patted Cloud on the back. "It is a beautiful day."

"It is," agreed Callie. "Professor?"

"Yes?"

"I uhh…I couldn't help but notice you and Arthur Winston appear to be good friends. I'm friends with him, too. We used to talk whenever he visited Vana."

Mara smiled. "Yes, he does seem to know everyone. He is a good man. He and I go back a bit."

"If you don't mind me asking, how so?"

"I don't mind." The professor sat across from Callie. "We used to be colleagues."

"Oh? I didn't realize you ever had a job prior to being a professor."

Mara laughed. "Of course! I was an anthropologist of sorts."

"But...he's a diplomat. Right?"

"Yeah, something like that. Our adventures together preceded his time as a diplomat."

"What kind of adventures?"

Mara laughed again. "We traveled a lot, to all seven cities of Khamara, of course. But the other nations and continents as well. Officially, we would go to establish trade lines or assist in the handling of special creatures, things of that nature. But unofficially, we were in constant search for the first relics."

"What?" asked Callie. "Are those even real? Did you find any?"

"What we found, I will keep a secret for another day," Mara smiled.

"I have to hear more!"

"How about this: I will ask a few questions about you, and you can ask me one in return?"

"Me? I'm boring. What do you want to know about me?"

"First, I want to know if you are going to winter cotillion."

"Ugh," groaned Callie. "I kind of have to for social dynamics class. But I have zero desire to, so I might skip it."

"Oh, come on, it will be good! Learning other cultures is important—even if it is the stuffy culture of the Rialians."

Callie laughed. "Yeah, I guess. I just don't think it's really my thing."

"I understand completely," said Mara. "Do you have a partner?"

"My friend Felix asked me. He's from Kipos."

"Felix Donegal? He is on the koroka team! A great guy."

"I don't like him like that, purely friends."

"That is fair."

"My turn," said Callie. "What was the greatest place you've ever been?"

"Greatest? That's a tough one. For natural beauty, I think the waterfalls of Ciyasan might be the most magnificent. For culture, I think the people of Milyakatsa were fascinating. Oh, and their food! It's incredible! But you, I believe Arthur told me you were from Elurra, is that true?"

"It's where I was born, yes. But I haven't been there since I was very small."

"The Ajke temples there are marvelous."

"I've heard the stories. Arthur told me all about how the priestesses ride on wild cats—and that some can control animals with their minds."

"Something like that, certainly. Have you any desire to see it for yourself?"

Callie looked down and picked at Cloud's fur. "Not exactly."

"Why not?"

"I just…I don't know. I guess I don't care."

Mara nodded, and the two sat in silence for a brief moment.

Callie gathered her thoughts and continued, "My mother, she was supposed to be a high-ranking Ajke priestess."

"That's so wonderful!"

"Yeah, but as I'm sure you're aware, Ajke priestesses are not supposed to have children."

Mara nodded in understanding.

"She gave me up to her brother, my uncle. He told me they don't know my father. And that I should never go back there and try to meet my mother. I would only ruin her life as a priestess. I wouldn't want that. I don't care enough to ruin someone else's life, someone I don't even remember meeting. I believe she did what was in both of our best interests at the time, so I should be grateful."

"And so your uncle took you to Vana?"

"Yes," said Callie. "He moved to Vana to keep me a secret from those back in Elurra. He used his Elurrian knowledge of animals and hunting to open up a pet shop, and he passed a lot of those skills down to me. Which is, you know, why I'm here and all."

"Why did you come all the way here to Riali? Why not stay in Vana? Do you miss your uncle?"

Callie let out an awkward sideways smile. "Not really. He's a good man, but I wouldn't say he loves me—or whatever that even means. It always felt like I was a burden for him more than anything else. I've always tried my hardest not to be." She looked up at Mara. "Why did you leave Arthur Winston? He seems like a great man."

Mara chuckled. "Oh, he's a great man, alright. It's complicated."

"That's not fair," said Callie. "If you're going to ask me all these questions…"

"Ok. Ok…We used to be lovers of sorts."

"Used to be…?" questioned Callie under her breath.

Mara rolled her eyes. "I had enough of that life. All the traveling and adventures—they were wonderful. Romantic, grand, I saw the world like I had always wanted to. But there comes a time when stability and consistency become an increasing priority. For me, I don't know, it just became too much. I wanted a place to call home, a place I could build for myself." She gestured around the sanctuary. "And I ended up back here. I didn't grow up like most of these entitled Langford students. When I met Arthur, it was my chance to finally escape."

"That sounds nice," said Callie. "I wouldn't mind making an escape. I suppose that is what Riali is for me."

"Is it? Or is it just another cage?"

"What do you mean?"

"Well, frankly, I don't really ever see you conversing with others. How are you supposed to learn and grow if you are hiding in your corner all the time?"

"Oh, that? I don't care what other people think of me. I don't care about chasing after popularity or whatever."

"Sure, and to some extent, that is admirable. But is your view an embracement of your individuality, a celebration of your own uniqueness, or is it simply a defense mechanism to avoid being hurt? I imagine you feel a sense of abandonment, a feeling of being unwanted. That is not the case, Callie. You are a brilliant young woman. You are full of life, and interests. Do not be the dove too afraid to sing, forever lonely it will sit."

Callie turned her head. "Thank you. But really, you are overthinking it. I just prefer being with Cloud and with the animals. They love me, they are loyal, I understand them."

"The Ajke priestesses. You descend from them. But have you heard of the Sudiso monks?"

"The ones exiled from Elurra? I know a little, but not much."

"Their philosophy in life is simple: to rid themselves of all earthly desires and impurities so they can reach a higher plane of morality and existence. To do so, they lock themselves away in temples. They do not communicate with the outside world—they hardly even communicate with each other. They simply farm their small plots of lands, meditate, perform the occasional ritual, and sleep. That is their life, that is their entire existence on this earth."

"Ok," said Callie. "Sounds pretty nice to me. What's your point?"

"They were kicked out of Elurra because they contributed nothing to society. They and the priestesses completely disagreed on how to live and coexist."

"Well yeah, the priestesses are warriors, of course they aren't going to lie down and do nothing. That kind of complacency would put the whole city at risk."

"That is not the point. The point is that these people, these monks, they were given the gift of life, and they continued to squander it. They do not live, do not experience, do not understand what it even means to be human."

Callie raised her eyebrows in confusion.

"What I am saying to you, Callie, is do not merely be an observer, do not shy away from life. Instead, embrace knowing that in order to experience joy, you will also have to know pain. Good will come; you just have to choose to step into life."

Callie nodded and scratched Cloud's ear. "I understand, Professor. You must really want me to go to this dance, huh?"

Mara chuckled. "I do! Do you have a dress?"

"Eh, sort of. I don't have anything fancy. Just a couple of nice shirts I brought from Vana that I don't wear often."

"Hmm...well, I have quite a large wardrobe. It could use some pruning. We are about the same size. Would you like to come look through my things and see if there is anything you like?"

"Oh, wow. That's really nice. I'm not sure I could do that. I would feel bad."

"Honestly, I have way too many dresses that I will never wear. Here, I was just headed back to the greenhouse. I can show you what I have, and you can ask your questions."

Professor Jones stood up and reached her hand toward Callie. Callie sighed, packed up her book, and allowed the professor to lift her up.

"Asher, now that my parents are gone, there is a power vacuum in the Maurinkos," said Nico as they ascended the staircase to the Catalano manor.

Asher stopped and stood outside the massive doors. "Are you worried they will try to take advantage of you?"

"Not so much. But they will assume I am weak; that I am just the spoiled offspring of people who achieved true success."

"Respect? That's your concern? Who cares about their opinions? You're a genius in your own right. They need you more than you need them."

Nico chuckled at the thought. "Thank you, Asher. You are a good friend. But I need to become what my parents wanted me to be. I need to be a leader."

Asher nodded, not in agreement, but to acknowledge the validity of Nico's emotion. "Ok then, let's show them the leader you can be, Nico."

Hanley opened the door and greeted them. The robotic butler had done an excellent job maintaining the house.

Since his parents had passed away, Nico had inherited the Catalano fortune, including the family business as well as the estate, making him one of the wealthiest men in Riali overnight.

Asher and Nico pulled on their masks and took their place at the table, Nico drinking one glass of wine after another as Maurinko members filed into the room. He had the music cut off and the lights dimmed. The mood became somber and dark. A few members came to his side to offer vague condolences, to maintain their illusion of anonymity. Others made tasteless jokes about his newfound fortune. Nico stared straight ahead, speaking minimally to the guests.

Father Bianok walked up. "Son. Your parents were a blessing to Riali and to the church. They were forever kind and so very charitable. Your father's faith in the First God brought great fortune to his business empire. And in return, his empire and generous offerings brought the Hilezkorra faith to prominence in Riali through a cyclical relationship of blessing."

Nico took a long drink from his goblet as Father Bianok continued. "I understand no amount of wealth could overcome the pain. But I do see your parents' greatness in you. Brilliant and ambitious minds, their spirit certainly lives on through you. And I trust your continued tithings will only bring about more blessings to your parents' eternal legacy."

Nico shut his eyes in an attempt to keep his patience. "Yes. Father. Thank you for the kind words."

Father Bianok bowed his head and walked away with a soft, "Blessings, child."

Nico looked over to Asher and shook his head. Before Asher could say anything, Sister Lilly leaned toward his ear to whisper something. Her somberness seemed entirely out of character to Asher. Her hand was placed gently on Nico's shoulder. He nodded as she spoke at length, eventually looking up at her. "Thank you," he said. "That won't be necessary. But thank you."

She scratched his back gently for a few seconds before turning around and walking off.

General Volkov took a seat on the other side of Nico and gave Asher a cold blank stare. Roman walked over and sat beside Asher.

"Sir," said the General in a low tone to Nico, "I am not sure what all you know about CAT Robotics' current ventures."

"I am well aware," said Nico sharply. "I might even have a demonstration for you tonight."

"Wonderful," replied the General.

"So then, it sounds like you are aware that your family's firm has been working with the military and local law enforcement to help catch Miasma?"

"And I know they have ongoing contract negotiations with you, General," said Nico, looking through the General's elaborate mask of machinery and breaking the protocol of anonymity.

Roman began speaking to Asher, rambling about koroka. Asher played along nonchalantly while trying his best to remain in earshot of Nico's conversation.

"The inter-city relations in Khamara have become tense. The Dyrian army has grown significantly larger since their alliance with the Hainlyal Islanders. And these attacks, it is heavily suspected they are Vanatian in origin."

Asher couldn't help but shoot a glance at the General as Roman continued to babble in his ear. Nico did not face the General when he next spoke. "And the Vanatians want to kill a candy shop owner?"

"Frank? That creep had it coming. No one knows if he was truly Miasma's first victim. It could really have been anyone who wanted him gone." The General saw Asher and turned his attention. "Ah, young man, do you have a lady friend to bring to Langford's Winter Cotillion?"

Asher shook his head. "No, Sir."

Roman interjected. "Well, I know Autumn is free..."

"What?"

"I know some people have their eye on her," Roman was being coy and not saying names, but his tone held a hint of sadness. "But she is single now."

"Autumn Vasiliev is a beautiful girl. That is unfortunate news," said Asher, attempting to offer cordial comfort.

Roman whispered into his ear, "Don't speak her last name."

Asher gave him a puzzled look.

Roman nodded over in the direction of a couple across the table. "Her parents," he whispered.

Neither looked much like Autumn. The father, balding and chubby, wore a simple mask. The mother, blond and plain, held herself with an air of regality. She was dripping with jewelry, and her mask was much more ornate, if not a bit gaudy.

Asher whispered back, "Does Autumn not come to these?"

"Not in a long while," said Roman, taking a swig of his wine.

The table conversations were ended abruptly by the sharp clinking of glass. Nico stood up, interrupting the ceremony. "Welcome, brothers and sisters. I thank you for your presence this evening as we commune together under the eyes of the First God and in my manor. As you know, a great sadness has overtaken us. For centuries we have been the guardians of Khamara, keeping peace and order when all else has tended toward chaos and anarchy. We are the great mind, but the body has become sick. It is time for a change. For starters, I choose to no longer be afraid of these growing threats against us."

Nico ripped off his mask and threw it down on the table. A collective gasp swept across the room as he continued, "Our enemies know who we are. We have operated in the shadows, and they have successfully brought us into the light, hoping we would fear it. But do we fear being known? No. I do not fear our wealth, our power, the good we have done for this city and for this nation. We have been the builders. But now, now we are forced to become the destroyers."

Nico turned and nodded at Hanley. A series of menacing, four-legged robots poured into the room and encircled the large dining table. They had domed heads with what appeared to be some kind of turret containing a small flame on top. Heat grazed the back of Asher's neck as he refused to turn in his seat to observe the armored creature closely. Instead, he chose to stare straight ahead at those seated across from him, who also had the large flaming wolf-like creatures behind them.

A man in a green mask stood up. "What is the meaning of this? Is this some sort of threat? What would your parents think?"

Hanley walked over to the man in the green mask until he was directly behind him.

"Don't you dare talk about my parents, Mr. Crann!" shouted Nico. Two of Hanley's arms wrapped around the man and forced him back into the chair as if being fastened by a steel seatbelt. The man did not speak but rather sat as still as possible despite his visible nerves.

"No, this is not a threat. It is a declaration. But first, before I get to the heart of tonight's meeting, I ask politely that you all remove your masks."

No one at the table moved. Asher wasn't sure if it was defiance or out of fear. He was baffled by Nico's behavior. *It was one thing for Nico to want to become a leader, but this...this was one extravagant display of power.*

He looked at Nico for some kind of clue, some kind of expression, but Nico didn't look his way. Hanley's free arms began to whirl, and the table watched the spectacle with bated breath. The butler drew one of his free arms toward Crann's plate and picked up a steak knife, pointing it at the man's heart. Hanley's hand spun rapidly, turning the knife into a powered drill.

"Please, please don't," pleaded the man in the green mask.

With his other free hand, Hanley lifted the man's mask, revealing a terrified Mr. Crann.

"Now, I *am* threatening," said Nico, still with no expression on his face. Asher instantly threw his mask onto the table. Nico looked over, and Asher gave him a forced smile.

He is not joking around, thought Asher. Nico was more than a bank account to be leeched, he was going to grasp his parents' position in the Maurinkos by sheer force. A completion of his inheritance. Nico smiled back and nodded as the rest of the Maurinkos removed their masks and placed them on the table.

"Tonight, I declare that the Maurinkos are at war. A terrorist has infiltrated our city, and they have been targeting wealthy and prominent members of Riali, many of whom are Maurinkos, and none more important than my own parents."

The table sat in complete silence.

"We will use every available resource at our disposal to find and destroy this terrorist and everyone associated with him. What you see around you is the latest in CAT Robotics technology, our new CAT Vanguard series. Highly mobile, unmanned combatants tailored to the needs and specifications of our great military. Currently, our sources believe the recent attacks may originate from the western cities, those whose alliance has been the least reliable since the great war. We have not confirmed these facts. But we will be prepared for whatever attacks may come as we hunt down Miasma. In the meantime, CAT Robotics has graciously agreed to allocate a greater amount of its focus and attention to ramping up military supplies and creating innovative new equipment for the Riali armed forces. In return, we have asked for full cooperation of the military in hunting down the terrorist. Simply, the Maurinko Society must be prepared to defend itself, which means Riali must be prepared as well."

The table murmured.

"Now," said Nico cheerfully, "let's begin!" He clapped his hands together, and the domed heads of the creatures opened to reveal heated steaks, potatoes, and veggies.

Dinner was served.

CHAPTER 17

Asher tugged at his uncomfortable collar to relieve the pressure around his neck. Winter cotillion had arrived: the punctuation at the end of their first semester at Langford.

"Ash, how many berries do we have left?" Nico asked, bobbing up and down, trying to capture the whole of his body in the narrow dorm room mirror.

"Not many. Why?"

Nico smiled. "Something to take the edge off. They should make dancing a whole lot more bearable."

Asher reached into their dorm room fridge and pulled out a small bag of frozen, spliced sussberries. "You think we should save any for Avee and Kiara?" he asked, plucking one out and tossing the rest into Nico's open hands.

"We can hold onto a few just in case." Nico grabbed a berry and shoved the bag into his tux jacket. "Cheers," he said, toasting with the berry.

The boys walked down the winding corridors, sharing scraps of knowledge they could remember from Madam Ederra's class.

"Archaic rituals," whined Nico.

Asher snorted. "That's funny coming from a Maurinko."

Nico gave Asher a sideways glance, "A Maurinko that is actively casting aside the inane formalities."

Asher hadn't mentioned the Maurinkos since the meeting. Nico was acting as normal, as though nothing had happened. *Perhaps*, Asher thought, *his new ambition of finding Miasma was the distraction he needed from the grief.*

The two reached the dining hall, which had been completely transformed for the winter cotillion. Warm, ambient lights hung from extravagant ivory chandeliers. Large white banners and gold chains crisscrossed above. Tables brimming with drink fountains and desserts had been pushed to the side of the room to make way for a dance floor. A small stage had been prepared in the corner for the band and orchestra. The boys walked through the room and outside, continuing on cobblestone pathways lit by tiny lanterns toward the sanctuary, where tables were set up for the evening's feast.

Nico had asked Avee, and Asher had asked Kiara. The girls had yet to arrive. The awkward tension of the night was palpable as other boys got up to greet their dates, offering their arms and pulling out chairs. "Huh," said Nico. "Did not know Callie had it in her."

"What?" asked Asher, turning around in his chair to see Callie enter the sanctuary on the arm of Felix Donegal. She wore a striking, dark green corset dress. Exotic feathers lined the front and came down to a point where the dress wrapped tightly around her legs before tailing out ever so slightly into an elegant train. Her hair was pulled into an elaborate bun, with curled auburn strands outlining her face. Asher made eye contact with Callie and nodded.

She quickly dropped Felix's arm and walked over. "Hey."

"Hey," said Asher, smiling widely. "You look great!"

"Thanks." Her voice was unamused. "Where's the food?"

"I don't think they've started serving yet," said Asher, his eyes wandering past Callie and toward the sound of bubbling laughter. Avee and Kiara walked in wearing matching pink dresses. Asher and Nico quickly went over and hugged their dates, then escorted them to the table.

Professor Ederra rose from the head table and gave a brief toast celebrating the first semester and the traditions of winter. After a round of cheers, the students dug into the feast: roasted hen with fingerling potatoes and buttered corn. Asher successfully kept up small talk with Kiara, but Nico's mind clearly had begun to drift. He stared blankly at the evening lights swirling above him.

"Nico..." said a frustrated Avee. "NICO!"

"What's up?" he said, snapping back to her attention.

"Are you high?" she asked.

Callie side-eyed the situation.

"Oh yeah, Asher and I forgot to offer," he smiled. "Did you all want any berries?" He looked at Asher, who gave a nervous laugh and shrug.

"I can't believe you'd get high at cotillion!" Avee said.

"Where did you even get those anyway? I thought you stopped making them after the whole Professor Redding incident," asked Kiara.

"I'd say you two could have learned from that mishap, but then we'd all be wrong," said Callie.

"We did," said Asher. "But we had a few left. We figured we'd use them to celebrate the end of the semester."

"Besides," interjected Nico, "I heard magical berries pair well with cabernet." He lifted his glass in mock elegance. Avee rolled her eyes. Kiara looked over at Asher. "If you screw up our dance, I swear…"

Asher did his best to focus his blue and green eyes on hers. "We'll be fine. I got this."

Asher shook off the hallucinations as if waking from a fever dream, trying to respond to whatever Kiara had just asked. "Yeah, yeah, I'm good."

The students finished clearing their plates and began piling onto the dance floor where the Langford orchestra was performing classical ballads.

"Don't embarrass me," Kiara whispered to Asher.

No pressure, he thought.

Sparkling lights fluttered around the room like wild birds. Large silk banners of white and gold laced around the ceiling and upper balconies where the teachers stood and observed the sea of students.

Asher adjusted his coattails, watching the light twinkle in the corner of Kiara's eye. The band struck up a waltz, and he took his cue, reaching out his hand in a polite gesture. She curtsied in return and took his hand.

The crowd began to whirl, swelling with the music, fast and light. Asher's head was a gyroscope, working overtime to right his body's course. He concentrated on his steps, focusing on the song's tempo and his spacing with the other dancers.

Professor Ederra weaved in and out of the students, using a ruler to correct postures and measure distances between partners. Asher paid her no attention. The air around him was an electric buzz. He could feel it all—the coolness of the breeze, the warmth of Kiara's skin, the melody rising within him, and then calm as the song came to its resolution. The room applauded for the orchestra, and Asher bowed to his partner.

"I'm confident we passed the professor's test, but did I pass yours?"

Kiara let out a sly grin. "Has there ever been a test you haven't passed, Asher Auden?"

Asher reached out his hand for a second dance, and Kiara kindly accepted.

The two continued dancing and spinning beneath glittering chandeliers. Around them, students broke rank, ebbing and flowing across the marble floors as a tangled mass, but Asher's euphoria was punctuated only by the applause for the band and the occasional exchanging of pleasantries with nearby friends. After a while, Asher saw Nico and Avee head to a side table to grab a drink. "Care to join them?" he asked.

Kiara nodded. "Yeah, I'm good to take a break." There was now a playfulness in her voice.

The two walked over to the concessions. Asher lightly tapped Nico on the back. "How're things going over here?"

"Good!" said Nico, taking a deep breath after a long swig of punch.

"Kiara and I are going to the ladies' room," Avee said, "We will be right back."

"How are things going with Kiara?" Nico asked with a gleam in his eye after the girls were out of earshot. "She seems to have lightened up a bit."

Asher blushed and poured himself a drink. "Yeah, the dancing wasn't all that bad. I think Professor was impre—" He was interrupted by the sound of a loud metallic crashing. "What was that?"

Nico scanned the room. A second noise erupted. "That was the main entrance," said Nico.

A third crash, and now the music had stopped.

The crowd began panicking. Asher turned his head toward the sanctuary doorway. It slammed shut.

Nico pointed. "That is all of the exits except the one on the balcony." The student's murmuring turned into a roar. Then came the sound of a piercing scream.

Asher turned toward Nico, "Could that have been Avee or Kiara?"

Madam Ederra stepped forward on the balcony and yelled over the noise. "Students! Stay calm and head to...to..." Her eyes grew wide before her body collapsed to the floor. A cloaked figure now stood in her place.

Asher saw the tubed gas mask, just as Callie had described.

Miasma threw grenade-like canisters from the balcony onto the ballroom floor. Professor Creed attempted to rush the cloaked figure, but he side-stepped the attack, and they both became lost in the cloud of smoke before Creed reappeared, a syringe jutting out of his neck. The professor fell to the floor, writhing in pain. Miasma continued to throw out more canisters of gas. Students fell in droves.

"Now is my chance. I am going to get him," Nico said.

Asher grabbed his arm. "No, there's nothing we can do right now."

"I don't care, I am not letting him get away."

"Look, the gas is purple. If this is the same gas Miasma used at the stadium, then we should be able to power through its effects with the berries."

Nico nodded. "Fine. So what is the plan? Play dead?"

"For now, I think that's the only play we have..."

"All right," said Nico, kneeling down. "But I am keeping my eyes open for this."

"ASHER!"

Asher whipped around at the sound of his name. It was Callie.

"Do you..." She collapsed onto the floor as consciousness drained from her face.

Nico threw him the bag of berries. Asher mushed one up and placed it between her lips.

"It's ok, Callie, you got this, come on."

She gulped it down, but it seemed to make no difference. Asher let her fall further onto the floor and looked over the crowd as panic gave way to a mass of unconscious students.

The once lively room had become stone silent, except for the cold clanking of steel boots. Asher's vision was blurred from the berries and the thick cloud of concentrated anticholinergic gas, but he could see Miasma's black cloak covering up a vest of weapons and canisters as he walked through the piles of still bodies. He stopped over one group, reached into his cloak, and pulled out a long syringe and vial.

Nico shifted his eyes toward Asher. Asher shook his head no; they shouldn't act. Miasma plunged the syringe into

Director Dolent's neck. Asher shut his eyes and grimaced while Nico continued watching, seething with anger.

Miasma went down the line of Langford's administration board, placing the syringe into the necks of one victim after another. The air was dense with thick purple gas.

Asher heard a stirring beside him. He looked over as Callie's eyes fluttered. He tried to push a finger to his lips to signal her to be quiet, but her groggy daze soon turned to panic. She shot up and looked around the room. "What...?"

Miasma, who had just finished injecting the last professor at the administration table, turned toward her. Their eyes locked, turning a second into an eternity. The terrorist pulled out a pistol and fired.

"NO!" Asher grabbed hold of Callie and pulled her down.

Miasma continued to fire, the bullets ricocheting inches away from them. Asher knocked a table over, and he and Callie pressed against its surface as more shots struck the wood frame.

The sound of the clip emptying was Nico's cue; he bolted upright and charged.

The berries and the smoke confused his judgment. Miasma sidestepped the tackle and flung Nico against a nearby gold-plated statue. Nico crashed hard and sprawled out onto the floor as Miasma took off through the exit.

Asher turned to Callie. "Check on Nico; I'll go after Miasma."

She nodded, and they sprinted off.

The berries were distorting Asher's senses, the staircase growing and shrinking with every step. He tried to focus, to prepare for the maze of winding Langford hallways, and concentrated on the loud clanking of metallic boots and fluttering flashes of a worn, black cloak ahead of him. He chased the figure into a clearing and stopped. Miasma was gone. He looked down the various corridors, weighing his options, when a sharp sting pierced his neck.

"Don't move," a distorted growl commanded.

Miasma grabbed the back of Asher's jacket with one hand and kept the syringe in his neck with the other. Miasma guided him to the staircase. Callie and Nico emerged through the doorway.

"Stop." Miasma's voice was calm but difficult to discern through the mask. Nico's head was bleeding profusely as he stood, barely conscious.

Callie spoke up. "What do you want?"

"I've gotten what I want."

The terrorist's voice was cold and inhuman.

"Let him go, or I swear to God I will kill you." Nico seethed.

"From what I understand, you plan to kill me regardless, Mr. Catalano."

Anger and confusion washed over Nico's face.

"You." Miasma shook Asher. "You found a way to counteract the gas. The berries, I presume?" He slowly pushed the syringe deeper into Asher's neck, he hadn't depressed the plunger yet.

"How?" stammered Asher.

Callie held onto Nico's arm to prevent him from rushing at Miasma and Asher.

Nico shouted, "You are not getting out of here alive."

Miasma's tone remained cold and calculated. "This contains a lethal toxin. By my estimate, Asher has three hours before his heart stops. A brilliant mind like his might work out how to counteract it. But chase me, and he will die. Consider this the last mercy I show you and your friends."

Asher strained away from the syringe as best he could, his face determined. "A brilliant mind, huh?" He grabbed Miasma's hand. "Let's see if I can change that opinion."

He shoved backward, sending himself and Miasma down the staircase and into the lobby below. Asher's vision was a blur of carpet and cloak as their bodies tumbled, one over the other. Each stair tread was a punch to the gut and a kick in the spine.

They reached the bottom. Asher pulled the needle from his neck. Its contents had now emptied into his bloodstream. He looked up. Miasma rose from the ground, looked at Asher, and quickly bolted through the doorway. Callie and Nico ran down the stairs to help Asher off the ground. The world was on fire around him, and this time he could feel every flame.

CHAPTER 18

By the time they reached the lab, Asher's limbs were numb. Cloud stood guard at the door while Callie and Nico buzzed around, taking orders from Asher. He started by draining five milliliters of blood from his arm. "We'll need all the blood we can get without jeopardizing my immune system." He started up the gel electrophoresis and prepared the strand displacement assay.

Asher could feel his tongue start to swell. "I can't tell what's the berries, what's the gas, and what's the toxin." He turned toward Nico and Callie. "You've both ingested berries and have been exposed to the gas but not the poison. Are either of your tongues swelling, or are you having trouble breathing?"

They both said no. "Ok...ok, it could be an allergic reaction."

Asher placed a few milliliters of his blood in a centrifuge and a few droplets of diluted blood on a slide. He peered into the microscope, gradually increasing the magnification. The red blood cells swirled around the slide and quickly coagulated as the water began to evaporate, forming intricate shapes that looked like tiny fires. He shook his head.

"Focus, Asher," he mumbled to himself. A large number of multi-nucleus lymphocytes began to coagulate. "Ok," he whispered. "Ok, looks like there's an increase of neutrophils."

"What do we know?" asked Nico.

"It will stop my heart, it's time sensitive, it's causing auto-immune type reactions."

Callie turned to Nico. "Nico, you need to find Nurse Kimona."

"There are piles of dead bodies in the ballroom. What the hell is the nurse going to do?" Nico fired back.

"I don't know! But find *someone*. Cloud and I will stand guard with Asher."

Nico looked over at Asher, who didn't bother acknowledging their conversation; his mind was fully engaged. Nico sighed. "Ok, I will figure it out. I will be right back. Don't let anyone in if you do not hear my voice."

He bolted out the door. Callie sat silently behind Asher, trying her best to stay out of his way while remaining attentive to his needs.

"I need cephalosporin."

"Ok. Where is it?"

"In the bottom drawer beside the acetone, in a gray bottle. Grab it. And the fluoroquinolone while you're in there."

Callie ran to the drawer and retrieved its contents.

Asher took one of the vials out of the centrifuge and pipetted the plasma into a hastily mixed solution. He placed it back under the microscope. "Alright. Ok." His breathing grew heavy, and his words began to jumble.

He grabbed four more vials off the centrifuges and pipetted various solutions into each one, gradually increasing the dosage. "Put these in the incubator. Set it to ninety-five degrees Celsius for three minutes."

He continued to make slides and place them under the microscope. "Callie, what do you feel?"

"Umm...terrified?"

"What? No. I mean physically. Come here." He pointed a small flashlight into her eyes. "What are your symptoms from the berries and gas?"

"Right." She hadn't put much thought into her own body. "My heart rate is very high. Everything is distorted—sizes and shapes, they don't seem to make sense. My stomach hurts a bit, but my head feels fine, even with the brightness of all these colors."

"Ok, good." Asher checked her pulse and breathing rate. She continued to list off her symptoms until a ding went off.

"That's the incubator," said Asher. "Let's see what's going on." He stumbled over to the lab bench, pulled a vial from the incubator, and raised it to eye level before it slipped from his fingers. The vial crashed onto the floor, Asher alongside it.

Nico sprinted through the Langford corridors, the hallways expanding and shrinking with every step. Ancient suits of armor appeared to reach out and grasp him, their metal bodies clanging among the dizzying sounds of clocks and spinning lights. He ignored it all and was soon greeted by the infirmary's locked doors.

He fumbled through his pockets, wrestled out the skeleton key, and stumbled in. He walked through lines of beds filled with patients, looking for one who seemed to be alert and conscious.

"Kiara." He said, seeing her open eyes at the end of the room. "What is going on? Where is Nurse Kimona?"

"Where have you been? Miasma attacked the winter cotillion. Langford is on lockdown."

"I am aware," said Nico. "Have the police arrived?"

"I'm not sure. Avee and I were attacked just outside the bathroom. There was gas everywhere. The people in here were not in the ballroom. Most of us ran straight to the infirmary."

She looked up at Nico with a tense nervousness. "What is wrong? What else has happened?"

Nico shook his head. "I don't have time to explain, I have to find help."

He bolted back out the door and headed straight to the ballroom. Residual purple gas lingered in the hallway, becoming heavier the closer he got. His disorientation wasn't improving, and he wasn't sure how long the protective effects of the berries would last.

Loud, marching steps headed toward the ballroom. Nico grasped for the walls, willing himself deeper into the purple gas. He could make out a brigade of soldiers with gas masks making their way into Langford.

"Hey!" he shouted, his voice weak and drowsy.

The soldiers were focused on rescuing the students and searching for traces of Miasma.

"HEY!" he shouted again, his voice louder but even more disoriented.

He approached the brigade of soldiers just outside the room before crashing down to his knees, taking a large suit of armor down with him.

A soldier turned. "What the...?"

"Freeze!" Another soldier shouted, pointing his rifle at Nico, "Don't move!"

Nico raised his hands sheepishly. "No. Look, I need help. I need medical help. Now."

One of the masked men stepped forward. "How are you awake?" He gestured for the other soldiers to lower their weapons, then handed him a gas mask. Nico could make out the faint grizzled voice of Sheriff Price.

"Sheriff. I have a serious situation. It's Asher, he needs to get to a hospital."

Price stared directly at Nico. "Bring him to our ambulances outside. We don't have the manpower to spare."

"We can't. Miasma pumped him with some kind of toxin. Said he had only a few hours to live. Asher is in the lab right now, trying to find a cure. He is going to die."

Price turned to his men and waved them off. They sprinted into the ballroom, and the sheriff looked back at Nico. "Miasma singled him out?"

"Yes," said Nico, taking a deep breath from behind the mask. "We chased Miasma, but he got the jump on us. He stuck Asher with a needle filled with something. He and Callie Saint are in the lab right now. He needs help."

The sheriff nodded. "Ok. Take me to him."

"Asher!" Callie screamed.

"I'm fine," he whimpered, rising to his feet. He was in his final hour. His vision was blurred, his body heavy. Sweat was pouring down his face from the fever and the effort of spinning from one table to the next, his eyes buried in microscopes, gels, and solutions. The color was drained from his face. His pupils were dilated.

Callie grabbed a wet cloth and ran over to him, placing it against his forehead. "Can you fix it?"

"I'm not sure," said Asher, the words barely escaping his lips. He stared into Callie's auburn hair, a waterfall of flame in his barely conscious eyes.

She nodded, dabbing at the sweat. Asher's shaggy black hair stuck to his forehead. His collared shirt was completely undone. His breaths were deep but unsteady.

"You said your hallucinations were gone?"

"Yes," said Callie. "It's nothing intense."

"Ok," said Asher looking past her. "Because mine are more vivid."

"Well…you took more berries than me?"

"Maybe." Asher put his fingers on Callie's neck. "But your heart rate is through the roof, which is a side effect of the berries."

"From the adrenaline, maybe?"

"No. My heart isn't. My heart is slow." He grabbed Callie's hand and placed it on his chest.

"It's counteracting the berries by acting as a sedative. But my hallucinations are more vivid, and it's acting as an anesthetic."

Callie narrowed her eyes. "I'm not sure what any of that means."

"It's binding to my NMDA receptors, and my plasma has a high concentration of CYP3A4 and CYP2D6 inhibitors."

Callie looked at Asher without saying a word.

He looked down, his eyes scanning the floor as if reaching the back of his mind. He looked back up at Callie. "It's a ketamine derivative."

"Ketamine?"

Asher spun around. "Yes. The kind they use for surgeries or antidepressants. But it's not pure; it's been diluted, probably with something like diethyl ether to help it spread; otherwise, I would have been on the floor already."

"Is there a cure?"

"CYP2B6 and CYP3A4 inducers could lower the levels of the ketamine in my blood."

"Great, do we have any of that in the lab?"

"Nico and I took some pharmaceuticals from the infirmary during our last visit. Go through the cabinet and see if you can find anything with benzodiazepine."

Callie rushed over to the cabinet and looked at the contents in confusion.

"No," Asher said. "The shelf over there, grab anything that is either a sedative or stimulant and throw it back on my bench."

She rifled through the cabinets and drawers, grabbing armfuls of various bottles.

Asher hobbled back to the workbench. "Ok…" He grabbed the surface and attempted to regain some composure. "Ok…"

Callie pulled up a seat and continued patting the back of his neck with a washrag. He began picking up and reading the labels. Finding what he wanted, he ground up several pills and diluted the mixture. His work was diligent and focused, but his body was showing clear signs of agony. "Callie, there's one more thing I have to ask."

"Of course."

"I don't want to ask it, but we're running out of time and—"

"Asher, what is it?" she interrupted.

"Ketamine, it's an enantiomeric compound."

"You know I don't know what that means."

"It means it's chiral. It means there's two possible solutions. One that will bind to the drug, inhibiting it from binding to more receptors. The other solution will bind directly to the receptors, making the drug more potent."

Callie made a go-on gesture.

"One of these will save me. The other will kill me."

The life drained from Callie's face. "I...No."

"I have no idea which will work. And there is no quick way to find out, except for one option. Callie..." Asher stumbled. "Callie, I'm so sorry."

She shook her head. "No. No, there has to be another way."

Callie stood in disbelief, her eyes piercing Asher. He turned his head away in shame. "If the solution is correct and it's safe, it won't bind to his receptors. It will just float through his blood and be filtered out in time. He'll become temporarily drowsy and a little incoherent, but he'll live."

"And the other one?"

"His heart will slow, and he will enter cardiac arrest. It will be quick and peaceful. If this happens, I take the other drug, and we pray. At the very least, it should buy me enough time to get medical attention."

Callie looked over to Cloud, who stood vigilantly by the door.

"It's the only way to know for sure. Otherwise, it is a fifty-fifty chance. We could guess, but if I don't do something, then I'll be dead within the next few minutes."

He raised the two syringes. "I put an extra ten milliliters in each syringe, so there's sixty in both. He only needs ten, and I need fifty milliliters. Do you understand?" Asher's head began to fall, his body visibly breaking down.

Callie's face was stern. She looked Asher in the eyes. "I understand."

She walked over to the door and knelt beside Cloud. She rubbed his back and whispered in his ear. Cloud followed her back over to the workbench, and the three of them sat on the floor.

"Do you have a guess which one will work better?"

Asher slouched against the table; his breathing was heavy. He looked at Callie from the corner of his eye. "I..."

The syringes rolled from Asher's limp hands. His eyes went white, spinning to the back of his head.

"Asher? Asher?" Callie grabbed his shoulder.

He moved his head slightly from left to right but couldn't speak.

She grabbed the nearest syringe. She pet Cloud with one hand and placed the syringe in the other. "I'm sorry, boy. Be brave for me."

Cloud sniffed at the syringe and looked up at Callie, his eyes wide with affection and understanding. She plunged the needle into his shoulder and released ten milliliters of the solution. He let out a whimper but didn't run. She pulled the syringe back out, and he curled up in her lap. Her hands glided along his head, down his neck and back. She watched as his breathing grew deep and heavy. Callie kept her eye on the clock and then back at Cloud.

His breaths grew deeper and deeper. His body, heavy on her lap. Cloud melted into her legs. Both her arms wrapped around the scruff of his neck. Her hand over his chest, her face pressed close until his whiskers grazed her cheek. She felt his heart flutter to a stop and listened as his long, fox snout released one final sigh.

She looked up at Asher, whose body had remained still for the past few minutes. She carefully placed Cloud's limp body aside, crawled over to him, picked up the other serum, and plunged it deep into his veins. His eyes snapped open. He looked at Callie, looked at his arm, and then looked down at the syringe she had chosen. His head wobbled, he was unable to speak, unable to express his sorrow. *I'm sorry, I'm sorry, I'm sorry,* was all he could think as his body collapsed onto her shoulder.

Callie held Asher's body up, placing her fingers across his neck to check for a pulse. It was faint, but he was alive. She steadied herself against the lab table, one arm propping him up, the other arm across Cloud's body. Wisps of wavy auburn hair streaked across her face, mixing with the taste of tears in each gasping breath.

CHAPTER 19

Asher woke up to the scent of starched sheets and juniper and the sight of Nurse Kimona, who was leaning over to adjust his pillows. "Asher, sweetie, you're awake!"

He groaned and tried to sit up.

Kimona grabbed a cup of water and placed the straw between his lips. "Drink. You need to get hydrated and flush out whatever concoction you put in your system."

Asher sipped from the straw. "Thank you."

He looked around at his surroundings. It appeared he was in the infirmary, but his bed had been quartered off with large curtains. He could hear a loud, bustling commotion coming from the rest of the room.

"It sounds busy out there."

"Yes," she said solemnly. "We've been at max capacity from the attack. The more serious injuries were rushed to Riali Medical Center. But we set up the infirmary here to help with those who are not in critical condition. It's been busy."

"I can imagine," said Asher, grabbing the water cup and taking another sip.

Kimona stood up and fiddled with Asher's IV bag. "Do you need another blanket or anything?"

"No. I'm fine, thank you."

"There are people here to see you. They wanted me to let them know once you were awake. But I…I told them it would be better for you to rest."

Asher smiled. "It's fine, Nurse. I appreciate it, but I can talk."

"Are you sure?"

"Yes, really, I'm feeling alright."

"Hmm." The nurse adjusted his blankets and placed the back of her hand across his forehead. "Ok. Wait here, I'll be right back with the sheriff."

As soon as Nurse Kimona walked away, Asher sat up and pulled back his privacy curtains. Rows of beds were filled with students and healthcare workers; only his had been protected with privacy curtains. Across the room, he saw Kiara and Avee sitting on the edge of a bed, watching over a body Asher presumed was Autumn. Asher turned his head toward the main entrance of the infirmary and was startled by the nearness of Sheriff Price.

"Are you ever *not* curious?" said Price in a gruff voice.

Asher tried to crack a smile but chose to look down instead. "Hi, Sheriff. No, I am always curious. But I suppose it's the same way for you?"

Price let out a muffled laugh, took off his hat, and sat down beside Asher's bed. Asher stared at his hands as he felt the sheriff's eyes studying him. After a few seconds of lingering silence, the sheriff pulled up a chair beside the bed. "Asher, you saw Miasma."

"Yes."

"Can you tell me what happened?"

Asher sighed. "Have you spoken to Nico and Callie? Are they alright?"

"They're fine," said Price, maintaining his eye contact. "Nico is waiting outside the door."

"And Callie?"

"I spoke with her earlier in the sanctuary."

Asher nodded, lost in thought.

"Asher, what did you see?"

"What parts of the story don't you know?"

The sheriff turned around to shut the curtains and spoke with a hushed voice.

"Nico said you had taken hallucinogens containing a stimulant and that you gave some to Callie when you saw Miasma walk into the room."

"That's correct."

"He said you three played dead and then chased Miasma. Miasma attacked Nico, grabbed hold of you, and injected you with poison. And you three fled to your lab. Callie told me you created a drug to counteract the poison."

"That's about it."

Price gripped his hat tighter. "Everyone else who was directly injected with Miasma's poison has died."

Asher looked away in distress. "I can help. I can show you the antidote I used."

"No, Asher, it's not about that," said the sheriff. His tone became more somber. "The terrorist got away. So far, the only people who have made contact with Miasma and lived are you and Callie. Some suspect these attacks are politically motivated, that the terrorist is specifically sparing the lives of Vanatians."

"That's ridiculous," Asher retorted. "I almost *died*!"

The sheriff waved his hand to try and quiet Asher. "I know, I know."

"And Callie, too!" Asher was becoming riled up.

"I'm aware. Look." Price leaned in closer. "The higher-ups have become paranoid. These have been high-profile targets, and Miasma has only grown bolder. People have every reason to be scared. But you need to stay out of this. You need to put as much distance between yourself and these attacks as possible."

"Of course, Sheriff. I never wanted anything to do with this. But if it's no trouble, Sheriff, I just have one question on my mind?"

"This investigation is still ongoing, I cannot divulge any non-public information to you, but I will try my best."

"The death serum. Is it what killed Nico's parents? It appears Miasma's mode of operation is to knock people out with the gas first and then use the serum."

"You're partially correct. The serum you experienced has been used in several attacks. However, each time it has been tweaked and modified, like they are solving a puzzle. In the earliest attacks we could contribute to the terrorist, the victims survived. Albeit, severely disabled."

"So then, Nico's parents?"

"The death serum isn't the only way Miasma has killed. I'll tell you what I told Nico. They died from carbon monoxide."

"How? That would take far too long?"

"Miasma had planted a pump on top of the booth, spewing monoxide into the small, confined room. Colorless. Odorless. No one would have known. But when someone went to open the door and noticed it was locked, Miasma put the second part of the plan into action: creating a distraction that delayed security from getting to the booth. They released the knockout gas in the stadium, wired to the koroka platform shoot, and wired one to the VIP booth. The monoxide caused a strange discoloration to the usual purplish nature of the knockout gas."

"My God," said Asher. "That's more clever than I thought."

"Right. But to my point, you need to see that I am not here to protect you. No one here can protect you. I'm only giving you this last warning. You and your friends have been at the center of multiple attacks."

"Am I a suspect, Sheriff?"

The sheriff paused. "These attacks began a few weeks before the academic year started, prior to yours and the other new students' arrivals. We know you are not the terrorist. But if you have any information that could lead to the capture...?"

"I don't know anything." Asher was annoyed at the sheriff's non-answer.

"Ok then. I'll be on my way and let you rest up. Play it safe, Mr. Auden. These are dark times here in Langford." Sheriff Price stood up and walked away, pulling the curtains closed behind him. Asher collapsed back into his bed with a sigh of exhaustion.

"Asher!" Nico's voice came from outside the privacy curtain.

Asher perked back up.

"Oh man, thank god."

Nico opened the privacy curtains, stepped into the partition, and leaned over the bed to give Asher a hug. Asher patted him on the back.

"How's your head?" Asher asked, seeing the bandage on Nico's scalp.

"Ah, my skull is pretty thick; I will be alright. How is your...everything?"

Asher laughed. "Like the worst hangover in the world."

"Ah, so just another Sunday. What did Price say to you?"

"The sheriff? Nothing good. The terrorist is still at large, and I need to be more careful. I think they suspect it's someone from Vana—"

"Vana? That doesn't make any sense. I guess I could *maybe* see Dyria..."

"Right. But why would Dyria or any of their allies be looking to attack Langford students?"

"Well...they didn't exactly attack the students."

"What do you mean," said Asher, adjusting himself in his bed.

"The only deaths were Director Dolent and a few professors. Some students outside the ballroom who got in the way were injured, but that is it."

"Interesting..." Asher nodded, his eyes wandering into deep thought.

"Everyone killed was a member of the Langford admissions board."

"How do you know?"

"My parents, they own—owned—a portion of this building, remember? I know all the board members, and I overheard Price discussing the casualties."

"Nico..." Asher groaned. "We can't do this."

"Do what?" Nico said defensively.

"We can't go chasing after Miasma. Sheriff Price already told me that all Vanatians are being watched. I won't be of any help to you if we have the police spying on us." Asher flopped back onto the bed and stared at the ceiling.

Nico stepped closer to the bed. "Asher, without you, I would have died."

"And without you, I would have died, too. But that doesn't make us immortal."

"No. No, you are right. If you don't want to join me, I can't make you."

"Sheriff Price will figure it out, Nico. And if not, then Vance Grimm will blow Miasma's head off with a shotgun."

Nico exhaled sharply in silent protest. Asher decided to change the topic. "Have you spoken to Callie?"

"No." Nico shook his head solemnly. "She is not talking with anyone."

Winter was beginning in earnest. Asher didn't care. Each breath brought a sharp sting of life to his lungs. The sanctuary's gardens had started their hibernation early, and rows of dead carnation petals lined the stone walkways.

He found her in the fox den. She knelt in the grass and placed a food bowl in a cage beside a small red fox. He watched, perhaps a few seconds too long. Her face hid her sorrow well, but her aura was a rain that flooded the room. He had a whole day to prepare his words, but no amount of rehearsing helped. His mind was blank.

"Callie," he said gently.

She did not turn to face him, only reached into the cage and pet the fox on the snout.

Asher walked up closer.

"Callie." His voice was even more faint the second time.

"Hi, Asher." Her voice was monotone, and she remained fixated on the tiny creature.

"How are you holding up?" He took a few steps closer.

"I'm alright. Looks like you made a quick recovery."

"Yeah." Asher sat on the ground beside her. "Nurse Kimona did an excellent job patching me up."

"Good."

"I'm sor—"

"No." Callie interrupted before Asher could speak a word. "Don't be sorry. Don't be anything. We did what we had to do."

"He saved me."

"Yes, you're alive. That's what matters."

Asher looked into the cage and watched the fox cub nibble at the food.

"I'm going back to Vana for Winter Break next week."

"Oh."

"Are you?"

"I'm not sure yet. Professor Jones could use my help here in the sanctuary."

"What about your uncle?"

"I'm sure he's doing fine. Say hi to him for me."

"Yeah." Asher let the silence linger, but eventually, curiosity got the best of him. "Have you spoken with him since you've been here?"

Callie stood up quickly, suddenly appearing angry. "No."

"You saved people, Callie. You saved me. You don't think he'd care?"

Callie grabbed a pail of meat beside her and threw its contents into a cage of knee-height lizard-like creatures.

"I haven't saved anyone, Asher."

The creatures went into a frenzy as they tore at the meat she had tossed into their cage.

"Ok," said Asher, agreeing only to pacify.

The two stood in silence, watching as the creatures fought for their meal, a huddled mass of beaks, fangs, and fat, spikey tails.

"Have you buried him?"

"Yes," said Callie. "Beside the greenhouse. Professor Jones helped me. Would you like to see him?"

"If you don't mind…"

"It's fine, we all deserve to say goodbye."

The two walked through the gardens in silence, the cold air whipping at their faces as they looked around, taking in the end of their first semester at Langford.

They approached a dirt mound beside Professor Jones's greenhouse. A small stone stood on top of it with no markings. Asher turned to Callie. For just a second, he could see her fight back tears, her stony face a shade softer than he was used to seeing. He knelt beside the grave and saw Cloud's collar. He picked it up, pressed his thumb against the metallic nameplate, and then rubbed along the inside—still lined with coarse, white fur. He examined a strand of fur thoughtfully, pocketed it, and set the collar back down before standing back up.

"I…" Asher struggled to find the words before turning to Callie. "He was a great fox."

"Snow fox," corrected Callie.

"Snow fox," nodded Asher, staring back at the grave. "The kind of snow fox legends are made of."

Callie stared at the dirt mound. Asher continued, "He was so intelligent. The way he would obey any command, he truly had a grasp on language."

Callie remained silent as Asher spoke, "I remember so many summers, growing up on the outskirts of the city near the woods, watching you two go for your romps through the wilderness. He was certainly a lover of squirrel chases, sunshine, adventure—"

"And food," said Callie. "He was a lover of food."

Asher smirked at the thought, "And ear scratches and belly rubs! There's not a soul in Vana who didn't know him, who didn't love him. He made himself famous here in Langford, too. But at the same time, he was fiercely loyal to the only creature odder than himself."

Callie cracked a smile as her head sank and her eyes closed.

"You loved him with all your heart, Callie. Everyone knows that. He knew that."

"I wish he had a chance to see Elurra. To see the snow and to meet others like him," she said, choking on the words.

"I will make this up to you, Callie. I know it may seem hollow now, but I promise you, I will find a way to make this right."

"It's not your place to do so, Asher. The pain without him is the greatest pain I have ever felt. But I know it doesn't compare to what my life would have been had he never lived. A snow fox, a hero, and my dearest friend."

"The immortal Asher Auden!" Roman approached with his arms stretched wide. "And the fearless Callie...Callie?"

"Saint," said Callie, staring him down.

"Saint. Right." Roman looked around. "Did I interrupt a moment?"

"We were saying goodbye to Cloud." Asher, now standing up, faced Roman.

"Oh no, what happened?"

"He died, dipshit," said Callie fiercely.

"I'm sorry about your dog, Callie." Roman paused. "Asher. I have a favor to ask."

"Do we have to do this now, Roman?"

"Langford is in the koroka playoffs, and we have been having such a great year. Honestly, I am not sure if we could have gone this far without you. Well, without me...but without me with your help. In any case, my teammates are garbage. You get the idea."

"Glad I could help," said Asher unenthusiastically.

"The injections have been great! In fact, I have been such a fan that I have used the last of them up."

"All of them?"

"Yeah..." said Roman. "Yeah, I have used all of them."

"Good lord, Roman, are you insane? We don't know the long-term effects of the injections. Those were supposed to last you the rest of the year."

"It's fine, it's fine. It's more than fine. I feel great. I feel better than I ever have; I have performed better, my body is in peak condition! You are a miracle worker, Asher."

"It's great that they're working, but I'm going to guess the favor you're asking and my answer is—"

"Is that I need more," Roman interrupted. "A lot more."

"No, Roman. I don't want to be responsible when your body collapses."

"No, Asher, you listen. We have something great! You do this for me, and I will get you in good with Dr. Rafe's lab. Full access, no questions asked."

Asher shook his head. "I'm not interested. I already have a great lab here that I share with Nico."

"Fine. Money then. How much do you want?"

"I don't need money, Roman."

Roman moved aggressively close to Asher's face. Callie stepped forward defensively next to Asher. Roman stared at her and laughed. "You two are ridiculous. What do you want, Asher?"

Asher turned around to break the tension. He looked over Cloud's grave, lost in introspection. Roman sighed behind him, impatient for a response. There were plenty of things Asher wanted—good grades, the respect of his friends, Cloud to still be here for Callie, a dead Miasma.

Asher turned back around. "Ok, Roman. I'll help you out."

CHAPTER 20

hree weeks away from Langford, from the big city, from molecular genetics tests, school lunches, sneaking off to the lab, and parties with Nico. Three weeks of no Miasma, no Maurinkos, sheriff, bounty hunter, general, nor the demanding rich kids. Asher dipped a clean paintbrush into a tin can of lacquer. The scent of cut pine and fresh paint filled the air of his father's workshop. Five days had passed since he'd stepped off the train and onto Vanatian soil.

He applied long strokes of finish to his dad's wood table—a piece commissioned for the mayor's office. It felt good to be back, unburdened. But despite the refuge, he felt like a stranger in his town and his parents' home. He'd gained more knowledge and experiences in the past five months than he had in his entire life prior, yet everything in Vana stayed remarkably untouched by the passing of time. The people, the buildings—how could he change so much in just a few months, but a place full of variables change so little?

"You should speak with Gus," Asher's father said while focusing on the shelves of a cabinet.

"Callie's uncle? What would I say?" Asher continued brushing lacquer onto the finished pieces of furniture.

"Let him know that you and she have been representing Vana well."

"Seems a little extreme, don't you think? He isn't even from Vana. And Callie isn't about the limelight. I think she needs to be the one to talk these things over with her uncle."

"Perhaps," said Asher's father. "I know I'm proud of you. Doing well in school, making friends, saving the day."

Asher laughed. "Thanks, Dad, but it's not like that. If anything, it's the opposite. There's a bit of anti-Dyrian and anti-Vanatian sentiment growing in Riali."

"Hmm. Well, to be honest, I do hope you take that sheriff's advice. Your intelligence and knowledge are blessings; people will be looking to exploit them in whatever way they can. Even if that means making you out to be their scapegoat."

"Oh, I'm aware."

"Are you? You're a good person, Asher. You're quick to trust."

"There is nothing I do that I don't want to do."

"Sure, but have you stopped to ask yourself why you're wanting to do them?"

Asher's mother walked into the workshop with glasses of sweet tea. "How are you boys doing in here?"

Asher grabbed a glass and smiled. "Good, Mom. Just about finished this table and Dad's putting on the detail for that cabinet."

"Is this the project for Mayor Hegelson?"

"Yep," said Asher's dad as he cleaned off his hands and grabbed the other glass.

"Professor Fenske came by earlier while you two were working."

"What? Why didn't you come get me?"

"He wanted you to drop by his office later. I told him you and your father were busy."

"Mom, it could be important! Did he say what time?"

"It's not more important than you and your dad catching up. You can go and see him later, he said he would be available after sundown. He'll be in his lab. I believe he's been working on a project for Langford."

"That's interesting...did he say what the project was?"

"No, but he's been asking a lot of questions about you and the attacks."

Asher chugged his tea and slammed it down, the ice clinking against the drained glass.

"I gotta go. I'll be back later tonight."

Professor Rupert Fenske's lab was located beside Oakard Academy, a humble university but the most significant one in Vana. The professor taught regularly at the academy, as well as at some of the more advanced courses in Asher's high school. His lab was dimly lit and adorned with large shelves stocked with glass jars full of various specimens. Thin brass pipes crisscrossed the ceiling in an incoherent, jumbled pattern. Asher took a moment to pause in front of two large vats, studying the intricate lever system that siphoned chemicals through the brass tubing. He followed it with his eyes, but before he could find the end of the maze, he caught the attention of the professor.

He outstretched his arms for an embrace. "The son of Vana returns!"

Asher smiled. "Hi, Professor, how've you been?"

"Oh, staying busy."

"I can see that. What project are you working on now?"

The professor motioned for Asher to come closer. "Come, take a look, I think you'll find this interesting."

Asher walked over to Fenske's lab bench, which littered with beakers and books.

"I was sent samples of the toxin used in the recent terrorist attacks."

"Oh…" Asher trailed off. "What I was attacked with, Professor. It wasn't just a sedative. It was some sort of serum."

The professor didn't seem to notice Asher's hesitance. "Yes, I'm aware. The knockout gas was some sort of tranquilizer, ketamine derivative. But the…the 'death serum,' well, I was provided some blood samples from Riali."

"I based my makeshift antidote on the sedative…"

"I heard about your concoction. Quite ingenious. The death serum itself, however, needs the tranquilizer to operate in order to stop the heart."

"So…what have you found?" asked Asher, now leaning over the workbench.

"I have narrowed it down to a few possibilities. But first, Asher, please tell me. This past one, what did you experience?"

"I…" Asher went silent. He had no desire to relive that night. He knew the professor meant no harm and that this was for the betterment of science. He mustered up his thoughts and recounted his experience. "First,

I was able to counteract the effects of the sleeping agent by using a psychoactive derived from kane mushrooms. It's why I was conscious during the stadium attack as well." Asher walked over to shelves of various chemicals. "However, the death serum was different. My heart rate slowed, a numbness came over my body, and overwhelming synesthesia resulted. I thought I was going to die, Professor."

Fenske nodded. "I'm certain you were, Asher, had you not been so quick on your feet."

"I barely got it right. It was enough to keep me alive until help arrived. But even then, the drug was a fifty-fifty at best. I should have died," said Asher.

"Yet you survived, Asher. You outsmarted a madman," said the professor enthusiastically. A heavy silence lingered as he continued his tinkering. He worked at a more furious pace, tossing chemicals around wildly, titrating various substances from the brass tubes above him. Asher fidgeted with some glass tubes while watching him work.

"Professor, I've met some people in Riali. Powerful people. They want me to work for them."

"That's exciting. Do I know these people?"

"Some of them, perhaps, but they want me to keep our connection secret."

"How interesting," replied the professor. "And how is Mionaar these days?"

"You know Dr. Rafe?"

The professor laughed. "Yes, we've been colleagues of sorts over the years. He was once a prodigy, much like you. Don't talk so much anymore."

Asher passed some glassware the professor was struggling to reach. "Why not?"

"Just went our separate ways, I suppose. A few disagreements here and there. All scientific, of course. Has he managed to rope Redding into his schemes yet?"

"No. Not to my knowledge."

"Right. Well, no matter."

"Professor, the people have asked me to help them with...with..." Asher struggled to put it into words. "Well, with immortality."

"So ambitious! They certainly picked the right man for the job," Professor Fenke laughed, a twinkle in his eye.

"Yeah. I'm not sure if it's exactly the right thing to do. Infinite life for select people. They want to become gods."

"Gods? No, nonsense. They wouldn't become gods. Gods would never be so cowardly."

"Cowardly...because they hide? Or because they fear death?"

"They are cowardly because they fear what they do not have."

"I'm fairly certain they have everything."

The professor looked up from his work and stared into Asher's eyes. "They have many resources, Asher. They have infinite wealth to fill up their stomachs and mansions. Infinite intelligence to develop their plans and trinkets. Infinite men to build their empires. Infinite power to retain their influence. But of all those resources, there's only one that they are lacking."

"Yes?"

"Time! Time. They must adhere to the same twenty-four hours as you and I. No more, no less."

"I'm restricted, too, Professor. I know I could solve food shortages or maybe cure some horrible disease. But my life is limited. I want to save the world—I want to fix it all!"

"No, Asher, you have to make a choice. What do you want your life's work to be, your great accomplishment? How do you want to be remembered? Do you even want to pay the price that comes with being remembered at all? Rarely does being a great man equate to living a happy life."

"I don't know," said Asher, now pacing between the rows of glass jars and specimens. "It's all a dizzying thought. Maybe…maybe they're right. Maybe I should help them. Buy us all some time. At least it is a direction, progressing the evolution of man."

The professor returned to his work and continued to speak without looking back up at Asher. "Have you considered that the heavens themselves do not contain any form of agency?"

"I'm not sure I understand what you mean."

"I mean, all things have their place and purpose. But what if the gods are not silent observers or all-knowing creators but rather forces pressing upon our universe in the same manner in which we press ourselves upon the world."

"Is the fact that celestials might not have free will supposed to make me feel any better about my own powerlessness?"

"Not at all," said the professor. "It is to liberate you from the burden of purpose and meaning without detracting from your own importance."

Asher turned a bottle over to read its label. "I've been told we are creators designed in the image of creators. My purpose is to build, discover, contribute…I don't know, to do something that makes this world a slightly better place than I left it?"

Fenske looked up from his desk, his eyes peering over the rim of his glasses as he observed his former student. "You are not the cog, Asher. You are the product. In the end, what you do doesn't matter. What others think of you doesn't matter. Your self-worth cannot be measured by grades. Or wealth. Or how desired you are. Or any other worldly metric. No, your existence is proof of a machine divine. The heavens are an engine, infinitely spinning, and that great engine created you—a spirit full of passion and talent. Selfish agendas wish to dictate how you use those gifts, but I tell you this, you should live the life you want to live, not the one expected of you."

Asher looked in the professor's eyes, hesitating before formulating his thoughts. "But I don't know what I want, Professor. I'm just figuring it out as I go."

"That's good," said the professor, smiling. "And where has that gotten you so far?"

"Well, I've created a modified growth hormone, some hallucinogenic berries, and I'm helping my best friend hunt down a terrorist."

"Are those things you want to be doing, Asher, or things others have placed upon you?"

"Yes. Well, I don't know. I guess so. I was told by the sheriff that I should stop, that it would be dangerous to go after the terrorist."

"If you're not sure, then why bother with such a dangerous task?"

"You tell me, Professor, you're assisting in the investigation too."

"You're right, Asher. I suppose there's a curiosity in me that can't easily be satisfied." He turned back to his equipment before adding, "There's a chance I will be coming to Riali."

"What? At a time like this, who would ever want to go there?"

"They have resources that I don't. There's a lot at stake with this investigation. Mayor Hegelson has offered Vana's help. I need to offer my assistance in any way that I can."

Asher shook his head. "I don't think it would be wise. Miasma could be anyone and could come after you if you try to find him."

"Aha!" shouted the professor.

"What? What is it?" Asher ran over to the desk.

"Got it, I got it!" shouted the professor before picking up a glass beaker.

"Yes?"

He handed the beaker to Asher. "This confirms it. I know what Miasma has been using in these attacks."

"And?"

"Mandu root. It's a very rare species of plant, not native to Riali. Very difficult to cultivate as well. A peculiar choice for poison."

Asher held the beaker closer to his face. "Mandu root..." he whispered. He examined the black liquid as it sloshed around the vial, his eyes focused and his head spinning with new ideas.

"No magical berries this time?" asked Liam as the two strolled through the woods.

Asher laughed and looked down at the ground. "No, not this time. Fresh out. And for good now."

"Hmmph. Seemed pretty handy to have around."

"I'm working on something."

"You always are," Liam laughed. "So, you ready to go back to Langford?"

Asher shrugged. "Eh, I don't know."

"Seems more your speed over this place." Liam threw up his hands to gesture around the forest.

"Perhaps, but Vana has its charm."

They continued their hike up the nearest mountain, which was more of a large hill. "Do you get bored in Vana?" asked Asher.

"It's definitely been more boring without you, but I don't mind. I saw the life you're leading out there in Riali. That stuff just ain't for me. The trees, the dirt. It's where I belong. You know?"

"Yeah, I know. You've said it a hundred times. I guess I just don't see things that way."

"You enjoy the chaos?"

"To an extent...yeah, I guess I do. The people and the city. I'm living at the pinnacle of man's great achievements."

"You know, I never really pictured you as such a people person. Growing up...you were always just kind of that weird kid."

Asher laughed. "And you weren't?"

"Weird? Nah..." Liam shook his head. "Just the fat kid."

"Yeah, well...if it wasn't for you, I'm not sure I'd be alive today."

"Now you're just being dramatic."

"The day you dragged me out of the lake. It changed me," said Asher.

"A story for another time, Ashy," said Liam dismissively.

They reached the top of the hill and found a spot that overlooked the Vanatian valley. Liam pointed at a rustling of trees in the distance. "I think that's Drvo."

Asher squinted hard at the horizon before Drvo's massive form emerged above the canopy. "Oh, yep, that's him, alright."

Liam opened his canteen, took a sip, and handed it to Asher. "What makes Drvo, like, a living thing anyway?"

"What do you mean?"

"You know, like he's a pile of rocks. Does he eat? Are there other creatures like him?"

"Oh..." Asher thought for a moment. "Yeah. Well, he was gifted to Vana from the priests of Saint Mazraea."

"Yeah, yeah, I know that part of the story. But why don't they just make an entire army of Drvos or something? Is he the only one?"

Asher thought about it a bit longer as he watched Drvo dip his massive granite hands into a stream. "Only thing I remember is that the priests had ancient knowledge obtained from the gods when they created him. He was brought to Vana just after the fall of Cha'rik Kai."

"Think he was meant to be a weapon?" asked Liam.

"That would make sense, given the time period. Kai was rumored to have been a collector of the relics. The priests have never been a technologically savvy bunch. But perhaps with ancient knowledge, the resources they had at their disposal, and the existential threat the world had just faced, they were able to experiment and create Drvo."

"Hmm," said Liam. "Funny to think a creature born for war and destruction is what brought so much life back to this forest."

They sat in silence and watched as the canopy swayed to the steps of Drvo. Plumes of sprites burst forth with each step, temporarily displaced before settling back into a new place of rest.

"About those berries, Asher…"

"You're really on about those things, aren't you?" Asher teased.

"Nah, it's not like that, I'm just worried. What happens if you run into Miasma again?" Liam had a look of pained concern on his face.

Asher sighed and continued to stare out over the forest. "Don't worry about me, Liam. I can take care of myself now."

"You're going to go after him, aren't you?"

"I think so, Liam."

"Why? You got so much other good stuff happening around you, why waste it on something like this?"

"For Nico. For Callie. For these people…"

"These Maurinko people? You barely know them."

"What they want is what would be best for me."

"Money?"

"Not just money, but resources to do great things. They need my help, and my help will be rewarded. I need to show them what I can do, and then I'll have their trust, and I can go on to do whatever it is I could ever want to do. It might help things here in Vana, too."

"Pshh." Liam rolled his eyes. "I ain't worried about Vana."

"Maybe not, but if Dyrian trade is hurt, it affects the lumber industry, too."

"Well, you can do this for Nico, and you can do this for Callie, but for the love of God don't act like you're doing this for me or your family. I know your parents don't want anything to do with this, they just want what's best for you, Ashy. And so do I. I trust you know what's best."

"Yeah?"

"Yeah, I do. You're smart like that. I know you have a plan."

Asher was silent. Liam turned back to him. "You do have a plan, right?"

"More like an idea…"

CHAPTER 21

Asher walked into his empty dorm room. It was just as he had left it three weeks ago—a desk full of notes, a dusty bronze mirror against the wall, Nico's trash scattered across his side of the room. He plopped his suitcase on the bed and walked out into the hallway, where he was promptly and enthusiastically greeted by Felix. "Hey, Asher! How was Vana?"

"It was good. Nice to rest up back at home. How was your break? Did you head back to Kipos?"

"Not this time, thought I would hang back and enjoy the city. Not looking forward to getting back to the grind..."

"Definitely. Hey, Felix, have you seen Nico? It looks like he hasn't been in the dorm for some time."

"Yeah, he's back at his house. He's been acting really strange lately..."

"In what way?"

"Just...I don't know. He's either incredibly outgoing or incredibly shy. Like there's no in-between with him."

"Right...he's still coping with the loss and all."

"Understandable. I'm sure he could use a friend right now."

Asher smiled. "Yeah, I'm going to try and find him. I'm off to see Callie first, though."

"Oh, she's around. I saw her in the sanctuary earlier. She's been a little off too, hasn't spoken to me or just about anyone this entire break to my knowledge. She's probably in her dorm if you're looking for her."

"Ok great, thank you."

Asher went off through the maze of hallways and corridors until he reached the women's northeast dormitory. He knocked on Callie's door, which swung open to reveal a surprised Callie. "Asher!"

"Hey, Callie," Asher smiled meekly.

"Come in."

Asher stepped into the dorm and left the door cracked behind him. Her room was much cleaner than his; it smelled of warm candles and glowed beneath soft hanging lights above the beds. She sat down on the mattress and pointed him to a small wooden rocking chair beside her desk.

Asher broke the silence. "How were things back here?"

"They were alright. I helped watch over the animals, got paid a little bit for the work. Winter is really pretty here in Riali, they actually get some snowfall."

"That's great..." said Asher, a hint of concern in his eyes.

"How was Vana?" asked Callie.

"Nothing changed."

"Yeah, nothing ever does."

"People asked about you."

"Should I care?"

"You should, people care about you."

"They don't, but it's fine. I don't need you to pretend, Asher."

Asher laughed and shook his head. Her pessimism was unbelievable, but what did he expect?

"How's Nico been? Have you seen him?"

Callie averted her eyes. "A few times. He's been having parties at the manor almost every night. He's been going all out. He invited me the first night of break right after you left. I decided to go and check it out…" Her voice trailed off for a minute. "It felt like everyone was there. It was packed. People were drunk and tearing up his parents' place. He didn't even care. The few times I managed to find him, he was blackout drunk and surrounded by girls. I think he needed you here, Asher. He needs someone or something to get his mind off his parents."

Asher shrugged. "I don't know, sounds like typical Nico. Just Vacation-Nico blowing off steam."

"No," said Callie sternly. "It wasn't like anything I've seen. One night, I was bored and hadn't really hung out with anyone in a while, so I thought I'd go over and check up on him. He hadn't invited me or anything, but you know, I figured it'd be alright."

"And?"

"I get there, and it was like how it usually was at first. People everywhere, drunk, having a good time. Singing in the living room, the shy ones gorging themselves in the kitchen, monotonous drinking games out on the patio— the usual. I walked around to see if I could find Nico, I figured he was in his bedroom or something with some girls, but then I heard a bunch of yelling and cheering coming from the main hallway. I ran out and saw that some kid had knocked over a suit of armor. Just some random kid, I don't know him. He apologized to Nico profusely, but Nico wasn't having it. He *laid* into him, all about how people were being disrespectful to his parents' stuff, but then his expression changed."

"How so?"

"Yeah, it's hard to explain, but he went from angry to relieved. He told the kid it was alright and asked if he liked the armor. The kid said yeah, trying to be nice. Nico said, 'Ok, well, if you want it, you can have it.' The kid obviously didn't want it, but Nico insisted that he not only take it but try it on. At that point, the kid tried walking toward the exit. There was something terrifying in Nico's eyes, just the way he was talking to the kid, like..."

"What was he saying?" asked Asher.

"He kept telling the kid to put on the suit. Then he grabbed another suit off the wall and threw it down. He started picking up the pieces and putting them on himself. Everyone else was cheering at this point. The kid tried to run away, but that robot butler grabbed him. Nico told the butler to put the suit on the kid, and then the butler's extra arms started coming out from his back and placing the armor on the kid. The kid was completely frozen stiff, unable to move as he was held in place being dressed in the armor."

"God..." whispered Asher.

"Nico finished putting on his suit and grabbed a sword and waited for the butler to finish dressing the kid. Once the butler finished, he dropped the kid, and the kid buckled under the weight of the armor. Nico kept screaming for him to get up and pick up his shield and sword. The kid was practically crying at this point. The crowd was just... just..." Callie started to pull into herself.

"It's alright, it's not your fault, Callie," said Asher calmly.

"I know! I know it's not my fault. It's just...God, Asher, it was awful. He charged the kid, there wasn't even a fight or anything. The kid fell down after one hit, and Nico just started bashing him. Over and over again. It was like he was an animal, letting everything out on this poor kid. He kept going—to a point where the crowd wasn't even cheering anymore. It started to get quiet, and then it went dead silent. Just the sound of his sword bashing the kid's helmet and ribcage. He didn't stop until he was exhausted." Callie paused. "Then the robot picked the kid up. Armor and all. Dragged him outside the house."

"What did Nico do then?"

"Took off the armor, and I think he went back to his bedroom after that, I don't know, I ran out. Haven't really been in the mood to talk to anyone since."

A silence lingered between them. "You should come with me to check on him tomorrow morning," Asher said.

Callie looked up at Asher. "I'd rather not."

"I think he'd want to see you. Besides, I have some news for both of you."

"Oh? What's that?"

"Professor Fenske and I spoke back at his lab. I think we have a lead on Miasma. And he might be headed to Riali."

Nico had spent his break locked up in the Catalano manor. By the time Asher returned to Langford, the stories of Nico's parties had become the stuff of campus legend. He had a buggy drop him and Callie off at the manor's front gate, its looming steps a testament to the success behind the Catalano name. He hit a buzzer beside the door. The massive doors swung open, and they were greeted by the well-dressed Hanley.

"Hello, Mr. Auden. Miss Saint."

"It's Callie," she responded coldly.

"Hi, Hanley. How are you?" asked Asher.

"Wonderful," said the butler in the driest of tones.

Asher peered into the house, unable to see much in the enormous, dimly lit corridors. "Is Nico here? I haven't seen him at school yet."

"Right this way. Apologies for the mess, I am still working on tidying up."

Asher and Callie dodged empty bottles and vomit landmines that caked the Vanatian wood flooring as Hanley took them up a flight of stairs to Nico's room. Hanley rapped on the closed door. "Master Nicholas, you have company here to see you. An Asher Auden and a Callendra Saint."

No answer. Asher took a step forward and knocked aggressively. Hanley turned toward the two of them. "Well, I'll leave you to it. There are other guests still on the floor of the dining room. I think it's best I begin to wake them."

They could hear a faint rustling on the other side of the door. Callie joined Asher in banging on the door until Hanley was out of the way. She then flung it open without waiting for Nico's permission.

His massive bedroom was in complete disarray. Sunlight poured through large windows over piles of books, scrap metal, liquor bottles, and cigarette butts.

Nico shot up straight out of bed, completely naked, a comforter just barely covering his torso and one leg. His hair was disheveled, and his face befuddled. Callie averted her eyes.

"Hanley, what are you doing? You can't just barge into my room!"

Asher waved slyly at Nico. "Uhh, it's us, Nico. Hanley's downstairs."

Nico laughed, groaned, and then fell back into bed. "Sorry about that, guys."

Asher laughed. "You're fine."

Callie slowly peeked through her hands to make sure Nico was decent.

One of Nico's arms blindly flailed around his nightstand, clearly in search of something. His hand fell upon a large switch that he slapped at aggressively. At once, several drones lifted from the corners of the room and began to perform various tasks. Lights were flicked on, trash was cleaned up, one of them dropped a robe across Nico that he proceeded to slip on. Another drone fetched him coffee. Asher counted roughly seven drones in total.

"Holy cow! Nico! You've been busy."

Nico took a sip of coffee and looked up at the whirling chaos above. "Yep. Yeah, these babies are my pride and joy. Just prototypes, but I plan to put them in production at CAT Robotics later this year if I get approval from the board."

"That's awesome news!"

"I've been able to improve their reaction time and inter-copter communication. Their ability to interact with each other is leading to all kinds of novel uses. Check this out."

Nico set down his coffee and slipped on a thick gauntlet of leather and wires. He waved the gauntlet in various gestures, and the drones danced in syncopation with his movement. His free hand pushed several buttons on the back of the glove, causing the drones to take on various formations and patterns. They began to circle over his head like a halo of whirring steel.

Asher shook his head in disbelief. "Incredible."

Nico pointed the glove at a nearby coffee pot. The drone picked up the pot and began slowly pouring a cup of coffee. His fingers flailed in complex patterns as the drone set down the pot, picked up the cup, and flew it over to Asher, who grabbed the cup and tugged slightly to draw the drone inward. He could see the copter self-correct instantaneously.

The drone's claws released the cup. The steam crept up Asher's upper lip and nostrils as he slowly took a sip. "And here I thought you were up to no good!"

Nico smiled and turned to Callie. "Would you like a cup as well?"

"No, thank you. Nico, we need to talk."

Nico sat down on his bed, pressed a few more buttons on the glove, and watched as the drone settled back down. "Alright, yeah. Come take a seat." He motioned over to a table pressed against a window.

Asher walked over and grabbed a desk seat. Callie sat on the table, the morning light reflecting off her auburn hair. Nico took off the glove and walked to his closet. "What's going on? If it's an intervention, then—"

"No, no," Asher cut him off. "It's not about that."

Callie butted in. "Well, I certainly think it's a good topic for discussion!"

"Not…not now." Asher glanced over at her; she rolled her eyes and focused on the clutter at the desk.

"I spoke with my old biology professor back in Vana. Professor Rupert Fenske. Sheriff Price sent him samples of the Miasma's sleep toxin to analyze."

Nico walked into his closet. "I'm listening."

"The toxin had a high concentration of a chemical that the professor believes is derived from mandu root."

"Mandu root? I've never heard of it."

"Exactly. It's rare and incredibly difficult to find."

Nico emerged from the closet, fully dressed. His face was stern. "Then there can't be much of a market for it in Riali. We might be able to find out who sells it."

Asher shrugged. "Maybe, but I doubt we'll find a seller in Riali. It's rarely used in any modern form of medicine. And even if it was, the amount they would need to create would be more than you could purchase at your local herb shop."

Nico turned back to Asher. "Did your professor tell you where the root comes from?"

Asher shrugged. "He didn't know. All he said was that it's rare, difficult to cultivate, and grows in colder climates."

Nico walked toward the door. "Once we figure out where it comes from, I can figure out who supplies it. When we figure out who supplies it, we will find Miasma."

Asher and Callie smiled at each other and followed Nico out the door.

CHAPTER 22

A sher stayed after class to speak with Professor Redding. His office was its typical storm of papers, the walls covered in half-finished, chalked equations. The two discussed the most recent class before Asher brought up what was on his mind.

"Professor, I've been looking more into the neuro suppressant used in the Miasma attacks."

Redding's face became stern. "Asher. You know you have to leave this alone. The sheriff asked you to stay away. Let him handle the situation."

"I know, I know…but hear me out." Asher shifted his weight as he prepared to explain. "I worked with Professor Fenske on deconstructing the death serum over our winter break, and we think we might have isolated an important compound. It acts similarly to the tranquilizer used in Miasma's gas, but it's extremely concentrated and much stronger. What do you know about mandu root?"

"Mandu root? That doesn't seem right," said Redding. "That is an incredibly difficult compound to synthesize. You would need a large quantity of diethyl ether to even begin making it soluble, and even then, there is only a handful of people in all of Khamara with the skills to prepare it properly. That would take extensive knowledge. No, we are most likely looking at something more of—"

"But Professor, if you don't mind me asking, what are you using in the tranquilizers used for the sanctuary? A tranquilizer capable of putting down an Ere must use something more powerful than standard medical aesthetics?"

The professor laughed. "That's…a very apt deduction. Yes, we do use trace amounts of it to boost our own formula, it helps with the larger animals. But mandu is a highly controlled and very expensive substance; any purchases I make have to go through the university. And the tranquilizer I make for Mara uses a ketamine derivative alongside the mandu root. Honestly, Asher, you need to drop this hunt before you wind up in a Riali prison or worse."

Asher sighed. "I understand. But can you at least tell me more about mandu? Is it something that can be grown in Riali?"

Redding rolled his eyes. "No, it's nearly impossible to cultivate, and any attempts to use an artificial environment generally result in poor yield and efficacy. It must be found in the wild, usually in cold mountainous regions. Pretty far from any climate around Riali."

"Saint Mazraea?"

"Yes, actually. Elurra a bit, too. But mandu has been used in various spiritual rituals, so the Hilezkorra in Saint Mazraea are known to value and harness the plant. The Ajke priestesses in Elurra are known to use it in animal rituals as well. In small quantities, it can cause certain neurological sensations. But, like I said, it is very difficult to distill into a solution."

"And the death serum? Do you think the serum used on me and the others also contained the mandu root?"

The professor's face looked pained. "I don't approve of where this conversation is headed. I don't know much about Miasma's death serum, and if I did, I would not be able to disclose that information to you." He paused. "I do have a question for you, though, Asher."

"Yes?" said Asher enthusiastically.

"How did you stay conscious during Miasma's gas attacks?"

Asher searched his words carefully, "I had taken a stimulant, I shared this information with the sheriff."

"What kind of stimulant did you use? One with psychoactive properties, I presume?"

"Yes, it was from kane mushrooms. It was just meant for fun."

"That's very interesting. Because, you see, I was poisoned by something very similar to kane mushrooms, and you figured out how to counteract the effects very quickly when I was poisoned. However, kane mushrooms do not contain a stimulant."

"Professor..." said Asher desperately.

"Tell me about the berries, Asher." The professor's eyes narrowed in on Asher.

Asher fumbled for words before he let it spill out. "I spliced the psychoactive gene from kane mushrooms into sussberries. I found that the psychoactive element of the mushrooms increases the stimulant from the berries quite significantly. But it wasn't me who made that cake, someone tried to frame me."

Professor Redding nodded, "I believe you, Asher. I do. But you must realize by now that the knowledge you possess is both incredible and terrifying."

"I never meant to hurt anyone," Asher pleaded.

"Of course not, but you did. Asher, you have such a bright future ahead of you. If you allow me, I can help guide you, and we can truly make a positive difference in this world. Not just making trendy drugs for your friends."

"I appreciate it, Professor, and yes, I could greatly use the guidance."

"Good," said Redding. "Let's start with you not chasing after Miasma, understood?"

Asher nodded. "I understand, Professor."

Callie sat up on a copper countertop, her legs swinging beneath. The lab made her uncomfortable; it was a cold place. "What are you working on anyway, Asher?"

"A new project."

"It is apparently a secret. He's codenamed it 'Cirrus-C,'" said Nico.

"Oh good," said Callie. "More secrets."

Asher went back to work. "It's not a secret, it's just...I'm not sure if it's going to work. It's a little ambitious and would easily be my greatest accomplishment to date, so I'd rather not say and get anyone's hopes up."

Callie shrugged, losing interest. Nico turned to Asher. "What did Professor Redding have to say?"

"About the toxin?"

"Yeah." Nico sounded impatient.

Asher turned back to his work. "He confirmed that Saint Mazraea cultivates mandu root. He also mentioned that it's a neurological agent commonly used in some of the Hilezkorra rituals."

"Wait..." Nico stopped his tinkering. "Which rituals?"

"I'm not sure. What rituals are there?"

"Well, the fact that it is a neurological agent makes me think they might be using it in the illumination rituals."

Asher's eyebrows raised. "What are the illumination rituals?"

"I really don't know much about them," said Nico. "Only a small sect of cardinals in the upper echelons of the Hilezkorra church partake. Them, and the Maurinkos, of course."

Callie stepped in. "And what happens during these rituals?"

"Honestly, all I have heard is rumors. It is a type of sacrificial fertility ritual. It has something to do with rebirth and immortality. I know it involves drinking something out of a supposed relic. It is usually reserved for the elders."

Callie's face was horrified. "What the hell are you rich, self-righteous pricks doing?"

Nico squinted. "You realize that the Maurinkos are the biggest contributors to the Hilezkorra church in the world, right? There is literally no reason why any member of the Hilezkorra order would want to attack Maurinkos or any high-status Rialian. If anything, they would go after predominantly heathenistic religions and cultures like in Elurra or Dyria."

"Not if you're drugging people in *fertility* rituals!" shouted Callie. "And what exactly are you sacrificing?"

"No one gets to that point without consent, you are thinking too much into this," said Nico defensively.

Asher put his hands up to stop the bickering. "We're not here to accuse anyone. We know the victims have largely been members of the Maurinkos. If you don't think it's a good lead, we can drop it."

Callie hopped off the desk and started heading for the door.

"No," said Nico. "No, you might be on to something. There has been a trade deal being discussed for over a year now between Riali and Saint Mazraea. I don't know the specifics at the moment, but I know it is something that has been in the works for a while."

Callie stopped and turned back around. "Who do you know that has access to the Hilezkorra offices in the Citadel?"

Nico looked up at Asher, who nodded, then turned back to Callie. "There's a church service next Sunday to celebrate the coming solstice. How are you with church?"

A door slammed, and the sounds of heavy footsteps resounded throughout the outside hallway. Callie's ears perked up, bringing the group's conversation to a quick halt. She stood still beside the door, listening to the other side, then immediately slammed off the lights.

"What are you doing?" Nico asked.

"Shhh! I heard Professor Fenske's name."

Asher and Nico crept closer to the door.

"I recognize one of the voices; I think it's Redding," Asher whispered.

Callie cracked the door open quietly.

The three held their breath and pressed closer.

Nico whispered, "The other voice, that's Dr. Rafe."

"And why does Rupert Fenske have samples of Miasma's concoctions again?" The voice was the distinct, smug tone of Dr. Rafe.

"We've been over this, Mionaar," said Redding. "Mayor Hegelson offered to help Riali with the investigation in whatever fashion. With all the accusations being levied against Vana and Dyria, the Mayor insisted that Riali send copies of the toxin for diagnosis."

"They think we can't handle our own diagnostics?"

"They're pretty proud of their scientific achievements."

"Oh please, one kid invents potent manure and now they're the forefront of scientific knowledge? Ridiculous." Rafe began to pace back and forth.

"You're certain Auden said the toxins were derived from mandu root?"

"Yes, that's what he said."

"Who else knows?"

"No one to my knowledge. But Fenske has been working on a cure. He will be in town within the week."

"Why am I just now finding out about this? Has no one been in contact with me or General Volkov?"

"I imagine he's going straight to Sheriff Price."

"Price? Ugh, the arrogance."

The sound of a distant door swung open.

"Ok, Redding, let's see what you got."

The door slammed closed.

Asher, Callie, and Nico sat in silence.

Callie whispered, "Nico, do you still have the skeleton key?"

"Yeah, why?"

"Because we need to get into Redding's office."

Asher protested, "What? No!"

"What do you mean no?" said Callie. "You heard their conversation. They didn't want you finding out about the toxins."

"I agree," said Nico, "I think we need to check it out."

"I've been in Redding's office a hundred times, there's nothing to find in there."

"Yeah, but when was the last time you were in his personal lab?" asked Callie.

"They're right next to each other, I've been in before."

Nico put his hand on Asher's shoulder. "Callie and I have no idea what we'd be looking at in that room. We need you in on this. Just like you said earlier, we're not accusing anyone of anything, we just need the facts."

Asher pressed his lips; he wanted to swallow his words. "Ok fine. We need to make it quick. If someone else finds us snooping around his office, they could assume we're tampering with the investigation. We already have enough heat as it is."

Callie and Nico nodded in agreement. Callie slowly closed the door and locked it, careful to be as quiet as possible.

The three waited in silence for half an hour before they heard Redding's lab door open and the men walk away. Asher counted down from sixty seconds, and then the three crept out as quietly as possible. They got to Redding's door, and Nico reached into his satchel and pulled out the large mechanical skeleton key. Its circular shape engulfed the lock as the sounds of pins and gears ground under its shiny, shield-like exterior.

The door opened with a pop, and they quickly and quietly entered the room. Callie was about to flick on the lights when Asher grabbed her hand. "No!" he hushed. "There could be security." He turned to Nico. "Can you pull out one of the drones?"

Nico let three drones loose so that they encircled the top of the lab, pouring light down from below. He handed Asher another drone to use as a flashlight. "It's not much," he whispered, "but that should do the trick."

Callie stood guard by the door as Asher made his way around the room, investigating the different vials and containers.

A large vat of purple liquid was titrating in the corner. Nico stared at it. "This looks like the tranquilizer that Miasma uses."

"Doesn't mean anything, he makes that same color liquid for Mara in the sanctuary. She's always in need of it," Callie whispered from across the room.

"Right..." Nico said to himself.

Asher wandered to a corner, looking over a series of mechanical containers. "What the...? Hey, Nico, get over here."

Nico rushed over, careful to keep his steps quiet. "What are these things?"

He picked up a silver, cylindrical tube with a series of small spouts on the outside. He fiddled with the capsule. "It looks like—"

A loud crack and the device opened. "There we go," he said. "It looks like a dispensing mechanism. Similar to the kind we keep in the domed heads of the new Vanguard robots. But it's been tampered with, ours usually just dispenses flame. There's a series of tubes here that lead out to various spouts. There's another area here to power the capsule that attaches to these miniature hydraulics that pump whatever is inside of it out."

Asher took a step closer. "And what's this here in the center?"

"I'm not sure." Nico shrugged.

Callie walked over and watched over their shoulders. "It looks like some kind of vial. The liquid is black.

Asher...I've seen this." Callie leaned in. "This looks like the serum Miasma used on you."

Asher plucked the tube from the capsule.

"Careful!" said Nico. "It's not powered, but I don't know what could set this thing off."

Asher examined the liquid. "Impossible."

Nico and Callie watched him. "What's impossible?" whispered Nico.

"The death serum," said Asher holding the tube up to the light of a hovering copter. "They found a way to aerosolize it."

CHAPTER 23

Every pew was filled. Asher, Callie, and Nico sat near the back, their eyes scanning over the congregation. Familiar faces populated the dense crowd. Felix waved to the group from a few rows up, but otherwise, their presence had gone unnoticed.

Asher kept his eyes on the choir. Autumn was in the second row, flanked by Kiara and Avee, her long, dark hair contrasting against a bright white dress. A bell sounded, and the congregation hushed. Sister Lilly came out from behind the altar, swinging a chained canister of incense from left to right as she walked up the aisle. The choir sang a hymn as the incense filled the room and Father Bianok approached the podium. The choir finished, but the heavenly sound continued to reverberate off the stone walls and stained-glass windows.

"I think this is our best opportunity," said Callie in a whisper. "No one will notice if we sneak out."

Father Bianok began to launch into his opening prayer, and the congregation bowed their heads in reverence.

Asher nodded. "Ok, let's go."

The three stood up and walked up a side aisle, careful not to cause any disturbance. Asher cracked the back door and was greeted by an imposing figure. "Roman!" he said, surprised, pushing his heel into the door to stop Nico and Callie from getting through. Nico immediately let go of the door and slunk back into the atrium before Roman could see them.

"Asher," said Roman in a low, grumbling voice. "Why are you not watching the sermon?"

"Bathroom. Just headed to the bathroom. And…you?"

"I was just headed in. I was helping my dad with some ushering duties."

Roman moved out of the way and waved Asher in toward the foyer. He shut the door behind the two of them.

"Asher, how is our little project coming along? First game of the playoffs is next week…"

"Actually, I'm really glad I ran into you." Asher lowered his voice. "I finished the batch last night."

"Batch?"

"It should get you through the finals and then some. And—the best part—I was able to make it to your specifications."

"So the effects will last longer?"

"Yes. They'll last longer, you'll think sharper, move faster. Everything is amplified. But I don't think I need to remind you how dangerous this can be."

"Have you tested it? Do you know if it works?"

"Only in animals. I did a few trial runs while I was in Vana. There's only one drawback."

"Ok?"

"I used a myostatin knockout to help increase the muscle mass. I was having a hard time distributing it evenly, so

I used a concentration made from the berries. You should see an even distribution of muscle mass increase, but it comes with some slight neurological side-effects."

Laughing so hard that Asher had to hush him, Roman wiped away a tear. "Oh, so you are telling me I will trip out while playing?"

"Come on, people will hear you. And no. Well...sort of. You will experience a temporary high, but it's very brief. Maybe an hour max."

"An hour? How am I supposed to play under those conditions?"

"Because the somatic portion is twice as potent as what I have given you previously. All animal subjects gained fifty percent more body mass and nearly two and a half times their normal strength."

"Whoa. That is impossible. How long did it last?"

"To be honest, I only had a few days to test the drug in Vana. By the time I left, the animals still retained their somatic advantages. You, of course, have a higher metabolism and..."

"The effects didn't wear off?" Roman asked, cutting off Asher.

"I didn't say that. I said the effects just lasted longer than I could observe. Honestly, we need more time to study the pharmacokinetics—"

"No," said Roman loudly. "It will be fine. If they didn't die and they saw those kinds of improvements, I am fine for a little extra fun the night before a game."

"I would advise taking one shot at least twenty-four hours before the game. Let's see how this first one goes for you, and if you feel you want to increase or decrease the dose, we can do that accordingly."

"I want all of it."

"I understand, you can have all of it, I'm just saying."

"Come by my dorm room tonight, I will pay you in full."

"Ok, ok, sounds good," said Asher. "Now, seriously, I really got to pee."

"Sure," said Roman. "Good to have you back, Asher." He gave Asher a strong pat on the shoulder and then pushed him out of the way as he walked into the atrium.

Nico and Callie exited from a side door so as not to raise Roman's suspicions, walked through the Citadel's hallways, and into the back offices.

"This one should be Bianok's," said Nico, testing the doors.

Callie looked around the hallway. "You're good."

He used the skeleton key, and they entered the office. It was cold and dimly lit by brass lamps. The walls were lined with bookshelves and statues of angelic creatures. A typewriter on the desk poked out from a mound of papers, and a brass bird cage hung in the back. Nico stared at the cage and watched as a sickly and decrepit cardinal stood perfectly still inside.

"We need to find a shipping ledger," Callie said, locking the door behind them. "It will tell us which docks Saint Mazraea is using in the Rialian Bay."

Nico tapped on the cage. The bird was unfazed by the disturbance. "Creepy," he murmured before walking toward the desk. "I will take a look over here, you check out those filing cabinets."

He used the skeleton key to open a few more drawers. He found keys, pocket watches, a small vile of green gems, a pistol, and more papers and books.

"Anything?" Callie called from across the room.

"No, nothing yet." He grabbed a stack of papers and began reading through the transcripts.

The doorknob turned. Callie stared wide-eyed at Nico. The two scanned the room for a place to hide as the door unlocked and swung open.

Callie ran over and stood beside Nico at the desk; the hooded figure looked up.

"Oh, hey guys!" a sweet, playful voice said from underneath the hood. Lilly dropped the hood and cheerfully beamed at both Nico and Callie. "What are you up to?"

"Ummm...nothing. Just looking to take a break from the service. It was becoming a little tedious, you know?" Nico's voice was slowly regaining its customary bravado.

"Oh, I see..." said Lilly, giving a sly smile. "You're not the first I've seen getting worked up on Sunday." She winked at Callie.

"Not like that!" Callie protested. Nico rolled his eyes at her inability to play along.

Lilly walked over to Callie. "I don't believe we've met. I'm Sister Lilly." She stuck out her dainty hand.

"Callie."

Lilly's skin was moon-pale, and her face didn't have a single blemish in sight. Heavy black makeup outlined bright blue eyes and contrasted against silvery hair. Callie noticed her hands looked to be scarred. Lilly withdrew her hand quickly before asking, "Callie, are you the one with the fox that Miasma killed?"

"His name was Cloud."

"Cute. You should have brought his body back to me. I would have loved to have met him."

"Why?"

"To make him alive again! I graduated top of class; that's why I was chosen to disciple under Father Bianok."

Callie looked over at Nico, perplexed.

"Necromancy," he said.

"Necromancy?" asked Callie in curious disgust.

"Reanimation!" Lilly playfully narrowed her eyes at Nico. "But yes, I could have made him as good as new."

"Thank you, Sister, but it's ok. Animals die. It happens."

"Well, I would love the practice. Let me know the next time another one of your pets dies!" Her face lit up at the thought and gesture.

"Thanks," said Callie plainly. "I'll be sure to remember that one."

A brief, awkward silence fell on the room before Nico chimed in with, "So what are you doing in the office? Would you like us to leave?"

Lilly paused before making her excuse, "I needed something for the service."

"Ah," said Nico moving toward the door, "fair enough, well, we will get out of your way then."

"Nuhuhh," said Lilly, holding up a finger to stop Nico. "How did *you* get in here?"

"The door was unlocked," Callie blurted out.

"No," said Lilly. "No, it was not." She walked up to Nico and began to examine his face closely. Nico slowly tilted his head to one side and smiled charmingly.

"Nico and I know a little about each other," Lilly said to Callie while maintaining eye contact with Nico. "He and I are part of a super-secret club." She began to run her hands down Nico's arms. "Personally, I find secrets kind of fun! You know someone's your friend when they trust you with information only the two of you keep." Her hands continued to wander seductively down Nico's side.

"Some secrets are well known. For instance, Nicholas here. He's clever. But I bet Callie knows that, too. You're so clever that you can build about anything. Just like your dad."

Nico's smile dropped.

"And you two. Callie has made it clear that you aren't here for the romance."

"I..." Callie tried to explain herself, but Lilly ignored her and grabbed the skeleton key. Nico grabbed at it at the same time.

"Oh my, is this yours, Nico?"

"What do you want, Lilly?" asked Nico sternly.

Her face stopped smiling. "I want to know why you are here." Her voice was cold and direct.

"Saint Mazraea has been importing mandu root to Riali. We want to know who has been making the purchases."

Lilly's smile grew wide again. "Well, why didn't you just ask! No need to be snooping!"

Nico took a deep breath and looked over at Callie, who was standing as if she were about to pounce. Lilly continued, "I'll trust you with a secret, but first, you have to trust me with one."

Nico smiled. "Of course, my mind is your vault."

"How did you get in here?"

Nico turned his head away as if to weigh the pros and cons of telling Lilly. He sighed and looked down at the key they both held. "This is a skeleton key."

"Good name."

"Yes. It can open any door or lock."

"Show me! Show me on that lock over there." She pointed to the bookshelf beside Callie. Callie turned around in confusion.

"Which lock?" said Nico.

"Over here." Lilly walked over and slid across a small wooden panel that had been on the side of the shelf.

"Umm…ok, sure." Nico grabbed the skeleton and placed it over the lock. He hesitated a minute. "You will let us know who is importing the mandu root if I do this, right?"

Lilly rolled her eyes. "Yes, Nico."

He began to fidget with the key as Callie watched Lilly walk behind the priest's desk and pocket something. She smiled at Callie and then turned her attention back to Nico. Various cogs began to spin on the outside of the key's shield. The clacking of grinding gears continued as it struggled. Lilly kept up her wide smile but gave a skeptical side-eye to Nico.

"Just be patient," he whispered. A few more seconds of mechanical whirring continued before the shelf finally clicked open. Lilly walked over, cracked it open, and reached inside. Nico and Callie both attempted to peek inside, but Lilly shooed them away playfully.

"Fascinating," said Lilly. "You really are quite the clever boy."

Nico sighed. "Ok, so now you tell me who's been making the mandu root purchases?"

"Sure," said Lilly. "Mandu root is found in the outskirts of Mazraea, it is very difficult to cultivate, but it is used quite routinely in various Hilezkorra rituals."

"I am aware of that much," said Nico annoyed. "But who else is purchasing it outside of the Citadel?"

"Well," said Lilly, mischievously rolling her eyes. "I don't have an exact answer."

Callie huffed in frustration. "Come on, Nico, this isn't going anywhere."

"But I can tell you this," she said, walking toward him. "There is a big shipment from Saint Mazraea coming in this weekend, and there is a chance your mandu root is on board. Saint Mazraea doesn't have too many exports, so there should really only be one or two ships. I suggest getting to the docks around sunrise, and you will be able to spot their buyers assisting with the offloading."

Nico smiled. "Thank you, Sister. I knew I could trust you."

"You're welcome," she said, her fingers now running through his hair. "But there is one more thing I need from you, Nicholas."

"I think that's enough favors today," said Callie.

Lilly did not avert her gaze but stared directly at Nico. "I need that key."

"What?" said Callie incredulously. "No. Nico, don't. We won't tell Father Bianok you were here, and you do the same, and then we're even."

Nico handed her the key. "It is ok, Callie, I can make another one."

"That's right!" said Lilly, smiling. "Forever the smartest in the room, Nicholas." She turned back around and stopped short of the door. "You see, now we are our own secret club." She looked over at Callie. "It's been a pleasure to finally meet you, Callendra."

CHAPTER 24

It was still dark out when pounding began at the door. Callie's voice came faintly through the dorm room walls. "Come on, get up!"

Asher rolled over, putting the pillow over his ears. Nico groaned and slid out of bed, opening the door.

"Ew, gross," said Callie. "Put on a shirt."

Nico looked down deliriously. "Yeah..."

Callie flicked on the lights and began throwing books at Asher on the bed.

"Ow, geez, ok. I'm up, I'm up."

"You were supposed to meet me in the lobby fifteen minutes ago!"

"Ahh..." creaked Nico. "Ok yeah, I am ready, let's do this."

As the sun rose over the eastern coast, the group departed toward the docks. "You know," said Asher, "all this time in Riali, and I've never made a stop to see the beach."

"It is not much of a beach," said Nico. "Cold, crowded, and most of the sand is imported."

"I don't know," said Callie. "This sunrise is a sight."

"Hey," said Asher, turning to Nico. "What was that thing you got called in for last night? I was just making some good progress on the Cirrus-C project when you left."

"Oh, that. There was a break-in at CAT Robotics over the weekend."

"What?" asked Callie, shocked. "What was stolen?"

"Not much," said Nico. "Nothing of great cost, at least."

"So then did they catch the guy?" asked Asher.

"Not quite. Someone stole six of the new CAT Vanguard robots. You know, the ones I presented at the Maurinko meeting."

"But that's military equipment," said Asher.

"It is not a big deal; we have about a hundred of them at this point. But yeah, apparently, Sheriff Price discovered one of them at the top of Riali Central Station."

"Whoa! Was it armed?" asked Asher.

"No, that is the odd thing," said Nico. "Sheriff Price didn't tell me what was in the head, but I know it didn't have the flames or explosive devices that are typically installed. Whoever operated it barely knew how to make it work, they got the coordinates plugged in correctly so that it could crawl, but that part is relatively easy. Any bonehead could do it."

Asher was deep in thought. "Is it possible to modify it with a different weapon?"

"Yeah, I suppose so. I mean, I did put dinner plates in thei—"

"Look!" Callie shouted.

Out in the distance, a fleet of ships began to swarm the harbor.

"Whose are those?" asked Nico.

Callie made out the faint violet and black of the flags. "Those are Dyrian warships."

Samira Raol stepped off the ship and walked with purpose, an entourage of scruffy, ex-pirate merchants trailing behind her. Her jet-black hair was pinned back with a gold headband, and she was dressed in red leather and adorned with an armory of guns, knives, and a rapier, all protected by the intricate gold armor of an established general.

She pushed aside a young Riali deckhand, unfazed by his attempt to assist with docking the ship, and made a beeline for the customs office. She flung open the doors of the office with a violent force.

"Where the fuck is Crann?"

Nervous onlookers pointed to a pair of large, gaudy doors. Samira and her entourage barged into the office. A short, pudgy man looked up from his desk with cold indifference. "Ah yes, I was told to expect a Dyrian shipment today."

"Check out the berries on this guy," she said, pointing to an unamused Mr. Crann, her crew laughing along. Security began to filter into the room behind Mr. Crann, rifles at their ready.

"And what can I do for you today, Ms. Raol?"

"You can start by telling me why the fuck your city is demanding twenty percent tariffs on all Dyrian imports."

"These are simply measures put into place to account for our losses due to the recent uptick in piracy and terrorism."

"You have targeted Dyria and Dyria alone. We are not responsible for any of these attacks."

"Oh, I beg to differ, I am aware of who your father is—"

"If you knew my father, then you would know he always thought the Crann Company ships were the most fun to rob. He said their men would cry and beg for their lives like a bunch of weak bitches. Cowards of the sea."

"So, you *have* committed piracy toward our company!"

"Don't play dumb, Crann. You and I both know that Dyria and the Hainlyal have been legitimate since the treaty. There's no need for piracy anymore, our islands are stronger than ever."

"Then it should not be too hard for you to pay the tariffs."

Samira turned to her second in command. "Order the harbor blockade. Let's show them what actual pirates look like."

Mr. Crann stood up from his desk. "A blockade would be an act of war, Ms. Raol. That would not be wise."

"Not an act of war, Mr. Crann, just a taste of what you're costing my company with these tariffs. Which, by the way, we will no longer be paying."

"Let me get this straight. You came all this way from Dyria to...*not* get paid? Surely you have some goods to sell?"

"Oh, and we'll sell them. I also saw a few ships from Mazraea out there coming in on the horizon. It would be a pity if they lost their cargo."

"Is that a threat?" asked a riled Mr. Crann, his security raising their rifles.

Samira stared him down intensely before turning to another member of her crew. The sailor nodded and presented a sack of gold coins to Mr. Crann's guards.

"Good," said Mr. Crann. "A bit crude to use a sack for your money, but I suppose a woman always needs her purse."

Samira grabbed a coin and flicked it at one of the guards. "You want my money? Riali, *the capital*, do you all want my money?" She slung another coin at a different guard. Mr. Crann let out a smug smile as he watched the antics. Samira tightened the sack back up and looked directly into his eyes. "Here's my FUCKING MONEY!" She swung the sack of gold and bashed it into Mr. Crann's face.

At the motion, her sailors moved quickly to disarm the guards and pinned them against the walls. Samira swung the bag again, this time breaking Mr. Crann's nose and sending a fountain of blood across his desk. She continued to beat him with the sack of coins, swinging mercilessly and without any fear of consequence. Blood soaked into the papers and documents covering his desk. Samira upended the sack and poured the gold coins over his unconscious body before walking out of the office.

At the door, she turned back to the frightened room of workers.

"There will be no more imports today at the harbor. By order of Samira Raol, Dyria has control of the docks for the next twenty-four hours. Once we have finished unloading, we will leave this pig shit of a city and you can all pray to your cockless gods that you never see my face again."

Asher, Nico, and Callie looked on as the Dyrian ships took up a blockade position around Riali's harbor. "What is going on?" asked Callie.

"I'm not sure," said Nico. "This looks like an act of aggression from Dyria."

"Regardless, it's going to be a lot harder to find the Saint Mazraea shipment with this mess going on."

"Maybe we don't need to find out where they are offloading."

"Then what's the plan?" asked Callie.

"If we can get to the ledgers, we can see if they are importing mandu root—and who is requesting it. Once we have that information, we might be able to figure out where it is going."

They agreed, and the group headed toward the customs station, arriving just a few minutes later. Inside, it looked like a war room, with armed soldiers hanging around the lobby and disheveled office workers cowering behind their desks.

"What the..." said Asher under his breath.

Nico walked up to someone who appeared to be a secretary. "I need to speak to Mr. Crann."

"You can't," said the unkempt secretary.

"Yes, I can. I am Nico Catalano of CAT Robotics, and I have important matters to discuss with—"

"No, you can't," she interrupted. "He has been taken to the hospital. He was attacked by that horrid pirate lady."

"Samira Raol?" asked Callie.

The secretary nodded.

"Where's his office?" asked Asher.

The secretary pointed out the room. The group walked in as a troop of soldiers walked out. "Just act like you belong," whispered Nico. "These grunts will not know the difference."

They entered the office, gathered up papers, and restored order to the room. "Over here," whispered Callie. "The ledgers for today's shipment."

They flipped through the blood-soaked papers on Mr. Crann's desk.

"The military, the Citadel, a pharmacy…you think Miasma could be with one of these groups?"

"I'm not sure," said Asher. "What's this one?"

"Frank's Candy shop," read Callie. "Wasn't that the first place that Miasma attacked, the one that no one could figure out why he targeted it?"

"Yes," answered Nico. "They didn't think he was an actual Miasma target since he was gassed then tortured, and no one else had been tortured. Frank was not a Maurinko, but he was well known in their circles."

"What was he known for?" asked Callie.

"To be honest, I don't know for certain. A lot of the Maurinkos appeared to be somewhat relieved when he died, I think he may have held blackmail on a lot of them. All I know is my parents never let me in that shop when I was a kid."

"Oh god," said Callie horrified. "He poisoned children?"

Nico sighed, "Perhaps. But why would a candy shop owner need mandu root?"

"First off," said Asher, "mandu root isn't strictly for killing. Smaller doses simply leave you unconscious and can erase your memory. Secondly, he must have been getting it routinely if no one is questioning the order. Lastly, and perhaps most importantly, this guy is dead. So why is his shop still ordering mandu root?"

"Sedating and erasing memory with candy..." Callie murmured in disgust.

"Even if it was for creating candy," said Nico, "this shop is importing nearly as much as the military. Not that it's going to get its shipment now. Dyria might be planning to turn away all imports into the city."

"It won't matter," said Nico. He dropped the papers and walked over toward the window; his eyes were distant in thought.

"What is it?" asked Asher.

"I know Miasma's plan."

CHAPTER 25

The following week of school was tense for Asher; his mind was in a constant state of connecting dots. Spirits for everyone else at Langford were high as the koroka team soared through their first round of playoffs. Nico had slowed down his partying and was spending most of his days in the lab. While he never spoke of his parents, Asher could tell their deaths took a toll on him. His charismatic tendencies were still there, but they felt forced—as if putting on a show.

Callie had been busying herself in the sanctuary when the trio wasn't together. She found solace tending to the animals and enjoyed learning about their various habitats firsthand from Fonzworth and Professor Jones. Unlike Nico, Callie wore her grief like an aura of dampened clothing, slowly but surely evaporating in the sunlight.

Asher wrapped up his homework and headed to the lab to meet up with Nico and Callie. It had become their chamber for bouncing ideas off each other and unearthing their anxieties. Between Asher's work on Cirrus-C and Nico's work on his minicopters, the room appeared to have been hit by a hurricane—spare mechanical parts were strewn across the room from Nico's tinkering, and random, unlabeled vials were flooding out of bookshelves and cabinets.

Callie twirled a glass syringe in her hand. "So what exactly is in this?"

Asher was arms-deep in his Cirrus-C project as he looked up to respond. "They're concentrated variants of what's in the berries. They'll act as an antidote and keep you conscious in the event of another gas attack. They should be able to keep you alive through the death serum as well, but I wouldn't test that theory for long. Those two are yours."

Callie pocketed the vials. "And do they have a psychological effect?"

"Yes. Considerably more potent than what's in the berries."

"Awesome," said Nico, taking a moment off from tinkering on his drones to admire a vial. "And how long does it last?"

"About three hours. But you need to save them for a rainy day, these really are for emergency situations only. Those ones are for you, Nico."

"Rainy day huh..." said Nico to himself, clutching the vial.

"Then why do we each need two?" asked Callie.

"We probably don't, but I figured it's better to be safe than sorry. I wouldn't advise taking more than two shots within an hour."

"Why not?" asked Nico.

"The hallucinogenic properties will increase exponentially with each dose. There's a serious risk of permanent psychological damage at those levels, potentially full-blown psychosis."

Callie's eyes widened. "Yeah, I don't plan on using this."

Asher opened his satchel. "Let's hope we never have to. But in case we do, I have plenty more."

They heard a knock and went silent, staring at each other questioningly. Asher shrugged, and Nico went to open the door.

"Yes?" asked Nico.

"I'm looking for an Asher Auden," an old man creaked.

"Sure," said Nico, swinging the door open and revealing a well-dressed Professor Fenske.

"Professor!" shouted Asher.

"Asher! Oh, and Ms. Saint. How are you two?"

Asher dropped his work and ran over to give the professor a hug; Callie waved from a distance.

"And what's your name, young sir?"

"I am Nicholas Catalano. You can call me Nico."

The two shook hands as the professor walked into the room. "Pleasure to meet you, Nico! Asher told me a lot about you during his break in Vana. I heard this is your lab!"

"It's my building..." said Nico, eyeing the professor suspiciously.

"What are you doing here, Professor?" asked Asher.

The professor began to explore the chaotic room and examine a vial. "I was just returning some equipment to Professor Redding, and he mentioned you had a lab down the hall. Thought I would stop by to say hi."

"That's wonderful and all...but I meant, what are you doing in Riali? I didn't think you'd be here so soon."

"I have a meeting with Sheriff Price tomorrow. I had some findings to share with him."

"You're meeting with Price tomorrow?" interrupted Nico.

"Yes," said Fenske. "Him and a few others."

Callie jumped off the table and approached Professor Fenske. "Professor, would we be able to join your meeting?"

"Why would you want to do that?"

"We have information about Miasma," said Nico. "We have been in the middle of all this stuff from the beginning. He killed my parents, and I have a right to know. Our intel is good."

Fenske looked over at the trio. "This is a confidential meeting, and the situation is very delicate. I think it'd be best you all sit this one out."

Asher shrugged off the comment. "I synthesized a potential antidote for the knockout gas, maybe they would want to see it."

Fenske sighed and nodded. "Ok. I'll bring you with me, but I can't promise they'll let you in on the conversation."

"Fair enough," said Nico. "Where should we meet?"

Having agreed to meet Professor Fenske at the sheriff's office, the three left the lab and made their way out of Langford. As they were passing through the grand hall, Felix flagged them down.

"Hey, Felix, what's going on?" Callie asked.

"Did y'all see that thing crawling up the side of the university?"

"What thing?" asked Asher.

"Like some kinda robot dog thing. I was comin' in and saw a creature crawl up the side of the school and into the bell tower. No one else was around, but I was hopin' someone else caught it."

"One of the Vanguards," Nico whispered to Asher and Callie.

"I didn't get a good look, it's gettin' dark and all. The thing disappeared once it reached the bell tower."

Asher snapped into action. "Felix, can you go to the sheriff's office? We were about to meet with him but let him know that one of CAT Industry's Vanguards has been sent to the top of Langford's bell tower. We're going to go check this out."

"Are you sure? I mean, I can back you up..." asked Felix.

"We'll be fine," said Callie. "Go on ahead, we'll meet up with you all later."

Felix nodded and ran off.

The three pounded up the seemingly never-ending stone staircase.

"It's what I thought; it's happening," said Nico frantically.

"There's no signs of him yet," said Asher as they neared the attics. "Let's just see for ourselves before we jump to conclusions."

"Hold up," Callie stopped the boys before they rounded a corner. She reached into her satchel and pulled out a small wooden box. "Grabbed this little guy before we left."

Opening the box, she sent an ahriman fluttering into the air.

"Gregory?" asked a perplexed Nico. Callie stuck out her hand for him to land and, with her opposite hand, pointed down the hallway. The ahriman took off. "He'll let us know if the coast is clear. I wouldn't want to run into an ambush."

"Good call," said Asher.

The ahriman flew back to her hand. She grabbed a treat and placed him on her shoulder. "Ok, we're all clear."

The three walked down the hallway and into the bell tower. Massive chains hung from every corner, like vines dripping off oak trees. The walls were lined with countless brass gears, all intended to rotate the automated chiming bells, and were punctuated with large arching windows that overlooked Riali. The gears clicked into place, pushing each other in an intricate system.

"Let's check out the center bell," said Asher.

"Look," said Nico, pointing to the top of the massive gold bell. "The current leading to it has been recircuited."

The ahriman flew up into the rafters and started to squeal.

"There," Callie pointed.

Asher walked over. "What the…? Nico, what is this thing?"

A cloaked robotic figure balanced on the rafters above the bell.

Nico grabbed onto some nearby chains and began to shimmy up. He climbed across the rafters and pulled back the cloak. "No…Oh, no…no, no, no."

"What? What's going on?" asked Callie.

"It is definitely one of the Vanguards," said Nico.

"Well," said Asher. "You helped build that thing, right? You can dismantle it."

"Yeah, that is the thing," said Nico. "The insides are supposed to be a turret or a flame thrower. But this does not appear to be either."

"What's in it, Nico?" asked Callie impatiently.

"A bomb."

"What?" shouted Asher.

Callie ran toward the edges of the tower, looking for signs of Miasma.

"Yeah, but it's not just a bomb…" Nico began to tinker with the machine. "There's a reservoir—similar to the one we found in Redding's office. The bomb itself will be enough to level Langford. But the toxin that would be released would flood out—and I have no idea how far, at least the eastern quadrant of the city."

"Would we be able to remove the reservoir?"

"Possibly. These things are designed to deliver their payload once they reach their pre-coordinated destination. The fact that this one hasn't gone off means it might be time delayed. Should be able to disconnect the battery and…"

Squeaking sounds came from the window. Callie looked over and saw the ahriman fluttering beside the arching window. She reached out her hand, grabbed the ahriman, and placed him back in his box. She looked back out the window as a glimmer caught her eyes: a reflection coming from the top of the Citadel. "Asher!"

"Yeah?"

"Can you come here really quick?"

Asher walked over. She pointed to the Citadel. "Over there, there's something climbing up it."

Asher squinted; he could make out the shape of another wolf-like creature clawing its way up the side of the great structure. "Nico! You were right!"

"I always am, but…uhh…what am I right about this time?"

"That Miasma was behind the break-in at CAT Robotics," said Callie.

"There's more of these bombs?" Nico's cursing echoed around the bell tower.

"Yeah, it appears so," answered Callie.

"Got it!" Nico dropped off the bell and dusted off his hands. "Saved the day."

"This isn't an attack on Langford," said Asher. "This is an all-out attack on Riali."

CHAPTER 26

Nico began to ramble. "There were seven Vanguards stolen from CAT Industries. Their bodies are one giant battery. Once it fully charges, it moves to its predestined coordinates and delivers its payload. But the power needed to charge even one of them is enormous; they would need an industrial power plant of their own. No way Miasma broke into a public power plant."

Callie walked away from the window. "We need to deactivate as many of these as possible and let the sheriff know. Felix is already there and telling him about this one, but he isn't aware of the others."

Asher remained in thought as the three made their way back down the Langford corridors. "Ok...ok. What about the Citadel?"

"What about it?" asked Nico.

"When Roman took us down to the catacombs, the entire area had its own independent power supply."

"What are the catacombs?" asked Callie.

"Not sure we have the time to go into all of it," said Asher. "Basically, there's an underground facility beneath the Citadel where the Maurinkos store dead bodies."

"Right, got it. The good guys. Dead bodies. Sure."

Nico rubbed his chin. "That whole area is off-grid, but there is enough power to conduct an operation of this magnitude. There's a million ways for the Vanguards to get out of the Citadel, but only one way into that room. If we get there soon enough, we may be able to stop the other remaining Vanguards from being sent out.

"And how does one get to this power plant of corpses?" asked Callie.

"There is a door at the end of the same hallway where Father Bianok's office is. It leads to another, smaller lobby. In that lobby are two doors, the left one is a mineshaft. It's down in there."

They headed to the edge of the sanctuary, nearest to the Citadel, and stopped as they saw a shadowy figure scaling its way down the side of the massive central tower.

"That is one of them. Looks to be headed toward the harbor," said Nico.

"Trying to cripple the Riali shipping industry, another blow to the Maurinkos," Asher thought out loud.

"I'm going to go to Sheriff Price; they need to know where the next bomb is located. I'll meet up with you all at the Citadel as soon as I can," Callie said.

"Ok," said Asher stoically.

"Be careful," said Nico. "We don't know if any other bombs have found their way into the city, and we don't know where Miasma is hiding. If he is even hiding at all."

Callie sprinted through the maze of hedges, pushing past groups of students without care. Dusk had begun to settle, and the streetlamps began to fire. She felt a sense of dreadful inevitably swell inside of her. An arm reached out from around the corner and stopped her in her tracks. She looked up at the concerned face of Professor Redding. "Professor! There are bombs…Miasma." She gasped deep breaths in between each word.

Redding shushed her. "Callie, Callie, listen. Stop, just listen. We know!"

She looked up, confused, his hands still on her shoulders. "You know what?"

"We know that Miasma has bombs over the city. We found one at the train station. I helped to disassemble it. You need to get out of here. Where is Asher?"

"Asher and Nico had an idea of how to stop the attack. Where are we all supposed to go?"

"What? No. You both need to get out of this city right now."

"Why us?"

"General Volkov has sent out an order to the Rialian military to round up every Dyrian and Vanatian in the city. They've taken Professor Fenske into custody. You and Asher are in danger, you can't be here for what is about to happen."

"I have to find Asher first."

"No, you don't have time. The last train leaves in two hours. You need to get to the station. Tell me where to find Asher, and I will get him out of here."

The sound of marching came from down the hallway.

"That is the Rialian forces, they're storming the University. Go, run!"

Callie turned around. The professor turned as well to approach and stall the oncoming soldiers. Atop the sanctuary steps, she could see toward the center of the city, where the station would be, but she had no choice. She was not leaving without Asher.

Asher and Nico raced through crowds of students, beelining to the Citadel. Sirens began to ring out through the city.

"What is that?" asked Asher.

Nico's face dropped. "That siren has not gone off in decades…It means the city is under siege."

"Good," said Asher. "Maybe it was from Callie's warning."

The rise and fall of the alarm echoed throughout the city, instilling an even greater sense of urgency within Asher as they continued toward the side entrance of the Citadel.

Nico turned to check the area.

"Asher, look!"

Asher followed Nico's eyes up one of the Citadel's sentry towers. Through its stone windows stood a shadowy hooded figure.

"We need to move quickly," said Nico, going through the door. "We need to get to the power supply before Miasma does."

He used a skeleton key to lock the door behind them, and they proceeded through the back hallways of the Citadel. It was much more cramped and poorly lit than Langford. Their steps reverberated off the stone and steel. Reaching the locked Maurinko lobby, Nico used the skeleton key once more. They entered the empty room and pried their way to the elevator shaft. "The power supply should be near the bottom floors."

They began their descent into the enormous cavern of perfectly symmetrical rings. Each level was outlined dark blue, like angelic halos. The metal elevator creaked precariously as Nico peered over the side, staring into the abyss of frozen bodies.

"Asher, if we cut the power, what will happen to these people?"

"There are more people in the city than bodies in the catacomb."

"So, they will die? For good this time?" asked Nico.

"They've already died. And in any case, they would not be protected from the blast of Miasma's bombs. The Citadel will surely be a target, and I doubt the air intake on these tanks is designed to filter for the gas Miasma is using."

"No," said Nico, looking out solemnly across the rows of bodies. "If I can get to the control room, I can reroute the power away from the Vanguards without losing power to the chambers. We don't need to shut the whole thing down."

Asher peered down into the cavern below, counting the floors in anticipation. Their platform continued to groan until it came to a sudden and jerking stop.

"Was that you?"

Nico shook his head slowly. The two looked up at the entrance. A figure stood, hands on the controls, silhouetted by the doorway. The silhouette was a massive and unmistakable outline.

CHAPTER 27

"Roman!" shouted Asher. "You have to listen. There's a bomb—"

"No!" Roman's booming voice reverberated down the metallic halls of the catacomb. "Everyone can hear the sirens. The police are calling to bring in all Vana citizens."

"We're trying to stop Miasma!" pleaded Asher.

"I've had my suspicions about you, Auden. Ever since you came to this city, these attacks have only gotten worse."

The elevator started to hum and pull them upward.

"We need to jump," Nico whispered.

"Roman, you know me. I have stopped Miasma before. I've been your friend every step of the way."

"My *friend*? You have been there for every attack. You gained access to the Maurinkos. How could you even call yourself a friend when I've seen the way you looked at Autumn? No, you are not a friend. You're a resource to be exploited. You were useful to me, to others, but you had zero intention of being a friend to any of us. You have no reason to be here. The Maurinkos were going to give you everything! Why they ever thought a filthy Vanatian could ever belong is beyond me. My own father knew it from day one. You were never here to save us, to help with the catacombs, to save the generations of Maurinkos. You are here to destroy them."

Roman's speech became even more mad and frantic as the elevator ascended to his level.

Nico grabbed Asher's arm. "Time to go!"

The two jumped off the moving platform and onto one of the levels, their bodies smashing against the metal grating. Rows of blue-lit cryo-chambers illuminated their path to the staircase. A loud crash echoed throughout the catacombs as Roman leaped from the platform onto the top of the elevator.

"GO GO GO!" Nico hurried Asher along as they ran full speed down the stairs. The elevator cables snapped, sending the car pummeling downward. Roman timed his jump perfectly and landed on the same level as Asher and Nico.

Asher turned to Nico. "You turn off the power. I'll hold off Roman."

"What, are you insane?"

"He's only after me, just go!"

Nico shook his head but took off. With Roman looming near, Asher could now see that he had grown nearly twice his normal mass.

"How much of the serum did you take, Roman?"

Roman walked slowly but confidently toward Asher. His boots thudded; the platform shook under his weight. "All of it."

"Of course you did. Too much of an ego to ever heed a warning."

"And when my dad has you as a prisoner, you will be serving your time cooking up more."

Asher went down another flight of stairs onto the next level, backing up slowly. Roman continued to advance.

"The serum is affecting your mind. You're not right, Roman. You're confused. I'm not the bad guy here!"

"Then you should have no problem explaining to my father what it is you're doing in the Maurinko catacombs during a siege."

Asher backed up into an occupied chamber, his fingers pressing against the cold glass.

"Roman, you don't have to do this, I'll come with you. But Nico and I, we can stop this attack."

Roman was now standing face-to-face with Asher. He threw his weight behind his fist, punching the glass next to Asher's head, cracking the window of the chamber. "I don't have to bring you back alive."

Asher didn't flinch. "I'm sorry, Roman."

Asher swung his arm from behind his back and plunged a syringe into Roman's sternum. Roman looked down, "What? What is this?"

"You've lost your mind, Roman. Just lie down. Nico and I will carry you out."

Roman's mind filled with the berry's hallucinogenic properties. He pulled a chamber off the wall. Gases and liquids spewed from the torn hoses of the ripped-out chamber. He threw the heavy metal box at Asher, who rolled away, narrowly avoiding being pinned down. Roman leaped over the chamber as Asher stood up to run. "Nico!"

Nico had reached the floor with the power supply. Generators buzzed around him, an electrical mess of pistons and conductors firing off into heavy cables. Several were latched onto two more of Nico's wolf-like Vanguard robots. Nico heard a scream, ran out, and watched as Roman grabbed Asher by the back of his shirt and threw him. Asher got up, his face bloodied. "Stick him with the antidote," he croaked.

"I thought these were for a rainy day only?"

"Nico!" shouted Asher in a frantic, garbled mess. "It is *fucking* pouring!"

Roman jumped down, landing between them. He gripped the railing and yanked out two steel poles from the floor. Asher crawled backward as Roman beat the two bars together and then scraped them alongside the grated metal flooring. The sound of metal grinding against metal resonated throughout the cavern.

"Roman, don't," Asher pleaded.

Roman's eyes were dilated and distant, his movements sporadic and unpredictable. He continued his march toward the bloody Asher, the metal pipes swinging at his side like koroka tonfas. He raised a steel pipe above his head, ready to strike.

"Argghh!" Roman fell to one knee before spinning around, revealing Nico's minicopter lodged into his back. Asher could make out the emptied antidote syringe. Nico stood wide-eyed behind Roman, a look of shock on his face.

"Asher, run!"

Asher stood up and ran to Nico, handing him his second syringe.

"Here, take my last one. I don't know how he's still standing. Another one of these could kill him if we're not careful."

Nico grabbed the syringe. "Go in the door behind me and turn off the power supply to the Vanguards. There's two of them in there, you'll need to power down the generators attached to them, otherwise, if you try and yank out the cables, it could cause the Vanguards to go off. Worst case scenario, there's a giant kill switch to the whole complex, you can't miss it. I'll take care of Roman, you're too injured to fight."

Roman used the pipes to dislodge the copter. Nico tried to fly it back, but Roman swatted it out of the air in an explosion of cogs and gears. Nico made a run for the stairs as Roman gave pursuit, his bulky body stumbled and crashed into the railing as his eyes rolled into the back of his head. They reached the ground floor, and Roman slipped on the steps and sprawled out against the concrete, sending the metal pipes flying. This was the only non-blue area in the catacombs. Instead, it glowed with a deep, dark red. Nico could see old and intricately decorated chambers for who must have been the most elite members of Maurinko society.

Roman stood back up in a belligerent haze.

"You...Nico..." His words were slurred and barely audible.

"Roman. Just stop. I can help you." Nico backed into an empty chamber. Roman's head drooped down as if it was weighing heavy on his body. He swayed back and forth, mumbling incoherently as he stumbled against the various chambers, leaving cracks in the glass. "Roman!" Nico pleaded. Roman stopped and made eye contact. Nico could see what appeared to be a few seconds of soberness in him. Soberness in the form of anger. "No..." said Nico. "Don't."

Roman lowered his shoulder and charged full speed at Nico, who sidestepped and threw the giant's body into an empty chamber. He stabbed him in the heart with the last antidote syringe. Roman looked down, then up at Nico, and then swayed uncontrollably as if his knees were going to give out.

"I'll come back for you." Nico grabbed a life support tube and stuck it in Roman's neck. Roman's eyes rolled into the back of his head. "I'm sorry," said Nico as he shut the glass door of the chamber.

Nico dropped the empty syringe and looked around the mysterious red level. He noticed a door he'd never seen before, tightly locked in a swirl of various cogs and gears, at the end of the hallway. Something so heavily protected must be unfathomably important, but what could it be? Perhaps it was a secondary backup generator? Even the skeleton key would not be enough to unlock whatever was hiding behind that mess of steel and engineering. He turned and walked back toward the staircase, his path illuminated by the bright-red glow of the chambers.

He continued up the floors, back to Asher, before stopping. Something was off about two chambers on the third floor. The glass on them had yet to be fogged over like the others, and the nameplates had been brightly polished. He walked over to them.

"No...Asher."

He scrambled over frantically to look into the second chamber.

"Asher!" he yelled louder. "ASHER, STOP!!"

Asher had located the main power supply, two more of the Vanguards were there charging. *Nico said seven of these*

were stolen, thought Asher, *I can at least stop these two.* Long electrical cables bore directly into the opened heads of the mechanical dog-like creatures. Asher peered inside. *The power is connected to the bomb; ripping out the cable could detonate the bomb and kill us all. But these machines are timed. Once they're fully charged, they will disconnect and go to their predetermined destination.*

The machine was fully entrenched in engineering beyond his skill set. He looked around the room and saw a wall of levers—off switches to the generators, as well as the master switch. Before he could kill the power, he heard his name.

"Asher! Asher, they're in the chamber. We can't shut off the power."

He leaned over the railing and looked down. "Nico? What?"

Nico opened his mouth to repeat himself, but a gas canister landed on the wall behind Asher. He instinctively ran over to the canister and kicked it over the ledge.

"Nico, get out of there!"

Nico frantically ran up the stairs, trying to get Asher's attention, but was interrupted by a second flying canister. He looked up to find Miasma standing on the landing platform.

"Nico!" Asher yelled down.

The canister landed beside Nico, who grasped for the additional antidote syringe Asher gave him to fight Roman. He plunged the needle into his skin and began to run up the stairs as canisters rained from above. The antidote coursed through his veins while the gas also took its grip. "Asher," he said weakly, "it's my parents..."

"Asher Auden and Nico Catalano, enough!" The booming, distorted voice of Miasma rang out through the catacombs. The boys looked up to see Miasma aiming a pistol at them.

"Who are you? Why are you doing this?" shouted Asher. A bullet whizzed past his ear and lodged itself into the glass of a chamber. He looked at the bullet, then back to Miasma, who was readjusting his aim. Time was running out. He ran back into the power room, several more shots ringing behind him.

He scanned the room for any sign of how to disconnect the Vanguards but was uncertain of what would do the trick. "There's no time," he thought out loud to himself. He ran to the wall of levers and pulled them each down, one by one. With every pull, he could hear pistons firing down and engines wheezing to a stop. He continued to pull until he reached the master lever. He flipped it down and the room went dark. The Vanguard robots dimmed to black. For a moment, the room's electric buzz went dead; a heavy and eerie silence in its place, abruptly punctuated by Nico's scream.

"ASHER! WHAT HAVE YOU DONE?"

Red emergency lights kicked on, and the sound of a few pistons went back to firing. *Backup generators, but not for the Vanguards*, thought Asher.

Disorientated, Nico dragged his heavy limbs up the stairs. "Asher…" he slurred. "Asher, don't do this…don't turn off the power."

Miasma leveled the pistol at the barely conscious Nico. The Citadel door opened.

Without hesitation, Callie rushed Miasma, pushing him into the railing. The gun dropped through the empty cavern.

Miasma turned around. "You! Why is it always you?"

"Well, for starters, it's pretty easy following someone wearing a cape." Callie sent a punch flying into Miasma's mask, knocking off the goggles. Bright blue eyes stared back at her in fierce anger. Miasma grabbed her by the shoulders and pushed her against the rail, sending a flurry of punches back. Callie grabbed a knife from her pocket and sliced at Miasma, who threw off the hampering cloak, revealing dark hair and a corseted figure. Miasma sidestepped, and Callie tumbled to the ground. She sat on top of Callie, ripped the knife out of her hand, and flung it across the floor.

Seeing the fight, Asher ran over. He kicked Miasma as hard as he could, tearing the mask partially off. "It's too late, I shut off the power. It's over." Asher picked up Callie as Miasma jumped back upright and turned to face him. Her mask was awry, revealing the unmistakable beauty it had hidden. Asher stood back in shock. "Autumn?"

The ground began to shake. "You didn't save anyone, Asher."

"Why? What do you mean?" The sound of explosions rang out in the distance.

"The Maurinkos, they are sick. The things they do. The things my parents allowed them to do to me, just so they could join their stupid society. I meant nothing to them. I was less than nothing. They used me, Asher, and they used you, too. And this city, this whole damn city, is their jewel and their shield. I am taking it all from them, Asher."

"Autumn, I didn't know. The gas you use..."

Autumn seethed. "It is over now. There is a backup generator on the bottom floor. When you disabled the main power, you shut off these catacombs, killing every last one of these monsters and setting off a bomb here in the citadel. I won." An explosion rang throughout the floors of the catacombs. Callie and Asher looked into the cavern and watched as the bottom floor ignited.

Autumn ran away.

"You go get Nico, I'll go after Autumn," said Callie, sprinting off. Asher ran down the flights of stairs as fast as he could. The flames had begun to rise, engulfing the bottom two floors, the chambers filling up with smoke and Miasma's gas.

Asher found Nico crawling up the steps, barely conscious. "Nico! Nico! Where's Roman?"

"Gone," mumbled Nico, barely able to move his lips. "They're gone."

Asher looked down at the flames, hoping to catch a glimpse of Roman's silhouette, but nothing appeared. The smoke began to blind him. "Ok, Nico, we got to go. Come on."

"No!" he said, shrugging Asher off.

"What? Come on, there's no time to mess around, this place is going to collapse."

Nico mumbled something incoherently. Asher grabbed him and put him on his shoulders, not making out Nico's mumbled protests.

"You're not making any sense. Come on, buddy. Let's get you out of here."

"You killed them, Asher. You killed them."

Asher dragged Nico's limp body out of the flames and into the Maurinkos' lobby. He could hear the sirens grow louder as they got closer to the clean, outside air. "I'm going to the lab. We'll be safe there."

Nico had passed out, his full body weight hanging on Asher. Ahead of them, Asher saw soldiers with gas masks. The sirens were deafening, and the sky was filling with smoke and ash.

CHAPTER 28

allie's lungs burned as she ran through the Citadel courtyard. The taste of smoke grew thicker with each breath. She paused briefly to inject Asher's antidote and watch as dying sprites rain-dropped from the sky above in streams of blues and greens. The sound of sirens pierced the dense, smoggy air, seeming to become louder as she continued the chase. Autumn was in her sights—her cloak tattered, her hair chaotic in the wind. Callie closed the distance between them as they reached the sanctuary, where rows of large hedges were illuminated by choked starlight.

Autumn came to a stop. She turned and faced Callie, pushing her goggles up and into her hair like a militant headband and shedding the last tattered remnants of her cloak. Callie did not stop. Instead, she continued her sprint straight at Autumn.

Autumn's eyebrows raised in bewilderment as she braced for the oncoming tackle. Callie lowered her shoulders and went straight through the much taller Autumn, then grappled her onto the ground. Autumn pushed Callie off, landing a strong punch to her nose. Callie fell sidewise, starting to bleed, then felt a kick to her stomach.

"Of all people, you should understand."

Callie crawled toward the wall. "There's nothing worth understanding here." The air had escaped her lungs; she could only squeak out the words. Autumn kicked her again and pulled out a thick syringe.

"I was not born wealthy like the rest of the Maurinkos. My parents wanted more than anything to regain their status in society and agreed to have me made in the image of my great-grandmother. Did I have any say? Did anyone ask if I wanted to be the carbon copy of some old singer? No. And when I didn't live up to standards, they let the Maurinkos use me however they wanted. My parents didn't care. Their rituals and their perversions. The Maurinkos are sick people, Callie. It was not enough that they already had everything, they still wanted my mind, my soul. And they will do it to others too. They have before and will continue to do so until the end of time. But I won't let them. And once I'm done? They will have nothing."

Callie's back was against the wall of an animal housing exhibit; she gripped a chain leash behind her. She looked up in fear and shock as Autumn drew nearer. Autumn lowered the syringe.

"I will put you down, just as Asher did to your fox."

Autumn plunged, and Callie dodged sideways, yanking the chain leash upward and tripping Autumn. Then, she quickly stood up and stepped hard on Autumn, breaking her wrist and causing her to drop the syringe. Autumn screamed in pain. She jumped up to face Callie, who quickly bashed her in the face with the steel collar, knocking her back down to the ground. Callie knelt beside the dazed Autumn and snapped the collar around her neck.

"What did you do?" asked Autumn, grasping at the collar.

"Do you *ever* stop talking?" Callie spat, then took a breath and turned around. She walked away into the animal exhibit flipping through the sanctuary keys in her hand.

"Come back!" yelled Autumn. "Don't leave me out here!"

Various animals came flooding into the sanctuary—snowshoe rabbits, gray wolves, birds of prey. A few minutes later, Callie returned.

"Oh God, I was never going to kill you, I swear. The syringe was only to sedate you. I was going to spare you and Asher. I like you guys. You Vanatians are not my enemy. The Maurinkos, they plot—"

"You had me fooled when you tried to gas me off the roof of Langford stadium. And when you poisoned my friend. And when your terrorism led to Cloud's death."

"I'm sorry," said Autumn, mustering sincerity. "I only wanted the Maurinkos to fall."

More explosions sounded in the distance. Callie turned around and watched as sections of the Langford sanctuary caught fire. The flames rose, reflecting in her eyes.

"Then why is this whole city on fire? They're blaming Vana for this, because of you!"

"This city *is* the Maurinkos. Everything about it is rotten. I could care less about the success of Dyria and Vana, but I want to watch Riali burn to the ground. They are only out to exploit other cities, just like they exploited me. Once something is of no value to them, it is either destroyed or discarded. I was lucky to be discarded. I was worthless to them and to my family, you have no idea the kind of loneliness and brokenness I felt!"

"And so you go to murder? You didn't get rid of your problems; you just made them worse! You could have left. You could have made a new name, a new life. You have intelligence, beauty, money. Why not leave these people behind? Instead of learning from the Maurinkos' mistakes, you learned how to be exactly like them. A killer with no regard for the lives of others. You are no better than the monsters that made you."

"I AM NOT THE SAME AS THEM!"

"You're right," said Callie, walking up close to Autumn. "You are so much worse. At least they provided some value to this world. You?" Callie paused as the sound of growling echoed through the animal housing. "You're less than worthless. You're selfish. Entitled. Yes, you are broken. All of us are broken, but to be alone in it, that is a choice. That is what I've learned since I've been here. But you want to play the victim, act like you have it worse, blame others—"

"You don't know me."

"I don't need to," said Callie, as the growling behind her took the form of two eres. "I know what you do. And this world could use less of it."

Autumn glanced warily at the eres before turning back to Callie. "You think you're so much better than me? Go ahead then, kill me. It might not stop the Maurinkos, but it would solve both our problems!"

Callie grabbed at Autumn's vest and tossed all her grenades, except for a single purple one, into a nearby trough. She held onto the last gas canister and backed up to the two eres. Around them, the sanctuary roared in response to the raging fire. She stared at the purple canister and back to Autumn. "Here," Callie said, holding the canister out, "throw this at the eres, maybe you'll be able to fend them off for a few extra minutes. Or maybe use it on yourself, and you might not feel them ripping at your skin as much. Either way, you only have about ten minutes before the fire reaches the far edges of the sanctuary."

Autumn grabbed the canister with her functioning hand and clutched it to her chest, her fiery eyes now faded and distant. She looked through Callie, through the eres, and fixated on the growing flames, "Why are you doing this?"

Callie started to walk back through the burning sanctuary, running her hands through the coarse sides of the eres. "For Cloud."

"I'll be right back," whispered Asher, setting the unconscious Nico down against the outside of the lab building. Inside, the emergency lights had been tripped, leaving the hall sparsely lit with every other bulb blackened. Doors had been flung open in a hurry, chairs were knocked over, papers were scattered in the chaos. Asher sprinted to the lab and tore through his work, packing all the Cirrus-C materials into his satchel. He looked through Nico's side of the lab and grabbed a prototype of the skeleton key. He scanned the room one last time and headed for the door, but he was stopped just short by the sound of clinking metal.

Asher peered through the slit of a window and saw tiny mechanical spiders scanning the rooms, squeezing themselves under the frames of shut doors and sliding through the open cracks of others. He looked for a place to hide in the lab. Nothing. The cabinets were too small, and the spiders would find him regardless. He only had one play: run.

He waited until the spiders disappeared into another room, then he slipped out quietly. He sneaked through the hallway to the next room over and cracked the door. Peering through the crack, he watched the spiders exit the previous room and scurry into his lab. Then he walked quickly and quietly through the hallway. *Almost there.* He heard the clanking of the spiders and tried to duck into another door, but his eyes widened with horror as the door rattled against the lock. He looked back to the lab as the first spider peeked its head out from the door. He was spotted.

Asher bolted toward the end of the hallway, chased by several mechanical spiders. They were too fast. They seized his ankle, causing him to trip and stumble. They swarmed, locking onto his feet and hands. He flailed his limbs desperately in an attempt to shake them off, but they dug in with razor-sharp legs. Asher managed to drag himself upright, his body straight as a board from the tight clasp of spiders around his ankles.

A figure emerged from the shadows in the hallway.

"Nico! You're awake. You've got to get me out of these things."

He stopped and stared at Asher, his darkened face void of emotion.

"Nico?"

Nico was illuminated by the glow of emergency lights.

"Nico, come on. I know you're in shock, you're processing a lot right now, but I need your help."

Nico didn't move. A second shadow emerged from behind him. Asher could make out the silhouette of a shotgun and trench coat.

A faint sound caught Asher's attention down the intersecting hallway, just beyond the corner he had tried to turn down. He saw Callie quietly make her way down the hallway, the two of them making eye contact. Asher shook his head no.

One of the spiders began to slowly crawl up his leg, gripping onto his shirt and skittering onto his face. "No," said Asher, still staring at Callie. A tiny buzzsaw emerged from the spider's body cavity. Callie continued to sneak toward him. Asher let out one last scream of, "No!"

Asher faced back toward the main hallway. Vance Grimm patted Nico's shoulder before making his way down the hallway. Nico shrunk back into the shadows, out of Asher's sight. *Was he the one who alerted Grimm?*

Grimm continued to march down the hallway, shotgun in one hand, black cap pulled down, the mason jar full of eyes bouncing at his side.

"Asher Auden," he growled in a low, raspy voice. "The General has been looking for you."

Asher turned back to Callie, who had remained hidden. "Don't," he pleaded.

"Don't? Don't what?" said Grimm, stepping closer to Asher. "I will admit that I am a little disappointed. I didn't take you for the groveling type. Must be a Vanatian thing—your dear Professor Fenske did the same."

Asher watched as a metallic hand appeared from one of the side classrooms and yanked Callie inward through an open classroom door.

With Callie safe for now, Asher focused his attention back to Grimm. His body had become locked in place, stiff, head tilted backward, his eyelid pried open, the legs of the spider digging deep into his flesh, drawing blood, and a tiny spinning buzzsaw hanging centimeters from his cornea. "I didn't do anything. I tried to stop it. It was Autumn Vasiliev, she is Miasma, I saw her in the Citadel—"

"SHUT UP!" shouted Grimm. He stood about a foot away, just close enough for Asher to smell the stale cigars and cheap liquor on his breath.

Callie turned to find Fonzworth leaning over her, Mara behind him. "Fonzworth will get you to the station. I'll get Asher. You need to go. Do you understand?" Callie nodded, Fonzworth's giant metal hand still over her mouth. "Good. Now go!" said Mara in a harsh whisper. She pulled a pistol from her pocket and crept through the door. She could see Asher and the spider's saw spinning above his eye. She was so close.

"I don't care about Miasma," Grimm spat. "The General has issued strict orders to bring in all citizens of Vana and Dyria. He specifically requested you and the girl. She has to come alive. You, on the other hand? Well, if all that's left is an eyeball, then I think we'll be alright." Grimm looked down at his arm and revealed a small panel of buttons. "I'll ask only once. Where is the girl?"

Asher stayed silent and perfectly still as Mara took careful aim at the spider above his eye. Grimm gave a crooked smile. "Thank goodness you found some courage after all! I needed an excuse to add to my collection. I think I prefer the green eye..."

The loud crack of a bullet firing ricocheted off the narrow school walls. The spider flew off Asher's face.

Mara quickly turned and let out a second shot at Grimm. He went down quickly, the bullet hitting his arm, but he lifted his shotgun with the other and fired wildly in Mara's direction.

Massive chunks of plaster and debris exploded off the wall. The spiders leaped off Asher and scurried for Mara. "RUN!" she shouted, taking aim at the mechanical spiders. Asher bolted down the hallway at full speed, blood blurring his vision, the sounds of gunshots echoing behind him.

One by one, the spiders exploded around Mara until her revolver was empty. She was grasping for more bullets in her pockets when Grimm rounded the corner. She ducked into a nearby classroom, slamming and locking the door behind her. The door exploded into a thousand splinters. A rogue piece of shrapnel buried itself in her leg as she dove behind a desk. The sound of nearby shotgun shells hit the floor as she finished reloading her pistol. Grimm laughed. "You know this is treason, Dr. Jones. I am here on government-sanctioned duty."

Mara kept her back against the desk, the gun drawn next to her face. "Killing students is your patriotic duty now?"

Grimm's face dropped back into a serious expression. He fired into the ceiling above Mara, showering tiles and debris on top of her. "Surrender yourself, or this next slug will go through the desk."

Mara closed her eyes. She slowed down her breathing and readied her pistol. Grimm stepped closer to the desk, his shotgun shouldered and ready to fire at the slightest flinch. "Such a pretty face, Dr. Jones, and such pretty eyes. Such a shame to turn it all into a red mist..." His voice trailed off as his finger found the trigger.

The sound of a pistol cocking came from behind him. "Drop the gun, Vance."

Grimm didn't move, the shotgun still pointed at the desk. "Sheriff. Have you heard the General's orders?"

"I have," said the sheriff, "and so you should know they were to round up Vanatians and Dyrians. Mara is neither."

Grimm didn't budge. "She is aiding the terrorists."

"Then you should let the authorities take it from here. Mara Jones, you are under arrest. Please put down your weapon."

Mara raised her hands slowly from behind the desk. Grimm lowered his shotgun, turned, and pressed his forehead against the sheriff's pistol. "If I didn't know any better, I would say you were aiding them, too."

The sheriff cocked back the hammer. "Are you done?"

Grimm grunted. Price continued to stare at him. Their eyes locked, not in a battle of will but in mutual understanding. "Traitor," growled Grimm as he pushed past Price before stopping in the doorway. "It's too late, you know."

"I know," said Price.

"The Vanguard has been released," said Grimm, now walking away with a crooked smile. "This is only the beginning."

CHAPTER 29

The streets were filled with gas-masked Riali soldiers. Callie pulled a cloak over her head and strapped on a gas mask provided by Fonzworth across her face. Fires raged around Langford, the orange hue of the sky punctuated by the purple and yellow wisps of Miasma's gas. She could see soldiers dragging families from homes as they rounded up civilians.

"Fonz, what happened? Why are they taking people away?"

"General's orders. They are arresting all Vanatian and Dyrian citizens in Riali."

"What do they plan on doing to them? None of this is on them."

"I am not sure. Interrogation, perhaps? The information I have is limited. I heard Arthur and Mara talking. Arthur believes the Rialian government knew this event was coming days in advance."

Callie turned her face away as a group of masked soldiers marched past. "Asher and I, we found Miasma. We stopped her."

"That might be so," said Fonzworth, "but I fear Miasma was only a symptom, not the disease."

Callie glanced across the burning landscape of Riali. The streets were littered with bodies of people who had fled their homes, desperate for a breath of fresh air.

They arrived at Riali Central Station, where guards blocked every entry and scanned passengers' eyes. Remnants of purple smoke swirled under the station's glass dome, and the once-elegant interior was desecrated by the chaos.

"Any ideas on how to get in?" asked Callie.

"Follow my lead, Ms. Saint." Fonzworth pushed through the crowd while reaching for something deep in his coat pocket. A guard stopped them. "No machines past this point."

"I'm the guardian of Elizabeth Crann. She needs to be on that train."

"Not without a retinal scan," said the guard.

Fonzworth puffed up his barreled chest. "How dare you! The Cranns will be appalled to know their daughter has been treated with such indignity."

"Sorry, we are under direct orders." The guard shoved the scanner toward Callie, but Fonzworth was quick to grab it.

"Hey!" shouted the guard, whipping a rifle with his free hand into Fonzworth's chest. "Let go, or you will be arrested for non-compliance of—"

"I say, you are the rudest!" shouted Fonzworth, purposely making a scene.

A small electrical pulse emanated from his hand and into one of Grimm's defunct spiders. Circuits within the spider sparked and fired, causing it to release a small ray of light that bounced into the scanner. Focused only on Fonzworth, the guard didn't seem to notice the malfunction. Fonzworth let go.

"Thank you," huffed the guard as he scanned Callie's eye. The scanner beeped, and the guard looked down at the results. "Huh?"

"What now?" asked Fonzworth impatiently.

"This isn't Elizabeth Crann."

Callie looked up nervously.

"Ha! Then who is she?" asked Fonzworth.

"Must be a malfunction, they have been dead for years." The guard slapped the machine a few times, and it beeped again, "Ok, got it, yes, Ms. Crann you are good to board."

Fonzworth put his hand on Callie's shoulder. "You're on your own from here on out. I look forward to meeting again."

"Thank you, Fonzworth. Tell Mara I said goodbye."

A somber smile lit his steely face as she touched his hand, turned, and walked onto the train.

A few minutes later, Callie was looking out of the overpacked train. Frightened faces crowded together, anxiously waiting for it to depart. *No sign of Asher.* A sudden sense of guilt washed over her. The ground began to rumble, but something felt odd. It was not the sound of a steam engine firing up. *An earthquake or perhaps another feyloom stampede?* The rumbling grew distant, as though it was moving away from the city even faster than her train. She squinted hard into the horizon as the train passed the city gate. All she could see was an ocean of glinting metal, reflecting off what was left of the burnt Riali skyline.

Asher had sprinted out of the lab, still carrying his satchel of supplies. He had spotted Fonzworth ahead but had to duck around a corner to hide from oncoming soldiers and lost track of Callie and the robot. He stayed low, plotting his moves from one building to the next, careful to avoid the battalions of gas-masked militia sweeping the Langford grounds. The streets were flooded with troops, and the road to the station appeared to be entirely blocked. It didn't matter; he had no other options.

He was making his way through courtyards when he bumped into two soldiers while rounding a corner.

"Stop!" said one soldier grabbing onto Asher's shoulder.

"What the..." said the other soldier pointing his rifle at Asher, "how are you breathing without a mask right now?"

"I...uhh..." Asher fumbled for an excuse.

"No matter," said the first soldier letting him go and reaching for something on his hip, "we need to scan your eye."

"I can't, I tripped and fell. My eye is full of blood, the scanner wouldn't be able to read it."

The soldiers examined him closely and saw open wounds still fresh from the legs of Grimm's spiders.

"Fine, the other eye then," said the soldier with the rifle.

Asher shrugged and presented his blue eye to be scanned.

"Nothing, you're not in the system. That's odd, no one should be in the city if they haven't been scanned."

The two soldiers conversed with each other, deciding on what to do, when a shadowy figure emerged from the courtyard gazebo. It didn't look like military personnel, but Asher kept a close watch as the figure approached.

"He is with me," called a voice to the soldiers.

They turned around to find Nico.

"Who are you, and how are you also without a mask?"

"I am Nicholas Catalano, go ahead and scan me, then leave us be."

The soldiers confirmed his identity, apologized, and went on their way.

Once the soldiers were out of sight, Asher stepped forward. "Nico…thank God. We need to get out of here. These soldiers are rounding up Vanatians. They took Professor Fenske. We can hide out at your house and wait for this to be over."

"No, Asher. We can't."

"What? Why? What's going on?"

"Why didn't you stop, Asher? I asked you to stop. I shouted at you, you looked right at me."

"What are you talking about? Stop what?"

"I saw my parents in the catacombs, Asher. I saw them, and I shouted for you, but you let them die."

"Nico, you're delirious. Miasma was there. She started firing off canisters of gas, and I had to pull the power to help stop the attack. You knew that. That was the plan."

"No, the plan was for me to reroute the power so that those in the catacombs would continue to be on life support. You didn't care if any of those people lived."

"Nico, I'm sorry about your parents. I truly am. But it was Autumn. Autumn killed them for being Maurinkos. They were murdered at the game. They've been dead for months now. It has nothing to do with me."

Nico looked down at his hands and a buzzing sound began to grow louder.

"I told you shutting off the power would kill those people, Asher. And when I was down there, I begged you to stop. But you wouldn't listen. You were the one who was supposed to save them, Asher. You were supposed to help us carry on our legacy."

"Nico, I'm sorry, I—"

"No!" Nico interrupted. "You don't get it. It was my parents who wanted me to be your roommate. They knew who you were before you even got here, Asher. The Maurinkos didn't want you staying in Vana, or worse, going to Dyria. So they had the Langford board accept you. Don't you get it? My parents made me be your friend, and you killed them."

"Nico, you're still disoriented. I...I don't even know what you're trying to say."

"SHUT UP!" A minicopter rose from behind Nico's back, a sharp blade attached to its body. Nico positioned it so that the blade faced Asher.

"The Maurinkos are why you are at Langford! They are why I was your roommate! They are why you had any friends at all, Asher. This whole year was because of them, because of me—"

"I put my life on the line for you, Nico! I was out here chasing after Miasma, FOR YOU!"

The minicopter went flying at Asher's chest. He sidestepped it and watched as it floated back behind Nico, hovering menacingly over his shoulder.

"You made Vana and Dyria rich," seethed Nico. "You and your professor, developing those crops. You didn't bother to make the creation public since it only worked in Vanatian soil. So what's going to happen to your city without you?"

Asher shook his head. "We didn't remove their ability to reproduce, they won't fail. Vana will be fine long after I'm gone."

A crooked smile came across Nico's face. "You don't think we thought of that? There is a contingency plan in place that is being implemented right now. We could have made you rich, Asher. We could have made you famous. You could have had everything you ever wanted, if only you worked with us. Now, it is all gone. I will make sure of it."

Nico sent the copter flying at Asher again, this time at full speed, intended to kill.

Asher leaped to the side, the contents of his satchel spilling out. He gathered them, not bothering to look back at Nico or the copter. The buzz of the copter slowly grew louder as the blade pressed against his throat. Asher continued to look down, refusing to make eye contact with Nico.

"Asher, you are no longer needed here."

Asher finally looked up and faced Nico one last time, his blue and bloodied-green eyes piercing Nico's with defiance. A burst of light exploded between them. The copter fell to the ground, its power drained. Asher turned around to see Arthur Winston placing down his staff. "You are correct, Mr. Catalano. Asher is no longer needed here. I will assist with bringing him in." Arthur extended his hand and lifted Asher from the ground.

"You will be arrested for treason!" shouted Nico.

"Unlikely." Arthur lifted Asher up. "Goodbye, Mr. Catalano." The two walked down the side streets, leaving Nico behind in the smoke and ash.

Arthur's airship exited the last of Miasma's clouds. The night air was sharp in Asher's lungs as he took off his gas mask. He could see the train pulling out of Riali's city limits in the distance.

"Where are we going?" he asked. "Vana?"

"No," said Arthur, finishing his readjustments to the burner. "It is too dangerous. We will head for Dyria."

"What do you mean dangerous? The city will protect me."

"Asher," said Arthur, walking over to stand beside him. "General Volkov has been planning for this day. I have reason to believe Vana is his intended target. It is possible, if not probable, they wanted this day to come so that they could justify an attack—an eye for an eye."

"What? If they were aware of the attack, then why didn't they do more to stop it?"

"Many believe a war between Dyria and Riali is inevitable. Vana is a resource, one that has provided a significant financial boost to the Dyrian economy. And, therefore, Vana will be the first casualty."

"What about my family?"

"Warnings have been sent. Vana will be evacuated and defended. Dyria is aware of the threat and has been prepared for mobilization."

Arthur scanned the horizon with his telescope before placing it back into his pocket and turning to Asher. "Your bag. Whatever is in it must be awfully important. You nearly died by Nico Catalano picking up its contents."

"Yes, it is important," said Asher. "It is a project I've been working on, Cirrus-C."

"Cirrus…" said Arthur thinking out loud, "like the type of cloud?"

Asher smiled, "A knowledgeable airman. Yes, like the cloud."

"And the C..." said Arthur, "I'm not sure about that part. But whatever it is, I cannot imagine any kind of cloud is worth risking your life."

"This Cloud is certainly worth risking—"

A rumbling sound cut Asher short. Arthur pulled out his telescope once more. "No..." he whispered.

Asher squinted in the same direction. It looked as though the entirety of the plains below them were covered in a dark tidal wave, a flood of creatures scurrying along the ground like an army of ants. Their movements were quick, far faster than the airship or the train.

"What are those?"

"I am not entirely sure," said Arthur, handing the telescope to Asher, "but I believe that would be the attack."

Asher zoomed in on the mechanical, dog-like creatures sprinting across the open plains. "It is the Vanguard," said Asher. "Nico developed these for the military. Miasma used them for bombs, but Nico had flames coming from the ones that he showed me."

"They look like wolves. I have never seen something move so fast."

"Where are they headed?"

Arthur watched as the moonlight flitted across the backs of machines—a flood of metal sprinting across the plains and into the night horizon.

"I think we both know where," he said softly.

"They will not be enough to take down Vana. Especially if they have been warned of an attack."

"You are correct," said Arthur. "But if what you are telling me is true—about the bombs, about the flames—then I don't think taking the city is the point. Asher...they will burn it down."

CHAPTER 30

The sirens came while the city was asleep.

Murphy Auden grabbed his rifle and went to see what the matter was.

"Murphy," cried Cara. "What is it?"

"I'm not sure. I'm going into town to see what I can do to help out."

Cara locked the door behind him as he rode into the black night. Murphy Auden was halfway into town when he saw the Vana militia swarming its way up the dirt path. He jumped off his horse when he recognized a familiar face. "Gus, what's going on? Who's coming?"

"It's the damn Rialians!" shouted Augustus Saint as he ran past.

Murphy scanned the crowd and then slowly turned back around to head back toward his house. The Rialians would be arriving from the east; his home was directly in their path.

"Mr. Auden!" shouted a young voice from behind him.

"Thank God. Liam, what's happening?"

"There was a terrorist attack in Riali. The capital is blaming Dyria and Vana for it. Rumor has it they sent out machines to do their dirty work."

"What kind of machines?"

"Not sure on that part yet," said Liam, "but we're setting up some makeshift barriers just over the ridge to try and stop anyone from coming into the city."

"They're blaming Vana for the attack, do we know if Asher is safe?"

"I don't know...but Asher is smart. He'll make it out."

"Right. Let's make sure he has something to come home to. You stay with the forces. I'm going to go fortify the house."

Liam nodded and ran up to the frontline.

He approached the wood barricade that had been hastily erected by the militia beside the starlit forest. A loud thud came from over a hill, shaking the earth as it drew closer.

"Ready men!" shouted the captain. Liam steadied his aim, watching as hundreds of trees cresting the hilltop began to sway fiercely.

"What is that?" asked Liam loudly.

"Wait...hold your fire," the captain ordered. The men echoed the command down the lines as Drvo emerged. He stepped toward the militia, then turned back to face the forest.

It started with one fire, deep in the distance, as if one tree had decided to spontaneously combust. The sudden burst of light gave some indication of fast-moving shadows.

"They're coming closer!" shouted the captain.

Another explosion, closer now, but further from the original. Then a third. And a fourth, far south. The landscape was catching fire fast.

They're going to burn down the whole forest, thought Liam.

The shadows moved out from the tree line and into the open. Large, mechanical, wolf-like creatures with spherical heads leaped impossibly fast through the air. Liam watched as one of them ran across the forest line, spewing flames thirty meters from its frame.

Liam didn't bother waiting for the captain's orders. He aimed for the head of the creature and watched as the machine exploded, sending flame and metallic carnage across the field, with shrapnel taking two other wolves off their programmed path.

"FIRE AT WILL!" yelled the captain. The militia opened fire as the metallic beasts exploded in enormous blasts. The onslaught persisted, wave after wave of mechanical wolves emerged from the forest. The forest itself became engulfed in flame, a swarming inferno swallowing the precious Vanatian woodlands.

Drvo grabbed a nearby oak and used it as a club to swing at the wolves, each swing resulting in streaking fire and crushed metal. The metallic horde pushed forward through the flames. A wolf leaped onto Drvo's back. He reached behind him and slammed it on the ground. The force of the explosion sent him tumbling, landing on his back with an earth-quaking thud. The wolves jumped at the opportunity, spewing flames onto the giant rock golem. Drvo stood back up and began to fight with a renewed fierceness, kicking and swinging as the Vanguard sent jets of liquid flame onto his foliage skin. Drvo became frantic, blinded by the fire and smoke and unable to see the onslaught attacking him. He stumbled backward.

"FALLBACK!" shouted the captain over roaring flame. "FALLBACK!!"

The ranks echoed the order. Drvo fell. Several soldiers leaped out of the way as his large, boulder body came crashing down. The wolves broke through the barricade, smashing wood planks, setting fresh ground ablaze. Drvo continued to fight while on his back. He grabbed wolves in his palm and crushed them, their oil dripping down his arms like blood. His body became a firestorm. The foliage burned, the rocks smoldered in the liquid fire. The wolves continued to pounce onto his body, smothering every inch of him as they exploded. Pieces of rock flew across the field as the men sprinted back toward the city line. A large chunk of Drvo flew past Liam's head. He looked back and saw Drvo being driven into the ground with each explosion. He watched until there was nothing left but a crater of dust and pebble.

Liam broke from the ranks and headed toward the Auden house. "Where are you headed?" shouted Augustus.

"Mr. Saint. I have to help the Audens. Their house is in the direct path of this thing." Gus nodded. "I'll come with you." Without hesitation, the two splintered off into the dark in search of Murphy Auden.

"It's Riali," Murphy said to Cara. "They sent some kind of advanced attack force to Vana."

Cara paced around the kitchen nervously. "Stay inside. We'll lock the doors. We'll barricade ourselves in if we have to."

"I can't," said Murphy. "They'll find a way in. I need to deter them from our land if they approach."

"Please don't. Please, I don't think this is a good idea."

"I love you, Cara." Murphy kissed her. "Lock the door behind me."

Murphy made his way to a wooden fence near the edge of his land. He propped his rifle against it and looked deep into the night. *Why is there so much fire?* he thought. It continued past the ridge and was making its way into the city. He could make out quick-moving shadows inside the flames.

"What the...?" whispered Murphy under his breath.

"RUN!" Liam shouted in the distance. "Mr. Auden, RUN!!" Murphy looked over and saw Liam sprinting toward the house with Gus.

"Liam! Liam, what are these things?"

Liam caught up, gasping for breath. "I don't know..." he breathed heavily. "They're some...sort of machines...they shoot out flame...you have...to get out of here."

A loud, metallic clanking came from the distance. The three of them turned.

"It's too late," said Gus.

Murphy ran back to the fence and steadied his rifle.

"It's no use," shouted Liam. "There's too many of them. You and Mrs. Auden, you have to run. Get away from the city!"

"I'm not letting this place burn down," said Murphy, steadying his rifle against the fence. The mechanical creature sprinted closer, Murphy could make out its legs and spherical head. Still too far to make a shot.

"Damnit, Mr. Auden, I'm telling you we need to get out of here!" shouted Liam. Even as he yelled, he ran to the fence beside Murphy. Gus joined them along the line, keeping his rifle steadied at the horizon.

The wolf was now in sight; Murphy took the first shot. A dirt cloud shot up. Miss. He cocked back the bolt and took aim for a second shot. All three of them began firing as the machine closed the gap between them. Shots ricocheted off its legs. The wolf began to spew flames, setting acres of grass and brush aflame. The boys reloaded and kept firing. A shot connected, and the wolf exploded.

"Nice shot!" shouted Murphy.

The others did not flinch, keeping their eyes on their scopes.

"Wait for it..." said Liam. "There will be more."

An eerie calm washed over the group.

A shadowy line emerged from the flame. Not one wolf, but a wave of beasts. "GIVE THEM EVERYTHING YOU GOT!!" shouted Liam.

Wolves continued to explode, spreading flames in a massive radius after each connected bullet. One down. Two down. Three down. The line drew closer and closer.

"How many of these things are there?" shouted Murphy.

"We can't do this, we're outnumbered," replied Gus. "We've lost the woods. We're going to lose the city."

"NO," shouted Liam. "Just keep firing!"

The men continued to fire, one wolf after the next exploding. A wolf broke through on the far side of the field and headed straight for the house. Murphy turned and fired, hitting it within yards of the house. "The fire is going to reach the house."

"If we stop now, we're dead," shouted Liam. "We'll be overrun." Murphy sprinted toward the house anyway.

"We need to retreat south," said Gus. "It's the safest route."

Liam agreed. "Go. I'll try and hold them off a bit longer."

Gus broke his gaze from the line to look back toward Liam, "This battle is lost."

"Go!" shouted Liam one last time.

Gus lowered his weapon, "Just be careful. Callie is still out there somewhere. I know she'll be alright, but we may need you to fight another day."

He took off south as Liam held out against the creatures by himself.

There were too many.

A wolf broke through the blaze, not yet spewing its flame. Liam fired. The bullet hit the corner socket of a leg, sending sparks flying and dismantling the leg.

"Oh no..." said Liam to himself as the wolf leaped into the air. It landed on Liam, pinning him to the ground, a large metallic pincer piercing his shoulder.

Liam shouted in pain. With his other hand, he grabbed the rifle and swept another of the wolf's legs, causing it to fall on its side. He pulled the other pincer free and rolled out from under the relentless machine. It continued to crawl toward the house. He smashed a third leg with the rifle. The wolf continued to crawl its way toward the house with its one leg.

"Determined thing, aren't you," said Liam, walking up and pointing the rifle at the last leg. "What's your plan now?" He blasted the fourth leg into pieces, disabling it for good. He put the rifle across his shoulders and smirked. A faint beeping began emanating from the head of the wolf. "No..." he said, slowly backing up. "No no noo—"

Liam started to sprint away as the wolf exploded. The blast sent Liam flying, his legs on fire.

"Shit, shit, shit." He dropped his rifle and began to strip off his pants. He stood up and stamped the flames out from his pants, then looked back up at the fire line. Several more shadows emerged. "Murphy," he whispered under his breath. He looked back at the house as Murphy started to break back inside. "I'm sorry." Liam ran off into the night and away from the fire.

Murphy tried his best to smother the flames beside the house. He looked back up through the field. The boys were gone. He watched as an explosion on his property set fire to his acreage of trees. There was no way for him to prevent this much fire from reaching the house. He knocked on the door. "Cara!" he shouted.

No answer. He smashed the rifle through a glass window and crawled inside. "CARA!" She ran to the stairs.

"MURPHY?" Her eyes were wide with fear. She had witnessed the horrors of what happened outside through the upstairs window.

"We have t—" A blast interrupted him. The front door went off its hinges, slamming Murphy into the kitchen counters.

"MURPHY!"

"CARA, RUN! Get out of here, go south!"

The kitchen was scattered with pockets of fire. Murphy did his best to stand back up, but he feared his legs were broken. He grabbed the rifle and leaned against the kitchen counter. A wolf emerged from the broken doorway. A second one followed. Then two of them, more methodical than the others, surveyed the room.

Murphy leveled the gun. "Cara," he said calmly, "please run."

Cara disappeared back upstairs. Murphy lowered the gun as the metal wolves advanced. One of the wolves stood on top of the counter, inches away from his head. It sparked up its flame. Murphy's face was caked with dirt and debris, his legs were mangled. He watched as the second wolf began to crawl up the stairs. Exhausted, he drew the gun up to his shoulder and took aim at the one climbing the stairs.

"Please be ok, Asher. Please just be ok. I love you, son." Murphy fired. The wolf exploded. Its flame and shrapnel hit the other wolf on the counter, setting off a second explosion.

Liam, limping away from the fight, turned and watched as the Auden house went up in flames.

CHAPTER 31

When morning came, Asher awoke to thick smoke in his lungs. He groaned.

"Good morning," said a somber Arthur, peering over the edge of his airship.

"Morning," said Asher. "What's going on?"

"We are almost there."

"Dyria?"

"No. Vana."

Asher stood up and walked to the edge. The forest was burnt down for as far as he could see. Vast miles of blackened tree stumps.

"No..." he said. "This can't be..."

"I am sorry," said Arthur. "Riali targeted the forest, Vana's most valuable resource. Without Vanatian timber, it will be difficult for Dyria to build up its Navy. Worse will be the inevitable food shortage."

"So this is war," said Asher, peering across the scorched earth.

"I am afraid so..."

Arthur pulled out his telescope and homed in on the approaching city. "Asher...You will not like what you see. Please, please remain calm."

Asher grabbed at the telescope and peered out. Anger swept over him. "They made a mistake. General Volkov. The Maurinkos. I won't let this happen for nothing."

Arthur sighed deeply. "Now is not the time for fighting, Asher."

"I can stop this! I stopped Roman. I stopped Miasma. I helped make Dyria the powerhouse it is today. Riali has no idea what it has done!"

Asher began to pace around the airship. Arthur turned, put his hand on Asher's shoulder, and looked deeply into his eyes. "Yes, you are brilliant, Asher. You have accomplished great things. But this is bigger than you."

Asher nodded, his lips still pursed in anger. Arthur began to descend the airship into the city. "Who are they?" Asher pointed.

"They look to be Dyrian forces," said Arthur.

Dyrian airships were dropping river water onto the remaining flames. Asher could see the tiny shapes of soldiers running house to house, salvaging and searching for survivors. The train rolled into the station just ahead of them.

"Can you take me to my house?"

"I have to go into the city. I don't advise going into the countryside right now, Asher. We can't stay here for long. Riali forces will be here in the coming days."

"Fine. But I need to see my family. I'll meet back up with you in the city."

Arthur nodded and worked to park the ship in the city square.

Asher walked out slowly into a city of charcoal. Behind him, Arthur was tampering with the controls of the airship, busying himself the best he could to avoid confronting the devastation. Blank-faced, Asher continued through the snowy ash. It was gone. All of it. The only traces left of the once elegant, cedar-built city were the ashes blackening the clothes and faces of now-homeless families.

Asher picked up his stride. Vanatian and Dyrian soldiers ran about, putting out fires. Civilians clawed through cinders in search of loved ones. His pace quickened again. He reached the edge of the city and was now in a dead sprint. The countryside. Riali had burnt it all to the ground. The homes, the crops, the forest. Everything the berries had shown him over the year had become reality. Asher looked out across the blackened ruin. He narrowed his focus, there was only one thing he cared about now.

He ran up the old, familiar dirt path that led to his family's home. *No*, he thought, *no…please not them.* Asher was staggering up to the remains of his house when a voice shouted, "ASHER!"

For a moment, hope fluttered in his ribs.

"ASHER!" shouted Liam, limping his way down the dirt path.

"Liam?" whimpered Asher. Asher looked past him and at the house.

"Asher, please don't. Don't go in there." Liam was now caught up with Asher.

"Why? WHY, LIAM?" His voice cracked as he yelled.

"Asher, I'm sorry." Liam put his arm around Asher to keep him from going further.

Asher pushed him off. "Why, Liam? Why shouldn't I go in there? TELL ME!"

Liam grabbed for Asher again but this time to hold him tightly. "I'm sorry. I'm so sorry. Asher, I tried..."

Liam's eyes were glazed with tears. "Please believe me. We fought them, Asher. Your dad and me. We fought them and they kept coming. I told him to run..." Liam's voice was breaking. "He didn't want to leave your mother. He went back to the house. There wasn't anything I could do."

Liam held on tightly as he beat his fists against Liam's large back. Asher gasped for breath while his tears soaked into Liam's chest. The familiar smell of sweat and smoke filled him. He breathed it in, minutes passed as he worked to calm himself down. "Did you see them?"

"Your father's body is in the house, Asher. I have not seen your mother."

"So, she may have lived?"

"I'm not sure. I went into the southern woods after we were overrun. I took out a few of them, but I was injured, so I hid by the river. I only just came back. I was going to head into the city, see what I can do. I can't believe you made it out of Riali."

"Yeah..."

"Let's head to the city center," said Liam. "We'll have people come back and help us with the house."

"Ok," he nodded.

Asher turned around, and they stumbled back toward the city.

Arthur kept his distance as Asher ran ahead. The mayor caught him walking along the path and joined him.

"Henry, do you happen to know where the battle took place?"

Mayor Hegelson pointed him to the spot where the Vanatian militia made its stand against the Rialian Vanguard. Arthur examined the burned-down barricade, his eyes scanning the horizon of the blackened forest. A glint caught his eye as he walked toward a pile of crumbled rock that once resembled Drvo.

"What do you see?" asked the mayor.

"Nothing," said Arthur, sifting through the rubble. "I just wanted to pay my respects to the soldiers and examine how this battle took place."

"Any suggestions as to what fortifications we can make for their next attack?"

Arthur picked up a piece from the rocks and examined it before answering the mayor. "It is questionable if Riali will attack again any time soon. I suspect they will first try to propose new trade agreements with Dyria now that they crippled their main supply of food and production. Once those talks fail, Riali will be back to claim Vana as their own. I would suggest placing artillery forts across the hilltops. It should slow them down enough for an evacuation. The refugees, though, they will not be able to stay here, it will only draw Rialian forces sooner." Arthur pocketed the rock before standing back up. "Mighty brave soldiers you have here in Vana."

The mayor nodded in agreement. "Shall we head back into town?"

"Yes, that would be fine."

Asher and Liam scanned the faces pouring out from the train. Anxiety crept through Liam. "You're sure she made it out, right?"

"I'm sure," said Asher. "She was ahead of me."

The faces of the people were shellshocked; they were a hysterical mass, desperate to find their loved ones.

A small bob of amber peeked through.

"That's gotta be her," said Liam, pointing and jostling to get a better view. "Yeah, Asher, it's her!"

Callie made her way through to them. Her eyes were on the ground, her face drained of emotion from the train ride through burned-down forests and decimated city. She looked up to find Asher and Liam, and the faintest of smiles appeared on her face. "Oh, hey, guys."

"Hey," said Liam meekly. The three of them stared at each other in a moment of silence and understanding. Suddenly, without notice, Asher embraced Callie. She reciprocated the hug, wrapping her arms around him and burying her face deep into his chest.

"I wasn't sure if you made it out, I didn't see you on the train."

Liam placed one hand on Asher's back and another on Callie's. "It's good to have y'all home."

Callie looked up. "Is that Arthur's airship?"

"Yes," said Asher. "He got me out of the city."

Callie began walking into the town, the boys following at her side.

Arthur stood beside the airship, speaking with Mayor Hegelson, Samira Raol, and a handful of others. Callie spotted her battered uncle beside his burned-down shop. "I'll be right back."

The boys continued toward the group beside the airship. Asher squinted as he approached. "Mom?" asked Asher.

A woman caked in ash looked down the road. "Asher!"

Asher ran to hug his mother. She cried, "Your father..."

"I know," said Asher. "Liam told me."

"Asher..."

"It's ok, Mom. It'll be ok."

Arthur walked up. "We can't stay here long. Everyone on that train is now a fugitive of the capital. They'll come looking for you and Callie."

"Where do we go?" asked Asher.

"Samira will take you back to Dyria. You'll be safe under her protection."

"And my mother?"

Arthur looked over at his mom, who shook her head. "I can't come with you, Asher."

Samira spoke up. "We have orders from Princess Nora that we only take the high-profile. Riali wants war with Dyria. If they hear we've taken in all of these refugees, it will give them more fuel for a direct attack. We need to spread the fugitives out across various cities, Asher and Callie would be safest with us."

"But it's my mother..."

"She will be safer by going south to Kipos. No war will hit them, and Riali will not find her there."

Asher looked back at his mother; she nodded in agreement.

"Don't worry about me, Asher. You're needed now."

Callie walked up to the group, a satchel across her shoulder and her rifle in hand. Liam looked at her and spoke up to the group, "I'm coming with them."

Arthur shook his head. "Didn't you hear Samira? Dyria will not be a safe place. Asher and Callie are political targets, they'll be coming for them."

"But they won't be coming for me, and I can offer my protection. I will pledge my loyalty to Dyria, and I will be a guard for Asher and Callie," said Liam as he looked over at Samira. Samira turned her icy expression toward Arthur and shrugged.

Arthur sighed. "Fine, but you are all now direct subjects of the Dyrian crown. You must do exactly as ordered by Princess Nora and her representatives." Arthur nodded toward Samira.

"We will," said Liam confidently.

"Good," said Arthur. "Then you are now aware of the danger. Samira will take you from here, I have other urgent matters to attend to, but I trust we will meet again."

Callie looked out over Vana, the city of cedar. A home that never felt like her own, now reduced to embers. But like the forest, it too would grow back in time. Different than what she remembered, but a place where others would thrive again. She looked out at the faces of the small group surrounding her. Friends, family, allies. All of them beaten, exhausted. All of them with their stories, their sadness, and their burdens. She felt an odd harmony, a beginning that only disaster brings. They were united. And that gave her hope.

"So then," she said boldly. "Should we keep moving?"

Asher smiled. "Yes, let's keep moving."

Derek Paul studied Molecular & Cellular Biology and Creative Writing at the University of Arizona. He is a former youth worship leader and singer/songwriter of the band The Breaking Pattern. Derek currently works in research, where he notably helped bring to market the mRNA-based covid-19 vaccine. If he isn't buried in scientific articles and delving into spiritual literature, you can find him residing in Chandler, Arizona, playing with his sheepadoodle Bailey Moo and writing poems about merlot.

A Machine Divine is self-published
by an independent author.

If you enjoyed the story, please rate and review, so that you can help the adventure continue!

Follow the Author
Instagram: TheBreakingPattern
Twitter: TheBreakPattern

Printed in Great Britain
by Amazon

25791050R00219